# WARRIOR AND PROTECTOR

## BOOK 1 IN THE SAXON WARRIOR SERIES

### PETER GIBBONS

Boldwood

First published in Great Britain in 2022 by Boldwood Books Ltd.

Copyright © Peter Gibbons, 2022

Cover Design by Head Design

Cover Photography: shutterstock

A CIP catalogue record for this book is available from the British Library.

Paperback ISBN 978-1-80483-461-9

Large Print ISBN 978-1-80483-457-2

Hardback ISBN 978-1-80483-456-5

Ebook ISBN 978-1-80483-454-1

Kindle ISBN 978-1-80483-455-8

Audio CD ISBN 978-1-80483-462-6

MP3 CD ISBN 978-1-80483-459-6

Digital audio download ISBN 978-1-80483-453-4

Boldwood Books Ltd
23 Bowerdean Street
London SW6 3TN
www.boldwoodbooks.com

*For my wife Fiona, for her support along the writer's journey*

Byrhtnoð maþelode, bord hafenode,
wand wacne æsc, wordum mælde,
yrre and anræd ageaf him andsware:
'Gehyrst þu, sælida, hwæt þis folc segeð?
Hi willað eow to gafole garas syllan,
ættrynne ord and ealde swurd

Byrhtnoth made a speech, raised his shield,
waved his slender ash spear, spoke in words,
angry and resolute gave him back an answer:
'Do you hear, seafarer, what these people say?
They are willing to give you spears as tribute,
deadly point and tested swords...

— AN EXCERPT FROM 'THE BATTLE OF
MALDON', AN ANGLO-SAXON POEM WRITTEN
TO CELEBRATE THE BATTLE FOUGHT AT
MALDON IN 991AD

# MAIN CHARACTERS

**Aethelhelm** Ealdorman of Cheshire
**King Æthelred II** King of the English
**Aflgar** Bastard son of Ealdorman Aethelhelm
**Beornoth** Saxon warrior
**Blaedswith** Inn Keeper at Knutsford
**Byrhtnoth** Ealdorman of Essex
**Eawynn** Wife of Beornoth
**Einar Ravenhair** Viking Warrior
**Erkenwald** Thegn of the East Saxons
**Imma** Warrior of the East Saxons
**Olaf Tryggvasson** Norwegian Jarl and Viking leader
**Osmod** Warrior of the East Saxons
**Osric** Son of Ealdorman Aethelhelm
**Sigurd Bearskin** Viking Warrior
**Skarde Wartooth** Viking Jarl
**Streonwold** Captain of Ealdorman Aethelhelm's warriors
**Theodred** Thegn of Cheshire
**Ulfketil Flatnose** Viking Warrior
**Wulfhere** Saxon warrior and friend to Beornoth

# GLOSSARY

**Burh** A fortification designed by Alfred the Great to protect against Viking incursions
**Byrnie** Saxon word for a coat of chainmail
**Danelaw** The part of England ruled by the Vikings from 865AD
**Drakkar** A type of Viking Warship
**Ealdorman** The leader of a shire of the English Kingdom, second in rank only to the King
**Einherjar** Vikings who have died in battle and have ascended to Valhalla
**Heriot** The weapons, land, and trappings of a thegn or other noble person, granted to him by his Lord and which becomes his will or inheritance
**Hide** An area of land large enough to support one family. A measure used for assessing areas of land
**Holmgang** A ritualised duel common amongst Viking peoples
**Njorth** The Viking Sea God
**Odin** The father of the Viking Gods
**Ragnarök** The end of days battle where the Viking Gods will battle Loki and his monster brood

**Reeve** Administer of justice ranking below a Thegn

**Seax** A short, single edged sword with the blade angled towards the point

**Thegn** Owner of five hides of land, a church and kitchen, a bell house and a castle gate who is obligated to fight for his Lord when called upon

**Thor** The Viking Thunder God

**Týr** The Viking War God

**Valhalla** Odin's great hall where he gathers dead warriors to fight for him at Ragnarök

**Weregild** Compensation to be paid, for example to the family of a person who has been killed

SOUTHERN ENGLAND, c.1000

N

GWYNEDD

MÔN (ANGLESEY)

RHOS

KNUTSFORD

CHESHIRE

DERBYSHIRE

YORKSHIRE

TERRITORY

OF THE

FIVE BOROUGHS

LINCOLNSHIRE

POWYS (NORTHERN)

POWYS (SOUTHERN)

SHROPSHIRE

STAFFORDSHIRE

TAMWORTH

LEICESTERSHIRE
LEICESTER

RUTLAND
STAMFORD

EAST

NORFOLK

ANGLIA

WORCESTERSHIRE

WARWICKSHIRE

NORTHAMPTONSHIRE

HUNTINGDON

CAMBRIDGESHIRE

CAMBRIDGE

SUFFOLK

DEHEUBARTH

DYFED

YSTRAD
TYWI

CYDWELI

GOWER

HEREFORDSHIRE

BEDFORD
SHIRE

HERTFORDSHIRE

COLCHESTER

ESSEX

GWENT

MORGANNWG
GLYWYSING

GLOUCESTERSHIRE

OXFORDSHIRE

OXFORD

WALLINGFORD

MALMESBURY

BERKSHIRE

SURREY

KENT

WILTSHIRE

SOMERSET

HAMPSHIRE
WINCHESTER

SUSSEX

DEVON

DORSET

CORNWALL

# PROLOGUE
## 989AD

The drakkar warship sliced through an iron-grey sea. Its clinker-built timbers flexed with the rise and fall of the white-tipped waves, and the ship's prow-beast snarled and cut its way across the Whale Road towards the Saxon coastline, as sleek and swift as an eagle diving for its prey.

Skarde Wartooth heaved on the tiller, feeling the strength and power of the Sea God Njorth in the resistance beneath his hand. He tossed his head back, enjoying the fresh chill of icy sea spray on his face as the wind whipped his long hair behind him like the pelt of a wild beast. He checked to his port where two similar drakkars kept pace with him, crashing and slicing through the surging sea, each one filled with four score of warriors. Skarde's warships darted towards the lands of the Saxons, where a gap showed in the shadow-shrouded promontory of its hills and cliffs. There, the country opened up into a wide estuary where a river yawned its mouth open to pour its waters into the wide sea. Skarde steered for that estuary and the river beyond, the watery roadway which would allow him to sail his shallow-draughted warships along its meandering course and deep into the heart of

Saxon Britain. He thought this part of the island of Britain was the old Kingdom of East Anglia, which was now part of the larger Kingdom of Wessex and nascent Kingdom of the English. But it didn't matter if it was East Anglia or Wessex. Skarde just wanted to kill Saxons. He reached for the small iron spear amulet at his neck and touched the metal for luck. Most men worshipped Thor, Njorth, or Týr. Skarde, however, worshiped Odin, the father of the Gods and Lord of Valhalla. Odin was the vicious and malevolent God of battle and victory. He was both cunning and fierce. Skarde closed his eyes, and in his mind's eye he saw Odin riding through the heavens on his eight-legged horse, Sleipnir, with the two crows Huginn and Muninn, thought and memory, perched on each of his broad shoulders.

'Hear me, All-Father,' Skarde whispered. 'Bring me battle luck, make my axe red with the blood of Saxon warriors. If I die, great Odin, let it be with blade in hand so I can join your Einherjar in Valhalla, and fight alongside you forever, until the day of Ragnarök.'

The ships banked towards the coastline and the wind whipped the sails, snapping the cloth taut and surging the warship forwards. It was late spring, which for men who went a-viking meant it was time to leave their wives and families and take to the ships in search of wealth and glory.

'If this is the right river, then there's a Saxon burh close to the coast,' Ulfketil Flatnose shouted above the din of the sea.

'Those old fortresses are rotting. The Saxons are lazy. Their King is weak, he usurped his brother and their earls are not united. I want to fight their warriors. My axe longs to drink their blood and test their mettle. We make for the burh,' said Skarde. His uncle, Arne, had lived in the north of Britain for a time: in the Kingdom of York, which, until recent times, had been under the control of Vikings for many years in the Danelaw. Arne had told

Skarde of the burhs, that network of fortresses built by King Alfred the Great, and expanded across the country by his warrior daughter Æthelflæd. Alfred built burhs to counter the threat of raiding Danes and other Vikings, to provide a chain of fortresses across the lands of the Saxons where local people could flee and enjoy the protection of Saxon swords and spears. The Great Heathen Army of Ivar the Boneless had taught the Saxons to fear Viking blades and had carved out a kingdom within the Saxon lands which had endured until the death of Erik Bloodaxe, thirty-five years earlier. Æthelred II was King of Wessex, Mercia, East Anglia and Northumbria now, which meant he was the King of what the Saxons now called England. Word had come north on the lips of merchants and trading ships that the kingdom was riven, the King had usurped the throne and his earls were divided into factions. It was ripe for attack.

'Will we fight today?' asked Ulfketil.

'We will if we can.'

'We fight today,' Ulfketil bellowed, and the crew cheered. Skarde nodded at their ferocity, their hunger to fight and prove their valour to the Gods. Odin wanted them to fight, Thor and Týr welcomed the blood and sacrifice Skarde and his men would offer up to their glory.

'Our Lord, Olaf Tryggvason, wants us to cut a swathe of war and fear across Saxon lands,' Skarde shouted to his men. 'Our people, my own kin, were butchered by the Saxons. Let them feel our fury now, let them feel the wrath of the blood feud. Death to the Saxons.' He pulled his axe free of the loop at his belt and held the blade aloft. His men cheered wildly and stomped their feet on the hull of his warship, the rhythmic pounding creating stirring war music. Skarde's Lord, Olaf Tryggvason, was striking at the same time further along the Saxon coast. Olaf had brought twenty warships to attack the Saxons, filled with warriors baying for war and glory. Skarde could smell the famously rich earth of Saxon farmland as they closed in on the coastline. He could smell victory and vengeance on the wind.

Skarde closed his eyes and remembered his aunt and uncle's faces. In the north, the Saxons had burned his own father's sister and her husband alive following the defeat of Erik Bloodaxe and his loss of the Kingdom of York to the Saxons. So, Skarde was here now, filled with war-fury and ready to bring the blood feud to all Saxons. They would feel the pain and suffering of his own kin, and Skarde would burnish his reputation brightly with the blood and bones of Saxon warriors.

The coastline drew close, cliffs rising high, topped by the famed lush greenery of Saxon Britain. Skarde saw riders there, small and skittish on the hillside, and he grinned to himself.

'Riders on the coast,' he said to Ulfketil. 'Let's find the nearest beach and go ashore, hopefully they have brought their best warriors.' The estuary and river beyond were the key to cutting deep into the countryside, but the chance to fight and kill Saxons on the beach was too good to refuse. His men had braved the dangers of the Whale Road to reach these shores, and he saw a chance to colour their blades with Saxon blood.

Ulfketil bellowed the orders to the crew, and the warship banked towards the lands of the Saxons. Skarde turned, and watched with satisfaction as his other warships made the same manoeuvre, making a sweep and following his lead like birds dipping and swooping as one flock in the sky. The wind whipped in the sails, and he felt the power of the sea beneath his hand again as his calloused palm gripped the tiller. It warmed his heart. The Gods were with him. Njorth gave him calm seas, and he knew Odin itched for blood and souls just as much as he did.

The golden sands of a Saxon beach rose into view beyond the rise and fall of the swell. Skarde raced towards it, watching the enemy horsemen pick their way down the hillside, spears and helmets glinting in the early spring sun. Ulfketil had the sail lowered, and the men withdrew the timber plugs from the holes along the ship's side, and made ready the long oars, removing them from their deck hooks and sliding them into place. Flatnose clashed his axe on a shield to beat time, and the oarsmen gave a clipped roar at each long pull. The ship surged towards the beach. Skarde could see men gathered there, a line of Saxon shields painted bright with the sigil of their Lord, making ready to meet Skarde and his warriors. His heart quickened in his chest. All his life, he had trained to fight. He was born to the blade and devoted to Odin All-Father. His chance to avenge his slaughtered uncle and aunt and burnish his own reputation was so close he could smell it above the salt of the sea, and the acrid sweat of his men.

The warship crunched on to a shelf of shale at the edge of the Saxon beach. Ulfketil threw the anchor stone over the side, and its seal-hide rope snapped taut. Skarde put one hand on the sheer strake and leapt over the side and into the sea. The icy cold bit at his chest, and for a brief horrifying moment panic flooded his senses as his head dipped beneath the water. He wore a mail coat and heavy war gear; if the water were deeper than head height he would drown before he could strike a blow in anger. But he pushed with his feet and his head burst through the surface. Skarde roared his defiance at the Saxon sea. The men aboard his ship cheered, and Ulfketil tossed Skarde his shield.

Skarde pumped his legs hard to push through the sea's resistance as quickly as possible, the weight of his soaked clothes, armour and weapons cumbersome. He stumbled as the tide tried to drag him back into its clawing embrace. He emerged from the water amidst a line of his men – vicious, hungry killers all – and he laughed at the timid Saxons. They should have killed him as he came stumbling from the water, but they waited on the beach behind a line of shields. Even their horsemen had dismounted to join the shield wall instead of riding Skarde and his men down before they could reach it. The Saxons hesitated, and they were afraid, and now they would die.

# PART I

---

# REEVE

# 1

Masterless warriors occupied Offa's Crag. A band of that lost caste of men, cursed to drift across the country as outlaws and sell-swords. Such men were warriors spat out by the constant petty feuds and cattle disputes which plagued the borderlands between the Saxon shires and the remnants of the old Danelaw. The Danelaw had been destroyed by the death of Erik Bloodaxe thirty-five years earlier, bringing an end to Viking rule in the Saxon north. But Danes were still as thick on the land as fleas on a grizzled dog. The Viking Danes had lived in the Danelaw for over a hundred years, descendants of the Great Heathen Army brought howling to Saxon shores by Ivar the Boneless and his brothers, all sons of Ragnar Lothbrok, in their savage attack on Northumbria, East Anglia and Mercia.

Beornoth pressed his right knee into his horse's flank, guiding her around a briar bright with purple thistles. She snorted and picked her way around the bush, taking a path across softer ferns and fallen pines. The mare was small and slow, too old to be riding up to the summit of the high valley which rose steeply from the glistening waters of the River Mersey. Offa's Crag sat high and dark in Cheshire, a newly created shire nestled in the borderlands between Northumbria, Mercia, and Gwynedd. Beornoth saw the crag through a break in the pine trees ahead, its grey stone flecked with white rock, jutting and prominent against the brown and green hue of the hillside. In the old days, they had said the crag was the lair of a Mountain Eotun, a monster who would sneak out of his high fastness in the night to terrorise the farm and village folk.

The only monsters up there now were the masterless men: brutal, desperate warriors looking for silver, food, women and ale. Beornoth did not know how many of the brigands there were, just that armed men had ransacked farms and stolen cattle, and that a shepherd had seen them marching for Offa's Crag. They were a ragged band of thieves and killers, and it was Beornoth's responsibility to bring them to justice.

A masterless man is a cursed thing, an outlaw who can be killed on sight. A warrior not attached to a Lord, a roaming soldier not sworn to serve a Thegn, or an Ealdorman, but carrying the strength of his arm and his blades to wherever there is trouble. There was always fighting in the north, especially around the borderlands between shires, and Lords always needed warriors. Masterless men without pay plagued Saxon lands, roaming and stealing, looting and killing, until they found trouble to profit from, or a Lord to pay them to fight.

'Go up there, confront them. We demand justice,' the farmers of Knutsford had said, wagging their thick fingers at Beornoth, their ruddy faces frowning and twisted with anger. There could be three men up there on the Crag armed with knives and clubs, or ten veteran warriors armed with spears and shields. The farmers didn't care how many men there were, or that Beornoth was just one man. Beornoth was the reeve, and it was his duty to bring down justice upon the criminals and protect the farms, known as hides, within his hidage.

He reached for the skin of ale at the rear of his saddle and grimaced as the effort of leaning stretched his bloated gut. Beornoth took a pull at the ale, and then another, tipping the skin upright to drain the last bitter dregs. He belched and cursed, throwing the empty skin into the undergrowth. He didn't care if there were three men or ten men. Either way, the bastards were going to meet his steel on Offa's Crag. His horse reached the edge of the pine forest and Beornoth emerged onto the hillside, a chill wind blowing against his face and stinging his ears. He pulled his threadbare woollen cloak about his shoulders. He had kept to the woodland during his ascent of the hills, to keep hidden from the view at the Crag's summit, even though that approach made the journey longer.

Beornoth moved the spear from his left hand to his right. The shaft was smooth from use, and he thought he must wrap the thing for grip once he returned to town. If they did not kill him on Offa's Crag. He could hear men's voices, the sound of laughter and chatter travelling on the wind. Those sounds told of men lolling and comfortable in their safety. Bellies, no doubt full of stolen beef and hands warming at a fire, telling each other old war stories and laughing at the weak farmers they had robbed. Unaware that the farmers had come for the local reeve, Beornoth, to ask him for justice.

He slid off the horse's back, and she curled her lip at him, snorting a gush of foul breath into his face. Beornoth produced an ale belch and blew its foulness at the horse in return. He would leave the poor nag here. Riding her up onto the Crag would just make the masterless men laugh. Beornoth was too big to ride her. His legs jutted out around the sides of her flanks and she was not a warhorse. If he still had his old horse, he would

have ridden the brute up the hillside and charged them. He
wondered where he was now, old Beorgan. That was a horse. A
beautiful, big, brave animal trained for war. Beorgan would snap
his teeth at enemy faces and crush men with his heavy hooves, a
horse fit for a warlord.

Beornoth rested the spear against his nag's flank and tight-
ened the straps of his breastplate. It was just a chest-and-belly
covering of hard baked leather. Not proper armour, not like a
byrnie mail coat, but it still offered some protection against a
spear or knife thrust. He untied the dented and misshapen half-
helm from the saddle and pushed it onto his head. It was tight,
and the rim dug into his forehead, so he raised his eyebrows
several times to loosen the fit. It was a terrible helmet, and he had
no leather liner to sit beneath it for comfort, but it was better than
no helmet at all. Beornoth's skull had been cracked a few times
over the years, and a blow to the head could drop a man, leaving
him vulnerable and open to a death blow.

He reached for his sword hilt, a reflex action built over a lifetime of war, and practice for war, but his hand only grasped at
thin air. Beornoth sighed. The blade was not there at his belt, and
had not been for years. His fingers yearned for it, for the comfort
of the leather-wrapped grip, to feel the balance in the hilt of the
long blade, and to raise her to his lips so he could kiss the iron
cross inlaid into the crosspiece. A sword was not just a weapon, it
was a warning to an enemy. It said that the wielder was a wealthy
warrior, made rich through war skill and the blood of his
enemies. It warned men that the wielder was a killer, and they
should be wary of him. A sword was an expensive weapon,
reserved for the most fearsome and skilled of warriors, and for
noblemen and Kings. It was a weapon only the finest smiths
could craft. Beornoth spat into the bracken at his feet. The sword
was gone, along with so much else. Instead, he pulled a war axe

from its leather sheath on the mare's saddle. The blade was pitted with rust and its haft was as worn by use as the spear shaft.

Beornoth took the spear in his right hand, hefted the axe in his left and began the trudge up the hillside towards Offa's Crag. The ground was heavy, covered in a dew resting there since morning and not yet burned off by the sun, so that after a few paces it soaked his boots through to his feet. He could hear the warriors talking as he grew closer, one high-pitched voice with a cackling laugh, another deep and rumbling. In the old days, Beornoth would have carried his war shield on his back, an iron boss surrounded by linden wood planking and secured with an iron rim. Now, he owned only a rusty axe, and a worn-out spear, but it would still be enough.

He reached the base of the Crag, where the stone emerged from the ground like a magnificent beast's claw grasping at the hillside so the monster beneath the earth could haul itself from the world beneath to terrorise the world of men. The world of men was not much better than the underworld. Beornoth had seen monsters stalking the world in defiance of the laws of God and Christ. Monsters disguised as men, burning, raping, killing and drenched in the blood of women and children. He held on to that thought, and his memories, conjuring terrible images to the forefront of his mind. Memories of fifteen summers as a warrior, and the dark pain of his own terrible loss. Normally, he pushed such images away, to a place where they could only haunt his dreams in the bleakness of night and sleep. But he needed them now. He told himself that the masterless men beyond the crag were the perpetrators of those horrific acts, of the burned, twisted bodies of small children. He told himself these men were the ones who had come to his land, back in the old days, and taken everything from him.

Beornoth was breathing heavily, though the march up the

hillside was gentle even for his ageing bones. It was the rage heaving at his chest, stretching at the cold leather breastplate. His thick and rugged knuckles were white with tension on axe and spear, knuckles smashed and healed countless times down the years. Beornoth clenched his jaw, his tongue slipping in and out of the missing teeth at the side of his face where an arrow had once shot him in the mouth, ripping his face open. He rolled his heavy shoulders to loosen the thick, corded muscle. Strength built over a lifetime of weapon work, sword work, axe work, murder, battle, and practise. He leapt up onto the Crag, and onto its top. Below him six men sat around a crackling fire, eating freshly roasting beef and sharing skins of ale.

Six bearded faces stared up at Beornoth, and they saw a big man armed with an axe and spear. The hillside was still. The only sounds were the crackling of their campfire and the whistle of the wind. Beornoth broke that silence with a roar, the bellow of a man who has seen murdered children and hurt women, the challenge of a man who has trained his whole life to fight and kill. At that moment, Beornoth projected the blame for all the atrocities and horror he had witnessed in his life on to those six men, and hate raged inside his belly like the flames of hell.

Beornoth leapt from the Crag and landed amongst them. He bent his knees to cushion the landing and stabbed the spear point into a bald man's eye, using the strength in his right arm to drive the spear point deep into the warrior's face until it met resistance at the back of his skull. He swung his axe backhand with his left hand so it chopped with a wet slap into the side of another man's head. Blood sprayed over the warriors around that man and he toppled, quivering, to the earth, his head a mass of red and black gore. Beornoth snarled and took a step forward to kick the flaming logs of the campfire onto two men opposite him. Sparks and cinder filled the air around the Crag, and a warrior's greasy beard and hair caught fire. That man screamed like the devil and rolled onto the grass, clutching at his burning face and eyes.

Three unwounded men leapt to their feet. One narrowly avoided the flaming logs Beornoth had kicked at him and rose with a wicked bladed seax in his hand. He was an enormous man. Bigger even than Beornoth, and with a scarred face twisted by anger and surprise. The smell of burning hair and flesh filled Beornoth's nose, and his ears rang with the mewing of dying warriors. He realised he was shouting incoherently, spittle flying from his mouth to fleck his beard, visions of massacred women and children still flashing before his eyes. He tugged on the axe haft, but it had lodged deep in the head of the dead warrior, so he let it go and grabbed his spear shaft in both hands and ripped it free of its victim's skull. The man closest to him ran, so Beornoth kicked at his heels and that man tumbled to the ground, screaming as he landed, and rolled in the blood of his dead comrade. The big man charged at Beornoth so he cracked him across the nose with the shaft of his spear, and kneed the warrior in the groin. Beornoth spun around the big man's creased-over torso to lunge his spear point into the belly of the final warrior who was coming at him armed with a spear of his own.

Beornoth twisted his spear in that last attacker's guts, and ripped it sideways and upwards so the blue coils of the warrior's insides slopped into the remnants of the fire where they hissed as they hit the hot, orange centre of the flames. The big man wrapped his arms around Beornoth's waist and tried to drive him backwards; Beornoth felt a hard, dull punch in his lower back, so he let go of his spear and hooked his foot around the big man's ankle and threw him over his hip. The big man thudded into the earth, and Beornoth stamped on his face, hard, and then stamped on him again.

Beornoth's chest heaved with the exertion, and a bead of sweat rolled down the side of his forehead and into his beard. The rage subsided; its void filled quickly with tiredness. Beornoth coughed and removed his ill-fitting half-helm and let it fall to the ground. He looked at the carnage, groaning at an ache in his left shoulder blade, and a throbbing in his right knee, old wounds sending him an echo of pain down the years. He wondered: if the farmers were to see the wounded and dying on the Crag, would they feel he had brought them justice? A whimpering sound snapped Beornoth from his thoughts. The man he had tripped was crawling on all fours, like a pig trying to escape the butcher. Beornoth stepped over the big unconscious man, and bent to pick up the haft of his axe where it protruded from the head of a dead warrior. He put his foot on that corpse's chest and yanked it free; the blade making a sucking sound as it tore free of brain and skull. He rested the axe on his shoulder and picked his way amongst the dead and dying, moving to the crawling man.

'Please, please, Lord. Don't kill me...' said the warrior, spinning to lie on his back and raising his hands.

'I am not a Lord,' said Beornoth. *Not any more, anyway.*

'You don't need to kill me,' said the man, blubbering. Tears rolled down his cheeks, tracing lines across the filth of his face. A bubble of snot formed in one of his nostrils. 'I'll go away, I'll never come back. We didn't mean to take the cows, or...'

Beornoth grunted as he brought the axe down over his shoulder, both hands on the haft for maximum force, and slammed the blade into the man's chest. Bones crunched, and a spurt of dark blood sprayed from the man's mouth as he died mid-sentence. Beornoth turned and retrieved his spear and used it to cut the throat of the man with the burned face, who lay silently quivering amongst a pile of ferns.

Five masterless men were dead, leaving one survivor.

Beornoth looked up at the shifting, dark sky. Clouds broiled, and he thought it might rain before nightfall. Below him, the valley spread out in a patchwork of brown farmland, golden crop fields, and bronze-topped woodland. Down there, people worked and lived their lives, peasants and serfs, honest people raising children and trying to find happiness amongst life's dull drudgery. They needed Beornoth. He protected them from the wolves. His savagery and war skill allowed them to sleep in peace, to laugh with their children and hold each other close on dark, cold nights. He felt no pity for the men he had killed. Once a man made the choice to take up arms, then he risked pain and death, and Beornoth had brought both to Offa's Crag.

When the big man woke, Beornoth would make him gather anything of value. He would tie the bastard to his horse and drag him down into the villages. The farmers would want to know that justice was delivered before they paid Beornoth, and then he would find a drink to dull the pain. The pain that covered Beornoth with a shroud of heavy sadness. Memories of a life lost, of what was and could have been, but could never be again.

## 2

Beornoth chewed on a piece of freshly roasted beef torn from a chunk of meat he had rescued from the campfire at the Crag. The juices ran into his beard, and he groaned in appreciation of the deep, earthy taste. He went to take another delicious bite when his nag jerked beneath him, and the meat flew from his hand to land amongst the nettles and brush. Beornoth cursed and twisted in the saddle. The big man was lying face down in the dirt, the rope tying him to the saddle taut and his arms stretched upwards from the ground as though he were prostrating himself in prayer. His falling had caused the horse to falter, and Beornoth sighed with disappointment.

'Get up, you lazy bastard,' he growled. The man didn't move. Beornoth sighed again and lurched from the saddle. He landed heavily on the ground, jarring his aching knee. He thought about picking up the piece of fallen beef, but it was caked in dust and soil, surrounded by stinging nettles, and his horse was nudging her wet nose at it. He walked to the big man and kicked him in the ribs. The masterless man groaned but didn't get up. Beornoth clenched his teeth and shook his head. He tucked his boot under the man's shoulder and flipped him onto his side, the sack on his back clanking as its iron contents shifted position.. His belly and thighs were filthy with the dirt and muck of the hillside and forest floor, his whole torso streaked with red blood and long, weeping grazes. Which was no surprise to Beornoth, because he had dragged the man naked behind his horse for most of the afternoon with a bundled cloak strapped to his back. The cloak was filled with weapons and anything of value Beornoth had stripped from the dead at the Crag.

The big man's eyes opened into slits, and he spat dirt and grass from his mouth. He looked at Beornoth from the corners of his eyes, without turning his head.

'Either get up and walk, or I'll cut your stinking throat and leave you here for the animals,' said Beornoth.

'Water, or ale?' the big man said, his voice rasping and little more than a whisper.

'There's no ale for dead men. Get up, brigand. I won't say it again.'

'For a warrior, Lord?'

'You're no warrior. You are a masterless, sell-sword bastard.'

Beornoth reached to his back and grasped the handle of the seax he had stripped from the big man. It was a fine weapon, well made and sheathed in a beautifully patterned scabbard which hung from the rear of his belt by two thongs.

'I am a warrior. I fought at Preston Brook, in the front ranks.'

Beornoth let go of his blade. He crouched, coming closer to the man and wincing at the pain in his knee as he did so.

'Don't lie to me. I was at Preston Brook.'

'I don't lie, Lord. I was with Cwichelm's men. He was the Thegn in Fernbridge.'

'Very well. If you were there, tell me, why did the Danes lose that day?'

'A big brute of a man drove a wedge of our warriors into their lines and broke them, then our horsemen charged from the flank and rolled them up,' said the big man, and coughed up a gobbet of dusty phlegm into the dirt.

Beornoth nodded and scratched at his beard. The man spoke the truth. Beornoth knew, because he was the man who had led that wedge through the Viking shield wall. A formidable line of overlapped shields, held firm by spear and sword. The Danes – long-haired, tattooed warriors – snarled and bayed, desperate to shove their sharp blades into his flesh and to spill his blood.

'A grim day,' said Beornoth. He reached around to his back and took a small skin of water from where it hung over his shoulder. He handed it to the big man, who sucked it down in great gulps and nodded his thanks. Beornoth stood and felt a throbbing in his side. He checked it with his palm and it came away bloody. The big man had cut him when they had grappled at the Crag. He had felt a blow there at the time but hadn't realised it was a blade. So many wounds over the years, it was hard to tell punch from stab sometimes. Beornoth had often suffered a dull thud in the heat and frenzy of battle and not realised the severity of the wound until afterwards. He had suffered a spear wound in his thigh that day at Preston Brook, and an axe haft had cracked him across the face, swelling his cheekbone. So many fights down over the years, too many cuts and rends in his flesh to remember. They came back to him as flashes of pain, of days lying in bed, or in fields, bleeding and sweating with fever. Often such memories were accompanied by visions of lost friends, the ones who had not been as lucky as he. Those visions would plague Beornoth's nights as vivid dreams: an old mate from the shield wall, carved open by an unforgiving enemy, or a boyhood friend seeping his lifeblood into a shadowed battlefield.

'Wulfhere is my name,' the big man said. Beornoth ignored

him and took the water skin back. He made sure the knotted cloak was secure on Wulfhere's back. He could sell the weapons in town, and the profits would keep him in ale, at least for a while. The big man heaved himself to standing, grunting under the weight of the sack, and held up his tied wrists to Beornoth, looking from the rope to Beornoth, and back again.

'Please Lord, for a veteran fallen on hard times.'

Beornoth mounted his nag and stroked her ear, and nudged her on towards the village. The rope behind him snapped taut, yanking Wulfhere forwards.

'Don't fall again,' Beornoth growled at him without looking back.

The village of Knutsford was a collection of wattle buildings topped by thatch in various stages of repair, from newly woven thatch shining bright gold under the afternoon sun, to deep-grey mottled, rotting thatch which was a haven for rats and lice. Knutsford was a village centred on a ford crossing a wide river which cut through the valley basin. The village boasted a blacksmith, a merchant, a tavern and a meeting hall. It served as the central gathering place for the surrounding farms in the valley. Beornoth rode his mare into the central square, which was little more than a patch of ground, trodden by countless horses and wagons to impacted mud, in between two lines of buildings. At the centre of the square was a raised timber platform used for announcements and such. The clip-clop of his mare on the hard packed earth road into the village caused curious faces to emerge from doorways, and bodies slunk from lanes and alleys, curious to see who had arrived in their village.

Beornoth ignored them. He was aware of bearded faces staring at him, whispering, and of the local women pointing and cackling at Wulfhere's nakedness. It was here at Knutsford where the farmers had appealed to Beornoth to bring justice to the masterless men who had attacked farms in the valley, and now he brought the proof of that justice for payment. He looked across at the tavern, a wide building with black timber structural beams showing through the wattle walls, and small, shuttered windows. He licked his lips, thirsty for the ale he planned to sup once they paid him. Enough ale to dull his memories, enough to send him into a dreamless, drunken sleep.

'The reeve has returned,' a shout went up from across the square, and three men approached, striding confidently with thumbs tucked in wide belts.

'I told you he would punish them, didn't I?' said a round-faced man with curly red hair.

'You did, Cenwulf, I'll give you that,' said another. This man was short and rotund, with a black beard and a bald head.

Beornoth slid from his horse and untied the rope from the saddle. The wound at his back stretched and Beornoth grunted at the pain. Wulfhere dropped to his knees in the mud, and the metal-filled cloak on his back clanked.

'Is this one of them?' said the short man.

Beornoth untied the cloak from Wulfhere's back and dropped it at the feet of Cenwulf the Merchant. It opened to reveal a collection of daggers, a short antler-handled seax, a spearhead, and two rusting cloak pins. Cenwulf grinned and itched at his belly.

'Must have been half a dozen of them, judging by these weapons,' he said, and whistled. 'And you on your own, Beo.'

'How much for all of it?' asked Beornoth. 'Except this.' He bent and picked up the seax, it was a fine weapon and the antler handle made a comfortable grip. Cenwulf sucked at his teeth and shook his head.

'Half a pound of silver?'

Beornoth sighed and pointed at Wulfhere. 'I could let him go, let him loose in the square. He'd have your guts opened in a heartbeat and your women carried off before nightfall.'

'Pay the man, Cenwulf,' said the third man, a broad-shouldered blacksmith. 'There's good iron there.'

'All right, all right. One pound of silver,' said Cenwulf.

Beornoth nodded and dragged Wulfhere to the central platform and tied him there. 'Don't escape. I'll just ride you down and kill you.'

Wulfhere gave a snort of laughter. 'These muck savages will kill me, anyway. Better to die well, I reckon.'

He was right, and Beornoth knew it. The villagers would call the farmers in from the hides around the valley and they would hang Wulfhere in the square, for all to gawp at him as he choked and dangled on the rope. It was no way for a warrior to die, especially one who had bled for his people, and fought the fearsome Danes at Preston Brook. If any man knew how it felt to fall on hard times, it was Beornoth. Wulfhere had lost his way somewhere in his life. Perhaps his Lord had died in battle with an enemy, forcing Wulfhere to flee. Perhaps a son had inherited from his father and looked upon Wulfhere with ill favour. There were a multitude of reasons for a warrior to lose his master, his ring giver, and become an outlaw, a man living outside of the structure of Saxon life.

Cenwulf held out a small leather purse. Beornoth took it and the jangle of the hacked-up pieces of silver within made his stomach rumble with the promise of food, and his mouth water at the prospect of ale. A rumbling sound coming from the west interrupted his reverie, like thunder rolling down the valley before a violent storm.

'Horsemen,' said the blacksmith. The three villagers all looked to Beornoth. He shrugged, not having any idea who was approaching. Just in case, Beornoth went to his mare and pulled his axe free of his sheath and tucked it into his belt, and he grabbed his spear. He turned to stand in the centre of the square. The sound of thunder grew louder, and Beornoth felt its thrum beneath his boots. A troop of ten horsemen cantered around the bend in the village main street and reined in before the central platform, their mounts snorting and throwing up clods of hardened earth.

One man wore a shining helmet chased with fur, and a thick wool cloak with a stole of fox fur at his neck. He had a sword strapped to his waist and a war shield hung from the saddle of his monstrous warhorse. Beornoth straightened his back. He knew the man. The villagers bowed their heads to the warrior and his men; Beornoth did not.

'Beornoth,' shouted the richly dressed warrior, his voice deep and full.

'Ealdorman Aethelhelm,' said Beornoth.

'Still at blade work?'

'Always, Lord.'

'Who is this?' said Aethelhelm, pointing at Wulfhere.

'Brigand. A group of masterless men were up on Offa's Crag. Up to no good, attacked a few farms.'

'So they sent you up there.'

'They did, Lord.'

'What is your place here, Beornoth? I mean, you are no longer a Thegn, of course.' The Ealdorman cleared his throat as he muttered the last words and straightened himself in the saddle. Beornoth scratched at his beard; Aethelhelm knew well that Beornoth was not a Thegn any more. He knew because Aethelhelm was the man who had taken that rank away from him. Beornoth did not hate him for it. He had left the Ealdorman with little choice.

'He's the reeve of this hidage,' said Cenwulf, head still bowed, but looking up at the Ealdorman, his tongue flicking nervously at his lips. An Ealdorman ranked below only the King, and Aethelhelm was the Lord of vast swathes of land in the newly created shire of Cheshire. The great Saxon Lords had forged Cheshire after the death of Erik Bloodaxe from what was the western Kingdom of York and the lands south of the River Mersey, touching the borders of Mercia. A lowly man like Cenwulf, without rank, might only get to address a mighty Lord such as Aethelhelm once in his life, if he was lucky. Cenwulf was not about to allow that opportunity to slip by.

'How many hides in this hidage?' asked Aethelhelm.

'Ten hides, Lord. Good farms, all of them.'

Aethelhelm looked at Beornoth, and for a moment Beornoth thought he saw a look of sadness pass across the Ealdorman's face. Aethelhelm had fought the Danes for as long as Beornoth, which was to say that he had been fighting from the time he was old enough to hold a sword steady. The Ealdorman would remember Beornoth as he was, in the old days, and Beornoth saw pity written across Aethelhelm's face. Beornoth sniffed and met his gaze. He remembered himself as Aethelhelm would remember him, garbed in a fine chain-mail byrnie, helmet gleaming and a long cloak streaming behind him as he galloped along on a warhorse, bright sword drawn and ready to strike. Beornoth had been a Lord of War, a Thegn, and men had called him Lord, in those days long ago.

'How many masterless men were up there?'

'A few.' Beornoth shrugged.

'That means two,' said a young warrior, tall and slim, who sat astride a beautiful grey mare. The surrounding warriors sniggered. The young warrior had golden hair tied back with a strip of woven leather, and he wore a byrnie mail coat polished to a burnished shine.

'There were six, my Lords,' said Cenwulf, pushing his shoulders back and glancing at Beornoth. 'There were six, and Beornoth went up alone. Only the prisoner here lives.'

'Six?' asked the young man. 'They must have been asleep, or as drunk as beggars on free mead.' Some of the mounted warriors laughed again. Beornoth recognised two of the older men, grizzled warriors. They did not laugh at the jest; only the younger warriors chuckled along.

'Old Beornoth against six men, eh?' said the Ealdorman, grinning. 'They stood no chance. Beornoth here was a Thegn in the days when the Danes were still thick across the old Kingdom of York. He rode with me as we cleared them out in the years following the death of Bloodaxe. He's the man we are here to see.'

Aethelhelm got down from his warhorse amid much creaking of leather and loud groaning. Beornoth had indeed ridden for years as a young man with Aethelhelm, scouring the land of the fearsome Danish outlaws. Erik Bloodaxe was their last King in York, and he had died in the time of Beornoth's father, but the fallout from the great Viking King's death had continued for decades.

'Walk with me, Beornoth,' he said, striding through the mud of the village square. They walked together until out of earshot of the villagers and the Ealdorman's retainers.

'A long way from the old days,' said Aethelhelm, looking around the drab squalor of the village. Beornoth said nothing. Memories of his old Hall with its golden thatch clawed their way up from the depths of his mind. Then a vision of his wife at the Hall doors, the sun shining in her hair and the sound of his children playing rang in his head. 'Terrible business, what happened to you and yours,' Aethelhelm continued.

'Yes, Lord.'

'Still. A man like you is bred for the blade. And there's always a need for killers to protect the sheep.'

'Yes, Lord.'

'They are back, Beo.'

'Who, Lord?'

'Who else? The Vikings. They're raiding along the south and east coast in large numbers. Fishermen report sightings of their cursed dragon boats. Fearsome men and warriors all.'

'So they're in Essex and Wessex, then. They must have a new leader?'

'Some young wolf called Olaf Tryggvason, from the far north, I hear. He will be a King one day, and you know as well as I that to be a King amongst the Northmen, a man must be savage, cunning and have a great reputation.'

'With a name like that, he sounds more like a Norseman than a Dane. At least they are down south this time, Lord. Away from your lands.'

'Could be a Norseman. They are down south, but the King has ordered me and the rest of the King's Thegns in all the shires to bring warriors south to help fight the enemy.'

'How many will ride, Lord?'

'All of my Thegns and most of my retainers. Not yet though. I have work to finish here in the north first. So, I will send a few men ahead, good men. Men who know how to kill Danes. Or Norsemen.' Aethelhelm stopped and put a gloved hand on Beornoth's shoulder. 'I want you to go, Beo, take some of my men and my bastard son with you. Kill some bloody Vikings and teach my bastard how to fight.'

Beornoth looked into the Ealdorman's rheumy eyes. Aethelhelm had been present in the maelstrom of Beornoth's life for as long as he could remember. He had been a good Lord, but also the man who had stripped everything from Beornoth in the dark days. He did not blame him for that, though; it was his duty as Ealdorman.

'If you go, Beornoth, and you fight well, when you return, I will give you back a Heriot, with weapons, a home and all the rights which go with it.'

The breath caught in Beornoth's chest. So, kill some Vikings, and all Aethelhelm had taken away he would restore. The inheritance and honour of Beornoth's family, going back to the time when his ancestors first came to the shores of Britain to win themselves a Kingdom, the Ealdorman would give back to him. His shame washed away with the blood of Viking raiders.

'Does Theodred still hold my Heriot?'

'He does. Your mail, your sword, your helmet, your warhorse and your old lands. All the things which belonged to your father before you.'

'Does he go south, to kill Vikings?'

'Not yet, but he will.'

'And you would take from him all that you took from me, my father's Heriot, my family's weapons and lands?'

'No, Beo. But fight, do what you do best and I will grant you a new Heriot, new lands and weapons.'

'Then I cannot go, my Lord. My place is here as reeve. You command Thegns, and a Thegn's purpose is to fight for his Lord and fulfil his oath. You grant the Heriot because the man who holds it must bring the granted weapons, his horse and the warriors from the lands he holds, to fight for his Ealdorman and for the King. So, Theodred can march south to mind your son and kill the sea wolves.'

# 3

'Turns out the stories about this man were fanciful horseshit, after all. Beornoth, the brutal warrior, champion of the Battle at Preston Brook,' said the golden-haired warrior with a smirk, his horse snorting and scraping at the earth. 'This reeve is afraid of the Vikings. We will go, the real warriors, father. We shall teach these damned heathens a lesson.'

'Beornoth has killed more Danes than you have had hot meals,' said the Ealdorman, and shot a frown at Beornoth. 'I can't force you. And you should be careful, turning down my offer with your prideful tongue. I am an Ealdorman, and I can force you if I choose. Don't let pride impede a chance to redeem yourself. The people down south need your sword. These are raiding Vikings. Hungry for war. They come with vengeance in their hearts for the death of Eric Bloodaxe and the many Dane and Norse farmers killed in the purges that followed. These men who sail to our shores are burners, killers, rapists and slayers of children. You know more than most what those simple people in the south face. They need Saxon wolves to stand up to the invader. The people need our own killers to protect them. You should be able to follow our trail for a few days if you change your mind. We ride west to gather more men from my lands, and then we go south. Follow us if you want to win back your Thegnhood.'

The riders wheeled their mounts around and thundered off, returning up the road from which they had arrived. Beornoth stood for a while and watched them disappear into the distance, calm returning to the small village once more. Everything Aethelhelm had said was true. The Saxon people would feel the pain of Viking savagery. If they were in the south to raid, then the long, sleek warships with their shallow draughts would sail up rivers, deep into the heart of Essex, Wessex, Mercia and East Anglia. They would strike fast, their goal to become wealthy, and kill, burn and cut a swathe of destruction across the country. Beornoth knew more than most the pain those farmers and peasants would face, and that they depended on the King and his network of King's Thegns, and the Thegns sworn to the Ealdorman of the shires to bring their swords and shields to fight the Vikings. But Beornoth didn't carry a sword, and nor did he wear a byrnie mail coat. Aethelhelm had taken them away, those weapons of great value and prestige, and given them to another man. Fighting on a promise of a new Heriot was not enough. It was not enough for him to ride with arrogant, young, untested warriors like that golden-haired fool amongst Aethelhelm's men. Beornoth imagined the pleasure in teaching that pup how to fight, rather than Aethelhelm's bastard, hours of strength training and weapons drills until he wept from the pain. Ealdorman Aethelhelm's men were all well-armed and well-mounted, and Beornoth would go to war carrying his rusting axe and old spear, and riding a nag too small for his hulking frame. They were the household troops of an Ealdorman and therefore ranked higher than a reeve. He might have fallen far, but Beornoth would be damned if he would take orders and allow himself to be mocked by a gaggle of snot-nosed bastards.

'Is there war? Are the Danes returned?' asked Cenwulf, a cracking nervousness in his voice.

'There's always war. The Danes will always return,' said Beornoth, his voice harsher than he intended. He turned his back on Cenwulf and winced at a stabbing pain in the small of his back. Beornoth strode towards the tavern. He needed to get his wound dressed, but more importantly, he needed a drink. His belly was sour, churning and twisting around Aethelhelm's offer. Kill some Norsemen, and the Ealdorman would attempt to make good all that he had taken away. It sounded so simple. These new Vikings, fresh from their harsh northern homes, would be pagan Odin worshippers, men who longed to die a glorious death in battle, hungry men looking for silver and glory and to please their Gods with blood. For them, war was their pathway to their heavenly hall in Valhalla. They fought prepared to die, craving glorious death in combat. Death in battle being the only way of securing their place in the feasting halls of their Gods. Beornoth had fought such men before, and it was no simple matter. The Danes in the Kingdom of York were mostly Christians, having lived in Britain for generations where, over time, they had learned to follow the one true God. The Christian religion had softened them. They were still hardy fighters and skilled warriors, but had lost the raw Odin ferocity of the wild pagan Northmen.

Beornoth stalked past Wulfhere, who huddled naked against the village's raised platform, filthy and cowed. No doubt the man had held honour and reputation once in his life, but now that life would end badly. He was a big man, and the scars on his forearms and face gave him away as a veteran warrior. The farmers and villagers would not be gentle with him. Beornoth tore his eyes away from the man, his plight a stark and visceral reminder of the fate waiting for fallen warriors, a masterless man brought to heel. Beornoth reached the tavern. He tried the double oak doors, but they were locked, so he rapped his knuckles on the thick timber. From inside the building, Beornoth could hear grumbling, and the scrape of furniture, followed by the clank and scratch of an iron door lock sliding free of its catch. The door opened a sliver, and the musty smell of stale ale and fire smoke wafted out to smother Beornoth's senses. He licked his dry lips and rubbed at his throat. A wild-haired, long-faced woman poked her head through the crack in the door. She frowned, deep lines in her forehead creasing upwards.

'I should have known it was you,' she said, and pursed her lips. A pattern of wrinkles carved the skin of her top lip, criss-crossing the space between her nose and mouth. 'You already owe me too much, Beo. I can't give you any more to drink.'

He raised the pouch of silver and jangled it. 'I need a drink, Blaedswith, and that cursed brigand I brought in cut me during the fight. Can you take a look at it?'

'Come on in, then. I must be bloody mad,' she said with a sigh. But she smiled and put a veiny hand on his shoulder, ushering him into the gloom beyond the tavern door.

Beornoth slumped into a chair at a table made from an upturned ale barrel with planking nailed to the top. He yawned and rubbed at his stinging eyes, Aethelhelm's offer still swimming around in his mind like a fish stuck in a weir trap. Blaedswith returned, clutching a tankard of frothing ale, and Beornoth took it from her hungrily. He took a long pull, savouring the honeyed flavours as it washed down his throat, satisfying not only his thirst but also his craving for the warmth the drink brought, the cloak of dullness it threw over the darkness in his head.

He nodded his thanks and cuffed away the froth from his beard.

'Off with it,' said Blaedswith, pointing at his baked leather breastplate and jerkin. He remembered the wound, and stood to strip to the waist, wincing at the sharp pain in his lower back. She helped him pull the breastplate over his head, and tutted at the wound, wrinkling her nose.

'You smell like a boar. You need a dip in the river, or at least a wash from a bowl of water.' Beornoth couldn't remember the last time he had washed himself. In his line of work, cleanliness was not high on the list of important attributes.

'Is it bad?' he asked, flinching as her fingers probed at the wound.

'For such a big, hard man, you squeal like a child. It's a long cut, I'll have to sew you up. Again. You've had more stitches than my winter cloak, Beo. You need to take more care of yourself.'

Blaedswith washed down the wound, and used a bone needle and gut string to draw the lips of the cut together and sew it closed. Beornoth swilled three tankards of ale during that time, and once she had finished and had helped him back on with his clothes and breastplate, she brought another pot of ale for him, and one for herself.

'Thank you, Blaedswith,' he said, and dropped the pouch of silver onto the tabletop.

'You can pay me for the ale, Beo, but the healing is free. I owe it to Eawynn. She was a fine woman, and a good friend, she looked after me when I needed it most and I do not forget that.'

Beornoth looked at the floor rushes and nodded. Blaedswith covered the floor of her tavern with rushes or hay to soak up the spillages and leavings of her customers.

'Such a shame.' She placed her hand on his arm and rubbed it in sympathy. 'What was the commotion outside? I thought I heard the Ealdorman's voice.'

Beornoth sniffed and took another pull of his ale, glad to

change the subject from his wife. 'I went up to Offa's Crag to deal with a gaggle of masterless men and brought one bastard back here to give the people their justice. Then the Ealdorman rode into town, with his men.'

'Justice. These cowards hide behind you, Beo, you know they are supposed to provide and arm a warrior from the hides. You do all of that for them.'

He waved a hand to dismiss her point. She was right, though. The villagers around the valley under the King's Law were supposed to provide and arm a warrior for every ten hides, which was every ten farms. They paid Beornoth as their reeve, and as reeve, his job was to keep order and provide justice, and he took the place of the armed warrior they were due to provide to the King if the order came for the army of the people, or fyrd, to muster.

'I know, I know.'

'You don't know. They have a former Thegn, one of the best warriors in the Kingdom, acting as their reeve. They should pay you more, Beo.'

'Maybe they should. I'll ask that shit Cenwulf to settle my tab with you next time.'

'Next time is never time. What did the old Ealdorman want, anyway?'

'The Vikings are back, raiding in the south. The King has sent for his Thegns to ride and support the southern shires. Aethelhelm will send warriors and go himself.'

'And he asks you to go?'

'He wants me to go,' confirmed Beornoth, draining his pot of ale.

'After everything, he asks you to fight the Vikings. For him. Did he mention your Heriot? You are, after all, no longer a

Thegn.' She held up her hands to apologise for mentioning the sensitive subject.

'He did. Theodred still holds my Heriot, raised up to it on the back of his father's wealth, the snivelling bastard. But if I fight well, then Aethelhelm will provide me with a new Heriot.'

Blaedswith's jaw dropped. 'He would create a new Heriot, a new Thegnhood. For you?'

'So he said. He wants me to take his bastard son along, to teach him how to fight.'

'That's by the by, surely?' she said, standing and rubbing her hands on her apron. She paced the tavern floor, a smile creasing her lined face. 'He would give you lands, a byrnie, sword, warhorse and such. It would restore you, Beo. Your father up in Heaven will rejoice.'

'I doubt that miserable so-and-so rejoices at anything, and if he's in Heaven, then there's hope for all of us,' said Beo, remembering his father for the brutal, surly and cruel man that he was. 'I said no, anyway.'

'You said no?'

Beornoth nodded and held up his empty tankard to Blaedswith. But she waved it away, and instead leaned close to him with her hands on her knees, peering deep into his eyes.

'All you ever talk about is your lost Heriot. How the Ealdorman took away your Hall, your byrnie, which had been your father's mail coat and his father's before him. He took your father's sword, spear and shield. He took away your warhorse and your shining helmet, and you were a Thegn no longer. You come in here every day, get stinking drunk. Talk to no one but me, and when you do talk, it's to moan about all that you have lost. Now, you have a chance to get it all back, and you said no?'

Beornoth sighed and looked at his boots. 'Aethelhelm was

right to take it away from me. I couldn't protect the people, or serve him properly in the mess I was in. Besides, it wouldn't be my Heriot, my family's Hall, lands and weapons. Theodred has that.'

'You sound like a child,' said Blaedswith, tutting and throwing her hands into the air. 'You would be a Thegn again, answerable only to the Ealdorman and the King. They would restore your family's honour. And you said no? So, your plan is to sit in here drinking ale all day until you fall down drunk, and continue as the reeve, killing and doing ruffian work for the local villagers for handfuls of silver?'

'Killing Vikings is no simple matter, Blaedswith. These will be pure Northmen, the finest warriors in the world.'

'What are you, if not a killer? The King needs his own wolves, his own savage men to fight the Northmen. How else can we win? Is he to send the fyrd against them, a gaggle of farmers and potters, to fight the sea wolves? The King needs men like you, Beornoth. Besides, Eawynn would want you to do it. She wouldn't want you wallowing in here pissed drunk every day.'

Beornoth thought of his wife, as she was in the old days. Quick to laughter, but also stern and strong. She had been a loving wife and a marvellous mother. He missed her every day. She would scold him if she saw how far he had fallen and what he was doing with his life. He pushed himself to his feet and stretched gingerly down to one side. The stitches were tight and itchy, but the wound would heal well. He took the purse and held it out to Blaedswith, but she shook her head.

'You'll need that for the journey.' She handed him a large skin of ale, the liquid inside sloshing as he took it. 'You'll need this, too.'

Beornoth nodded his thanks and strode to the door. He turned to check Blaedswith wasn't looking and left the pouch of coins on a table by the door. She deserved it. She was a good woman and a good friend. One of the few friends Beornoth had left in this miserable world. He walked across the square, where a spiteful rain began to fall, bouncing in the mud in thousands of tiny splatters. Beornoth made for his home, the small bed at the back of Cenwulf's merchant's store which he rented from the villager. He ducked under the door lintel and pulled off his breastplate, and stacked his weapons against the wall. Lowering himself onto the pallet bed filled with straw, Beornoth touched at the stitches. They were rough and crusted with blood, but Blaedswith had done a good job. There would be a scar there. Another line of raised scar tissue on his body. To add to the countless others, each told a tale of men killed and blood spilled. Beornoth grabbed the large ale skin, and, as he did most days, drank himself into oblivion.

'Wake up, Beo,' said a gruff voice, accompanied by a boot nudging his shoulder. 'Wake up. Jesus and the saints in Heaven, but you stink. Have you pissed yourself?'

Beornoth groaned, his head pounded, and he swallowed against a stinging, dry throat. He opened his eyes a slit, but torch-light hurt his eyes. 'Bugger off,' he croaked, to whoever had disturbed his drunken slumber. He guessed it was early evening.

'I won't bugger off. We paid you today, and you owe me coin for food and your regular repayments, which are most irregular.' It was Swidhelm, then. Beornoth owed the man silver. He had borrowed from him to pay Cenwulf for his lodging, amongst other things, but he had no silver left to pay him. He pushed himself to sitting and heaved over the side of his bed. The contraction of his torso produced nothing, but he heaved again, this time his whole body convulsing and pulling against the fresh stitches. A sour trickle of thick yellow liquid dripped from his mouth into the floor rushes and Beornoth wiped his hand on the back of his arm.

'I don't have it,' he groaned, pressing a hand to his throbbing head.

'You're a disgrace. A piss-stinking, drunken embarrassment. To think you were once a Thegn, lauded by all. Little wonder God punished you as he did. You and your wife deserve little better if this is the level of your moral fortitude.'

Beornoth looked up at Swidhelm. The tall man sneered and made the sign of the cross. 'What did you say about my family?' Beornoth said. He ground his teeth and peered up through half-closed eyes.

'I said you are a disgrace, and no wonder God punished you and yours if this is the level of your godliness,' said Swidhelm, tucking his thumbs in his belt and raising an eyebrow. 'You owe me...'

He didn't have time to finish speaking. Beornoth rose and grabbed Swidhelm by the throat, squeezing the soft skin of the villager's neck in his enormous fist. He felt the lump of Swidhelm's Adam's apple against the callouses of his palm and squeezed harder, driving him against the wall. Swidhelm's eyes bulged, and he clawed at Beornoth's arms, but he was weak. Beornoth leant in close to him.

'You don't talk about my wife or my children, ever. Your God forsook me and mine.'

Beornoth looked into the blue of Swidhelm's eyes, and anger twisted his mouth into a rictus of hate. All his life he had protected these people, brought his sword and strength to keep the wolves away. Yes, he was drunk, and he had pissed himself in his drunken sleep, but he was a warrior and he was sick of sheep such as Swidhelm, taunting and judging him. A vision of his wife, brown-eyed and beautiful, cradling one of his baby daughters, flashed before his eyes. He roared in Swidhelm's face and threw him to the hard packed-earth floor. Beornoth stamped on Swidhelm's belly. He dropped to straddle Swidhelm and headbutted him twice, feeling Swidhelm's cheekbone crack and shatter against his forehead. Swidhelm yelped and twisted away, his legs scrambling in the floor rushes. Beornoth grabbed Swidhelm by the face, his hand grasping the flesh of nose, cheek and eye, and he wanted to smash his head into the ground and crush his skull. Beornoth ground his teeth but caught his anger before it turned to murder, a crime he would surely hang for. Instead, Beornoth punched Swidhelm beneath his ear, sending him into darkness.

Beornoth knelt and put his hands on his knees to catch his breath. He had hurt a freeman, an honest man. Swidhelm had spoken ill of Beornoth's family, but assaulting him was a crime, an attack that might yet be murder if he didn't wake up. Reeve or not, Beornoth would either have to pay a weregild to Swidlhelm's family in recompense for the crime – but he had no wealth and the price would be high – or he would hang. Beornoth told himself that Swidhelm was a bastard, and that he deserved it. A memory of children laughing tried to force its way into Beornoth's mind, but he pushed it away. Beornoth knew what he was, and he was a killer. Blaedswith was right. They needed him down south; they needed men like him to fight the Vikings. His life here would be over anyway, now that Swidhelm was badly beaten, possibly dead. So he searched Swidhelm's body and took two pouches of silver. He stripped Swidhelm's clothes and tipped a jug of water over his own head to wake himself up, and across his trews to wash away the piss stains. Outside was Swidhelm's horse, so Beornoth took that, too. He retrieved his own horse and strapped his weapons to the saddle.

Beornoth led the two horses by their bridles into the village square. Rain drifted from the hills, slanting from a patchwork sky of bleak darkness mixed with bright white cloud. A gaggle of urchins were poking at Wulfhere with sticks and throwing stones at him. The children hooted with laughter at his nakedness, and screamed with delight whenever he lashed a foot out at them.

'Get away, you filthy little toads,' growled Beornoth, and the children scattered to the corners of the village, laughing as they went.

'Piss off, watch you don't fall over or piss on your boots. Alehouse rat,' one brave child called from an unseen hiding place, and the others cackled their amusement.

Wulfhere curled up into a ball, shivering in the rain. His wrists were red raw where Beornoth had tied them to the high platform. He scowled up at Beornoth. Red welts covered his body where the children had struck at him.

'If you want to live, swear an oath to be my man,' said Beornoth, and threw the bundle of Swidhelm's clothes into the mud next to the big man. 'I go to fight Vikings, though. So make your choice. Die here like a dog, or swear to me and kill Norsemen.'

'I'll be your man,' said Wulfhere, grinning with a gap-toothed smile. 'Better to die on a Viking blade than on the end of a rope here in this shithole.'

So Beornoth cut him free, and Wulfhere pulled on the clothes. He was a large, broad-shouldered warrior, and the smaller man's clothes were short on his arms and legs. Beornoth knew he must swallow any bitterness for Aethelhelm. He had to. If there was a chance to win back his honour and his family's status, then he must take it. He might not have the chance to fight for his old Heriot back, but to be a Thegn again would at least restore something of what he once was. If he was to make the journey south, then it would be with the Ealdorman's hearth-troops who had taunted Beornoth in the village square. Those men would not accept Beornoth as one of them. They would always see him for what he was: a fallen man. Wulfhere, at least, would be his man, and Beornoth hoped, someone that he could rely upon in a fight. Beornoth wiped the rain from his face and thumbed the edge of his axe. He would ride after Aethelhelm and fight the Vikings. Blaedswith was right, he would kill the raiders and win back his family's honour, or die trying.

# 4

Beornoth caught up with Aethelhelm and his men south of the ancient Roman city of Chester. Aethelhelm had traversed his landholdings, calling his Thegns to arms, and so had taken a longer road south. That great walled city lay outside of the Ealdorman's shire but it offered the last opportunity to provision the men and horses before their long journey south would take them into Mercia and then on down through Britain's midlands and towards Wessex and East Anglia. Each of those lands had once been a kingdom in its own right, ruled by great Kings reaching far into the distant past to the time when the Saxons first arrived on Britain's shores from across the sea beyond Frankia to drive the native people back into the corners of Wales and Cornwall, and to forge kingdoms for themselves.

During the ride south-west, Beornoth and Wulfhere had stopped at the town of Rumcofa to find more suitable clothing for Wulfhere. But Beornoth had instead used the small amount of silver he still possessed to buy ale, and so spent the journey from Rumcofa to Chester swaying in the saddle and swigging from one of the three ale skins he had purchased. Wulfhere scowled and itched at Swidhelm's jerkin and trews. They stretched tight across his chest and thighs, and rode high on his calves and forearms, and Beornoth taunted him for looking like a King's fool, chuckling to himself in a mumbled drawl. They found the Ealdorman and his men at a ford across a tributary of the River Dee, which ran in wide, meandering curves around the Roman city before flowing south and west into Wales.

'Good to see you saw sense, Beo. I must ride east across more of my shire and gather more men. I'll follow you south in a week. You have brought a companion,' said Aethelhelm, sneering down his long nose at Wulfhere, who looked every part a beggar, with only his sheer size and scarred face marking him out as a warrior. 'You will take my youngest son, Alfgar, under your wing. Teach him what you know, Beornoth. I had hoped he would find a place in the clergy, but alas, he is not a man of letters. So you must teach him to fight. My eldest son, Osric, will go with you, and the captain of my men, Streonwold, will take command. Search out Byrhtnoth, who is the Ealdorman of Essex, and a friend. He's a warrior and will lead his men into the fight against the Norsemen. Join your swords to his until I ride south.'

'I have your word, Lord, on all that you promised?' Beornoth asked, reluctant to question Aethelhelm's word as an Ealdorman, but also keen for assurance that the Heriot was still promised in return for Beornoth's commitment to fight.

'Of course you have my word. Is that good enough for you, Beo?' Aethelhelm said, frowning. 'Streonwold, my son Osric and others here are all aware of my promise to you, Beornoth. Am I not renowned as a fair Lord, and ring giver?'

'Yes, Lord,' said Beornoth, and he bowed his head, his face flushing from the Ealdorman's frown, but content that others had heard that which was promised.

The Ealdorman rode east with four of his retainers, leaving

Beornoth and Wulfhere under Streonwold's command. Streon-wold was a short but stocky warrior of an age with Beornoth. The two men had fought side by side many times, and Beornoth would have considered him a friend in the old days.

'Welcome, Beo,' was all Streonwold said to acknowledge that Beornoth had joined his group of riders. But it was enough. Beornoth was not expecting a smile or a clap on the back from the surly captain.

'That's all we need, a drunk and a bloody beggar,' said the golden-haired warrior amongst them. Beornoth was dismayed, but not surprised to learn that he was Osric, the Ealdorman's eldest son and heir. Beornoth belched and straightened himself in the saddle. An insult like that was intended to spike a warrior's pride, but Beornoth's pride had fled long ago, swilled away by ale and the humiliating loss of his Heriot. Osric shook his head. 'Try to pull yourself together. We ride to war.'

'Alfgar,' growled Streonwold.

'Here,' came a callow voice from the rear of the horsemen.

'Show yourself, lad,' said Streonwold. A tall, thin youth wearing an ill-fitting leather breastplate and a leather helmet liner on his head urged his horse forward alongside Streonwold. The captain's dark warhorse snorted at the youth's mount, and it jerked sideways, causing the young man to topple. He only saved himself from falling to the ground by awkwardly clinging on to the pommel of his saddle. The surrounding riders sniggered, and Osric laughed aloud, and urged his horse onwards, followed by two companions.

'Alfgar, this is Beornoth. He's an old friend, and a warrior. Listen to him, watch him, and learn from him. You will stick to him like shit to a sheep's arse and do as he says. Now go on and catch up to your brother,' said Streonwold.

The youth nodded and offered a wan smile to Beornoth before riding after Osric.

'He's a bit soft, and the Ealdorman wants him toughened up. He wants him in harm's way, Beo,' said Streonwold, giving Beornoth a hard look.

'I bet he does,' said Beornoth, watching the youth wobbling in the saddle. The Ealdorman was no doubt sending his gentle bastard to fight the Vikings knowing that he would return as a toughened, experienced warrior, or not at all. A second or third son of an Ealdorman, or a bastard son, was a problem. The first son would inherit and become Ealdorman himself one day, but the others must either find a place in the Church, or become a warrior. There was no place in an Ealdorman's world for anything in between.

Beornoth reached for his skin of ale and took another pull. Drips poured down his beard, and he closed his eyes, feeling his senses dulling and eyes heavy under the influence of the yeasty brew.

'Try to stay sober, Beo,' said Streonwold, and Beornoth saw the look of disdain on his old friend's face. Streonwold, like Aethelhelm, would remember Beornoth as he was, and the sight of him now was but a shadow of his former self. Beornoth took another swig of his ale and nodded to Streonwold.

'Don't worry. I can still fight.'

The group began the journey south, riding through the valleys and dales on the borders of the Kingdom of York before entering the old Kingdom of Mercia, which was not a Kingdom in its own right any longer, and formed part of the Kingdom of Wessex, which was essentially the Kingdom of Angle Land, or England, which ran from the island's south coast all the way to where the northern borders edged the wild lands of the Picts and Strath Clota.

Alfgar rode between Beornoth and Wulfhere, and kept himself to himself, the silence welcome as Beornoth continued to make his way through the remnants of his ale. Beornoth felt his heart grow heavy as they reached the midlands and approached the lands surrounding the city of Tamwerthie. Passing this way meant he had to pay a visit to a convent in the environs of the city, a visit that would raise ghosts and tear at his memories like a monster from the depths of hell. Beornoth told Streonwold he would make the detour, and Streonwold did not object, knowing the nature of the visit Beornoth must make, and on the condition that he return to the group by nightfall. So, Beornoth took Wulfhere and Alfgar and rode for the convent of St Brigid.

They reached the high timber walls of the convent by midday; the sky was the pale blue of bluebells and a light breeze carried the sound of bees at work in the conical hives which dotted the edges of the place of worship, where it stood in a bright, peaceful glade.

'I hope we aren't here to say prayers,' said Wulfhere, scowling at the high cross on the building's gable, and making the sign of the cross on his chest.

'You two will wait out here. I won't be long. You could do with saying a few prayers for God's forgiveness,' said Beornoth, frowning at Wulfhere. Alfgar crossed himself but remained silent, and Wulfhere slid from his saddle to stretch his back. Beornoth left his horse with the two men and walked to the gate. He glanced up at the high cross where it reached out towards Heaven and the power of God. He crossed himself half-heartedly, more from reflex than respect, and the act made him feel guilty. Beornoth had not seen the inside of a church for many years. God had forsaken him, and he had given up on God and Christ in return. He knocked on the door, and it banged against its black painted iron hinges. After a while, a small, square opening in the gate slid open, and a pale face with pursed lips peered out at him.

'It's you,' said the nun.

'I'm here to see her.'

'Well, I assume you are not here to say confession. Have you been drinking?' she asked. She sniffed and then scowled at him, but did not wait for a response. 'Wait there.'

Beornoth could hear the grating and sliding of bolts behind the timber gate before it swung open to reveal a bright courtyard filled by a vegetable garden, where nuns knelt tending to plants, and a small grove of fruit trees. Beornoth's heart lifted to see the place. It was a haven of peace and tranquillity, and he told himself that he was glad she was here. Shielded from the world's cruelty and, he hoped, distracted from the horrors of her memories, which lay locked inside her head like a caged bear.

'This way,' said the nun, and she set off at a brisk walk with a set of iron keys attached to a wide loop jangling at her waist with each step.

'Is she well?' asked Beornoth.

'As well as can be expected.'

They walked through the courtyard and on into a stone-floored hallway with doors on either side. Beornoth's boots echoed off the stone floor and around the timber ceiling of the hallway, and he wished he had cleaned them before entering the convent. Glancing behind him, Beornoth saw the trail of mud he had left. He ran a hand through his hair to get some of the knots out, and through his beard to smooth it out as best he could. The nun stopped outside a door halfway along the corridor, and took a key from the large iron loop and slid it into a dark lock, but before turning the key she glanced at Beornoth.

'Don't upset her. She has been calmer of late. She still might not recognise you, so don't expect too much. It was a terrible thing. She has been through so much. Only by God's grace is she still with us.'

Beornoth swallowed and clenched his fists. God's grace. He had seen little of that in his life. He pushed the door open, and the nun stepped aside, peering around him and tutting at the muddy trail he had left down the corridor. He turned his shoulders sideways to get past her, and ducked under the door's lintel. His heart caught in his chest as he saw the outline of a woman with long hair against the bright glare of an open window, the shutters opened wide to allow the light and earthy smells of the courtyard to imbue the room with a sense of freshness and cleanliness.

He edged around the room until he came alongside the woman's profile. The sun shone on her long dark hair and the familiar shape of her nose and chin. She turned to him, and the gorge in his throat rose, and he flinched from her. She looked at him, dark brown eyes empty, her mouth slightly open, but no sign of recognition on her face. A jagged scar ran from her throat up across her cheek, and she turned away from him to look out of the window once more.

'Eawynn,' he breathed, almost whispering. 'It's me, Beo.'

She didn't move. He took a step closer to the woman who had been his wife, his everything, for that first, joyful part of his life.

'It's the girls' birthdays soon,' he said, but she didn't move. 'Our little ones would have been fourteen summers old this year.' Only they weren't. They were forever frozen as they had been when they died, small children filled with laughter. Running around Beornoth's Hall and lands, playing and bringing joy to all.

'Eawynn, please, my love,' he said, and reached out towards her, but held his hand back. He looked at it, scarred and calloused, shaking in the space between him and her. All Beornoth wanted to do in that moment was take her in his arms and hold her tight, take her away and look after her himself. But the time for that had passed, he had instead found his solace in ale and the Ealdorman had sent Eawynn south to the convent, to be cared for by the sisters of St Brigid's. It was for the best, because when she had needed him most, he had left her alone and slipped into the warm embrace of drunken anguish. He had not been there on that terrible day, when their world was ripped apart, and he had not been there afterwards to pick up the pieces either.

'I'm sorry,' he whispered. She turned to him again, that vacant look still on her face, but this time a solitary tear rolled down her scarred cheek. Then she quivered and then shook. Her face turned from serene emptiness into a twisted mask of grief and hatred. She lunged at him, beating on his chest and clawing at his face.

'You left us. We needed you and you weren't there. I hate you; I curse you; I hate you!' she screamed, the words hurtling from her snarling mouth. Beornoth tried to hold her back, but she had become feral and, with the strength of the mad, she drove him backwards. Outside of the door, a bell rang, and moments later, six sisters charged into the room and grabbed Eawynn and dragged her off him. Beornoth watched them pull her to the ground, shouting to each other to tie her and secure her. Beornoth just stared, open-mouthed and horrified. An image of her on their wedding day came to him, yellow and blue flowers in her hair, and her smile beautiful. Then another image of his Hall as a charred mess, with the bones of his children in the ashes, and his wife used and cut by Viking raiders.

Beornoth strode from the room and dropped what remained of the silver he had taken from Swidhelm on a small table by the door. He walked through the courtyard so fast that he almost ran. His chest heaved with the horror of it, the pain of her being left like this to suffer. Why did God not help her? All of her suffering, and the loss of his children, lay at the feet of the Viking men of war. Brutal men who lived by the sword and the law of their pagan Gods. The Northmen were back, and their raiding meant more burning, death and suffering. Beornoth would take his blades and his strength and avenge the past and protect people of Saxon England. He would soak the earth with the raiders' blood and throw them back into the cruel, dark sea which spewed them forth.

# 5

Beornoth and the rest of Streonwold's riders made the journey across the heartland of central Mercia in a few days and without incident. The chill mornings and fresh greenery of late spring turned into early summer, and morning hoar frost over grass and ditch gave way to bright, hazy days where the sun warmed Beornoth's face. The worst Beornoth had to face during the ride was the sneers and hushed laughter of Osric and his band of loyal followers. They were careful enough to say nothing offensive within his hearing, and at the evening campfires Beornoth drank enough ale to drown out their bragging talk of the brave deeds they would accomplish, and how they would strike fear into the hearts of the fearsome Norsemen.

The journey took the riders south-east, heading towards the corner of Britain known as Essex, the lands of the East Saxons, where Ealdorman Byrhtnoth ruled in the name of the King Æthelred. Streonwold rode at the head of the small column, and as the riders crested a heather-topped hill, Beornoth rode along-side the captain of Ealdorman Aethelhelm's men.

'The land of the East Saxons,' Beornoth said, looking down

into the lush green valley stretching below them. Hamlets and farms dotted a sweeping, fertile view of green, brown and golden fields.

'We need to find Byrhtnoth as soon as we can, and add our men to his,' said Streonwold. Beornoth took a long pull at an ale skin, one of three he had purchased for hack silver borrowed from one of Aethelhelm's men the day before. He had drunk two already, and this was his last skin. He passed it to Streonwold, but the warrior held up a hand to refuse, and looked from the skin to Beornoth with an arched eyebrow.

'Do you know Byrhtnoth?'

'I've met him before. He's a tough old dog, a fighter. His lands run from the river Thames in Lundenwic all the way to the east coast, so he's also a rich old dog.'

'Lots of men, then.'

'He keeps warriors in the field. It's not ten years yet since they killed the last King, and the new King came to power. Byrhtnoth supported the old King, so I imagine he's had to do a bit of fighting to protect his lands.'

'And now the Norsemen are here.'

'They are, so all we need to do is look for smoke or ships.'

The riders were a half day beyond the town of Celmersfort, and heading for a river which ran through the lands of the East Saxons and on to the sea. Streonwold had asked men labouring in a field for any news of Byrhtnoth, and they had pointed east and said they should make for Ceolmaer's ford. It was on the way to that ford that they first saw the signal they looked for, a column of smoke snatched here and there by the wind, winding its way above a treeline in the distance.

'There, smoke,' Wulfhere called, his keen eyes spotting the smudge on the skyline.

'That's just a Hall fire,' said Osric. 'No need to be afraid. We should go there and enjoy their hospitality. Some fresh meat and warm bread would be welcome. And if it is smoke, I hope there are Vikings there. I'll give them a taste of good Saxon steel. My blade, Heartcrusher, will take some heads before this fight is over.'

'That's no Hall fire, that's burning thatch,' growled Streonwold. Beornoth thought Streonwold was right. There was too much smoke to be a simple hearth fire. They urged their mounts on towards the pillar of smoke. Osric talked in a hushed voice with his men, who sniggered along with him at whatever words he uttered, but kept from the rest of the group.

Beornoth smelled the village before he saw it. The greens and browns of the countryside gave way to a smear of grey and black desolation. It had been a collection of short, thatched wattle buildings, but all that remained were smoking piles of charred timbers. A group of a dozen people with soot and ash-blackened arms and faces huddled at one end of the village where they knelt together, praying. A stubble-tonsured priest in a long brown smock said words over them, his face looking bright white against the black darkness of the smoke-damaged folk. Beornoth gagged as he approached. The smell of roasting meat hung in the air, and he held his hand over his nose at what was the stench of burning human flesh. He could see twisted, small figures between the smoking timbers, their skeletons shrunken by the flames and their limbs grasping and desperate. It was a familiar smell, nauseating and forever etched into Beornoth's mind as a reminder of the horrors of his past.

'The smell,' hissed Osric, bringing his own hand to his nose.

'The smell of the Vikings. Get used to it,' said Beornoth. He stepped down from his horse and walked towards the gathered survivors. The priest saw him coming and nodded in his direction.

'Protection is here. The Lord has sent warriors to protect us from the marauding heathens,' the priest said and made the sign of the cross above the kneeling people. They turned to him, the whites of their eyes bright against their blackened faces, features drawn by the horror. Tears had streaked pathways of grief down their cheeks.

'When did this happen?' said Beornoth.

'They came at first light. They were among us before we knew it,' said a thin man with missing front teeth.

'Did they take anything?'

'Our women, they took two of our daughters. They took the young ones for slaves, killed others, left us old ones with nothing but ashes. Please, Lord. Help us,' sobbed a woman, then buried her face into the shoulder of the man kneeling next to her.

'How many ships?'

'One, Lord. A big ship with a dragon at its prow,' said the thin man.

Beornoth turned and stalked back to Streonwold. Alfgar walked towards him, his mouth slack and his footing unsure amongst the ashes. He looked at Beornoth, but could not meet his gaze, his eyes moving to the ground to avoid eye contact. Alfgar licked his lips and raised his hand slightly, but then clasped both hands together, wringing them and shaking his head.

'What is it?' barked Beornoth, taking a step towards him. 'Spit it out.'

'Should we not say something to these people, help them?' said Alfgar, looking from the kneeling people to the ruins of their lives amongst the ashes. He spoke softly, and still could not meet Beornoth's eye.

'What can you say to make things better for them?' said Beornoth.

'I don't know. I... we... should help them.'

'It's too late for them. Best thing for us to do is follow the river and find the bloody Vikings.'

'How can you not care about these poor people?' Alfgar said, as Beornoth walked past him. He ignored Alfgar, trying not to lose his temper with the young man.

'They took some women, either for slaves or pleasure. Nothing else, spits, ploughs, anything of value is still here,' Beornoth said, standing alongside Streonwold.

'Bastards were just here for murder,' said Streonwold, and spat into the ashes.

'Aye, there will be a dozen of such places ravaged if we don't catch up to them soon.'

'We find Byrhtnoth first. Join up with him.'

'The ship can't be far away, if we ride upriver...'

'We find the Ealdorman. The few men we have here can't fight a crew of Norsemen. We join the local forces, that is the command of Lord Aethelhelm. We can't charge off to fight on our own, Beo. I want vengeance just as much as you do. But we stand a better chance of defeating the Vikings if we join forces with the men of Essex,' said Streonwold.

'Get on your horse, drink your ale, and try not to fall off. We find the Ealdorman,' said Osric. He looked down at the villagers, not even attempting to hide the pitiless sneer on his face. 'It's not our fault their Thegns left these people unprotected. Bloody southerners. This wouldn't happen up north.'

'Fool, boy,' said Beornoth under his breath. The village was still smouldering, smoke rising from the charred remains of children. Osric was the son of an Ealdorman and had therefore lived a life of privilege. He knew nothing of the hard lives these people eked out, or the pain they felt at the murder of their loved ones.

'What did you say?' said Osric, straightening his back in the saddle and reaching for the grip of the sword he wore buckled at his waist. Beornoth bristled and took a step towards Osric, but Streonwold put a hand on his chest.

'Take your hand off your sword, Osric. I've seen men killed for less. We ride out. Now,' Streonwold growled.

Osric looked down his nose at Beornoth, the corner of his mouth twisting. He turned to his two friends and muttered something out of earshot. The two men laughed, and they rode on past the praying, distraught villagers.

That night the riders camped west of the burned village. Beornoth had kept to himself throughout the journey south. He had barely spoken to any of Streonwold's men, distancing himself even from his sworn man, Wulfhere, and from Alfgar. His only companion through the long days and evenings had been ale, or mead, or whatever mind-numbing drink he could get his hands on. It was a warm evening, and two of Streonwold's men cooked rabbit over a small fire. Beornoth sat with his back against a sycamore tree. He twirled one of its fluttering seeds between his fingers, hoping the spinning of the small leaves would distract him from the overwhelming urge to take a drink. It wasn't working. An ale skin lay beside him on the grass, but he hadn't taken a drink since the village. The charred, smoking corpses at the raided village were a harsh reminder for Beornoth that he was at war again. He had spent the last few years rounding up or killing masterless men and cattle thieves or settling small family feuds in the valley in return for his pay as a reeve. This was different. This was war. To fight well required more than skill at arms, and as Beornoth scratched at his dry throat and licked at cracked lips, he knew the drinking had to stop. The Ealdorman wouldn't grant a Heriot to a drunk. That was what had cost Beornoth his land and inheritance in the first place. If he was to win back his family's honour, and become a

Thegn again, then he would need a clear head and a steady hand.

Beornoth closed his eyes and saw again the rage on Eawynn's scarred face, the fury in her eyes as she had clawed at him, spitting her hatred. His hand reached for the ale skin, but he pushed himself to his feet instead, he had to become sober. He needed something to take his mind off the pain, the shame deep inside him, and the harrowing cries of his mad wife and the nightmare of his dead children.

'Alfgar, come here,' he called to the Ealdorman's bastard. Alfgar looked up from where he sat cross-legged, close to the fire. His mouth hung open, and he just stared at Beornoth. 'Come here and bring your spear.' The lad looked at the other men, then leapt to his feet and grabbed his spear. The Ealdorman had tasked Beornoth with teaching the lad to fight, so teach he would.

Alfgar walked towards Beornoth. He was pigeon-toed and walked in small shuffling steps with his shoulders hunched and his eyes fixed on the ground. Beornoth saw Osric and his men giggling and pointing at the youth. The heir and his two companions had been a thorn in Beornoth's side all the way from the north-west down to the land of the East Saxons. They had chided and mocked the other warriors, safe in the knowledge that they had the protection of their Lord and ranked above the other men. It had not bothered Beornoth too much, largely because he had been drunk for most of the journey, but now that he was sober and his head throbbed with the thirst of it, the three men were getting under his skin.

Alfgar stood before Beornoth, holding the spear at his side, its butt resting on the grass. He did not meet Beornoth's eye, but stared at his own boots, and for a moment Beornoth thought the lad might cry.

'Did your father teach you to fight, boy?' said Beornoth.

Alfgar muttered and covered his mouth with his left hand so that Beornoth couldn't hear him.

'Speak up, I can't hear you.'

'I said no, Lord.' Alfgar spoke louder, but Beornoth still had to crane his neck to hear the words.

'I am not a Lord. Just call me Beo. Why were you not taught to fight?' They taught all boys of rank the use of weapons. Any lad whose father was a Thegn, a household warrior or retainer, would learn how to use axe, spear, shield and bow. Weapon craft would be how they made their living once they became men, and skill at arms was a sure way to keep a man alive.

'My father wanted me to join the Church, so I learned my letters.'

'So why didn't you join the Church?'

Alfgar shuffled his feet and shot a glance over his shoulder at the men around the fire to make sure they weren't listening.

'I fear God does not look favourably upon me. I pray and worship and am a godly man, but I fear God does not hear my words. And the Church... was not what I had hoped it would be. I did not feel the grace of God.'

Beornoth stared at the lad. He guessed Alfgar had seen close to twenty summers, which was old for an unmarried young man. At his age he should already be an experienced warrior with a wife and part of his father's hearth-troop. He was of average height but narrow in the shoulder. Beornoth thought Alfgar looked like a priest, and could see him with a tonsure and wearing the brown, drab robes of the clergy. Beornoth himself was no longer a man of God, which was rare, so he didn't question the boy further on his beliefs.

'Show me how you thrust that spear.'

'What, here?' said Alfgar, and threw another glance over his shoulder. This time, the men were watching him.

'Yes, show me a solid thrust.'

The Adam's apple in Alfgar's throat bounced up and down, and he shuffled his feet. He placed two hands on the weapon and pushed it forward, but with no commitment. Beornoth shook his head.

'I will show you how to use that, then the shield, and then the axe. Give it to me.'

Alfgar handed him the spear.

'Thrust, parry, hook, low, high,' said Beornoth, grunting as he showed the key movements.

'Watch out, you might fall over, you sack of mead,' shouted Osric, and his men hooted with laughter.

'Ignore those fools. We practise each morning and evening until you get it right. You will need to learn if you want to live.'

Alfgar nodded, and Beornoth saw the hint of a smile on his pale face.

'Wulfhere, bring your spear,' he called. The big man stood and grabbed his weapon, which was propped up next to him. He approached, rolling his shoulders. Beornoth had all but ignored the man since taking his oath. That, too, was something he would need to change. If it came to shield-wall fighting, which Beornoth knew and hoped it would, then he would need a trusted man holding the shield on his unprotected right side.

Beornoth stood next to Wulfhere, and they went through the drill of spear craft. The drill any self-respecting warrior did regularly to keep his skills sharp and his arm strong.

'We will do this together, the three of us each day. Bring me a shield.'

Wulfhere fetched Alfgar's shield and handed it to Beornoth. He grabbed the rim, one hand on each edge of the iron band which ran around the edge of the shield. Beornoth lifted the shield high and held it there, then lowered it and repeated the movement until he could lift the thing no longer.

'Do that twice a day, and you will get stronger. You will need your strength.'

Which was true, because the next day they met the Vikings.

**6**

Beornoth woke the following morning with a pounding head and a sour feeling in his stomach. He had awoken to such discomfort countless times, the heavy penance for drinking too much the night before. But that morning, the opposite was true. He had drunk nothing but water that night, but now he craved ale, or mead. He needed it, the want of it overwhelming and painful. Most men carried ale to drink instead of water because it was easier to keep fresh, and less likely to give them poorly guts, so it would not be hard to find. Beornoth, however, had promised himself that he would stay away from ale, he knew he drank too much, and the burned village had been a stark reminder that he needed a clear head if he was to fight effectively, and he would need to kill fierce Viking warriors if he was to get his Heriot back.

Alfgar carried a horn of water, and Beornoth took a thirsty pull at it before taking the lad through his morning practice. Wulfhere, Alfgar and Beornoth found a patch of open scrubland close to the camp and went through the same drills as on the previous night. The movements of the spear and strength work with the shield. Then, at the end, Beornoth strapped the shield onto Alfgar's left arm and showed him how to brace himself behind it and use the spear to counterstrike over and under the iron rim. Alfgar was clumsy and unsure of himself, and could not hold the heavy shield steady for long, but he listened and tried patiently to follow Beornoth's lead.

Streonwold gave the order to push south-west in search of Ealdorman Byrhtnoth, and they rode out as a chill morning wind whipped across the East Saxon hills. The treetops rustled and swayed, and Beornoth pulled his old woollen cloak around him. His hands and face were sweating, but he was shivering in the saddle. Every step his horse took felt like a knife stabbing behind his eyes, and as they crossed hills and dales, all Beornoth could think about was how much he wanted a drink.

Mid-morning came and Beornoth saw the shining coils of a river meandering in the distance, glittering under the sun like the scales of a writhing dragon. The water was the thoroughfare by which the Vikings made their attacks inland, so Beornoth was glad to see it, because it meant they were closer to the enemy. They stopped to rest the horses, and Beornoth huddled against the base of a fallen oak tree, hiding his shaking hands beneath his cloak. His mind was drowning in his thirst for ale or mead. He needed it, craved it. Beornoth pushed the desire deep down, and told himself that he had spent enough time at the bottom of an ale jug. The time for drinking was over.

Wulfhere and one of Streonwold's men went to forage for berries and mushrooms in a nearby woodland so the men could eat whilst they rested.

'You look like shit,' said Streonwold, coming to stand next to Beornoth. Beornoth grunted and pulled his cloak tighter around him. 'There should be another town to the south, according to the priest at the burned village. No doubt we will meet Byrhtnoth either today or tomorrow.'

'When will Aethelhelm ride south?'

'In the next few days, he should have gathered enough men by then.'

'Will Theodred ride?'

'He's the Thegn with your old Heriot?'

'He is.'

'Maybe. The Ealdorman won't send all of his Thegns and warriors south. Just one for every ten hides. You came, and you're a reeve. If he can get a few more like that, then he can leave some Thegns in the north to protect his lands whilst the rest of us are away.'

'For what? The fighting is here.' Beornoth knew how Aethelhelm was thinking, just as much as Streonwold did, and it made sense for the Ealdorman to not leave his lands unprotected whilst he rode to war. But Beornoth wanted Theodred in harm's way. He wanted the bastard skewered on a Norseman's blade. That way he could win his old lands back, instead of fighting on the promise of a new Heriot the Ealdorman had promised to create for him.

'Lord Aethelhelm can't leave his lands unprotected, some Thegns must remain in case any attacks come from Ireland or the north. I know you hate Theodred, but he was granted your old Heriot, he didn't seek it.'

'He got it because his father paid Aethelhelm. He is a rich man's second son and a turd, and I want him in harm's way.'

'You were in no fit state to be a Thegn, Beo. You know it. The Ealdorman stripped away your Heriot and granted it to Theodred. He stays in the north to protect Aethelhelm's lands and we are here, that's just the way it is.'

'Can Theodred fight?'

'He has a hearth-troop of men who can, and he knows his weapons. That's enough now, I'll say no more on it. What the bloody hell are they doing?' Streonwold huffed, looking at Osric and his men, who were wrestling and rolling on the ground like boys at a summer fair. He strode over, bellowing at them to stop and get a grip on themselves. Beornoth ignored them.

'Water?' said Alfgar, holding his horn to Beornoth. 'It's fresh, there's a brook back there, I just refilled it.' He didn't meet Beornoth's eyes, and kept his gaze on his boots. But Beornoth nodded thanks and took a drink, trying to stop his hand from shaking whilst he held the horn.

'You used to be a Thegn?' asked Alfgar, and then his face flushed when he noticed Beornoth's frown. 'I'm sorry, you don't need to answer. I'll go...'

'I was a Thegn, as was my father before me and his father, going back through the generations until our people first came to these shores. I lost it, lost my family, my lands, my Heriot. Everything.'

'What is a Heriot?'

'Bloody hell, boy. Does your father teach you nothing? A Heriot is the gift the King or an Ealdorman grants to a Thegn for his service. His land, weapons, a horse. It's usually passed on through the generations, but it's the Ealdorman's right to grant it or take it. In return, a Thegn looks after the hides under his protection, and fights for the Ealdorman and the King whenever they call.'

'A hide is a farm?'

'Yes, it's a bloody farm, enough to feed one family. So ten hides are ten farms, or ten families.'

'So how did you lose your Heriot and hides?'

'Enough bloody questions for one day,' growled Beornoth, and handed the horn back to Alfgar. The boy plainly knew little of war, or how the warrior hierarchy worked. 'What did you learn when you were a child?'

'My letters. The Bible and the word of God.'

'So why did you not become a priest, then? You are a little old to be only learning how to fight now, most lads your age should already be seasoned fighters, married and settled.'

'I am a godly man. I pray and try to be virtuous. But I simply did not feel God the way the other students did, it is a lot to give up one's life in service of the Lord. To sacrifice oneself to chastity, to forego wealth and be devoted to God alone.'

Beornoth laughed at that. 'There are not many priests in my experience who forego wealth, and who keep their vow of chastity. Most of them have fingers thick with rings, and they live and eat like Kings.'

'That was also part of the problem, Lord. My father wanted me to join the Church so I could eventually hold some of the land owned by the Church. Land ceded to them by him and our forebears. The abbeys and monasteries own lots of good land across the north-west. So I would have become a priest or Bishop landowner, wealthy and rich.'

'And your father wants to keep it all in the family, the profits will still flow to him. Men would kill for such a life of comfort, Alfgar.'

'Yes, Lord. But that is not the word of God.'

'You are better off becoming a fighter, lad. Simpler work.' Beornoth shook his head. The word of God might be good for soothing the pain of a mother's loss of her child, or a widower's loss of his wife, but it would not stop the Vikings from raiding and killing. Beornoth had been a man of God. All Saxons were. But the pain of his life had forced him to question God and Christ. How could God allow all the suffering in the world when he could take it all away whenever he wished? These days, Beornoth saw God more as a crutch for the bereaved and the hopeful, if it comforted people to believe that their dead loved ones were waiting for them in Heaven, where they would one day be reunited, then it made no difference to him. For generations, Ealdormen and men of power across the Saxon lands had granted swathes of land to the Church in return for God's favour. Down the years, this practice had made the Church extremely wealthy, and also deprived Ealdormen and Thegns of good land. Aethelhelm was no fool, he wanted his son to own much of that land so that the income it generated would still flow through his family, and not into the already overflowing coffers of the Church.

Beornoth turned at a crunch of foliage and crack of fallen branches over his shoulder. Wulfhere came bursting from the forest's edge, red-faced and out of breath.

'Vikings, in the wood. Foraging,' said Wulfhere, squeezing the words out between huge sucks of breath. 'Cwicca spotted them, then I saw them, too.'

Cwicca was Streonwold's man, a thin warrior who carried a bow slung over his back and had a face pitted from a childhood pox.

'I reckon there's about three of them looking for grub, just like us,' said Cwicca.

Beornoth stood and strode to his horse. He pulled his war axe from its sheath in the saddle and took off his cloak. His head still pounded from the ale-longing, and the pain made him quick to anger. If there were Vikings ahead, then he wanted to fight them, to sate his fury for all their kind had wrought upon him.

'What the bloody hell are you doing?' asked Streonwold, hands on his hips.

'Going to kill Norsemen, that's why we're here.'

'What if there's more of them in the woods? It's too risky and our orders are to join up with Byrhtnoth.'

'I'm here to kill Norsemen, and there's three of the bastards in there. Wulfhere comes with me. The rest of you do as you like.'

He ignored Streonwold's complaining and walked towards the forest. Wulfhere fell in alongside him, as did Alfgar, clutching his spear to his chest. Osric and his two warriors also followed, which surprised Beornoth. Streonwold was not a coward. Beornoth knew him to be a brave and skilled warrior, but he would follow Aethelhelm's orders to the death and would never deviate from them, and Beornoth expected Osric to side with his father's captain.

'Where did you see them?' Beornoth said. He rested his axe on his shoulder for a moment to make sure the antler-handled seax was loose in its sheath at the back of his belt.

'This way, the forest thickens and then opens out into a glade. Buggers are in there. Follow me,' said Wulfhere. He led them on through the undergrowth until they reached a large thorn bush. There Wulfhere crouched and placed a finger to his lips. 'I saw them over there, so best go quietly now,' he whispered, and moved cautiously. Beornoth followed his lead, walking carefully, making sure not to tread on a rotten branch or twig and alert their prey.

Wulfhere held up a hand, and the line of men stopped. The big man reached up and tugged on his own earlobe, and pointed ahead of him. Beornoth held his breath and turned his head to listen. Sure enough, he could hear Norse voices talking some distance before them. He set his teeth and his hand clenched on the haft of his axe. Beornoth waved the others in close to him.

'Me and Wulfhere will approach from this side. Osric and Alfgar, head west, you other two go east. When you hear the signal, charge in from the flanks.'

'What signal?' asked Egbert, one of Osric's men.

'When the fighting starts,' said Beornoth.

'I'm not going with this idiot,' hissed Osric, sneering at Alfgar. 'He couldn't fight off an angry chicken.'

'Do as I say, or piss off back to Streonwold,' growled Beornoth. Osric was about to protest again, but he kept his teeth together once he saw the steel in Beornoth's eyes. The others crept off in opposite directions, and Beornoth and Wulfhere pressed ahead, still taking care where they put their feet.

The talking grew louder, and Beornoth could make out some words despite the distance. He spoke good Norse. There were still many Viking families in settlements across the Kingdom of York and he had spent most of his life fighting or dealing with trouble-some Vikings, and so had picked up the language along the way. They crouched behind a moss-covered boulder on the edge of the glade Wulfhere had described, and sure enough there were three Vikings foraging around in the undergrowth, pulling mushrooms and placing them into a sack. They talked and laughed at ease and relaxed, even though they were in a foreign and hostile land.

Beornoth stood and rolled his neck and shoulders. He took two deep breaths and strode forward into the glade. The three men wore breastplates made of baked leather and wore their hair long and elaborate. They shaved their heads at the back and sides, with plaits and beads woven into their beards and hair. Each man had an axe looped at his belt and they went about their work without lookouts, joking and laughing. That annoyed Beornoth. They were so confident of their superiority over the Saxons that they hadn't even bothered to post lookouts whilst they foraged. He allowed the memory of his murdered children and broken wife to flood his mind, which kindled a fire in his belly. He touched his hand to his chest, feeling the wooden locket he wore there as a reminder of that horror and loss.

One of the Vikings looked up, hearing footsteps crunching on the fallen leaves and soft bed of the forest floor. The man stood and shoved a large cup mushroom into his sack. He smirked at Beornoth and Wulfhere.

'Look, some peasants,' said the warrior, speaking Norse. He was tall and hatchet-faced. His two friends came to stand with him and they rested their hands on their axe heads.

Beornoth kept walking until he was within striking distance of the Vikings.

'They have weapons. Let's kill the bastards and take what they have,' said a short Norseman with a tattooed face.

'Hardly worth it for a rusty axe and a spear. Maybe they could be your bed salves, Toki,' said a broad-shouldered man. The others laughed.

Beornoth thrust his axe out to punch its flat head into the tall warrior's nose, sending the Viking reeling, off balance. Beornoth slid his hand up the haft and brought the axe around, keeping its momentum going to hook its head around the neck of the tattoo-faced man, and dragged him towards Wulfhere. The broad-shouldered Viking slipped his axe free, and let out a roar. There was half challenge and half fear in that shout, and Beornoth felt the battle calm washing over him, the calmness that came to him in the clash of arms. That calm mixed with the heightened joy of fighting, of testing his skill and savageness against another man, and Beornoth felt alive. His headache and sweaty palms vanished.

He brought his axe up to parry a strike from the broad-shouldered warrior and followed that with a kick to the man's groin. The warrior crouched and threw himself to the ground, rolling away and groaning at the pain between his legs. The hatchet-faced man drove his shoulder into Beornoth, sending him spinning backwards, but Beornoth let himself spin and brought his axe around in a wide sweep which the warrior ducked underneath. Hatchet-face lashed out with his axe and it sang past Beornoth's face, allowing him to step in and headbutt the Norseman full in the face. Beornoth shoved the man away and whipped the seax free from its scabbard at his back. He drove the broken-backed blade into the hatchet-faced man's ribs in four short, hard strikes, and the Viking yelped and fell to the ground.

Beornoth glanced over his shoulder to see Wulfhere jabbing at the third Dane with his spear, and that man circled the big Saxon warily, keeping beyond the reach of the leaf-shaped blade. The broad-shouldered man was back to his feet and charged at Beornoth in a whir of axe and knife thrusts and cuts. Beornoth parried high and low, blocking with his axe haft, or dodging the blows. The man was fast, and his attacks were skilful and had strength behind each blow. Beornoth edged away and waited for his enemy to over-lunge or push himself off balance. A shout of pain came from behind him, and Beornoth knew Wulfhere had dealt with his foe. The broad-shouldered warrior saw that fight, and realising he would now face two enemies, his onslaught increased in ferocity. That caused the man to overstretch. Beornoth let his axe fall and grabbed the warrior's wrist, punching his seax once into the man's armpit and then dragging the blade across his throat in one swift motion. Hot blood flowed down the seax blade and over Beornoth's hand and he flicked it away into the leaf mulch of the forest floor. The broad-shouldered man fell to his knees, clutching at his throat, and Beornoth put a boot on his chest to kick him to the ground.

'It feels good to fight again,' said Wulfhere, looking down at the dying Viking whose blood leaked dark over his neck and face. Osric and Alfgar appeared from the woods to their left, and Osric's other men from the right. They all had weapons drawn and came on gingerly, staring at the dead and dying Vikings.

'You missed the fighting,' said Beornoth, picking up his axe and pointing it at Osric.

'We only just arrived, I...'

'All the way from the north to here, I've listened to your piss-

and-wind talk of how many men you're going to kill, and how men will fear your fancy blade. Here was your chance, and you hid in the trees like a frightened fox.'

'You can't to talk to me like that,' stammered Osric, his face flushing.

'I just did. Next time there's fighting to be done, you'd better get to it, boy. Otherwise it will be my axe you face.'

'How dare you threaten me, you drunken bastard? I will be Ealdorman one day, and I won't forget your impudence. Why, I'll have you hung for the way you spoke to me.'

Beornoth marched to Osric, his bulk towering over the Ealdorman's son and forcing him back two paces. Beornoth raised his axe, dripping and coated with thick, dark blood and gobbets of flesh.

'Don't threaten, boy. Act. I'm here whenever you want me.' Beornoth wiped the blood from his axe with his hand and smeared it on Osric's face. The young warrior let out a cry and cowered away, pawing at the blood on his cheek and nose.

Osric stared at the dying Vikings, one of which had begun to cry, making a mewing noise between sobs. Beornoth knelt and picked up the broad-shouldered man's axe. It was a fine weapon with a rune-carved blade and leather bound around the haft for grip. He tucked it into his belt and walked to the man he had stabbed. He was bleeding out and stared at Beornoth, eyes sunken in a pale face.

'I take it you have never killed a man?' Beornoth said to Alfgar, who shook his head. His bottom lip quivered, knowing what Beornoth would say next.

## 7

Alfgar held his spear in an overhand grip, blade pointed at the dying Viking. The hatchet-faced warrior squirmed in the leaf mulch and his eyes quivered, watery and glistening.

'Do it now. Aim for his chest or his throat, and stab him hard,' Beornoth said. Alfgar looked from him to the Norseman. Alfgar was shaking and the tip of his spear wavered. 'This bastard has sailed here from the hard north. He is a killer of men, children, and a raper of women. Without a second thought, he'd gut you. He made those corpses in the village we passed. So kill the bastard and send him screaming to hell,' Beornoth growled.

Alfgar closed his eyes and shook his head.

'Do it, now!' Beornoth roared. Alfgar jumped with fright. He screamed and stabbed the spear at the Viking. The blade caught the man under the chin and cut deep into his gullet, ripping open the soft skin in a wash of blood. Alfgar opened his eyes and dropped the spear, falling to his knees and watching the man in his death throes as he jerked and twisted in the dirt.

'Now the Vikings know we can fight as well as they do. Now they will fear our blades and our wrath. Search them for coin and weapons.' Beornoth pointed a finger at Osric and his friends. 'When we fight the Vikings, there must be no mercy. No hesitation. We must take everything from them, hurt them, drive our steel into their flesh and rip out their lives. They are here for our wives and daughters, to take our land and make it theirs. So next time you hesitate, I'll kill you myself.'

They just stared at him, wide-eyed and open-mouthed. Osric's face had turned ashen as he looked at the three corpses, and the blood and gore spattered on Beornoth's face and hands.

'Wulfhere, arm yourself properly. There's good iron here,' Beornoth said. Wulfhere took a bearded axe and a knife from a dead Norseman, and pulled a stout breastplate from another. He sat on the ground and pulled the boots from a dead man and measured them against the sole of his own foot and grinned.

'Good fit,' he said, winking at Alfgar and pulling on his new boots.

With his new clothes and war gear, Wulfhere looked more like a warrior, and the group trudged through the forest towards Streonwold and the others.

'You fought well,' said Beornoth, and Wulfhere nodded thanks.

'It's good to be fighting on the right side of things again,' he said, grinning a gap-toothed smile. 'I haven't thanked you.'

'For what?'

'For freeing me from those villagers, it would have been a terrible death. The snivelling little soil-scrabblers would have hurt me, and then hanged me.'

'Don't thank me. Just keep your oath and fight hard.'

'Well, thanks anyway. I wasn't always a man with no master,' said Wulfhere. 'Once I served my Lord in Mercia. I was a warrior, but my Lord died and he had no sons. A neighbouring Thegn took his lands and cast us warriors out. The new Thegn had no use for us who served the old one. I had to eat, to live...'

Such stories were common, and a man of war faced little choice if he had no Lord to serve. It was a terrible fate to be a masterless man, and one that all warriors feared. Beornoth was glad to have Wulfhere at his side. He was a stout fighter and seemed like a good man.

'Keep your eye on Alfgar. We need to make a warrior out of him.'

'I'll look after him. Keep his training going. You might regret what you did to the Lordling in the woods, Lord. You showed him up in front of his friends. He won't like that.'

'Osric is a little windbag. All talk of glory and what he's going to do, with his rich man's sword and its bloody fool name. When it came to it, he hung back like a sheep on shearing day.'

'He's the son of an Ealdorman. Haven't you ever named a weapon?'

'No. A weapon is a tool. It doesn't need a name. It just needs a firm hand to wield it.'

Beornoth gnawed at his beard. He had been hard on Osric in the woods, and smearing a dead man's blood on his face was probably too harsh a lesson. Beornoth comforted himself, knowing that they needed harsh lessons. If the young men were to learn about war, they would need to learn quickly. War was hard and brutal, and if they were going to survive, then they must be tempered like hard steel.

Streonwold and his men had broken camp and prepared the horses to push on. When he saw Beornoth emerge from the forest, he craned his neck to look over Beornoth's shoulder, and when he saw Osric was unharmed, he let out a visible sigh of relief.

'Well?' said Streonwold.

'Three of the bastards dead,' said Beornoth. 'Alfgar killed his first Viking. He's a warrior now.'

Streonwold looked at Alfgar, who trudged towards his horse with slumped shoulders and eyes fixed on the ground.

'Aye, he looks like it,' said Streonwold, shaking his head. 'Any sign of the rest of them, or their ships?'

'We didn't look.'

'Let's move on, then. We'll find Byrhtnoth today.'

They found the Ealdorman and his men at a town. Its dwellings and buildings spanned a ford across a wide river which cut through the lands of the East Saxons. The town had sprung up around a burh, but spread beyond its dilapidated walls to cross over both sides of the river.

Beornoth led his mare by the bridle through the entranceway to the burh, which cut through a bank of earth as high as Beornoth's head, and the path carried on through the ditch beyond and on into the fortress itself. The bank was timber-faced, but many of those timbers were rotten and had either fallen down completely or were in the process of doing so. Byrhtnoth's men worked at digging out the ditch and replacing the rotten timbers, so that the air was filled with the sound of sawing timber, and the smell of freshly cut wood.

Inside the burh, the entrance led on to a series of straight, muddy pathways, each leading to a central square and surrounded on each side by thatched buildings. Beornoth saw men patrolling the fighting platform atop the wooden walls inside the ditch.

'The Ealdorman knows what he is doing,' said Beornoth. 'No warriors idling here. They are all either busy repairing the fortress, or patrolling it.'

'Keeping them busy keeps them out of trouble. They have left this old fort to rot for too long. I hope they are not all like this down south,' grumbled Streonwold.

'Streonwold, you find us somewhere to stable the horses. I'll find the Ealdorman,' said Osric, and beckoned his men to follow him. He threw a scowl in Beornoth's direction as he went. Beornoth watched the young man canter along the long central street which passed through the burh. The local people bowed as he passed. He was sure the golden-haired heir would do all he could to slither up to Byrhtnoth and ingratiate himself before his father arrived.

'Come on,' said Streonwold, patting his stomach, seemingly unperturbed that Osric had given him an order, when he was the captain of Aethelhelm's warriors. 'There must be food here somewhere.'

They stabled the mounts on a line of horses outside the burh. Ruddy-faced boys had a rope tied between trees and a long line of large, glossy warhorses, alongside smaller regular mounts, munched on bales of hay whilst children brushed their coats. Streonwold found some meat and fresh bread, and they made a small fire beyond the ditch where other groups of warriors sat to take a meal. Beornoth tore into a loaf of bread, hoping its doughy thickness would soak up the sourness in his belly. It had been a day and half since he had last taken a drink of ale, and he thirstily watched the others take turns on a skin of mead Streonwold had purchased inside the burh. Beornoth did not take a drink himself, fearing that once its hoppy taste passed his lips, he would fall back to drinking it all day, every day. He couldn't afford to have dulled wits, when his purpose here was to reforge his reputation and win back his Heriot. He had to be sharp if he was to prove himself and become a Thegn again, restoring his family's honour. So, instead, he shared a horn of water with Alfgar, which the youth had pulled from a well deep inside the burh.

Beornoth's hands and face had stopped sweating, but his stomach was still sickly and his head still pounded. He craved ale, but he steeled himself against that need. The fight in the forest had given him a chance to show his worth. He had killed Vikings. He had enjoyed killing them. It meant three fewer murderous hunters raiding up and down England's coastline and three fewer men to fight if it came to a shield-wall fight. Beornoth reckoned Byrhtnoth had close to forty men in and around the burh. It was a good number, but not enough if the Vikings had anything over two crews' worth of warriors. The Saxons would need at least a long hundred men to put up a fight, the first and most difficult task being to find the Vikings and pin them down. In Beornoth's experience, raiding Vikings did not want to fight battles. They preferred to hit and run and preserve their numbers for another day. Their leaders, or Jarls, only had the men they sailed south with. A shield wall was a terrible place of blood, death and pain. If a Jarl lost too many men in a battle, he would need to wait for more ships to sail south and reinforce him, or retreat to the north and wait until the spring raiding season next year before attacking again.

'It was a brave thing, to kill your first man. You will never forget that moment and it will haunt you. But you must see it as a service to your people, as a thing that must be done,' Beornoth said to Alfgar, handing him the horn of water. Alfgar looked at him, his eyes quivering.

'I killed a man today, a man who couldn't defend himself. Murder is a sin. God will have seen me,' he said, and made the sign of the cross.

'Vikings kill defenceless Saxons all the time. Do you think God loves the heathens? Do you think he wants us Saxons to become worshippers of Odin and Thor?'

'Well... no,' said Alfgar. He sat up straighter.

'Do you think it makes God happy to see his people burned, killed and raped by heathens?'

'No.'

'He would want you to strike back, to protect the land of his flock.'

'An eye for an eye. Isn't that what Jesus said?' said Wulfhere.

'Yes, that's right,' said Alfgar. He reached behind his jerkin and drew forth a wooden cross. It was a small thing carved from pale wood. 'So killing pagans could be God's work. Do you think so?'

'Killing Vikings is as much God's work as praying or delivering a sermon,' said Beornoth.

'God bless us all, then,' grinned Wulfhere through a mouth full of roast chicken. 'Did you make that?' He pointed at Alfgar's pendant.

'No, one of our household servants made it for me when I was a boy.' Alfgar tucked it back into his jerkin. His eyes looked brighter, and the hunch had gone from his shoulders.

A commotion at the gates of the burh caught Beornoth's attention, and he saw a group of men striding through the gateway and out across the ditch. He could see Osric there, marching confidently next to an enormous bear of a man. The big man was of late middle age, with a clipped beard which was white around his neck and chin and black in the moustache and cheeks. He wore a shining helmet, with two bushes of curly black hair poking out of either side. His Byrnie mail coat was burnished to a sheen, and he wore a sword belted at his waist in a red scabbard. He looked like a Lord of War, and Beornoth rose to greet him.

'Ealdorman Byrhtnoth,' said Streonwold, and bowed his head, as did Beornoth and the others.

'You are welcome,' said the Ealdorman of Essex. 'Osric here

tells me you have all come south ahead of Ealdorman Aethelhelm's force.'

'Yes, Lord,' said Streonwold.

'He also tells me you helped him kill three of the cursed pagans close to here.'

Beornoth looked at Osric, who purposefully ignored him and looked from Byrhtnoth to Streonwold.

'Streonwold is my father's finest warrior, Lord. He will kill many of the Viking scum,' said Osric.

'Good, young Osric. Your fight in the forest is our first strike back at them. First blood. The only good Viking is a dead one. Now, I hear our sentries spotted riders from the ramparts and it looks as though we have more warriors to swell our numbers,' said Byrhtnoth, pointing to the fields beyond, where a group of riders approached.

'It's my father. I would know his warhorse anywhere,' said Osric proudly. He finally caught Beornoth's eye, and a smile played at the corners of Osric's mouth. He edged closer to the Ealdorman. Osric had spun a tale to Byrhtnoth of how bravely he had fought and killed three savage Vikings. If Osric had fought, if he had even lifted his blade in anger, the lie would not have troubled Beornoth. It was a nobleman's privilege to take the credit for the deeds of his warriors. But Osric had taken no part in the fight with the Norsemen. Beornoth and Wulfhere had done the hard work. They had risked their lives and crossed blades with the deadly Vikings and spilled their blood. A Thegn or an Ealdorman, any warrior of rank and leader of men, must show his warriors that he shares their risks, that he fights and risks his life alongside them. Beornoth hoped Osric hadn't fought in the woods because the violence had surprised him, and he was not used to seeing blood spilt. If not, it meant he was a coward, which would be a problem if

Osric was to lead any of his father's warriors in the fight against the Vikings.

Ealdorman Aethelhelm rode towards the burh at the head of a line of horsemen, the ground rumbling under their hooves. The warriors in and around the fortress cheered their arrival and Aethelhelm drew his sword and raised it in salute. The sun twinkled on the blade, and the lift in mood around the burh was palpable. He and Byrhtnoth shook hands and exchanged pleasantries, and Beornoth's heart warmed. Now that the riders swelled their numbers, it surely meant it was time to take the fight to the Viking raiders and let them feel the edge of Saxon blades.

# 8

The morning following Aethelhelm's arrival in Essex, he and Byrhtnoth agreed to split their force in two, one heading east along the river towards the coast and the other heading west, deep into the lands of the East Saxons. They sent scouts ahead to as many towns and villages along the river as possible, with orders to seek news of the Viking boats, or sightings of mounted Viking forces in the countryside. It was as good a plan as any when facing Viking raids, and Beornoth knew from fighting such an enemy himself that the hardest part of stopping the Northmen was actually finding them and committing them to battle. Their swift ships made them extremely mobile, and they could appear and strike by surprise along one river, and then strike again at any point along the coast just days later.

Beornoth rode with Aethelhelm and Streonwold in the party heading east, and Osric and his men joined Byrhtnoth in the group marching to the west. Beornoth was pleased to see the golden-haired son of the Ealdorman heading in the opposite direction. The boy had ingratiated himself with Byrhtnoth based on a tale of stolen deeds, and the rift between Beornoth and Osric grew deeper with each day. Every time Beornoth saw Osric, he felt his brows furrow and his hands itch. It was a feeling Beornoth realised he would need to control. Osric would be an Ealdorman one day, and an Ealdorman was a powerful enemy, ranking below only the King, and any man who got on the wrong side of such a powerful foe was likely to wind up dead.

'Fine land down here,' said the Ealdorman, looking around at the lush hills and valleys of Essex. 'Good for wheat and animals.' Aethelhelm himself, being an Ealdorman, owned vast swathes of land in the north-west of England and much of what was formerly the Kingdom of York. Beornoth breathed in the soft air, bees hummed at their work, and birdsong drifted on the breeze. It was easy to see why the lush, verdant valleys and thick soil were as much of an attraction to the Vikings as a honeycomb to a child. The Norseman had attacked and ravaged England's coastlines for generations, and all men knew the Vikings craved and envied the fruitful lands of Britain. Their Northern home, or so Beornoth had heard, was a cruel, cold and rock-filled country where farming was hard and living was worse. The lush lands of Wessex, Essex and Devon were the breadbasket of the Saxon Kingdom, and the Vikings desired it for their own.

'Any word of more ships, Lord?' asked Beornoth.

'Yes, more's the pity,' replied Aethelhelm. 'More raids on the south coast, so I hear. That's why the King has his Thegns spread thin across the country. We have to fight the Vikings, Beo, if we wait for them to form an army, we could wait years, enduring their raids up and down the country.'

'So they're just softening us up, then?'

'Probing for weaknesses, testing our mettle and the King's strength. No doubt their leaders are looking for a place to strike, somewhere where we show meekness or reluctance to fight.

That's where they will pour their ships and warriors into our lands and take a foothold.'

'We'll show them strength, then.'

'So we will, Beo. King Æthelred is in the south, with the Thegns of Wessex and his ships, and we are here to protect our western coastline, and our rivers the cursed Vikings use like roads.'

King Æthelred had come to the throne a dozen years earlier, as a boy of twelve summers. His father, King Edgar, was known as the Peaceful and had enjoyed a reign largely free of Viking incursions. Æthelred's reign had commenced following the death of his brother, the rightful heir. Beornoth thought better of asking Aethelhelm about that murky ascension, as it was widely known that Æthelred's brother had been murdered, and the powerful Ealdormen of the realm were implicated in the slaying.

'Did Theodred ride south with you, Lord? I did not see him amongst your riders.' Beornoth did not know the man to whom Aethelhelm had granted his family's Heriot, he had never even met him. But Beornoth was here to fight for that inheritance, and whilst he would gladly accept the new lands and weapons in the Heriot the Ealdorman had promised, he still yearned to recover his old lands and Hall. If the Vikings intended to invade and take a foothold in Essex, then men would die in the shield walls and skirmishes of that war. If Theodred marched south and stood in the shield wall, and a Viking blade ripped his life away, then maybe Aethelhelm would not need to create a new Heriot for Beornoth.

'He did not,' said Aethelhelm brusquely. 'He stays in the north to protect my lands there. Forget him, Beo, forget your old lands. You fight now for a chance at a new life, new lands. Do not talk to me about Theodred again.'

Beornoth chewed at his bottom lip. He had pushed the

Ealdorman too far, and it had been a mistake. It irked Beornoth that Theodred was safe and warm by his fire, whilst he was here risking his life in the fight against the Vikings, but Aethelhelm spoke clearly, and Beornoth would not talk of it again.

Aethelhelm twisted in his saddle, the leather of his trappings and belt creaking as he turned. The Ealdorman grinned through his greying beard. Then a rising sound of men's voices further back in the column caused Aethelhelm to pull on his reins and turn his warhorse towards the commotion.

'The Vikings!' came a shout. A rider thundered up the marching column, repeating his warning, as his horse's hooves threw clods of soil over the marching warriors. Once before the Ealdorman, the rider yanked hard on his reins, and the horse bared its teeth and dragged itself to a stop, its flanks flecked with sweat.

'Where?' growled Aethelhelm. The rider tried to catch his breath and pointed behind him.

'They sail towards us, Lord. Three ships heading for the coast.'

'We have them. Praise be to God for delivering our enemies,' said Aethelhelm, setting his jaw. 'Streonwold, find a pinch point or a narrow turn in the river and cut down a tree to throw across the banks.'

'Yes, Lord,' said Streonwold. 'How far away are they?'

'They will be here before noon,' replied the rider.

Streonwold set off hard eastwards, taking a company of twenty riders with him. Aethelhelm ordered the scout to be given a fresh horse, and sent him west to Byrhtnoth to tell the Ealdorman to bring his East Saxons, because Aethelhelm would force the Vikings to fight.

'Three ships means there could be a long hundred of them, Lord,' said Beornoth.

'I know it, Beo, we have the numbers to match them.'

'Where is the King's fleet? Will he not send ships to fight the Vikings?'

'The King's ships are in the south-west. More of the bastards are attacking there. So here in the east, the King is trusting to our blades and valour to throw the heathens from our shores.'

'Half of our men are from Byrhtnoth's fyrd.'

'We will do the fighting, Beo, the warriors amongst us. The fyrd just make up the numbers. God will give us the strength to be victorious.'

Beornoth frowned and scratched at his beard. The fyrd was a force of common men forced to fight by their Lords. Each group of hides had to supply men to fight in time of need. They were not Thegns, reeves or household warriors. These were farmers, blacksmiths and millers, armed with a spear, who would now stand against the professional warriors of the far north. Beornoth rode silently next to Aethelhelm. The Ealdorman knew as much about fighting Danes and Norsemen as Beornoth, so it wouldn't serve him well to point out the obvious to Aethelhelm. The Vikings on those ships would all be warriors, each man the equal of a Saxon Thegn or household warrior. Men in the Viking home-lands who wanted to farm, or be potters or blacksmiths, stayed there, and the lovers of battle, the sword-and-spear Danes, Svears and Norsemen, sailed south in search of reputation and war. Beornoth turned to make a count of their force. Aethelhelm marched with forty warriors, and then Byrhtnoth had provided around sixty men of the Essex fyrd. So, when it came to the fight, it would be forty Saxon warriors against one hundred savage Viking pagans. If the Vikings overwhelmed the forty Thegns and household troops, and got amongst the men of the Essex fyrd, then they would make a great slaughter.

The column marched alongside the river, the water not

visible beyond the rushes, trees and briars of the riverbank, but the sound of the water babbled above the murmuring and chatter of the army.

'The men seem happy,' said Wulfhere, as the column halted at a point where the river's narrow turn would make it slow for the Vikings warships to follow its flow and navigate the sharp bend, and where Streonwold's men had felled a long beech tree, and dragged its dark trunk across the river's span. The trunk's long, grasping branches rustled in the breeze as small leaves in various shades of green were dragged into the flowing water.

Streonwold had picked a place where the river narrowed on both banks. Towards the west the banks were thick with drooping willow trees, dipping their light green leaves into the water and spanning a full third of the river's width, which meant the Vikings would make that turn blind to what lay ahead. At the point where Streonwold had laid the tree trunk, both banks of the river edged out towards each other, banks thick with reeds and deep, sprawling grasses which made a natural pinch in the river's flow. On the bank where the Saxons formed up was a flat field with low heather, dotted here and there with purple and blue flowers. The field led on to a wood edged with silver birch trees, whose trunks shone in the sunlight. That wood rose slowly up a shallow valley and on into rolling hills stretching away south across the fertile land of the East Saxons.

'The men are confident. Likely they haven't fought Vikings before,' said Beornoth. He dismounted and adjusted his axe in its belt loop. It was the shorter, rune-bladed weapon he had taken from the Norseman in the forest. It was a better-weighted weapon than his old axe, and its leather-wrapped haft felt comfortable in his grip. The old long axe, pitted with rust, remained in a sheath in his saddle. Beornoth handed the reins of his mare to a boy, took his spear and went to help form the lines of battle.

'So, we think Vikings will jump from their ships and fight us here on the riverbank?' asked Wulfhere.

'Seems that way,' replied Beornoth.

'Do you think they will?'

'Well, they can't get out of the river with us in front and Byrhtnoth's men behind. Byrhtnoth will block the river to the west. So, to get away, the Vikings must remove that tree. To move it, they need us out of the way, so yes, there will be a fight.'

'What about Alfgar?'

'You and I will stand in the front line, if Aethelhelm permits us. Alfgar will stand behind us. Find us good shields, Wulfhere. Alfgar's task will be to hold one above our heads if the Norsemen have archers.'

'Why stand in the front?' asked Wulfhere. Beornoth stopped walking and stared into the big man's eyes. He did not see fear there, but he knew that there were not many men who, like him, loved to fight, and pushed their way into the front lines to bathe in the heart-thumping welter of danger where senses became heightened at the moment of risking one's life. For most men, the prospect of an enemy thrusting or slashing a blade into your flesh was horrifying. More than that, the terrible wound that would cripple a warrior and turn him into a beggar was enough to force a man back in the lines. Those men would look to strike a blow with their spear, striking over the heads and shoulders of the men in the front line, the war lovers. Beornoth had always fought in the front, where the dangerous men gather.

'We stand at the front, and we fight and kill. Now, find three shields.'

'Why not let others...'

'I do not leave the fighting to others. I have a Heriot to reclaim, and the only way to do that is to stand in the front and kill Norsemen. So, that is what we will do.'

Wulfhere held his gaze for a moment, then nodded and called for Alfgar. The two men went off to find shields and Beornoth helped organise the fyrd into lines along the riverbank.

The men were becoming restless as the dragon-prowed Viking warship eased around the bend in the river. Men had stood in line for a quarter turn of the sun across a pale blue sky, and many had broken ranks to piss or scoop a drink of water from the river. An overhang of riverside foliage obscured most of the turn, but a splash of oars moved the Saxon warriors to silence as a snarling beast head emerged from the bushes. The clinker-built timbers of her hull rose like the belly of a great monster, and the beast's head showed its teeth as the ship cut through the river water like a serpent.

'Only one ship,' muttered Wulfhere. Beornoth felt a twinge in his belly. There should be three ships, three ships of Vikings, to trap on the banks of the East Saxon river. But he could only see one, and on that ship, he couldn't see any warriors. The surrounding men were silent. He heard a man cough three lines behind him and Beornoth craned his neck to see who rowed the ship and where the warriors were. Only three banks of oars were dipping into the water, dragging the ship along. That meant only six men rowed her, and Beornoth had expected between thirty and forty killers to be aboard, baying for blood and brandishing axe, sword and spear.

A flaxen-haired man appeared at the prow. He wore shining mail and stood with one arm around the beast head. The ship drew closer, and he drew a shining sword and waved it above his head. Beornoth froze. It was a signal, a sign to his men gathered out of sight to attack, and where the Saxon plan had seemed so simple and impossible to fail, Beornoth knew the Vikings had sprung a trap of their own, and everything that seemed so easy was now torn to pieces.

'Bastards are on our flanks,' he said, and he felt Wulfhere stiffen beside him.

The Norse warrior barked an order, and three more oars appeared on the side of the ship closest to the Saxons. The Viking warrior let out a whoop and stepped over the ship's side to stand on the oar closest to him. He held his arms out wide for balance, still carrying his sword, and took long steps from oar to oar. When he reached the sixth oar, he turned, wobbled slightly and came back the same way. The few men on board his ship roared with delight at their leader's feat, and the Saxons jeered and shouted and clashed their weapons on their shields. The din rang in Beornoth's ears, and he clenched his teeth.

'Arrogant to do that in sight of an army gathered to kill him. These Viking bastards have monstrous pride,' he muttered.

The flaxen-haired Viking popped up at the prow of his ship again, and suddenly his arm whipped forward and he launched a spear at the Saxon lines. It flew in a high arc and thumped into the chest of a Saxon warrior close to the riverbank. A thunderous roar went up from the forest on the Saxon left flank, and Viking warriors came howling from the wood like a flood of charging wolves.

'Shield wall,' shouted Aethelhelm, and he and Streonwold tried to bully the ranks to wheel around and face the threat from their south side. The men had lined up to face the threat from the river, but the Vikings must have sent scouts ahead, ranging across the countryside, looking for the Saxon attack which they knew must come. Beornoth cursed Aethelhelm for not sending scouts of his own to check the surrounding area, especially the high ground. Aethelhelm had been so fixated on the river and trapping the Viking ships that he had been blind to any threat from the landward flanks.

'Move, you whores,' Streonwold bellowed, shoving men with

his axe. Beornoth turned and took three deep breaths. He hefted the shield which Wulfhere had found from Aethelhelm's supply carts and overlapped its edge with Wulfhere's shield. The big man nodded at him, and Beornoth could see the muscles of his jaw working beneath his beard.

Up and down the line, men were praying, calling on God to protect them and grant them luck. To Beornoth's left, he saw the Viking leader had made it to the riverbank and sprinted now across the Saxon lines towards his men. He barked an order and the wild charge halted. They stopped dead at his command and made a shield wall of their own. A warrior handed the leader a shield while he joined their front rank. The leader beat his axe upon it, and his men followed. They marched towards the Saxons in time with the beat of their blades on wood, chanting as they marched.

The rhythmic chanting rattled across the riverbank, and Beornoth gripped his spear shaft. He glanced down to make sure his axe was safely at his belt, and he wished he had a helmet to protect his skull.

'Alfgar,' he said, but there was no reply. 'Alfgar,' he shouted.

'Yes, I'm here,' replied a high-pitched, quaking voice behind Beornoth.

'They are just men, and we are going to kill them. You use your shield to protect mine and Wulfhere's head. Do you understand?'

'Yes,' came the whimpering reply.

Beornoth heard men crying out behind him. He could smell piss wafting on the breeze where the men of the fyrd realised what they faced. Beornoth hoped the Ealdorman was right and the proper warriors in the Saxon line were enough to defeat the ferocious Viking warriors.

The enemy shield wall grew closer, and Beornoth could see

the men opposite him. Big men, armed with shields, axes and spears. He could see some wore mail byrnies, and most wore helmets. Four more steps and he could see the whites of their teeth snarling within their beards.

'Hold the shield wall,' he shouted, more for his own courage than anyone else's. 'Hold the charge and kill the bastards.'

'For God, and King Æthelred,' bellowed Aethelhelm from along the line, and the warriors cheered and set themselves for battle.

A shield slammed into Beornoth's own, and he felt a boot scrape down his shin where the man opposite him kicked at him. He could smell the man's foetid ale breath over the shield rim and pushed back, shouting as he did so. A spear blade snapped past his face and the fright of it took his breath away. The Vikings shoved forwards, and the Saxons shoved back. The press was tight, and it was hard to breathe. Beornoth had his spear held above the press. He held the weapon overhand, with the point resting on the iron rim of his shield. So as the Viking's boot stamped on his foot, and the foul smell of his breath blew into Beornoth's face, he jabbed his spear forward and it punched through the jelly of his attacker's eye and on into his head. Beornoth felt resistance as the point crunched on the Viking's skull, so he wrenched it back and blood spurted from the dying man's face across his shield to splash warm and thick on Beornoth's cheek.

The attacker fell away, and Beornoth raised his shield and shoved the boss into the face of an enemy who hacked at Wulfhere's shield with an axe. Beornoth shoved and stabbed, slashed and wounded and his heart pounded in his chest at the horror of it. Screams and shouts filled his ears and Beornoth did what they had trained him to do, what he was born to do. He killed.

From the corner of his eye, he saw the flaxen-haired Viking leader hacking into the Saxon shield wall. He saw men fall away from his ferocity.

'Skarde, Skarde, Skarde,' the Danes chanted, and their leader hammered his way into the line. Suddenly, a great cry went up from the Saxon lines.

'The Ealdorman, the Ealdorman is down,' came the cry.

Beornoth turned towards the shout, but he couldn't see where Aethelhelm was amongst the crush of bodies. He felt a sharp thud on his left thigh and he cried out. To turn had been a mistake. He had taken his eyes off the shield wall for a heartbeat and now a spear point tore into his thigh like a white-hot blade fresh from a blacksmith's forge. Beornoth slammed his shield down to snap the spear, and its point jerked out of his leg. The Viking opposite him reached below his shield to grasp for an unseen weapon, but Beornoth stabbed his spear into the warrior's throat and pushed him back. He drove the spear on and put his shoulder behind his shield to drive into the enemy line.

Suddenly, everyone around him moved slowly. They were slow and heavy, caught in time, and he was fast and light. He felt the elation. This was the battle joy, the fleeting moment in the clash of blades where a man's soul danced on the edge of life and death. Beornoth snapped his spear across his shield rim where it had stuck in his foe's throat, and the man's neck was a black mess of torn flesh and gouts of blood. He jammed the broken spear shaft into the face of the man who beat on Wulfhere's shield, and that Viking reeled away as the shattered wood punched through his cheek and shattered his teeth. Beornoth whipped his axe free from his belt and surged into the Norsemen. He felt a thump on his shoulder and a blade hammered into his shield, but Beornoth was moving fast, cutting and slashing at eyes, necks and faces. The enemy fell back from him, and he suddenly realised he was bellowing the names of his dead daughters, roaring their names into the dying Viking faces, wreaking vengeance for his loss on the countrymen of their killers.

Beornoth realised he was ahead of the Saxon shield wall. They were moving back, shaken by the loss of their leader, and he could hear Streonwold shouting for him to get back. Beornoth dropped his shield and took his axe from its sheath at his back and beckoned the Vikings to come and die. A huge, red-bearded man came at him with a long-handled war axe, and Beornoth swayed away from a lunge and ducked under its mighty back-swing. Before the enemy could bring his axe back around, Beornoth crouched and hacked his axe blade into the warrior's foot, hearing the crunch as the bones inside his boot shattered. The warrior howled and Beornoth drove his seax into the man's belly, dragging it across to find a gap beneath his breastplate. The long knife drove into the soft flesh between red-beard's belly and breastplate, and Beornoth sawed it back and forth with all his strength. The warrior shrieked like a cat in the dark of night, and he looked down in horror as the purple coils of his guts slopped across Beornoth's arm and onto the mud-churned battlefield.

The man fell and Beornoth shouted his challenge at the Vikings, realising that they had backed away to create a space between their shield wall and the Saxon shield wall, and into that space came their flaxen-haired leader, Skarde. He was armed with an axe and long knife, just like Beornoth, and the two men circled each other. Skarde had piercing blue eyes in a face that was all sharp edges and flat planes on his cheeks and forehead, like he was cut from stone. The Viking leader sprang at Beornoth in a whir of blades, and Beornoth held his breath, trying to deflect the blows, but the man was too fast and his knife cut across Beornoth's forearm and laid open his cheek so that

Beornoth tasted the iron tang of blood in his mouth as it washed down his face.

Beornoth lunged with his axe, and Skarde parried it. The Viking expected Beornoth to cut low then with his knife, but Beornoth charged him. He headbutted his enemy and bullied him. Skarde was of similar height, but was lighter across the shoulder, and Beornoth used his size to force Skarde back. He headbutted him again, feeling the gristle of Skarde's nose give way under his forehead, and Beornoth bit at his face, sinking his teeth into the Viking leader's cheek and clamping his jaws down. Skarde howled and spun away, into the safety of his own shield wall. They held there, enveloping Skarde into their ranks and reforming a solid wall of overlapped shields, whose brightly painted symbols were splashed with Saxon blood and scored by Saxon blades.

Skarde was the fastest and most skilled warrior Beornoth had ever fought, and the pain of the wounds he had taken suddenly weakened him. Where the Viking was skill and speed, Beornoth was all brutal savagery, and he dared to think he had given as good as he had got. He limped back to the Saxon shield wall, and saw the enemy attacking the flank by the river. He was thirsty, so thirsty.

The Vikings roared, and Saxons fell back, and Beornoth's heart sank because Ealdorman Aethelhelm was dead.

# 9

Aethelhelm's loss hit the Saxons like a hammer blow, and their lines fell back from the Viking shield wall. Once the shout went up that the Ealdorman had fallen, the front rank of Saxons shuffled backwards away from their enemy. The fight drained out of them with the loss of their leader. Streonwold and Beornoth called for them to hold the line and keep the shield wall intact, but the Norsemen broke through at the flanks and the sea wolves got amongst the fyrd inside the bend of the river. Once the hard warriors from the north brought their axes to bear against the farmers, bakers and smiths of Essex, the slaughter had truly begun.

Beornoth grimaced as Alfgar tied a scrap of cloth around the wound in his thigh, where a Viking spear blade had torn deep into his muscle. During the retreat, Beornoth and Streonwold had wheeled the front lines around so that they could make an orderly march back towards the woodland. The warriors amongst the Saxons held the line and took small steps backwards, keeping their shields and faces towards the enemy, but the men of the fyrd broke into an all-out run towards the trees. Skarde's Vikings allowed them to retreat, bellowing and howling their victory at the defeated Saxons. The Vikings had the river, and it was a simple matter for them to drag away the trunk Streonwold had thrown over it to block their path to the sea.

'They were laughing at us,' grumbled Wulfhere. He sat next to Beornoth, washing the blood from his face and bald head with a handful of river water.

'Thank God they didn't pursue us,' said Alfgar, tying the makeshift bandage and wiping his bloody hands on his trews. 'The slaughter was horrific. Such pain and suffering...'

'Wasn't much sign of God today,' said Beornoth, checking the other wounds on his body to make sure there weren't any still bleeding. 'Seems to me that the Viking Gods were stronger.'

'God will have his vengeance on the heathens,' said Alfgar, crossing himself and shaking his head at Beornoth's blasphemy. Alfgar had knelt and prayed over his father's body, he had not wept, but he had been even more withdrawn than usual since Aethelhelm's death. Alfgar stood and walked to help other injured warriors nearby, and Beornoth saw his hands were trembling.

'Look after him,' Beornoth said to Wulfhere. 'Being a bastard is not easy, but Aethelhelm was still his father. Get him a drink and some food, if there is any.' Wulfhere nodded.

Two Viking warships emerged from behind the drooping willow branches and rowed slowly downriver. The victorious Vikings massed along the sheer strake of each vessel, waving and taunting the Saxons gathered at the edge of the wood.

'Bastards are away now,' said Wulfhere. 'Off to strike somewhere else, to kill some more of our people.'

'Help me up,' said Beornoth, groaning as he tried to get to his feet. Wulfhere stood and grabbed Beornoth's wrist and Beornoth allowed the big man to haul him upright. Wulfhere followed as Beornoth picked his way around the seated warriors, each man tending to his own wounds or helping a friend. There was an eerie silence over the group. The sound of the cheering Norsemen travelled across the blood-soaked battlefield where bodies lay, some still twitching or crawling towards them. Beornoth saw a warrior sobbing, clutching at the stump of a handless wrist, bloody wrappings barely stemming the flow of blood. Another man rolled in the dirt, hands over a face cleaved open by an axe blade. The Saxons watched the dragon boats sail past, their faces contorted into grimaces of hate, pain and shame at the defeat. Beornoth felt it, too. It twisted in his guts like an ache from rotten food.

'This is war, lad,' Beornoth said over his shoulder to Alfgar. 'This is why we learn our weapons and practise every day. There will always be war, always be Danes or Norsemen, or some other bastard trying to take something: your land, your family, your wealth. If you want to live, and protect those you love, learn to fight well.'

'Yes, Lord,' said Alfgar in a whimper. The boy was tripping as he walked through the wounded, the horror and screams of the fallen making him weak.

'I am not a Lord,' growled Beornoth. 'If you don't want to end up like these poor souls, learn to fight. Practise your weapons.'

'You fight like a demon,' said Wulfhere. 'That Viking chief back there was as skilled a warrior as I've ever seen, and you almost killed him.'

'He almost killed me, too. He killed Aethelhelm as well, so let's see what Streonwold wants to do now.'

They found Streonwold bent over the body of Ealdorman

Aethelhelm. Streonwold knelt with his hands clasped together as he whispered a prayer over his dead Lord. Streonwold's hands shook, caked in dark, dried blood. Crusted flakes of other men's lifeblood tangled with the dark hair on the back of his hands and under the sleeves of his jerkin. Streonwold looked up and sighed as he recognised Beornoth and rose to meet him.

'Bastards got a blade into his gullet,' said the warrior. His byrnie mail coat was filthy from the battle, and his face looked drawn and pale. Alfgar dropped to his knees, and began to pray over his father's body once more, rocking back and forth as he whispered to God.

'They outfoxed us. We should have had scouts in the trees,' said Beornoth. He looked down at the white face of the dead Ealdorman. Someone had washed the blood from his face and neck, so that the wound was like a second mouth, smiling at his throat. Beornoth thought Aethelhelm looked older, and smaller, now that he was dead. His hair and beard looked whiter, and his shoulders narrower. The Ealdorman had loomed large across Beornoth's life. Beornoth had succeeded his father as Thegn and Aethelhelm had confirmed him in the family Heriot. Beornoth remembered kneeling on the cold stone of the church floor as Aethelhelm went through the ceremony of presenting Beornoth with the mail byrnie, sword, helmet, spear, shield and warhorse. Each of which the Bishop had blessed, and Beornoth had served his Lord well, until the Danes attacked his lands and cast all of that asunder. Then, in Beornoth's grief-stricken fall into desperate drunkenness, Aethelhelm took that Heriot away. Even though Aethelhelm had been the man to cast Beornoth down, and take away his inheritance, Beornoth did not hold it against him. An Ealdorman needed Thegns who could fulfil their oaths, tend to their lands, and fight when needed. Beornoth looked at the long nose and grey eyes of his former Lord. He hoped the old boar was in Heaven and that all the coins he had paid to the Church over the years had bought enough prayers to get him there.

'We had scouts up there. We're not fools, Beo. The Norsemen must have found them and killed them.'

'The Vikings fight well.'

'They do.' Streonwold glanced at Alfgar and took Beornoth by the arm. 'Walk with me.'

The two men walked towards the river, and towards the edges of the mud-churned battlefield. Beornoth watched the Viking warships disappear behind a bend in the river, the remains of their oar strokes rippling across the water's glassy surface.

'Osric will be the new Ealdorman now,' said Streonwold, spitting towards the riverbank reeds and running a hand through his sweat-soaked hair.

'Hadn't thought about that,' said Beornoth. He rubbed at tired eyes and sighed, realising that his hopes of a new Heriot now lay in the hands of Osric.

'He doesn't like you. Aethelhelm was fond of you, Beo, he knew you as a fighter. Osric's different. He doesn't know much about war. He's a little turd, and he hates you for what you did to him in that forest.'

'He will soon learn about war. The Vikings will be back.'

'They will,' Streonwold agreed. 'Osric will want the lad gone.' He jutted his chin in Alfgar's direction.

'I'd almost forgot, he's Aethelhelm's bastard.'

'He is, which means he had a claim to be Ealdorman, and any man who doesn't like Osric could get behind Alfgar and use him to take the shire from Osric.'

'So Osric, the Ealdorman, will want Alfgar's throat cut.'

'So watch him, Beo, the old man loved Alfgar. The lad should have gone to the Church, and spent his life with words and God, but now he's here with the likes of us. Keep him alive and away from Osric.'

Beornoth nodded. 'Not much chance of Osric granting me a Heriot.' He recalled the confrontation in the forest where Beornoth and Wulfhere had killed the Viking foragers.

Streonwold laughed and shook his head. 'The old man would have done it. He would have made a new Heriot for you. He hated taking your father's lands from you. I'll miss the old bear.' He knelt to pick up something which had caught his eye in the grass. It was a slim leather thong with two beads attached to it. 'Must have snapped in the fighting.' He spat on the beads and rubbed them clean on the forearm of his jerkin, where it covered his arms below his byrnie.

'He still took it away, though, even if I deserved it. What do you want those for?'

'I keep them, for my children,' said Streonwold, and tucked them into a pouch tied around his neck beneath his armour and clothes. Beornoth touched at his wooden locket, hidden from view. He remembered the laughter and joy of his own children, and grimaced at the harsh bitterness of the world.

'Riders,' said Streonwold, pointing downriver. He strode away on his bandy legs, his rolling gait hurrying towards the oncoming force. Beornoth walked back to the others, where Wulfhere and Alfgar stared towards the new arrivals.

'That will be Ealdorman Byrhtnoth, too late for the fight,' said Wulfhere.

'With your brother,' Beornoth said to Alfgar. 'Stay close to me. He's the Ealdorman now.'

The riders reined in, and their leaders spoke to Streonwold. He gestured at the battlefield and then pointed upriver in the direction the Vikings had disappeared. The riders dismounted and Byrhtnoth, flanked by Osric and his household warriors, strode towards where Aethelhelm lay.

Beornoth braced himself for Osric's malevolent aloofness to brush aside his hopes of land and Heriot, but he didn't have the chance. Before the Ealdorman had taken ten paces, a shout of terror went up from the injured men at the forest's edge, because the Vikings had returned to finish their slaughter.

# 10

The Norse warriors appeared over a rise to the east, their massed ranks singing in sonorous, deep voices, the sound of their war hymn to Odin rumbling down the river's shallow valley to turn the Saxons' hearts cold.

'There's more of them,' said Wulfhere. Their numbers looked swelled, and Beornoth saw the prows of two of their warships beating oars upriver, returning from the direction in which they had sailed following their earlier victory. Warriors thronged the decks, brandishing weapons and shouting their defiance at the Saxons.

'They mean to surround us, form up, shield wall, shield wall!' Beornoth bellowed. He tried to run to where he had left his shield amongst the wounded, but his injured thigh forced him into a hurried limp. He saw the fear etched on the faces of the Saxons sat on the grass at the wood's edge. The men had fought and lost already, and now they must fight again, or they would all die beneath Viking blades. Cries went up amongst the Saxons, the anguish and despair falling over them like a heavy net.

'Get up, rise and fight again, or we will all die this day. Men will pour from those ships and they come to kill you. If you don't fight, we will all die this day, fight for your lives!' Beornoth hefted his shield and strode towards Streonwold, Byrhtnoth and Osric, who stood staring at the Viking forces.

'They have returned to kill us,' said Streonwold, his voice wan and distant.

'Must have met their other ships just off the coast and come back to finish us off,' Beornoth said.

'They have more men, even with our numbers combined,' said Byrhtnoth.

'They mean to surround us, Lord,' said Beornoth. 'They'll sail those two ships upriver and attack us from the rear whilst we fight facing East.'

'That's their plan,' agreed Byrhtnoth, and he tucked his thumbs into his belt, eyes darting from the ships to the advancing army.

'Osric, take the horsemen west and stop them from disembarking. Harry them, and hold them, whilst we make the shield wall and fight the first lot here,' said Beornoth.

'Lord,' said Osric. The men around looked at the golden-haired youth with raised eyebrows and open mouths. 'My father is dead, so I am Ealdorman now. So you call me Lord Osric.'

Byrhtnoth sighed and shook his head. 'Your father's corpse is still warm, lad. What he says is right, take the horses west, stop the bastards from attacking our rear.'

Osric's face flushed, and he glared at Beornoth with pursed lips. 'Very well,' he said. 'Streonwold, fetch me my father's sword.'

Streonwold looked at Beornoth and shrugged and then ran to fetch the blade. Osric's horse stamped its legs in the mud and the new Ealdorman savaged its reins, he drove his heels into the horse's flanks so that horse and rider stomped towards Beornoth and he could feel the beast's hot breath as it snorted and bobbed its head. Osric leant over the saddle to stare at Beornoth, and a joyless smile played at the corner of his mouth.

'You can forget the Heriot my father promised you, reeve,' Osric said, allowing the words to drawl. His eyes searched Beornoth's own, looking for pain and disappointment to glory in, but Beornoth just met his gaze with a cold stare. 'You and my bastard brother will return north after this is over. I am the Ealdorman now, and I will find a suitable place for you both. You will never be a Thegn again. I will have need for a man to empty my pisspot each morning.' Osric laughed and wheeled away, and Beornoth felt his chest tighten as his dream joined Aethelhelm in death.

'Make the shield wall,' bellowed Byrhtnoth, and the warriors around shouted their ascent in a clipped roar.

The Vikings aboard the warships rowed past the Saxons, shouting and jeering across the bows. Amongst Byrhtnoth's riders were six men armed with bows, and those men fired shafts into the baying Norsemen, which reduced their baiting after one Viking fell into the water with an arrow in his throat. Beornoth watched the ships row past, bile rising in the back of his throat at the despair of it. He was wounded, weakened and tired. His ale craving thundered in his head, and the horrible remains of the earlier battle still sprawled across the riverbank. The Northmen would never stop. They would always come back raiding, killing and stealing, and it would never end until they were all dead. He banged his axe on the iron boss of his shield and felt his heart pound. His leg throbbed and the wounds on his arms and back stung and tore at him as he moved, but he pushed his way through the mass of warriors to the front rank, and Wulfhere stood beside him. Alfgar took up his position behind him and Wulfhere, and Beornoth felt the touch of his shield on his back.

'Remember, lad, protect our heads from the high blows,' he

said, and heard Alfgar's muttered acknowledgement.

The Viking lines drew closer, chanting their war songs in unison, sending a deep and rumbling tremor through Beornoth's chest. He saw their leader, the man he knew to be Skarde, stride out beyond the shield wall, his face bloody from his fight with Beornoth. A hulking warrior barged his way out of the Viking shield wall, stripped to the waist with whorls of dark blue tattoos across his chests and arms. The tattooed warrior raised his shield and axe, turning to his own warriors and then to the lines of Saxons. The Norsemen held their line, only twenty paces from the Saxon shield wall, and the warrior edged forward. Skarde slapped him on the back and shook his weapons at the Saxon line.

'What in all Satan's hell are they doing now?' said Wulfhere.

'The big one wants to fight, man against man, a test of champions,' said Beornoth.

'Look at the size of him. He's even bigger than me.'

And so he was. There would not be many men who would want to fight the Viking giant.

'Ashwig and Cwen,' Beornoth whispered. Then he repeated the names of his dead daughters again louder, and louder. He could feel Wulfhere staring at him, but the madness of war fury was descending upon him, and Beornoth pushed his way out of the front rank to meet the Norse giant.

'Get back in line. I know you're brave, but I'm the Ealdorman, so I'll fight him,' came a deep, sonorous voice from Beornoth's left. It snapped him from his anger-fuelled daze, and Beornoth turned to see Byrhtnoth striding forward to meet the enemy. He marched with his bright sword drawn, and his shield hanging low at his side, his helmet burnished as bright as the North Star.

'Byrhtnoth, Byrhtnoth,' Beornoth called, and the massed Saxon ranks behind him echoed the chant. Beornoth's heart swelled. It was a brave and noble act for the Ealdorman to fight the Viking champion. To show the men that he not only shared their risks, but to go out alone to fight the brutal tattooed giant filled the Saxons with pride and respect for their leader. Beornoth stepped back into the line and watched as the Ealdorman stopped and raised his shield to face the Norseman.

'I've never seen the like, a nobleman fighting alone, risking his own skin,' said Wulfhere. The men around were still roaring and shouting for their leader to kill the Viking.

'Let's hope he wins,' said Beornoth. If they lost Byrhtnoth, so soon after losing Aethelhelm, then the men's fighting spirit would crumble, and the Vikings would slaughter them like lambs.

The Norseman took a stride forward, his eyes wide and protruding from his bushy-bearded face. He lunged at Byrhtnoth, and the Ealdorman took the blow full on his shield boss and followed the block by driving forward behind his shield to force the Viking backwards. The huge warrior took two backwards steps, hooked the beard of his axe blade around Byrhtnoth's shield and yanked it downwards and heaved forward with his own axe. It punched into the air where Byrhtnoth's head should have been, but the Ealdorman had ducked and brought his sword up to cut across the Viking's chest, carving a long red gash. The Norseman roared and kicked at the Ealdorman, but Byrhtnoth smashed his iron shield rim into the warrior's shin, and he fell to one knee. He tried to scramble to his feet, but Byrhtnoth used his shield boss to punch the giant full in the face, and as the Viking reeled from the blow, Byrhtnoth plunged his sword point into the warrior's belly. The Viking stared wide-eyed, and his mouth fell open in shock at the wound. He dwarfed the Ealdorman, but the Viking's monstrous size made him slow and Byrhtnoth was lethal and fast. Byrhtnoth dropped his shield and gripped his sword two-handed to rip the blade up the tattooed man's torso, splitting him open like a butcher would a pig. The wound was terrible, and the giant fell to the grass, almost cut into two, slopping his insides onto Saxon soil. The Saxons roared for their leader, and the Vikings fell silent.

Byrhtnoth picked up his shield and marched back to his men, holding his sword aloft.

'Kill them all!' shouted the men around Beornoth. The Ealdorman had won, and Beornoth felt the confidence surge in the Saxon lines. But they remained outnumbered, and the Vikings came on, the shield wall edging closer, urged on by their flaxen-haired leader Skarde at the centre of their line.

The shield walls clashed, and good men died. Beornoth pushed and shoved with his shield, he cut with his axe, and enemy blades cut at him in return. He took more wounds on his neck and forearms, and more than once Alfgar did his job and protected his head from spears and axes aimed above the shield wall. The fighting raged for what seemed like an entire day, but before the sun had moved a fraction in the sky, the lines parted and both Saxons and Vikings took steps backwards. The ground between the lines was a mess of mud, piss and blood. Corpses lay twisted and trampled and the injured screamed, moaned and crawled towards their own lines begging for help.

'They will come again. Prepare yourselves,' Byrhtnoth called, out of Beornoth's sight but still in the front line.

'Are you wounded?' Beornoth asked Wulfhere. The big Saxon gasped for breath, doubled over his shield.

'A few cuts, but still alive. Just need to catch my breath.'

Wulfhere stood, his eyes wide and white, face and breastplate splattered with red and brown gore. It was hard to see his own wounds, so thick upon him was the blood of his enemies. Beornoth himself was breathing hard, sweat heavy on his jerkin beneath his hard baked-leather breastplate. He looked behind him and Alfgar was still there, his slim shoulders pushed inwards and his face drawn and pale. Beornoth nodded at him. The boy had done as well as any other warrior in the Saxon lines. He had stood his ground and more than once had deflected high blows from Beornoth's and Wulfhere's heads.

The Vikings came again and again, and the shield walls clashed. Beornoth lost all sense of time. Slowly, the Saxon lines fell back under the press of the larger Viking numbers. The battle lines pivoted so that the Saxons backed on to the treeline again, and the Norsemen filled the space along the riverbank. The day drew on, men died and the lines thinned. So many dead, so many wounded. Beornoth fought in the front line in each encounter, and as more warriors fell, he found himself with his shield locked against Streonwold's, and Ealdorman Byrhtnoth one further along the line. Wulfhere held fast on Beornoth's right, hard and resolute.

At another lull in combat, Beornoth took a drink of water brought by a boy, a thin waif of a child with water skins hung over his shoulders and around his neck. The river water was cool in Beornoth's throat, and he poured a splash on his face, where the sweat stung his eyes and the iron taste of blood washed his lips

'We can't hold much longer,' said Byrhtnoth. The Ealdorman wiped his sword blade with a clump of grass torn from the earth. They stood at the wood's edge. There was a strange eerie quiet, the men treating wounds and preparing weapons, long past the point of exhaustion.

'Neither can they,' said Beornoth. He looked across the battle-field at the carnage of the day's fighting and the Vikings were as subdued as the Saxons, no more chanting or shouting, just exhausted, grim preparation for the next assault.

'They have lost as many as we have, so why haven't they left the field?' asked Streonwold.

'Pride? Hatred? You are right, though, Vikings normally avoid a fight like this unless they think they can win. Too many losses weakens them. If they lose too many men, their campaign is over. We should kill as many of the bastards as we can, send them screaming across the sea,' said Beornoth.

The Vikings formed up again, Skarde still at their centre urging them on to the fight.

'God help us,' said Wulfhere. A collective sigh went up across the Saxon lines, and Beornoth saw why. The two Viking ships were coming back upriver, creeping past the drooping willow branches with the same steady oar strokes as Skarde's ship had earlier that day.

'Osric must have held them,' said Streonwold.

'He should bring his horsemen here, then. A charge into their flank would win the battle,' said Beornoth. Byrhtnoth stared at him and nodded. He shouted behind them for a boy to run and find the new Ealdorman downriver and bid him bring his horsemen east.

Ahead, the ship-borne Vikings disembarked and swelled the Viking numbers facing the Saxons by two crews' worth of fighters, a long fifty or sixty men. The Norsemen shouted their fury at the Saxons once more, and their shield wall formed up and edged closer across the bloody mess of the battlefield.

Byrhtnoth strode forward and turned to his men. He said, 'Once more, men. Hold the line. Throw the heathen bastards back into the river. We fight for our women and children, for our homes and mothers and fathers. For God and the King! Pick up your blades once more, and fight!' He raised his sword aloft, the men cheered – a ragged, exhausted roar – and the lines formed up slowly.

Beornoth took his place between Streonwold and Wulfhere, and Byrhtnoth took his place next to Streonwold and they made the shield wall firm. Beornoth's leg screamed at him to stop, to sit down and rest. His other wounds burned and throbbed, and his eyes were weary. But he whispered his daughter's names again, and thought of their little burned bodies in the remnants of his Hall and the fury came to Beornoth once more, burning away his exhaustion. They moved forward, right leg and left leg shuffling in unison, keeping their shields overlapped, and the weight of it burned Beornoth's shoulders. So he whispered those names again, and pictured his little daughters running through the fields laughing and full of joy, until the Danes had come and torn all of that away.

'Where is Osric?' said Beornoth, glancing west upriver. If the Vikings had been unsuccessful in leaving their ships further upriver and their plan to outflank the Saxons thwarted, then Osric had done well. But the Norsemen had found time to row downriver back to the battlefield, and still there was no sign of the new Ealdorman.

'Hopefully waiting for the right time to strike,' said Streonwold, his voice hoarse from shouting orders at the men all day long.

'Now would be good,' grumbled Wulfhere.

The shield walls came close and Beornoth braced himself for impact, but the Viking lines halted upon an order from Skarde and their wall parted to let a line of warriors burst through armed with long-handled Dane axes. Those men sprinted across the distance between the lines and swung their axes overhand so that the blades hooked over the top of the shield rims of the Saxon front line.

'Brace your shields,' Streonwold roared, but just as the words left his lips, the Vikings yanked down on their axes and they tipped the Saxon front line shields downwards and forwards. From behind the axemen then came another mighty shout and a line of spears erupted from the Norse lines, spitting like venom from a serpent. Beornoth had got his left knee behind his shield and so could keep it high, and a spear thudded into its top boards, driving it back into his shoulder. The spear blade throw held so much force that it pierced Beornoth's shield's boards, its point ending only a handspan away from his eye. Beornoth heard screaming around him and felt the resistance of the shield wall give as the combination of axe and spear attacks decimated the Saxon front rank. He glanced left to see Streonwold being pulled back into the ranks behind him, his face a mask of blood where a spear had split his nose and cheek open. Beside him, Wulfhere had dropped his shield and gutted a Norse axeman in front of him with his seax.

Beornoth dropped his own shield to loosen the axe hooked over its rip and punched his own axe forward to cut the blade into the face of the Viking in front of him. That enemy shrieked in pain and Beornoth kicked him in the groin. Beornoth shuffled left and joined his shield to Byrhtnoth's. The Ealdorman had taken a wound to his shoulder, tearing his mail byrnie in a ragged, bloody mess. He had dropped his sword and his right arm hung at his side, useless and dripping blood.

'We can't hold them,' growled the Ealdorman, and Beornoth saw it was true. The Vikings had decimated the Saxon front line, the fiercest warriors in the Saxon army swept aside. One more push and the Vikings would break through, and then they would be amongst the fyrd, and that would be a slaughter.

'If I am going to die here, let me die as a Thegn once more, Lord,' said Beornoth, suddenly seeing a chance to resurrect his hopes for a return to honour. A Viking snaked out of their line and thrust a spear towards the Ealdorman, but Beornoth hooked his axe around the shaft and pulled the blow wide, then reverse cut the axe blade across the attacker's throat.

'You were a Thegn?'

'I was, Lord. My family held a Heriot. I was a Thegn sworn to
Aethelhelm. But that Heriot was lost to me. If I am to give my life
here, let me do it as a Thegn. Let me take up your sword and
make my ancestors proud.'

'Take it, man. I've lost Thegns here today. You have fought like
a King's Thegn. Take up the sword and honour your forefathers.'

Beornoth sighed. The surrounding battle slowed. The sounds
of screaming and shouting, the clash of iron on wood, metal
against metal, became dull, like listening to the sea in a beach
shell. He thought of his father, so proud and so brave. He thought
of his dead daughters, and his wife driven mad by the pain of loss
and assault. Beornoth dropped his axe and knelt, his hand
squelching in the mass of mud, blood and piss at his feet until he
grasped the hilt of Byrhtnoth's sword. His hand curled around the
hilt of finely sanded wood riveted to the blade's tang. He saw a
pommel of round iron inlaid with a cross chased with silver. The
long blade came up, and the balance was welcome, like a lost
limb restored. Beornoth dropped his shield and snatched his seax
from its sheath at his back.

Beornoth let out a war cry, a bellow which erupted from the
depths of his stomach and washed over the battlefield like a
mighty war horn from the poets of old. Men around him paused
and stared, and suddenly the battle sped up, and Beornoth fought
like a Lord of War.

He charged into the Vikings, cutting and ducking, slashing
and shouting. They fell away from him, and he stabbed at their
flesh, every spot of blood, every cry of pain a satisfying tribute to
his lost family. It happened in a blur. He knew blades struck at
him, and he was ready for the death blow, welcoming the warmth
that death would bring to his sad heart, but he fought on. He was
amongst the enemy, driving into them, killing and maiming.

From the corner of his eye he could see Wulfhere had followed him, the huge warrior cutting and slashing with bravery and skill.

A horn sounded, loud and clear, over the din of battle. The Saxons behind roared, and the surrounding Danes edged back towards the river, slowly at first, but then Beornoth found himself cutting and lunging at nothing. He realised he was keening the names of his daughters and fighting empty space. Beornoth fell to his knees, wounded and exhausted; Wulfhere collapsed next to him gasping for breath but still alive. Beornoth felt a rumble beneath him and heard the thunder of hoof-beats. Osric had brought his horsemen to the fight, and they crashed into the fleeing Viking flank like a warmed knife in fresh butter.

Beornoth felt a shadow looming over him, and he looked up to see the figure of Byrhtnoth staring down at him, nodding.

'Rarely have I seen such bravery. You will be a Thegn again, Beornoth. I grant you a Heriot and lands here in my service. Will you swear to me and become a Thegn of the East Saxons?'

Byrhtnoth held out his left hand, and Beornoth took it and swore to serve him. He kissed the Ealdorman's hand, and the Ealdorman placed it on Beornoth's head and whispered a prayer.

The Vikings fell back, retreating behind an organised shield wall on to their fast ships. But they would come again, and as he knelt in the battlefield's filth, Beornoth looked up at the shifting mass of milky clouds above. He knew he would need to be a War Thegn. The Vikings would never stop, and the people would need protection. He had won a Heriot, not his father's, but a Thegn's Heriot all the same. To return north with Osric meant death or a life of hell for Beornoth and Alfgar, and he had avoided that grim fate through the slaughter of the battlefield. He had brought honour back to his ancestors, but a sourness curdled that honour, for Beornoth knew that this was surely only the beginning of the war with the Norsemen.

# PART II

# THEGN

## 11

Beornoth leant over a deep bowl on a table in his chambers and washed his face with cool water. He took a bone comb with a finely carved, tiny boar's head at one end and brushed it through his beard, and then through his hair. He tied his hair at the nape of his neck with a thin strip of leather and took a drink of water from a burnished tankard. The servants at first had questioned why their new Lord would not drink ale. Everyone drank it to avoid the risk of stomach sickness inherent with water from rivers and wells, but Beornoth growled and barked at them, and so water it was.

He had not taken a drink of ale for over a year, but he still yearned for its thick yeasty taste every day, and for the haze of peace it brought, even if that peace was fleeting. Beornoth stretched his torso and looked at the scars on his body, arms and legs. The deep wound in his thigh was still lurid and red, but the rest of the cuts taken at the battle by the riverbank a year ago had healed well enough. He pulled on his byrnie mail coat and shrugged it into place. The weight was familiar and welcome. When Byrhtnoth had presented Beornoth with the mail coat,

Beornoth had struggled to get used to its weight, having not worn armour for so long. The daily wearing of a byrnie made a warrior strong. It was hard work just to walk around all day in the coat made from hundreds of interlocked rings, which covered him from neck to thigh.

In the days following the Battle of River's Bend, as it became known, Byrhtnoth had presented Beornoth with the accoutrements of his new Heriot at the land and hidage at Branoc's Tree, which included a sword. It was a fine weapon, the long groove of the fuller ran along its length, its crosspiece was plain and unadorned and the handle was two plates of horn wound about with leather to cover the tang. The weapon's pommel was a curved lobe of metal, shaped into four columns tapering out from the central and longest column. Beornoth wore a belt buckle shaped into a horse's head and burnished to a shine. Beornoth looked down at himself, in his byrnie, fine buckle and sword, and felt like a Thegn again. Like the man he once was. His old breast-plate and dirty clothes were long gone, burned in a pit behind his new Hall. The day he had burned them, Beornoth had felt his self-pity and self-destructive darkness trail up into the sky in the wisps of smoke, and he hoped it was the end of his days of drunkenness and deep melancholy. Every morning his belly and throat still cried out for ale, urging him to find a skin of it and suck it down. But he had left that part of his life behind. The longing for the mind-dulling effects of ale followed his nightly slumber, still plagued by nightmares, visions of his burned children and damaged wife visiting him vividly every night whilst he slept. He reached behind his byrnie and pulled forth the small locket. Beornoth twisted open the face and rubbed his thumb across the soft golden hair beneath. He closed his eyes and hoped his daughters were both looking down on him with pride, in the afterlife, now that he had found his station again, and he promised them he would never forget them. He might have burned away the self-pity, but the deep sadness remained, and he knew in his heart that it would always be there. Just as his daughters would always be the age they were on the day the Vikings had taken them from him.

Beornoth walked from his chambers and along the dark timber-lined corridor, lit only by a flickering torch which sent shadows crawling around the close space. Beornoth strode out of the corridor and into the Hall beyond. The people in the Hall all stopped what they were doing and bowed their heads as he passed. Beornoth remembered how the children at Knutsford would taunt him for being a drunk, and how the villagers would look down their noses at him, the fallen man. They would not mock him now. He nodded to the servants, maids and boys in his Hall, and walked past the raised dais where his solid oak chair stood proudly. He skirted around the circular firepit at the centre of the room, where men piled logs and poked at the crackling flame, which never went out. In the high eaves, smoke danced in the shafts of light which forced their way through the smoke hole cut into the roof's thatch and Beornoth could smell baking bread and hear the familiar sound of crunching, where at the Hall's edges the people ground oats and barley.

Beornoth stepped out of the double doors, carved with whorls and crosses and secured to the Hall's timbers by huge iron hinges, and out into the central courtyard of his burh. He nodded in satisfaction to hear the clang and bang of weapons, and the grunts of warriors as his men practised with axe, spear and shield. Every day they trained with weapons, one against one, and in the shield wall, they worked on all the drills and movements which formed the key elements of fighting. Beornoth would join them most days, but today was different, today was the day of the week when the people within the hidage under his protection would come to him with their gripes and complaints, and he would propose decisions, and try to provide justice for his people. Beornoth watched Alfgar. The young warrior performed a perfect lunge with his spear, and kept his shield up high, just as Beornoth had shown him. Since River's Bend, Alfgar had taken to weapons training like a foal to the field. He had grown thicker in the shoulder, and he did not look out of place amongst the warriors of his hearth-troop. Alfgar drove a grizzled veteran back with his shield, and Wulfhere clapped his approval.

A clutch of figures dressed in drab cloth, with wooden crosses at their necks and frowns on their faces, hurried across the courtyard towards him, and Beornoth cursed. He saw Wulfhere grinning at him from where he stood, stripped to the waist and sweating from his practice. The huge warrior held a shield painted with yellow and brown spirals, and a spear with a wooden blade instead of iron, to keep the daily practice free from bloodshed. Once Byrhtnoth had conducted the ceremony to make Beornoth a Thegn, in front of the Bishop and the important people of Essex, Beornoth had made Wulfhere the captain of his household troops. Wulfhere grinned now because he saw the women heading in Beornoth's direction and knew them to be harridans, and the bane of Beornoth's new life. Wulfhere winked at Beornoth, and Beornoth chewed at his bottom lip.

'They are at it again,' screeched a small, plump woman at the centre of the group. Her face was red and her cheeks bulging like ripe apples, her frown enough to curdle milk.

Beornoth sighed and tucked his thumbs into his belt. 'What is it, Aethelberga?'

'Those ruffians of yours, banging and clanking at the third hour,' she said, throwing her hands in the air and making the sign of the cross over her heavy breast three times in rapid succession.

'We must practise our weapons, if we are...'

'It is the third hour, which is the time of mid-morning prayer, as you well know. It is sacrilege that you and your men don't follow the proper times of prayer.' Her shoulders shuffled, and her chins quivered, and the women about her nodded and whispered amongst themselves.

'My men pray, my Lady. But they must also fight, unless you want the pagan Vikings as your Lords and you as their slaves.'

'God preserve us. My Helmstan always followed the...'

'Helmstan is dead,' barked Beornoth, growing tired of the way she constantly harped on about her dead husband. Helmstan had been the Thegn of Branoc's Tree before he had died at the Battle of River's Bend, and Aethelberga was his widow, and now Beornoth had taken Helmstan's place and Heriot. Aethelberga talked of her late husband as though he were a saint, and Beornoth's surly, harsh manner drove her to despair.

'You are a cruel and godless man. What evil must I have done to the Ealdorman for him to thrust you upon me?' She wept, and before Beornoth could speak again she waddled off, limping from a gripe in her hip which gave her constant cause for complaint.

Beornoth watched her go, followed by her gaggle of womenfolk, bustling towards the church with its cross mounted on the high gable end, and no doubt into the arms of her sycophantic priest. Byrhtnoth had made Beornoth Thegn of Branoc's Tree, but with that title and its Heriot, he had inherited Helmstan's widow. She was childless, and so when Helmstan had died with a Norseman's axe in his skull at River's Bend, the land and all that came with it fell to Byrhtnoth, as Ealdorman, to appoint a new Thegn. At the Heriot ceremony, Byrhtnoth had handed Beornoth his new sword, byrnie, helmet, spear, shield and riding tack, along with a magnificent white stallion trained for war.

'She's a shrew, that one,' said Wulfhere, strolling over to join Beornoth.

'She's a pain in the arse,' said Beornoth.

'You have fine lands here now, men to command and wealth. Byrhtnoth honoured you.'

Which was true. Branoc's Tree was a Hall, church, grain store and an ample huddle of wattle-and-daub housing for his men and servants, all within a stout timber palisade. Beornoth was now responsible for one hundred hides around Branoc's Tree. Branoc's Tree was just one of the many hundreds which, together, constituted the shire of Essex, all under the Lordship of Ealdorman Byrhtnoth. Branoc's Tree and its environs were good, fertile land south of the salt fens and high enough to avoid flooding from the nearby river in winter.

'Its spring now, the Vikings will return soon, we can count on it. They might have returned to Jutland or Norway for the winter with their plunder and burnished reputations, but I fear they come to our shores for more than just raiding. Are they ready?' Beornoth said, nodding towards the men at practice.

'They are good men. They'll fight hard, Lord.'

Along with the land, Beornoth had also inherited Helmstan's household troops. The Vikings had been quiet following the Battle of River's Bend, largely because the brutal fight would have left the Norsemen with too many dead or injured warriors to continue effectively raiding, and so the rest of that summer had passed in peace, giving time for wounds to heal, and for Beornoth to settle into his new lands. He and Wulfhere had trained the ten household troops hard, forging them into skilled and organised warriors. The household warriors knew their weapons already, and Helmstan had equipped them well with stout spears and solid shields, but to fight the Vikings they would need to be the best and most organised of fighting men.

'King Æthelred's warriors saw off Olaf Tryggvason, but from what men say, this Olaf wants to make himself rich on the fat of Wessex, make himself a King even. Æthelred wintered in Winchester and I know Ealdorman Byrhtnoth went to him to make sure the burhs across the coast would be strengthened before the Vikings returned with the good weather. So, our men will need to fight hard. Byrhtnoth didn't make me Thegn here to sow oats. The Vikings will be back, and when they do, we will be in the thick of it.'

'No doubting that, Lord.'

'How is Alfgar coming along?'

'Good, see?' said Wulfhere, and pointed to the youth. Alfgar was now a tall and broad-shouldered young man, and Beornoth watched him moving through the spear movements, and he did it well. He was straight-backed, and his thrusts and parries were all executed with power and control.

'Let's hope it's enough to keep him alive.'

'Let's hope. At least he is away from his shit of a brother.'

Beornoth had noticed that Wulfhere held himself straighter now. No longer was he the cowed masterless man Beornoth had dragged from Offa's Crag. He was a proud warrior again, and a fine one at that. He was one of the few men around him that Beornoth felt he could talk to, in moments where it wasn't awkward, and Beornoth welcomed the company.

After River's Bend, Osric had demanded that Alfgar return to the north with him. Alfgar was Osric's half-brother and his to command in his new position as Ealdorman. Beornoth knew, however, that once Osric got back to his lands in Cheshire, that Alfgar was a dead man. An Ealdorman would not want a bastard brother around for his enemies to rally around and who might become a rival for Lordship of the shire. So Beornoth had made Alfgar swear an oath to be his man, and then asked Byrhtnoth to allow Alfgar to remain with him as his oathman. Byrhtnoth had allowed it, much to Osric's fury, and he had ridden away in a flurry of horses and curses. Beornoth liked Alfgar. He was quiet and callow, but he had shown bravery at River's Bend, and the lad knew how to read from his time with the Church. Beornoth himself could not read a word, so that skill alone was of value to a Thegn who could expect to receive written orders and proclamations from his Ealdorman.

Groups of people trickled into the gates of Branoc's Tree, and Beornoth looked up at the clear blue sky. There had been no frost that morning, and the sprawling oak tree which gave the land its name showed green shoots. Spring was bursting from the darkness of winter, which also meant the campaigning season had arrived. Beornoth clapped Wulfhere on the back and walked towards the Hall. It was time to take his raised seat and allow his people to bring their petitions before him. Beornoth rolled his shoulders as he walked. He had never enjoyed this part of being a Thegn. He had always been more of a fighter than a justice of the peace. He remembered as a boy that he would sneak into his father's Hall and watch the old boar preside over his court. Laying down decisions, agreeing to ride out and settle disputes himself. He remembered his father as a cold, harsh and brutal man, but he had the respect of his people and Beornoth had always strived to emulate that.

Beornoth climbed the dais inside the Hall, feeling the warmth of the fire where the flames crackled and spat. A servant had left a luxurious dark wool cloak over the back of his chair, and Beornoth draped it around himself, fastening it at the shoulder with a silver cloak pin. He sat and beckoned to the back of the Hall, where Aethelberga had entered and was clucking and fussing with the folk gathered at the dark corners of the Hall's entrance.

Beornoth had allowed her to keep most of her roles and duties around Branoc's Tree, and continue on as the Lady of the house. He had no steward, and no desire to appoint one. Beornoth was from the north, many days' ride from the lands of the East Saxons, and so he neither knew nor trusted any of the people in or around Branoc's Tree. Which meant he trusted no one beyond Wulfhere and Alfgar. But Beornoth had noted early on that the people seemed to respect Aethelberga, and she was a clever and confident woman, even if he found her shrill and annoying. She enjoyed her position as the female head of the household, and she was good at it, so Beornoth saw no reason to change the existing arrangement.

Beornoth did, of course, have a wife of his own. He thought often of Eawynn, who had once been his beloved. She had been everything to him until their lives were torn asunder. He imagined her as she was in the old days and daydreamed that she was here in Branoc's Tree. Her hair would catch the sunlight from the smoke hole, and her smile would warm the room like a summer's sun. He told himself that she was in the best place where the sisters could look after her. Eawynn was not herself, not since that dark day so long ago.

Aethelberga cleared her throat loudly, snapping Beornoth from his daze.

'Ordlaf of Birch End is first before you today, my Lord,' she said, presenting a short man with a warty nose and bent back. Beornoth sighed and listened to his complaint of a dowry not fully paid, an accusation laid against a man named Eafa who also stood before him. Beornoth listened patiently to both sides as they made their arguments, and then ordered the dowry paid in full.

'If it's not paid by the full moon, I will ride and make sure it's paid myself,' Beornoth said. Both men bowed and walked away.

And so it went for most of the morning, mundane disputes over border hedges cut down, field walls moved, and cows stolen. Until a man limped into the Hall, propped up by his two sons. Aethelberga let out a yelp and ran to the man, fussing at his injuries.

'This is Peada, who is, or was, cousin to my Helmstan,' she said, shouting above the mumbling and pointing of all those in the Hall.

'What happened to you, Peada?' asked Beornoth.

'Men attacked my lands, Lord. Armed men from a different shire.'

A rumble of murmuring and collective intakes of breath undulated around the Hall.

'How many men, and what makes you think they were from a different shire?'

Peada took a drink from a ladle of water brought by one of Aethelberga's maids, and he supped it thirstily, coughing and clutching at injured ribs.

'There were six of them, my Lord, and they spoke... well...' he said, looking from Beornoth to Aethelberga and then at the floor rushes.

'Speak up, man. They spoke like what?'

'Like you and your captain, Lord,' Peada said, and every face in the Hall turned to look at Beornoth.

'When did they attack?'

'Yesterday, Lord, they hurt my daughter,' he said, and began sobbing. Aethelberga put her arm around him and pulled him towards the fire to warm him.

'That's all for today. I ride out for Peada's holdings. Saddle the horses!' Beornoth called, and he strode from the dais, leaving the remaining petitioners with their problems unresolved.

Beornoth burst into his chambers and searched for his riding boots and travel clothes. The door behind him slammed, and then swung open again. He turned to see Aethelberga standing in the doorway wringing her hands.

'Not now, woman,' Beornoth said, sighing and digging around in a deep chest, searching for his thick, woollen cloak.

'What do you think this means?' she asked, ignoring his request to leave.

Beornoth stood up and stalked over to her, his frame big and looming in the small chamber. 'It means men have come to my lands with blades, and it's my responsibility to drive them out, or put them in the ground.'

Aethelberga, to her credit, did not flinch away from Beornoth's venom. She placed her hands on her hips and frowned right back at him.

'They sound like northerners. Are they men who have followed you here?'

'They could be masterless men from anywhere.'

'But they are not from anywhere, they are from the north, your homeland. I am not asking you these questions to harry you, Beornoth. I am asking you because the people look to me for answers. They look to you for your sword and for justice, but to me for support, and for food when their farms are destroyed.'

'You are no longer the wife of a Thegn, so...'

'How dare you say that to me?' she said, her cheeks flushing red. 'I am still the Lady of this house, and of this hundred. Helmstan and his forebears protected this land for generations. You stroll in here, from God only knows where, scowling and cursing at all and sundry. You might have impressed Byrhtnoth with your ability to kill, my Lord, but there's more to being a Thegn than fighting.'

'Do not tell me about my business. I was a Thegn in the north for many years, and my wife ran the estate just as you do here. I know how it works, but I am the Lord here, and your husband is dead. So let me do what I do best, and clear these killers from my lands before they hurt someone else.'

'You were a Thegn, and had a wife?'

'I was, and am. And, yes, I have a wife.' He swallowed hard, regretting losing his temper with the woman. He suddenly realised he had barely spoken to her since arriving at Branoc's Tree. In fact, he had avoided any type of conversation at all. Beornoth's attitude to Aethelberga was that she should be grateful to him for not packing her off to a convent to see out her days in prayer. He had kept her around because she was useful, and what she said was right, a Thegn's wife performed duties within the hundred which were just as important as the protection of a Thegn's sword. Looking at her there in the doorway, Beornoth knew he had to change the way he treated her.

'Your wife is still in the north?' she said.

'She is, but she is ill. Very ill.' Beornoth sighed and rubbed at his temples. 'Listen, I have treated you harshly. I think an enemy of mine from the north has sent these men, but to find out for sure, I need to find them and question them.'

'Will she come to Branoc's Tree?' asked Aethelberga. Beornoth just stared at her. He had not considered fetching Eawynn from her home at the convent. She was safe there, and well cared for. But, despite everything which had happened to her and between them, she was still his wife.

'She is very ill, but maybe one day we will bring her here. She can never run the house, I am afraid. So your position is safe. Whilst I am gone, listen to the people, take appropriate decisions in my absence. I will ride for Peada's farm and from there try to pick up the track of these raiders. If you hear talk that riders have been seen, or have attacked somewhere else, send a messenger to me.'

She nodded and set her jaw. 'I'll have the servants prepare food for you and the men for the journey,' she said. Beornoth inclined his head and sidled past her and through the doorway. He hoped there could be a truce between them now, and he would take extra care to pay Aethelberga more respect in the future. But first he had to find the men who had violated the people under his protection, and discover if what he suspected was true and that Osric was behind the attack.

## 12

Beornoth stroked the ears of his white stallion, the horse nodded his head and Beornoth patted his muscular neck. His name was Ealdorbana, which meant life destroyer, and Helmstan had named the beast well. Beornoth's predecessor had trained Ealdorbana for war, so he would not fear blood, or noise, and he would snap his teeth and trample foes under his huge legs. He was sixteen hands, had powerful hind legs and was one of the finest horses Beornoth had ever seen. Beornoth's mind wandered to his old nag, lost following the slaughter at River's Bend, and he hoped the beast had found a full pasture somewhere to see out her days.

'A beast like that is worth more than a mail byrnie,' said Wulfhere, watching Beornoth stroking the animal.

'You haven't sold yours yet, I see,' said Beornoth, pointing at Wulfhere's mail coat, and Wulfhere laughed. Byrhtnoth had distributed the armour and arms stripped from the dead at River's Bend amongst those who had distinguished themselves in battle, so Wulfhere was the proud owner of a byrnie mail coat stripped from a dead Norseman, and a burnished helmet with a nasal protector which he carried now tied to the saddle of his horse.

'We've come far since that day on the Crag.'

'We have,' allowed Beornoth, remembering how he had dragged Wulfhere naked across the hills and dales of north-west England. 'And now we must find and kill men from my old home.'

'Do you think they are Osric's men?'

'Who else?'

'But why, because of Alfgar?'

'That, and because he won't be happy that I'm a Thegn again. I insulted him in front of his friends, and he hates me for that. I saw it in his eyes. He wants us dead, and I'll wager you a fistful of hack silver he sent these bastards south to harry us.'

'Why not just kill Alfgar?'

'Easier said than done. They'd have to get past you and I first,' said Beornoth, and Wulfhere laughed again.

They sat atop a hill drenched in early spring sunlight; the sky was clear, and the sun was as bright as on a midsummer's day, but it was cold and Ealdorbana's breath misted from his nose in great plumes. The hill was a high sheep pasture topped by a small copse which afforded a view across the westernmost portion of Beornoth's hundred. They were close to Peada's farm, and Beornoth searched the valley for a sign of enemy riders. The farmers had told Beornoth that there were six men, all mounted and well-armed. They had attacked another farm only a day earlier and so must be close. Their horse's tracks led this way and had not been difficult to follow. The raiders had spent the night at the farm they had attacked and then rode out at first light. So Beornoth and his men waited in the copse for any sign of the riders. He had brought six of his household warriors, including Wulfhere and Alfgar.

'What will you do with the shrew?' asked Wulfhere.

'Aethelberga? She's not that bad. She runs a good house.'

'So you're thinking of marrying her, then?'

Beornoth turned and thought about punching Wulfhere. The hulking warrior saw the threat in his eyes and gave a wry, gap-toothed smile, holding his hands up to apologise.

'I'm thinking about bringing my wife down here, where I know she's safe.'

The humour vanished from Wulfhere's broad face, and he looked out across the valleys below. 'You think Osric would hurt her?'

'He might. He's a spiteful little weasel.'

'So, when shall we get her?'

'After we sort this rabble out, maybe I'll send Alfgar for her.' Beornoth wanted Eawynn close. Since his altercation with Aethelberga, he had felt guilt like a heavy stone in his chest. Eawynn might have been driven to madness through her pain and suffering, and Ealdorman Aethelhelm had been right to send her to the convent for her own safety and care, but she was still Beornoth's wife. He should have brought her south the moment he had taken over Branoc's Tree. No matter how hard it would be to hear her shrieking and to see the hate in her eyes every day, whilst all the time being reminding of what she was in the time before, of her beauty and the love they had shared, Eawynn should be with him. 'Have you ever been married?'

'Once,' said Wulfhere, and rubbed a hand across his face. 'When I was young. She died, giving birth to a son. The boy died with her.'

Beornoth nodded solemnly. Childbirth was as dangerous for a woman as the shield wall was for a warrior, and Wulfhere's loss was a hard thing to bear and a tragedy for his dead wife and son.

'There, Lord,' Alfgar called, leaning over the neck of his

piebald mare and pointing to the east. Sure enough, there was a line of six riders emerging from the cover of a pine forest and ambling down towards a brook which wound its way down the valley on its journey towards the river.

'We have them now,' said Beornoth, and he curled his hand around the leather-bound hilt of his sword, gripping it tight.

Later that day, deep in a pine forest which bordered the lands around Branoc's Tree, and as the chill darkness enveloped the land, Beornoth and his warriors crouched behind moss-covered rocks above a gulley surrounded by blackberry bushes. Once they had found the enemy, it had been a simple thing to track them from a distance until they stopped to make camp for the night. The men had travelled south heading for Beornoth's Hall and then diverted west for the cover of the pine forest to make their camp for the night.

Beornoth watched them, six men making their meal over a small fire. Sharing a joke and supping ale, men who had attacked Beornoth's lands. Their horses safely hobbled and the eaves of the dense pines around them hiding the smoke from their fire. They thought they were safe, and they thought they were clever. They thought they could ride into his lands and take what they wanted, unsettle Beornoth's people and disrupt his new station as Thegn. He watched them, and he wanted to hurt them. They had raped Peada's daughter mercilessly. Beornoth deplored violence against those who could not defend themselves, and no woman deserved that most terrible of fates. He knew all too well what the pain of that violent ordeal did to a woman's mind.

'We go soon,' he whispered to his men. 'Remember, we are justice and vengeance for the people of Branoc's Tree. I go first. I want one left alive, just one. The rest we kill and bring their corpses to show our people what justice looks like.'

The surrounding faces nodded and checked weapons and

shield straps. Wulfhere was whittling at a piece of golden wood with a short knife. He was forever whittling at something, making toys for the children at Branoc's Tree, or pipes for the young women. Wulfhere blew the shavings from his current piece of work and ran his fingers over the smooth wood. He took a thong of leather he had tucked into his boot and passed it through a hole he had made at the top of his creation. It was a cross, the size of a man's middle finger, and Wulfhere had carved it with intricate spirals and whorls. It was fine work and Beornoth had noticed his captain working on it for weeks.

'Here, Alfgar. For your prayers,' said Wulfhere, and handed the cross to the young man.

Alfgar took it, and his thin face lit up in a broad grin. 'It's magnificent, Wulfhere. Thank you, and God bless you,' he said.

'Maybe you'll say a few prayers for me, lad,' said Wulfhere. 'For the man I was.' His eyes flitted to Beornoth and back to Alfgar. 'I fell into sin, did bad things. So say prayers for me, and maybe I'll go to Heaven when it's my time.'

Beornoth slipped his sword gently from his scabbard, careful not to make a sound.

'Let's go. Keep quiet on the way down, and remember, I want one of them alive.'

They set off down the slope between the pine trees, treading carefully so as not to snap a rotten branch or slip and alert the enemy below. Beornoth trusted Wulfhere would fight. The big warrior had proved himself more than once to be a skilled and ferocious fighter. Alfgar had shown promise in training across the winter and had stood firm at River's Bend, and he had taken a life in the forest before the battle. The other men were untested. They were Helmstan's household troops, who Beornoth had inherited. Each man had sworn an oath to fight for Beornoth and do his bidding, but he had not seen them fight yet. They trained well enough, and showed skill and experience in arms, but training was one thing and the fury of battle was another, where an enemy uses all his skill and strength to hurt you, to spill your blood, and to rip your life away.

One of the six raiders served as a lookout, and he paced around the edges of their camp whilst eating a haunch of stolen lamb. Beornoth didn't care that the lookout might see their approach and warn the others. He was close now, down the slope, and they would die anyway. Beornoth stood from his crouch and held his sword in front of him, rolling his neck from side to side to loosen his shoulders.

'Time to test all that practising,' he said to his men behind him. Beornoth strode forwards and saw the lookout turn towards him, his mouth hanging open and juices from the lamb dripping into his black beard. He dropped the meat and fumbled for a seax sheathed at his belt.

'Warriors!' the lookout shouted; the words garbled by the food in his mouth. Beornoth quickened his pace, taking four long strides. The man freed his seax and brought its broken-backed blade up before him, but Beornoth was close and he brought his sword up two-handed and batted the seax aside. As the man stumbled from the force of the sword blow, Beornoth kicked him in the side with his heel and drove him into the fallen pines and leaves of the forest floor. The enemy around the fire scrambled for weapons, their confidence and laughter turning quickly to cries of alarm.

The black-bearded man rolled down the forest hillside towards his friends, and Beornoth snarled and marched after him. The fallen man looked up at him with big eyes, he dropped his seax and raised his hands, but before he could beg for his life Beornoth slammed the point of his sword into the warrior's beard, piercing his gullet and spraying blood into the twilight.

One was dead, and five left. Beornoth had his men at his back, so victory was not in doubt. It had been a long winter trying to fit in with and get used to the people and way of life at Branoc's Tree, so it felt good to do what he did best.

A tall, broad-shouldered warrior charged at Beornoth. He ran clutching a spear two-handed and snarling, his aim to run Beornoth through like a pig on feast day. The attack was clumsy, and Beornoth swayed aside and used the blade of his sword to guide the attacker past him, trusting that Wulfhere would take care of him. He heard Wulfhere roar his war cry behind him and knew his captain was attacking the spearman. The remaining four enemies fanned out, each armed with spear or axe, and one man brandished a sword. He was a short, swarthy man with a balding pate and heavy brows. The sword marked him out as the leader, and a warrior of note, but Beornoth resisted his urge to charge forward and engage the swordsman. A furious charge would leave him open to a blow from the other enemy warriors, and there was no need to risk that, Beornoth knew the fight was already won. He stopped himself amid the melee and let his men charge past him. They did so and then halted to raise shields and spears towards the enemy in an organised charge practised so many times on the training field.

'Don't wait, just kill the bastards,' Beornoth shouted. The eldest of his warriors, a tall, spindly man named Osmod, glanced at Beornoth and encouraged the men onwards. Alfgar took up a position in their midst, armed with his spear. Wulfhere came up alongside Beornoth, his gore-covered axe head held before him, and the enemy spearman dead behind him. Beornoth put a hand on Wulfhere's chest to stop from joining the fight.

'Wait here,' he said.

'Why, I want that bastard's sword,' said Wulfhere, and made to move past Beornoth.

'You can have it. I already know you can fight. I want to see what this lot can do.'

Wulfhere nodded and grinned, and kept his place at Beornoth's side.

The stand-off between the two lines of men continued, with a man from each line occasionally darting forwards with a feint, but without committing to the attack.

'They're afraid of us, lads. Bloody soft-bellied southerners,' growled the swordsman.

Beornoth felt the small hairs on the back of his neck stand up. The delay in fighting was giving the enemy warriors confidence, despite their inferior numbers.

'Useless,' Beornoth said and barged through the line of his men. Osmod spun around and nearly fell over from the force of Beornoth's shoulder. Beornoth marched straight for the swordsman, and an enemy warrior jabbed a spear at his face, but Beornoth grabbed its shaft with his left hand and pulled the warrior towards him, headbutting him and connecting with his eye socket. He heard the bone behind the warrior's eye crack beneath the blow and he let go of the spear as the warrior reeled away in pain. Beornoth lunged at the swordsman, and the swarthy man parried the blow and cut his blade low at Beornoth's shin, but Beornoth's blade was there to block the cut. The man whipped a dagger from his belt and slashed it at Beornoth's face, so he ducked to avoid the blow and brought his blade around to attack his enemy in a flurry of cuts and lunges. The smaller man edged back, bullied by Beornoth's speed and size, and Beornoth continued to press him backwards until the retreating swordsman's heel caught on a rock beneath the foliage of the forest floor and he tumbled to the earth.

Beornoth caught movement in his peripheral vision and from the corner of his eye he saw an axe swinging for his neck, but

Alfgar darted in just in time to block it with his spear. The young warrior keened a high-pitched scream, more fear than threat, and he attacked the axeman, wildly stabbing at him with his spear. Beornoth ignored that fight and swung his sword hard to connect with the hilt of the fallen man's blade to send it spinning away into a hedge. The warrior snarled up at Beornoth but did not beg for his life, and did not flinch as Beornoth raised his sword for the death stroke. Instead of killing the man, Beornoth placed the blade behind his knee and made a cut through the tendon there, then dropped his sword and pulled his seax free from the sheath hanging from the back of his belt. He knelt on the man's chest and used his free hand to grab one thick, hairy wrist and with the other he sliced open the flap of skin attaching thumb to forefinger, and then did the same on the warrior's other hand. That was a painful wound, and one which Beornoth knew would stop the man wielding a blade.

Beornoth stood and picked up his sword and saw Alfgar crumbled in the leaf mulch, kneeling next to an enemy writhing with Alfgar's spear in his guts. Alfgar was half sobbing and half sucking in gulps of air. Wulfhere had despatched another man, which left one enemy warrior standing. Osmod and the household troops surrounded that man, and he threw down his weapons and knelt for mercy.

'If you bastards want to live under my roof, and you and your families want to eat my bread and drink my ale, then you need to fight. My men will always go where the fighting is thickest, and you lot need to learn to strike, or find a new Lord,' said Beornoth, and Osmod and the other men looked at each other and at the man kneeling between them.

Beornoth strode to the warrior writhing in the dirt with a spear in his belly and without breaking stride he slashed his sword to open the warrior's throat, whose groans stopped immediately as his lifeblood gurgled and poured amongst the fallen pines. Osmod and the others parted as Beornoth approached.

'Please, Lord, I beg you for my life,' said the kneeling man. He was young, with a threadbare fair beard and bright blue eyes, not much older than Alfgar, Beornoth thought.

'Who sent you here?'

'Ealdorman Osric sent us, Lord, he paid us silver. Please, spare me. I have a wife...'

'What did he order you to do?'

'Keep quiet, Barra, shut your cheese pipe,' shouted the swarthy man.

'Who raped the farmer's daughter?' Beornoth asked, and Barra's eyes flicked to his companion, but he shook his head and clenched his eyes tightly closed. 'What did Osric order you to do?' asked Beornoth again. This time he raised his sword so that the gore-splattered point was a handbreadth from the kneeling man's face.

The man gulped, and a tear rolled down his cheek. He said, 'He bade us kill the man Alfgar, who is his bastard brother, and create havoc in your land, Lord.'

'Osric said those words?'

'Yes, Lord, he hates you. He says you belittled him, and you are a drunk and coward who leaves his mad wife to rot in a convent and goes whoring every night. He says you are the enemy of God.'

The words stung Beornoth like a whip. A drunk he may have been, but the rest was poison dripping from the Ealdorman's mouth. It had been a mistake to scold him for his reluctance to fight that day in the forest, and a mistake to stand up to him at River's Bend. There was an obvious reason for Osric to want Alfgar dead, to remove him as a potential rival. But Beornoth saw now how much he had hurt the young nobleman's pride, and now they both had reason to hate each other.

The swarthy warrior shuffled and seemed about to speak until Beornoth made a quick turn and swung his sword backhand. He felt resistance as the hard blade passed through the man's neck and heard the thud as his head hit the ground in a spray of blood. Osmod gasped, and at least one of the household troops put his hand to his mouth and closed his eyes.

'I said one survivor, and that's him,' Beornoth said, pointing his sword at Barra. 'Alfgar, you fought well today. The weapons and silver these men carry are yours. Wulfhere, find the sword and it's yours. You lot had better learn to kill. The Vikings will come soon, and they will reap your souls like wheat if you let them. We have enemies in the north and enemies across the sea, and both must learn that we are hard men to kill.'

'Father, forgive us,' whispered Alfgar, and he clutched his new crucifix to his lips, staring at the dead warriors.

'Forgive us nothing,' barked Beornoth. 'Remember, these men raided Peada's farm and raped his daughter. If that was your daughter, you would want me as the man to bring vengeance and destruction on these men. And that's what I've done.'

Alfgar made the sign of the cross at his breast over and over. Beornoth could see fear in his eyes, not just the shock of the slaughter. His half-brother wanted him dead, and had sent men deep into Essex to make that happen. Alfgar knew his brother must hate him to send men so far south. Beornoth put Barra on a horse to send back to his master to tell the tale of his failure, and then ordered his men to drape the corpses of the dead across their mounts. He would ride back to Branoc's Tree and show the people what happened to men who attacked the lands in his hundred.

# 13

The people of Branoc's Tree gathered beside the gnarled trunk of the village's ancient oak. The folk were hushed as they stood and gawped at the bodies of the five dead men which Beornoth had laid out for all to see. Women feigned shock, with gasps and hands over their mouths at the sight of blood and terrible wounds, but Beornoth saw the twinkle in their eyes, and the animated but hushed conversations they had in groups as they walked away from the grizzly spectacle. He saw nods and hands curled into fists. He saw approval. Beornoth made sure his warriors stood with him to watch the reactions. This was justice and vengeance, in all its visceral brutality, and Beornoth had delivered it for his people.

Beornoth stood at the entrance to his Hall and dipped his head in a barrel full of rainwater. The liquid was cooling and, as he came up, he ran his fingers through his hair and beard to wash out the grime from the journey and the fight in the pine forest. A light spring wind felt chill on his neck, and he felt like a warrior again, now that he was back to performing his duties as Thegn. He might not be in his ancestral lands in the north, but that could never be possible now that he had the enmity of Ealdorman Osric. A smiling servant came to him and bowed his head. He offered Beornoth a freshly baked loaf of bread, which he took graciously. He unbuckled his sword and seax and handed them to the man to be cleaned.

He caught sight of Aethelberga shuffling towards him across the open space at the centre of Branoc's Tree, and he thought about ducking inside the Hall to avoid her, but he reminded himself of their last meeting, and remembered his commitment to be more respectful towards her. The priest of Branoc's Tree joined Aethelberga in her march. He was a small mouse-like man with protruding yellowed teeth and long, wild eyebrows which curled up at the ends.

'I see you caught the offenders, my Lord,' said Aethelberga as she drew close. She raised a fist and shook it in his direction. A satisfied smile split her face, and Beornoth wondered at the contrast of pious people who preached peace and love, but also expected the full force of the law, which meant death, to apply to any who deviated from an honest path.

'Thank the Lord that you stopped these awful sinners before they could cause any more harm,' said the priest, and he raised his hand to make the sign of the cross before his face.

'They won't be hurting any more of our people,' said Beornoth, doing his best to keep his voice light and as friendly as possible.

'Were you able to discover the origin of the foul creatures?' asked Aethelberga.

'Yes, an enemy in the north sent them. But don't worry, it's all settled now,' Beornoth lied. He didn't want to tell them that Alfgar was the intended target, or that he was the bastard son of a dead Ealdorman. Nor did he want to elaborate on his own dark history and the new, powerful enemy he had found in Osric. Those facts would just cause idle chatter and worry, and both were things outside of the control of the people in Branoc's Tree.

'Will we see you in church, now that you have returned victorious, my Lord?' asked the priest, Father Tondbert.

Beornoth frowned at the little man. He knew the people fretted and worried about his absence from the church, but he had not been in one since God had forsaken him, and he had no intention of entering one now. He knew, of course, that the people of Branoc's Tree were just as pious and god-fearing as the people in the north, and that his absence from church gave rise to fears that he was at best a sinner, and at worst a pagan or heretic. Luckily, Beornoth spotted Alfgar striding towards the church, his hands clasped about the new crucifix around his neck.

'I think there is one there who needs your spiritual attention, Father,' said Beornoth, jutting his chin towards Alfgar and the church. It was a thatched building with a large cross raised high on its gable end. The church was the central point in any town, and its importance, or the power a priest had over the people, was not lost on Beornoth.

'Ah, good Alfgar. Such a fine boy, and very learned in the history of the saints of this blessed island. I should go to him. Please excuse me, my Lord,' said Father Tondbert.

Beornoth nodded, and the priest hitched up his long robe and scuttled off towards the church, chasing Alfgar, who was distraught that he had killed his second man and had, therefore, committed a sin which required confession and absolution.

'The people are happy, my Lord,' said Aethelberga, halting Beornoth as he was about to disappear inside the Hall. 'They can see now that you will protect them.'

'That's as it should be. I am their Thegn.'

'Forgive me for mentioning it, but the good father is right. Why is it we do not see you in church?'

Beornoth sighed. He didn't want to tell her the tale of his life, but he also knew that questions would be asked. 'I won't be attending church, not now, not ever.'

'Well, why ever not?' she said, becoming flustered, fussing with her hands in front of her chest.

'I tell you this now, Aethelberga, not as a tale for fireside chatter. But just so you know my mind and my reasons.'

'Of course, of course.'

'I was a god-fearing and worshipful man my whole life. Until one day the Danes came to my lands whilst I was away performing my duties elsewhere. They burned my Hall and ravaged my people. My children were slain and their bodies burned, and my wife assaulted and left with nothing but the terrible visions of that day in her head, which drove her mad.'

'My Lord, I am so sorry...'

He raised a finger to stop her. 'God did not protect my family that day. He abandoned them to the pagans and their heathen Gods. I can never forgive that. I swore an oath never to set foot in a church again, and I won't.'

Her face contorted, switching between sadness at the horrors he had described, and the desire to convince him that salvation lay with God, but she could tell by the look on his face that such words would be wasted.

'My wife lives with the sisters of a convent, far from here. They care for her and tend to her grief. I intend to bring her here to Branoc's Tree so she can be close to me, and I can see that she is looked after. Aethelberga, I would have you keep your roll as the Lady of the house, albeit as Helmstan's widow. I will never marry again, so your place here will always be secure. Do we have an understanding?'

She stared at him open-mouthed, and then nodded and clasped her hands to her chest. 'Yes, yes, we do. Thank you, my

Lord. We will make your wife as comfortable as we can and care for her every need.'

Beornoth nodded and went into his Hall to warm his hands at the fire.

A messenger galloped into the gates the next day, his piebald mare lathered and his clothes travel-stained. Beornoth was at daily practice in the yard with his household troops, stripped to the waist and sweating from the exertion of weapons practice. Since the fight in the pine forest, Beornoth had determined to push his men hard. Their hesitation to fight that day wasn't cowardice. Most men fought that way, content to remain behind their shields and try to strike a blow at the enemy without exposing themselves to attack. That was the right way to fight, unless one was reckless and ready to die. But Beornoth was a battle-lover, he was a front-line warrior and his men must be the same. So he drilled them hard this day and planned to do the same every day. He and Wulfhere clubbed and drove them with weapons wrapped in cloth, or wooden practice weapons. Osmod and the men found themselves bruised and battered, but they were learning when to snake out of their defensive positions and strike, and how to kill an enemy.

Beornoth handed leadership of the training drills over to Wulfhere and strode across the yard to where the messenger stood, dusting himself down. A servant took his horse to water the beast and brush it to clean off the dust and dirt, and pointed the man in Beornoth's direction. The messenger came towards him with hurried steps, bowed and cleared his throat.

'Ealdorman Byrhtnoth sent me, my Lord. He had me ride with upmost haste.'

'What's the message?'

'The Vikings have returned, Lord,' he said, and took off his woollen cap to wring in his hands.

'Where?'

'All over the south and east, Lord. Their leader is a prince of the Norsemen, a man named Olaf Tryggvason. They have attacked in many small groups of ships. Lord Byrhtnoth bids you to ride to River's Bend. He says you will know where that is.'

'I know, sure enough. Take some food and ale, rest your horse and then return. Tell the Ealdorman that I will meet him there five days from now.'

'Osmod, Wulfhere,' Beornoth called. The lanky warrior and the big northerner came forwards. Osmod's eye was swollen and bruised from a blow he had taken the day before, and Wulfhere had a practice axe resting on a broad shoulder. 'The Vikings are back. The Ealdorman orders to muster. We ride to River's Bend to meet Byrhtnoth in five days.'

'The Vikings will always be back. One day, we should sail to their homeland and lay waste to their homes,' said Wulfhere.

'There's nothing there but rocks and ice, or so I heard tell,' said Osmod.

'They will return, and it's our job to kill them. You two ride across the hundred. The people know their oaths and their duties. I expect two armed men for every tithing, so that's two for every ten hides, plus one more for every ten to ride to Branoc's Tree to hold the walls in case of attack. I'll meet you in two days' time at the ford near Rabbits' Hollow.'

'Yes, Lord,' said Wulfhere.

'It is springtime, so there might be problems with...' said Osmod.

'Be there with twenty men in two days' time. If any resist, then it's your duty to punish them. I know they have farm work, but if the Norsemen get loose in the shire, then there won't be any farms. Just piles of ash and dead Saxons. A firm hand from you now is better than a Viking blade in their belly or their farm on fire later.'

Osmod swallowed, his Adam's apple visible in his thin throat like a bucket rising and sinking in a well. He nodded, and the men made preparations to ride.

Four days later, Beornoth and his mounted troops arrived at River's Bend. The spring days were becoming warmer, and the East Saxon countryside was blooming with greens and browns, the hedgerows were thick with berries of red and deep black, and newborn lambs bounded in the fields and hills. The river itself brought back memories of that grim fight against Skarde and his ferocious warriors only a year earlier. Beornoth rubbed at the wound he had taken in the thigh that day. It still throbbed and ached in the cold and he had taken fresh scars on his forearms and hands in the grim battle. The fields around River's Bend were busy with the men of the fyrd armed with spears, pitchforks and wood axes, as well as the more heavily armed and organised household troops of Byrhtnoth's Thegns.

Beornoth saw a big man waving to him from across the throng, close to the forest's edge where they had taken respite during the fight with Skarde. Beornoth could make out simple lean-to shelters there now, and smoke rose from a smattering of small cooking fires. He clicked his tongue and led his riders towards the forest, and was glad to see that the waving man was Wulfhere, and the surrounding men were the men he and Osmod had rallied from the Branoc's Tree hundred.

'Good to see you, Lord.' Wulfhere grinned, and tossed a piece of bread to Beornoth. He caught it and nodded thanks.

'How many did you get?' he asked, scanning the men lolling about on the grass. They wore the simple clothes of serfs and farmers, wool jerkins and hooded caps.

'We got the twenty, had to crack a few skulls, but we have

twenty,' said Wulfhere, and he stroked Ealdorbana's nose. The
horse snorted and nuzzled Wulfhere, and he fished a carrot out of
a pouch at his waist and fed it to the warhorse. 'They are all
armed with spear, or axe.'

'Good. Where's Byrhtnoth?'

'He rode out early. There were rumours the Vikings were
already up the river, that they had left their ships by the coast this
time and rode inland on horses captured from local farms. He
went to investigate.'

'So, who is in command whilst he's gone?'

'There's a little weasel-faced so-and-so over by the riverbank.
He's a King's Thegn and his name's Erkenwald. I think he's in
charge.'

'I'll go talk to him, look after the horses and try to find food
for the men,' said Beornoth, and he slid from the saddle, handing
the reins to Wulfhere. He walked through the camp, wishing they
had gathered such large numbers together the summer previous.
They would have outnumbered Skarde, and the gathering of such
a force might even have been enough to deter the Norsemen from
attacking. Beornoth knew from experience that they only fought
when they believed they could win. A large Saxon force in Essex
provided the Viking leaders with a simple decision to sail their
warships on to find easier prey further along the Saxon coastline.

Beornoth found Erkenwald by the river, just as Wulfhere had
said. He was a short man with a thin face, his chin was clean-
shaven and he wore a byrnie, which looked too big for his slight
frame. A thick belt cinched it at his narrow waist, and a sword in a
red scabbard hung over the belt, its hilt contained sparkling
stones which twinkled in the sunlight.

'I am Beornoth from Branoc's Tree,' he said, standing before
the smaller man, and looking over the well-armed men
around him.

'Welcome. These are the other Thegns summoned by the Ealdorman,' Erkenwald said, speaking with a slight lisp. 'You are the new Thegn, appointed at the battle here last year?'

'That's me.' Beornoth nodded greetings to the Thegns, who stood at their ease, talking between themselves. All men in byrnie mail coats, armed with swords or axes. These were the warriors of Essex. The professional fighters of the East Saxons come with their household troops, just like Beornoth, to fight and kill the Viking raiders.

'Me and most of the others here missed the battle here last year. I heard it was a rare fight.' The Thegns around Erkenwald grew close to listen, each man nodding his head at Beornoth when the Battle of River's Bend was mentioned.

'It was a hard day. Many brave men fell,' said Beornoth.

'Helmstan was a good man, we'll miss his sword,' said an ageing Thegn with thinning hair, followed by much grumbling and stroking of beards from the others.

'Will the King send ships this time, to block the river?' asked Beornoth, changing the subject. He did not know any of the Thegns of Essex who stood with Erkenwald. They would all know each other well, having grown up together, fought together, and met as the Witan of Essex together. The Witan was a gathering of the Lords of Essex to advise the Ealdorman, before he attended the King's Witan to advise the King himself. It was the same in the north, where Beornoth knew most of the Thegns in Cheshire, and the old Kingdom of York, but here he was a stranger, a new man who had taken up Helmstan's sword.

'Byrhtnoth says not. This prince of the Norse, Olaf, is also raiding across the south coast and the King's fleet is there. He hasn't sent for the northern Thegns either. There are worries the Vikings will also attack there,' said Erkenwald.

'Sounds like the beginning of a new invasion, a new Great

Army maybe,' said a tall Thegn with a scar running the length of his face. The other Thegns blew out their cheeks and shook their heads. The Great Heathen Army, under the Viking leader Ivar the Boneless, had attacked England in the time of Alfred the Great and cut a swathe of blood and destruction from the walls of York down to the churches of Winchester. Their victorious invasion had brought the old kingdoms of Northumbria, Mercia and East Anglia to their knees. The forced peace that army had agreed with Alfred had been the start of the Danelaw. There, Dane and Saxon lived on either side of Watling Street and divided the island in two. That Danish rule had only ended fifty years earlier with the defeat of Erik Bloodaxe in York.

'Let's hope not,' said Erkenwald. 'But they must see us as weak. Burhs have fallen into disrepair and they have not attacked us in a generation. They are probing for gaps in our defences. Somewhere they can get a foothold and pour into our rivers with ships and axes.'

'Byrhtnoth says our numbers might frighten them off. There might not be a fight at all,' said a young man in a shining byrnie. He had a long, soft face and shoulder-length hair tied at the nape of his neck.

'They come to fight and kill, make no mistake,' said Beornoth. He glowered at the young man, and fixed him with a stare, to make his words as clear as possible. 'I've fought Vikings all my life. They aren't like us; they aren't like their kin who settled here and took on our ways and our Gods. These are pure Northmen; their Gods urge them to violence and they glory in battle. These men want to kill Saxons like you and me. They want to rape your women and enslave your children. So we should want to fight them. If they don't strike here, it will be somewhere else. So steel yourself to it, lad, harden yourself to what must be done. Your people need your sword to strike at the invaders and to take the strikes of their blades on your shield in return. We are all that protect the gentle people of our hills and dales from the unforgiving, savage ravagers from the cold, hard north. We must be more brutal, and more ferocious than them, if we want to drive them out of our lands.' Beornoth realised he had raised his voice, and that the men about were staring at him, some were nodding, and others looked stunned. He cleared his throat and waited for someone else to speak.

'How many men have you brought, Beornoth?' asked Erkenwald, breaking the silence which had fallen over the gathering following Beornoth's impassioned speech.

'I bring ten of my household men, mounted and armed, and twenty fyrd men from my hundred.'

'Good, we have five Thegns here now and have a sizeable force. Keeping them all fed, and making sure men don't foul the river water, is another matter. We can probably stay here for another day or so before we need to find the enemy, or find more food.'

'Any sign of the enemy?'

'A few sightings. A shepherd came in just after Byrhtnoth left, says he saw riders in the east.'

'Has anyone gone to check?'

'No, Byrhtnoth ordered us to wait here.'

'I can go with my mounted men. I'll be back before sundown, I'll leave my fyrd men here under your command.'

Erkenwald scratched at his chin, and peered around at the gathered force. 'Go on, then. The shepherd came from beyond that rise, he said head for Widow's Rock. It's a jutting rock face between two valleys, just before the sea. Looks like a widow's face in a hood, from a certain side, at least.'

Beornoth left his fyrd men at River's Bend, and rode out with his horsemen. Whilst part of him hoped the riders the shepherd reported seeing were just Saxons marshalling to join Byrhtnoth's forces, a bigger part of him, the part that yearned still for vengeance, wanted it to be the Vikings. He wanted them to have made landfall and be abroad in Essex. He wanted that, because he wanted to kill them and make their blood run thick and deep into the grey, wild sea which brought them howling down from their northern home.

## 14

Beornoth led his riders in a column, following Erkenwald's instructions until he came around a rolling hillock of farmland thick with golden crops. A dip opened up before him where two valleys joined, and between the rolling overlap of their sloping hillsides he saw the jutting rock face of Widow's Rock.

'Looks nothing like a widow,' said Wulfhere as they cantered through a field of wheat. 'Looks more like a hunchback's arse to me.'

'How do you know what a hunchback's arse looks like?' came a voice further down the line. Beornoth recognised it as Imma, the youngest member of his household troops. The other men laughed, and even Alfgar let out a giggle.

'Watch it, lad, or I'll give you a thick ear,' growled Wulfhere, but he had a smile on his broad, flat face.

The rock face was a dark mass of ledges and crags falling from a flat peak down into a dense forest at its base. It protruded at its centre, where the rock was a lighter grey than the dark brown of the surrounding crags, and Beornoth supposed it looked a little like a nose and chin. People liked to give their landmarks names, there was no other way to navigate or explain the land to one another, and places across Saxon lands had names like Widow's Rock, or Offa's Crag, or Rabbits' Hollow. In most cases, people had forgotten who exactly had lent their names to the countryside, and what the names meant, but they persisted as an effective way of marking boundaries, and describing directions.

Beornoth led his men onwards towards Widow's Rock, keeping to the high ground and searching for any sign of Viking raiders. They were far from any of the rivers which ran through Essex, and so if there were Vikings in the vicinity, they would be on horseback and looking to strike hard and fast in search of plunder and food. To help their campaign, the Vikings would also send scouts deep into the countryside, looking for towns and villages, and building up a picture of what the surrounding area looked like. Beornoth knew from his many years fighting the Danes that their reputation as aimless raiders was misplaced. They were clever, careful masters of war-planning and campaigns.

'Do you hear that?' said Alfgar, reining in his horse and leaning his head forward.

'No, nothing,' said Wulfhere.

'Sounds like thunder,' said Alfgar, and looked up at the pale blue sky. 'Doesn't look like a storm is brewing, though.'

'I hear it now, and it's riders not thunder.' Wulfhere pointed east past Widow's Rock.

'Let's go. Keep together and hold the line,' said Beornoth. He dug his heels into Ealdorbana's flanks, and the horse bunched his powerful hind legs and launched himself forward into a run. They rode hard down the valley, circled around the foot of the Rock where it dropped into a dense forest of ash and elm. The sound of the riders ahead of them grew louder, and became intertwined then with shouts of men, and cries of women and children. Those all too familiar sounds of war rang inside Beornoth's skull and he urged Ealdorbana on to a faster gallop, visions playing in his mind of the devastation the raiders would wreak on the peaceful Saxon towns in the valley.

Ealdorbana leapt over a low briar hedge, and Beornoth saw a small settlement ahead. It was nothing more than a collection of four low thatched timber houses, one of which billowed smoke from one end. He drew his sword and saw a woman race across the open pasture beyond the houses. Two warriors brandishing axes pursued her, their long, plaited hair betraying them as Vikings. Beornoth roared his war cry and urged Ealdorbana towards them. The horse covered the space in five heartbeats, and the Vikings saw him coming too late. A blonde-haired man turned to him with a look of surprise on his buck-toothed face, and Beornoth let Ealdorbana crash into him at full tilt, the huge muscles of the warhorse's chest hurling the warrior into the air. He fell heavily on the ground, and Ealdorbana trampled the Viking beneath his heavy hooves. Beornoth yanked on the reins and the horse skidded on the grass, keeping his footing and turning to snap his monstrous teeth at the fallen man's face.

Beornoth saw the rest of his men ride into the village. One of them swept up the fleeing woman to ride behind him, and the sounds of clashing weapons filled the air. The Viking ahead of him watched Ealdorbana savage the warrior on the ground. Blood splashed across the white flesh of the horse's legs and dripped from his maw. The warrior dropped his axe and turned to run headlong towards the village. Beornoth set off after him, feeling the power of Ealdorbana beneath him. The warrior turned to glance over his shoulder and Beornoth saw the whites of his eyes as he brought the edge of his sword down hard on the man's skull, splitting the bone with an audible crack.

By the time Beornoth reached the houses, the fighting was

over. Four Vikings lay dead in the worn earth pathway between the buildings, and one more sat propped up against the side of a barn, holding his stomach with both hands where a wound leaked his lifeblood onto the green grass. The villagers huddled at the opposite end of the settlement; the men holding their women and children, who sobbed and shook from the shock of the attack. Beornoth leapt from the saddle and stroked Ealdorbana's nose. The beast whinnied, and he left him to crop at the grass. Beornoth kept his sword drawn and stalked to the injured warrior, who looked up at him with a long face.

'What's your name?' said Beornoth in Norse.

'Bjarki,' said the man, and coughed up a glob of this blood.

'You're a Norseman, then.' Beornoth had lived amongst and fought Vikings his whole life. He knew the connotations of a man's name, and how it showed where he was from. He knew their Gods, their customs, and their ways.

'Yes, from Levanger. Do you know it, Lord?' Bjarki's face was pale, and his hands shook. Beornoth saw blue and purple coils beneath his fingers where he held his insides in. He called Beornoth Lord because he saw the sword, byrnie and helmet and knew Beornoth was a warrior of stature, a wealthy leader of men.

'No, I don't know it. Who is your Jarl?'

'Skarde Wartooth,' said Bjarki, and coughed again. So Skarde was back. Beornoth remembered the skilled and savage flaxen-haired leader from the Battle of River's Bend. 'I dropped my axe, Lord. Can you give me a blade to hold? I feel my time is almost up.'

'Who killed you?'

'The tall, thin man,' said Bjarki. Beornoth called for Osmod, and the warrior strode across the settlement with long, languid steps.

'Where did you get your horses, and where is your camp?' asked Beornoth.

Bjarki laughed and grimaced from the pain. He said, 'I can't tell you that, now, can I?'

'You will if you want a blade to hold. Tell me, and I'll give you an axe to hold so you can go to Odin's Hall.'

Bjarki eyed Osmod's axe.

'What's he looking at my axe for? Let me finish him, Lord,' said Osmod, not understanding the Norse tongue.

'You did well today, Osmod, you fought, and you killed. He believes that if he dies holding a weapon and in battle, he will go to the afterlife with his God, Odin, and live forever in the hall of warriors. If he dies without a blade, then he goes to his God's hell.' Beornoth reached over and took the axe. He held it towards Bjarki. 'Tell me where your camp is, and I'll give you the axe and finish you quickly.'

'A day's ride from here, north and east, in a cove by the sea. Our ships are there. Most of our crew were here only moments ago, but those with horses have returned to camp.'

'How many men and ships?'

The Viking coughed and licked his dry lips. 'Many ships, Lord, many men,' he said, and smiled.

'Is Olaf Tryggvason there?'

'No, he raids further west from here, around the coast of Wessex. Skarde is sworn to Olaf.'

'Will Olaf invade Essex or Wessex?'

Bjarki coughed and groaned, wincing at the pain in his guts. 'I don't know of such things, Lord. I came for silver and reputation, but my time is up. Please, I told you what you wanted to know. Give me a blade.'

Beornoth handed him the axe, and Bjarki smiled. Beornoth placed his sword at Bjarki's throat and sliced it open, sheeting blood down his jerkin and leather breastplate, and sending him to Valhalla.

'Gather up their weapons, leave any valuables here for these people,' said Beornoth. Osmod nodded and ripped his axe from the dead Viking's hand. Beornoth strode to where the villagers huddled, and he saw the long looks of desperation on their faces.

'You can't stay here. They will be back. Head east to where our warriors gather by the river. You can return to your homes once the Vikings have gone.'

'But this is our home, Lord,' said an ageing man with grizzled hair and a long beard. 'We can't leave. It's all we have.'

'You have your lives. If you stay here, you'll die. Make your own decision,' said Beornoth, and he turned and left them. He was hard on them, but they needed to hear the truth.

'Beornoth,' Wulfhere shouted from across the settlement. Beornoth heard a crashing of leaves and his men hurried to the sound. For a moment, Beornoth thought the Vikings had returned and his hand fell to the grip of his sword, but as he came closer, he saw Wulfhere helping a man from the saddle of a horse whose sides were splashed with white foamy lather, like the surface of a scummed pond. The horse's forelegs shook and its head bobbed as the beast struggled to breathe.

Wulfhere helped the man to stand. He wore a mail byrnie, torn and bloody at his shoulder and chest, and his bearded face was a mask of dried blood and fervour. Despite his injures and blown horse, the man pushed and bucked against Wulfhere as though he wanted to continue on his journey. Beornoth knew him for a Saxon by his short hair and clipped beard, and his byrnie marked him out as a Thegn or a Lord.

'Calm, calm,' said Wulfhere, whispering. He had one arm around the wounded man's shoulder and another on his belly to stop him toppling over.

'I must keep going, my...' He coughed and bubbles of blood showed at the corners of his mouth. Beornoth put a hand on his uninjured shoulder and bent at the knee to look into the man's nut-brown eyes. Those eyes locked on to Beornoth. They shook and trembled, and the man's bottom lip quivered.

'You are a Thegn?' asked Beornoth.

'Yes.' The man nodded. 'Thegn of Teotan's Hall.'

'Is that far from here?'

'East.' The Thegn's head snapped up, and he looked frantically around the village. 'The Vikings are here, hundreds of them. They've landed at the sea. Please God, my children.'

'What about your children?' said Beornoth. He felt a pain stab in his chest and the tug of his locket beneath his byrnie and jerkin. The Thegn sobbed, and he shook his head, looking at the ground. Beornoth shook his shoulder. 'What about your children?'

'Gone. Taken. They came, killed everyone. Took the women and children away. My Hall burned; my men killed.'

'How far from here?'

The warrior shook, and his sobs turned to anguished cries.

'How far?' Beornoth shouted this time, and the Thegn looked into his eyes again. Beornoth looked deep into the dark brown pools of despair. In those eyes he saw himself, as he was long ago. He saw sorrow and horror and loss. Beornoth realised his hand was on his locket.

'A day's ride, by the sea,' whispered the Thegn.

Beornoth turned away and fingered at his locket, pushing the smooth wood open to feel the soft hair inside. He remembered his little girls. He heard their laughter ringing in his head, and the joy of their smiles in his heart.

He clenched his teeth and closed the locket, securing it beneath his jerkin. He felt the anger well in the pit of his stomach, and let it kindle into a flame of fury. The Vikings had taken children, the children of a Thegn, and burned his Hall. They were taking women and children to sell as slaves at their great markets on the Jutland peninsula. It was like the horror of his own misfortune playing out again. He glanced back at the wounded Thegn and saw himself, as he had been, stumbling in the ashes of his ruined life and dead children.

Beornoth would not let the Vikings take this man's children, or any children. As long as he could wield his sword and draw breath, he would stop them.

## 15

The Thegn bled out, coughing and spluttering in the village ruins. Alfgar knelt with him, holding his hand clasped between his own, Alfgar's pale skin in contrast to the dark, blood-encrusted Thegn's hand. Alfgar prayed, and the Thegn stared deep into his eyes. He coughed and shuddered, and his eyes flickered wildly as he stared. His breath gave out in a wheeze, and his head slumped to one side. Alfgar sighed, made the sign of the cross above the dead man and kept hold of his hand, clenching it tighter now that the warrior was dead. The young Thegn would never see his children again, and that was a pain Beornoth was all too familiar with.

Beornoth envied him. The Thegn's pain had been brief. It had burned bright and fierce and became extinguished as his lifeblood leaked into the dirt beneath him. There could be nothing worse than the pain suffered by a parent at the loss of a child. It was a hollowing, overwhelming suffocation of sadness and despair. Beornoth had lived with that feeling for years, and he had often wished that he too had died that day, on the day his own children had burned to death. He had even contemplated taking his own life many times. But Beornoth had instead opted to drink himself to death, and that sadly had not worked either. It had dulled his pain for a few hours at a time, but he was still alive. All he had left of his beautiful daughters were memories, and the locket of hair held at his chest. Beornoth sighed and rubbed at his eyes. He tried to recall the faces of his daughters, but the pictures would not come. All he could conjure was the sound of their laughter, and their golden curls bouncing as he tickled them on his knee.

'Get him on his horse. We'll bring his corpse back to River's Bend for the Ealdorman,' said Beornoth.

'What about these people?' said Alfgar. He carefully laid the dead Thegn's hand to rest by his side and rose to stand with Beornoth. Beornoth noticed that Alfgar's spear rested against a nearby fence, and its tip was dark with blood. The young warrior had fought and traded blows with the professional warriors of the north, and he had survived. He had grown broader in the chest, and the hard work Alfgar had put in across the winter, working at his weapons and strengthening his body, had kept him alive.

'I already told them to head east to where our forces are. They say they want to stay here.'

'If they stay, they'll die, or the Vikings will take them as slaves.'

'They must decide their own fate.'

'We can let them march back to River's Bend with us.'

'We can't. We ride now and move fast.'

'But, if we leave them...'

Beornoth didn't allow him to finish. 'Besides, you and I aren't going back to River's Bend. Wulfhere will lead our men back, with the Thegn's body, to rejoin Erkenwald and Byrhtnoth.'

'So, where will we go?'

'To the coast, to find his children. You, Osmod and I.'

Alfgar frowned and looked from Beornoth to the dead Thegn. 'I want to see those prisoners freed as much as you, Lord, but what good can you and I do alone against hundreds of Viking warriors?'

'Are you questioning my command?'

'No, I have sworn an oath to serve you, Lord, and would do whatever you command. But surely we must discuss the sense of what you are suggesting?'

'A year ago you could barely meet my eye, and now you think to challenge me?'

'It isn't a challenge, Beornoth, I would never do that.' Alfgar's cheeks flushed red, and he took a step back.

Beornoth scratched at his beard. He unfastened the strap beneath his chin and removed the helmet and its liner to run his hand through his sweat-soaked hair. It wasn't Alfgar's place to question his decisions, but he knew Alfgar to be an honest lad, and if he was going to drag him deep into lands patrolled by Viking warriors, then perhaps he should explain why. The lad was no longer the callow, thin Ealdorman's bastard. He was a warrior now.

'The Vikings will have made a camp. It appears they have done so by the coast, maybe on or close to a beach. If they are riding out this far, then they have secured enough horses to range throughout the lands within a day's ride of the sea. They can't be ashore long since that first sighting of their ships, so they won't have been able to build a fortified camp. Now is the best chance we have of getting the prisoners out of there.'

Wulfhere approached, cleaning the blade of his axe with a strip of cloth torn from a fallen Viking's cloak. 'So you want to bring this poor soul back to River's Bend?' he said, but his easy manner evaporated as he sensed the tension between Beornoth and Alfgar.

'Yes, Byrhtnoth will need his horse and arms for the Heriot. There's land around here somewhere now without a Thegn. Tell him what happened here, and that the Vikings have made camp by the sea.'

'Will you not be there to tell him these things yourself, Lord?' asked Wulfhere, and his eyebrow raised slightly, eyes flicking from Beornoth to Alfgar.

'No. I'm going to their camp, and Alfgar is coming with me.'

'If you want to scout them, then maybe me and Alfgar could do it, or me and Osmod. Leave you to talk to the Ealdorman. Make plans and such.'

'We're not going to scout,' said Beornoth. 'We're going to free the prisoners.'

'But how...' began Wulfhere, before Beornoth cut in.

'This is not a discussion. Follow your orders.'

'Of course, Lord. It's just that...'

'I dragged your arse down from Offa's Crag when I could have split your skull and left you there to feed the crows. I freed you and allowed you to live. You have a sword strapped to your waist and a fine axe, you have a helmet and silver in your pouch. You are the captain of my household warriors. All I ask from you is the respect your oath demands.'

Wulfhere bowed his head. He said, 'You have my oath and my respect, my Lord. I did not intend to anger you.'

Beornoth cursed under his breath. The young Thegn's death, and the story of his lost children had made his temper flare, and he knew he was being harsh on his men. He reached beneath his byrnie and pulled the locket free. Beornoth ran his fingers over the smooth wood. He had been hard on Alfgar and Wulfhere, and he knew they were right to be surprised by his orders. It made no sense for him to leave Wulfhere to go back to the Ealdorman, or for Beornoth to infiltrate the Viking camp with only his sword, Osmod and Alfgar.

'I can't let those children be sold into slavery. I won't let the Vikings take them north and sell them at a stinking market like cattle to God knows who.'

'Why not ask Byrhtnoth to bring all of our forces here and attack the camp in force?' asked Wulfhere.

'By the time the army gets here, the Vikings will have erected a ditch and palisade. It would take twice our number to assault it. I've seen before how they fortify themselves once they get a foothold. Besides, if they think we're going to overwhelm them, they have their backs to the sea and can simply sail away to strike somewhere else.'

'If only the King would send his fleet to Essex, that would stop the bloody Vikings,' said Wulfhere.

'His ships are likely more than matched by this Olaf Tryggvason in the west, the larger Viking force is probably probing the south and south-west looking for gaps, searching for weaknesses so they can strike like a dog at a wounded animal,' said Alfgar, and made the sign of the cross. 'God save us from these pitiless heathens and their savage warmongering.'

'Alfgar, get the horses ready. Make sure we've enough food for two or three days, and some water,' said Beornoth, and Alfgar nodded and went to his work.

'He fought today, one of the bravest of our lot,' said Wulfhere, watching Alfgar as he busied himself.

'He fights, and that's enough.'

'He's clever as well, all that learning he did with the priests as a child. He's as quick as a whip.'

'That's why I'm taking him with me. If I fall, he'll know to ride to Byrhtnoth. He'll also know what to do to make sure the people at Branoc's Tree are safe.'

'You won't fall, Lord,' said Wulfhere, and rested his axe on his shoulder and looked deep into Beornoth's eyes. 'Just don't take too many risks. I know you lost your little girls, and now you've a chance to save others. It's a chance to save what was lost, in some way. But the East Saxons need your sword if we are going to beat the Vikings, so make sure you live.'

'We can't always fall back against these heathen bastards. We can't always pay them off. Too often when we fight them, they win or flee to strike again. It's time we struck at them, time they feared our blades for a change.'

'You are the Thegn, and you have my oath and the oath of all the others here. I'll follow you into the depths of hell, if you command it, and so would the others. When you came upon me, I was the lowest of the low. I should be dead now, swinging from a gibbet. No one would care if that were so, and there'd be no place for me in God's Heaven, not with the things I've done. You gave me another chance, a chance to be a good man, to make something of my life. So, let me come with you, Lord. Let us all bring the fight to the Vikings.'

'I know you would come if I asked it. But our orders are to stay with the army. If I bring you all with me, it denies Byrhtnoth a band of fine warriors. If he saw that as disobedience on my part, then he could take Branoc's Tree away, and my Heriot away. So, I need you to bring the men back and fight for Byrhtnoth and do as he commands. Tell him I go to scout the enemy, nothing more. I'll get those children out, Wulfhere, or I'll die trying.'

'Very well, Lord. I'll do as you say.'

'One more thing, Wulfhere. If I fall, I want you to go north, to the convent we stopped at last year on our journey south. My wife is there: Eawynn. Bring her to Branoc's Tree and make sure she's safe. She's never been the same since... what happened to our lands, to our children and to her. It took a heavy toll on her mind.

She left herself there in the charred ruins of our Hall. She saw our children burn.' Beornoth was whispering, his throat thick and his heart heavy. 'So, if I fall. Look after her Wulfhere.'

'I will, my Lord, you have my word,' said Wulfhere. The big man's jaw set firm, and Beornoth saw from the glassy look in his eyes and the certainty in that broad, flat face, Wulfhere would do as he asked.

Beornoth watched his men head west to rejoin Byrhtnoth's forces, and he shook his head at the stubbornness of the villagers, so determined to stay here in the remnants of their village, even though they knew the Vikings would be back, and the carnage would begin again. It was their home. He understood that. Without their home, what would they be, after all? He climbed into Ealdorbana's saddle and stroked the horse's soft ears. He tucked the locket containing the pieces of hair of his beautiful, dead children behind his armour, and set off to rescue prisoners. Knowing that if he failed, those people were doomed to slavery and a life of living hell.

# 16

The four men crested the hill with the sun at their backs. After a brief pause, they ambled down its slope, picking their way around divots and brambles at their ease. The men fanned out into a wide line, shouting jokes and insults at each other, accompanied by raucous laughter. They spoke in Norse, and Beornoth watched them from beneath the boughs of a sprawling beech tree. He knelt in a grove where a hedgerow edged the grass-covered slope down which the Vikings strolled.

'They are coming this way,' whispered Alfgar, crouched next to Beornoth.

'Ready yourself, and watch the archer,' said Beornoth, noting that one of the Norsemen had a bow slung across his back, and a quiver of arrows at his belt.

'They'll hear the horses, and see us at any moment.' The tone of Alfgar's whisper heightened.

'They will.'

'You mean to fight them? I should have guessed.'

'There's three of us and four of them,' said Osmod, his head twitching and hands wringing the shaft of his spear.

Beornoth meant to fight them. His first instinct had been to charge up the hill and attack them from Ealdorbana's back, but he was unsure what lay beyond the peak of the hill. Maybe the Viking camp sprawled just over the rise, and he would ride to certain death, leaving the captured children to a life of slavery and God only knew what other depredations. So he waited beneath the ancient tree, waited for the Vikings to get closer, close enough so that if one of the Norsemen raised a call to any larger force nearby, then he had time to ride away. Beornoth also wanted to be close enough to kill them quickly and not allow any to escape.

'We are going to fight them, and before they die, they are going to tell us where their camp is.'

Alfgar crossed himself and whispered a prayer. Beornoth wondered at the boy's piety. Beornoth had never been a godly man. He had gone to church and followed all the festivals and holy days in the same way that all Saxons did. He had seen too much death and suffering in his life to have any genuine faith in God. What God could allow all the world's cruelty to happen and allow worshippers of Pagan Gods to triumph? Why would God permit such suffering amongst his flock? The Viking Gods encouraged the Northmen to battle and rewarded brave warriors with a place in Odin's eternal warriors' hall, Valhalla. All the experiences of Beornoth's life had taught him that the peace and forgiveness the Christian God preached had no place in this world, it was a place of cruelty and darkness, and a man must meet violence with more violence if he wanted to live, and his people to be protected.

A small, broad-shouldered Viking suddenly stopped in the field. He called to his friends and pointed towards the tree where Beornoth, Alfgar and Osmod huddled, barely concealed beneath the leaves and branches. Their horses hobbled behind the trees.

'They've seen us,' whispered Osmod.

'Now we punish them for coming to our lands, for killing our people and taking our children,' said Beornoth, and he strode from cover, dragging his sword from the scabbard at his waist. The blade scraped on the wooden lip at the scabbard's throat, and the sound made Beornoth's heart beat faster. Once the shining blade was naked, violence must follow, and Beornoth wanted it. He wanted to spill the Northmen's blood and hear their cries of pain. He wanted them to feel the same terror the people in Essex felt during their raids, and he wanted them to feel the horror of impending death that his own children had felt beneath the eaves of his burning Hall.

'Should I take the one on the left, or the one on the right?' stuttered Alfgar, running to catch up to Beornoth, spear at the ready. The archer was on the right, and he posed most danger to their attack if he could get a shaft or two away, the range of his weapon giving him an advantage.

'Go left,' Beornoth said flatly. 'Try to kill one of the bastards, or at least keep one busy until I can kill him. Osmod, you go for their centre.'

'There's four of them, and three of us. You can see that, Lord?' said Osmod, but Beornoth just frowned at him.

The short Viking shouted to them in Norse. Beornoth couldn't catch the words. His head was roaring with the competing pressures of fear, hate and anticipation, which drowned out any other noise.

Beornoth passed his sword to his left hand and whipped his antler-handled seax from its sheath at the rear of his belt. He brought his right arm back and launched the broken-backed blade overhand, grunting at the force of the throw. The weight of the seax was all in the wide point at its tip, so it sang through the air with a soft whistle and slammed into the archer's chest with a thud. The man looked down at the metal protruding from his body and sucked in huge gulps of air, falling to his knees. Blood coughed from his mouth and into his beard.

'Three,' said Beornoth, and he charged at the small Norseman at the centre of their line, the man struggling to draw an axe from his belt and backing away from Osmod, who threatened him with his spear. The Viking held up a hand as if to calm Beornoth or keep him back, but Beornoth shifted the sword to his right hand and swept the blade up in a long arc. The tip of the sword cut through the short man's chin and sliced up through his teeth and cheek in a wash of blood and a gurgled cry of terror. Beornoth put his left hand to the hilt, and ripped the blade free, opening the short man's face like a terrible flower of gore. Osmod looked from the Viking's corpse and back to Beornoth, his mouth open and slack.

Beornoth glanced left and saw that Alfgar had attacked the leftmost Viking with his spear, and the final Viking was shaking his head and taking steps backward from Beornoth and his bloody fury. The Norseman turned and ran, but it was too late and Beornoth sliced his sword across the rear of the man's calves, dropping him to the earth. The Viking flipped over, his eyes wide with fear and his teeth clenched so hard Beornoth thought they would shatter.

'Where is your camp?' Beornoth barked at him in Norse, holding his blood-smeared sword at the Viking's face. The man shook his head and grasped at his wounded legs. Beornoth pushed the sword forward and sliced the man's cheek open. He screamed at the pain. 'You are a killer of women and children. Tell me where your camp is or I'll cut off your manhood and let you die without a blade.'

'The camp is only an hour away, beyond that hill. On the beach,' the Viking said in a whimper.

'How many men?'

'A long two hundred.'

'Is Skarde there?'

'Yes, yes, he is. Please...'

Beornoth didn't let him finish. He drew back his sword, took a step forward, and raised his boot high. He stamped down with all his weight on the Viking's throat and felt the crunch of his windpipe under his foot. The Viking croaked and coughed and made a screeching noise as he choked to death. Beornoth closed his eyes, another death to lay at the altar of his sorrow.

Alfgar had wounded the final Viking, but had taken a cut to his own shoulder from the enemy's axe. The Viking had his back to Beornoth, and he jerked like a fish when Beornoth drove the point of his sword into his back to burst out of his chest. The Viking toppled to the grass, and Beornoth yanked his sword free of the corpse and wiped the blood from the blade on the dead man's beard.

'My shoulder,' said Alfgar, putting his hand to the wound and bringing a bloody palm to his face.

'It doesn't look deep, you'll live,' said Beornoth. 'Their camp is an hour from here.'

'God help us, Lord, but you are a savage killer,' said Osmod, and Alfgar made the sign of the cross over the dead Vikings.

'These men burned houses, killed innocent people, and took others for slaves. If we hadn't killed them, they would do it again. They don't deserve your pity. Take anything of value and let's get a look at this camp.'

Beornoth and Alfgar left the horses tied in a small wood to the west of the field where they had killed the four Viking warriors. Beornoth stroked Ealdorbana's muzzle and whispered in his ear that he would be safe, and that he would return as soon as he could. He took the saddle from the horse's back and brushed him down with a handful of dry grass before leaving a pile of grass for the horse to eat. The big white warhorse dipped his head and Beornoth embraced him to his chest. He stalked away from Ealdorbana and hoped that no cursed Vikings found him whilst foraging or patrolling the area.

'Do you think they'll be here when we return?' asked Alfgar, peering back at the beasts.

'We can't bring them with us. They'd be heard across the hills, and any self-respecting scout would have us picked off before we got within fifty paces of him.'

'If we return,' said Alfgar. He held his spear in the crook of his arm and fumbled with a belt clasp he had taken from one of the dead Vikings. It was a thick belt with a loop for an axe, and a scabbard for a long-bladed knife. Alfgar had the knife and the axe secured, and he fussed at the copper belt buckle fashioned into a boar's snout and tusks.

'War can make you rich, lad,' said Beornoth. Many soldiers came back from campaigns laden with booty taken from fallen foes, and for household troops they depended on that as well as the gifts of silver and gold they expected from their Lord to make their living.

'Or dead,' said Alfgar.

As afternoon turned to dusk, and a red glow showed on the horizon, Beornoth, Osmod and Alfgar lay upon an outcrop of rock where below them the land fell away into a bowl-like valley, rising on each side to cliffs overlooking the sea, and ahead of them the fields changed into sandy dunes topped by long grass waving in the breeze from the rolling grey waves beyond.

'We must stay low now and be careful. Your young eyes can see further than mine, Alfgar. Look for their scouts and guards,' Beornoth said. Over the dunes, he could see the top of a palisade under construction on the beach. The Vikings had cut staves twice as long as a man from surrounding woodland, and chopped the ends into spikes. Those staves were now being secured into the sand in deep holes, and the tips of the rising timbers wavered and moved like the back of a giant hedgehog.

'They are digging themselves in,' said Osmod, squinting and using his hand to shield his eyes from the setting sun's brightness.

'They always do,' said Beornoth. 'They're no fools when it comes to war. There will be a deep ditch in front of that palisade, and men will patrol it day and night.'

'I can see five ships' masts,' said Alfgar.

'That means a long two hundred men, just as we thought. Making a camp here on the beach allows them to sail away easily if they feel under threat.'

'How come you know so much about the Vikings, Lord?' asked Osmod, making eye contact with Beornoth but then looking away as though he regretted the question.

'I've fought them all my life. The north is full of Danish and Norse families. They might have been here for three generations and worship God instead of Odin, but they are still Vikings. Then the wild raiders still howl down across the north-west coast, hitting and killing and sailing back to the islands north of Pictland or back to Denmark or Norway with their plunder. The Irish Vikings raid, as well. It never ends. Always fighting, always killing.'

'I thought the Danes were gone from the north, when Erik Bloodaxe was killed, in our father's time?' asked Osmod.

'They aren't gone. They are just part of us now. Part of the Kingdom of York and what was Northumbria. They named towns and villages there in the Viking tongue. They'll never be gone.' Beornoth sighed and ran his fingers beneath the neck of his byrnie, where it chafed at his beard as they lay on the cold rock. 'Look for their guards and scouts. When it's dark, we'll work our way down to the dunes and look for where they hold the prisoners.'

'Do you still mean to go in there, Lord?' asked Alfgar.

'I do. I won't leave those children there.'

'The Vikings take slaves all the time. Why are these people so important?' Osmod said, but then he saw the twist of Beornoth's mouth, and stared at the rock beneath him. 'I'm sorry, Lord. I didn't mean to question you.'

'They will take those women and children north to their great trading town at Kaupang, or just across the western sea to Dublin. There, they will sell our people as slaves. If they are lucky, they will go to work on farms in Jutland, or the far Norse isles, or somewhere in Frankia. If they are unlucky, they will be sold to the men of the south, where the sun burns hot and who will take them to their beds and the beds of their warriors. I won't abide that, not if there's a chance we can free them.'

Beornoth saw Alfgar and Osmod exchange a look, and he saw the fear on their faces. He was asking them to attack a camp of two hundred fierce warriors, and so Beornoth supposed he should give them more of an explanation. 'Years ago, whilst I was away fighting for your father, Vikings raided my land. They killed my people, hurt my wife, and burned my children in my Hall. My wife lives a life of pain and madness in a convent in the north, and I lost my ancestral Heriot in the years following the attack. As long as I draw breath, I will always fight and kill these raiders and sea wolves. I will always use my sword and my men to protect our people from the Northmen. So, we will go in there when its dark and free those prisoners, and if we die, then we go to your Heaven having died trying to protect good god-fearing people from the wild heathens. So, prepare yourselves and look for patterns in how they patrol the beach. Tonight we kill Vikings, and free the people who need our protection.'

## 17

The moon was a sliver of light in a malevolent sky of greys and blacks. Dark clouds shrouded the stars in the deep darkness, with only the shifting and swirling mass of the sky itself visible above a black beach. The only sound was the gentle, relentless sigh of the sea as small waves lapped at the East Saxon shore.

The Viking camp was lit by myriad small fires across the beach. Where they had completed sections of the palisade's construction, torches lit the timber posts, with more fires across the length of the ditch where the wall was still under construction. Beornoth could also see a fire lit on each of the cliffs rising to the right and left of the beach, where Viking scouts would stand guard throughout the night, watching for a Saxon attack.

'Do you think they have men out on patrol?' asked Osmod, tutting as he fussed at sand which had got into his beard. The three Saxons lay belly down on the sand dunes thirty paces from the Viking camp. They had slowly crept closer to the dunes once darkness fell and were now hidden beneath the long spiky grass which grew across the small hills and pathways of the sand dunes.

'No,' said Beornoth. 'It's too dark. If they did, they would carry fire and we would have seen them by now. They will feel safe enough behind that ditch.'

'I think that's where they have the prisoners,' said Alfgar, pointing to the south where they had spotted a fenced area butting on to the edge of the sea when it was at high tide. The tide was out now, and the fenced paddock was roughly ten paces from the water, and lay between two warships which tugged on their moorings as the tide tried to drag them out to sea.

'Could just be animal pens, pigs and sheep for eating,' said Osmod.

'It's where we'll start,' said Beornoth. He had seen no other likely places where the Vikings would keep their prisoners unless they were aboard the warships themselves. He trusted Alfgar's young eyes, and so he raised himself to a crouch and dusted the sand from his byrnie and scabbard. Alfgar and Osmod did the same, and Beornoth led them in a slow, crouched shuffle through the pathways within the high dunes. He headed south, planning to go slowly and make a wide sweep across the beach, and come to the camp from beneath the cliff on that side.

'So what do we do if they see us, if they raise a shout?' whispered Osmod.

'If we are still on the beach, then we run,' said Beornoth. 'If we are in the camp, then we fight our way out.'

Beornoth took his time, taking twenty paces and then pausing to listen for any sound of the enemy, and to scan around them for the glare of torchlight. Once he was satisfied that they would not stumble into some Vikings in the darkness, or that the night guards had not spotted them, he moved on. Time became fluid, and the three men moved through the dunes in silence.

Beornoth came to where the dunes gave way to rising cliffs and made his way on to the beach itself. It was a mix of soft sand

and long strips of small pebbles and shale. The shale would crunch underfoot, so Beornoth made his way slowly and carefully, keeping to the sandy areas and treading as carefully as possible. As he crept along, his head shrunk into his shoulders from the fear of the Viking guards atop the southern cliffs. They were at his back now, and his heart beat fast, waiting for the shouts to erupt from above and behind. If that alarm went up, it could mean nothing but death for Beornoth, Alfgar and Osmod. The Norsemen would storm from their beds and charge across the beach, hunting them down mercilessly. If the Vikings caught them, Beornoth would fight until they overwhelmed him, until the cold steel of Viking blades plunged into his flesh to tear his life way. The only alternative was torture. The Vikings were famed for their elaborate tortures: the blood eagle and other horrifically painful ways to die. Ivar the Boneless had once cut the blood eagle into King Aelle of Northumbria's back. He had opened the flesh of the king's back, chiselled away his ribs, and opened up his ribcage so that the splayed bones and flesh resembled an eagle's spread wings. That grisly work was all performed whilst the unfortunate Saxon king was still alive, until Ivar strung him up and his own splayed ribs burst his heart. Beornoth pushed those thoughts from his head. If it came to that, he was sure he would die fighting. They would not take him alive.

'Stop,' whispered Alfgar, putting his arm across Beornoth's chest. They halted, and Alfgar pointed ahead. Beornoth followed the direction of Alfgar's finger and saw that the depth of the night's shadows ahead had changed. It had grown darker, which surely meant they were approaching the ditch the Vikings had dug deep into the sand around their camp. Any attackers would need to fight their way up that slope, where Viking blades would strike down from above as they tried to make the climb up the sandbank, with its treacherous footing. The three Saxons stopped and waited because in the time they had spent watching the camp, Beornoth knew a guard would stroll past at any moment, torch in hand, to check the camp's perimeter. Beornoth stared ahead at the deep darkness of the ditch. The Vikings had dug it to the depth of a man's height, and it had to be deep, because seawater would seep from the wet, heavy sand and fill the ditch's belly. It would also be less effective for the Vikings than a ditch dug into the earth, because the sides would crumble and the thing would collapse before long, but that only showed Beornoth that the Vikings did not plan on staying here long, otherwise they would have made their camp further inland and beyond the precariously temporary dunes.

'Careful, when we cross. Do not splash into the water of the ditch, the sound will carry to the guards. We have to jump across and climb up the sides,' said Beornoth. 'Secure your weapons. Make sure there is nothing loose about you that will rattle or shake as we grow closer.'

'There,' hissed Osmod, and Beornoth saw a torch floating in the darkness, like a spirit emerging from the sand to weave its magic. The light gave way to show a guard trudging across the sand, holding a wooden stave torch in one hand and swigging from an ale skin held in the other. Beornoth licked his lips and his stomach growled at the thought of the ale in that skin. He missed the peace drinking brought him, and the welcome oblivion of drinking until he passed out. But he didn't miss waking up in pools of his own vomit and piss, and having to scrounge a miserable living from men who had once called him Lord.

The guard reached the edge of the ditch where it ran into the sea. He looked at the black darkness of the water and turned to make the return journey of his watch. Beornoth pulled his locket from beneath his byrnie and brought the smooth timber to his lips. He kissed it; the wood warm from where it had been resting against his chest. Beornoth imagined it was his daughters in that Viking camp waiting to be sold to the highest bidder. That thought caused his teeth to clench, and rage to kindle in his chest. He slid the seax slowly from its sheath at his back. He said, 'Follow me,' to Alfgar and Osmod and then set off at a dash towards the ditch.

Beornoth ran, taking long strides, and leapt over the wide gap in the sand and landed on the other side with a grunt. He dug his free hand into the sand for grip, and for a moment thought he would slip down into the seawater in the ditch's belly, but he kept his feet and clambered his way up the sandbank. He paused in a crouch, heart pounding in his chest and the rush of blood thumping in his ears. The guard paused and then turned to peer in Beornoth's direction. He lifted his torch and leant forward, peering into the darkness to see where the noise came from. Beornoth didn't hesitate. He rose from his crouch and charged towards the guard. The guard saw Beornoth approach through the gloom, rushing like a ghost into the torchlight. Before the man had time to react, Beornoth launched himself at the guard, who was smaller than he, which was the case for most men, and Beornoth whipped his right hand upwards. The seax sank into the soft flesh underneath the guard's chin and drove upwards into his mouth and the hard bone beyond. The guard wriggled on the end of the seax and made a choking sound before collapsing into a heap on the sand. Beornoth dragged his seax free in a gout of warm blood and rolled the dead guard into the ditch.

'I don't think anyone heard,' said Alfgar, picking up the torch from the sand and leaning into the camp, bending his ear to search for the sound of onrushing Vikings coming for their blood, but it did not come. Beornoth strode towards the enclosure, which he hoped was where the prisoners were being held.

Alfgar and Osmod followed, and they reached the fencing without challenge, and without coming across any more guards. Alfgar raised the wooden torch, and its warm light forced the darkness from the enclosure. There in the far corner, prisoners huddled together, lying on the sand and trying to sleep. Beornoth leapt over the fencing, which was no higher than his waist, and approached the prisoners. They stirred and looked up at him, fear showing in their wide eyes and pale faces. He saw children amongst them and reached out his hand towards them.

'I am a Thegn. I have come to set you free,' he said. The closest prisoner to him was a young woman with long black hair. She raised her hand to her mouth and stifled a sob. She reached out and took his hand, and Beornoth helped her rise to her feet. The others stayed where they were, another woman shaking her head and looking towards the Viking tents.

'Come, now, we must hurry,' said Osmod, entering the enclosure and urging the others along. 'Why are you waiting?'

'They are afraid that the Vikings will come,' said Beornoth. He knelt and looked at the children. 'I won't hurt you. Come with us, and we will bring you to your families.'

A small girl stood and ran to Beornoth. She wrapped her arms around his leg, and he placed a hand on her head. He felt the gorge rise in his throat and a catch in his chest. Such a small, innocent child destined for a life of suffering and pain, unless Beornoth could set her free.

They coaxed the prisoners out of the enclosure and hurried towards the ditch, planning to escape in the same direction from which they had entered the camp. Alfgar leapt across the ditch, and Osmod stood in its centre to help the prisoners cross one at a time into Alfgar's arms. There were four women, and three made it across. The fourth helped the children, of which there were five, across to Osmod and Alfgar. Beornoth sheathed his seax,

believing they had done it and that the prisoners were safe, when
a shout went up from the camp behind him, and he closed his
eyes and let out a heavy sigh, the brief dream of a fast escape
across the night-darkened beach torn asunder.

More voices sounded, and Beornoth turned to see movement
in the darkness where the Viking tents stood in neat rows.

'Take them and go, don't stop. Get the horses and get back to
River's Bend,' he said.

'Where are you going?' said Osmod, staring up at him from
the ditch.

'To keep them busy. Now, go.' Beornoth took up the flaming
torch from where Alfgar had laid it to rest on the sand and ran
past the enclosure. He ran to where the ships bobbed in the rising
tide. Beornoth drew his sword and hacked at the nearest rope. It
was thick and heavy; a twisted coil of seal hide attached to an
enormous stone sunk deep into the wet sand to moor the
warship. Three blows and the rope snapped. Beornoth threw his
torch onto the deck of that ship and nodded as he heard the
warship crunching on the shale beach, as the strength of the tide
dragged it into the sea's embrace. He ran to the second ship, and
this time it took five swings of his sword to cut the mooring rope.

Beornoth turned then and let out his war cry. He stood on the
wet sand, set his feet and roared into the darkness. He shouted
his challenge and begged the Vikings to come and be killed.
There was nothing more precious to a Northman than his ships,
and Beornoth knew that all thoughts of pursuing the prisoners
would evaporate when the Vikings saw their ships slipping out to
sea, and he hoped that would be enough to get the prisoners to
safety. He shouted and roared and eventually bearded faces
appeared out of the gloom, some held torches and some held
axes. Beornoth smiled at them.

'I am Beornoth. I have killed your guard, and I killed your

men in the fields beyond. I have cut loose your ships, and I am here to send you to Niflheim.' That was the Vikings' hell, where warriors who died badly and without honour would wander as wraiths for eternity. He spoke in Norse, his voice as loud and deep as a war drum over the undulating sigh of the tide. A Viking bellowed at him from the gloom and came charging. He had a long, plaited beard and held his axe high, ready to take a monstrous swing at Beornoth's chest. It was a wild swing, one that an untrained farmer of the fyrd might make, not a skilled, war-hardened axeman from the harsh north. It was all anger and spite, and Beornoth laughed. He couldn't help it. The laugh came from deep in his belly and shook his body. Just like his daughters would tremble and wriggle when he would tickle them. Beornoth laughed because he knew the Viking would die. He had lost control in the fog of anger and now Beornoth would kill another Viking to bleed on the pyre of his vengeance.

Beornoth simply took a long step forward and knelt on his leading leg. He lunged upwards and forwards with his sword, and braced the back of the pommel with his left hand. The Viking ran on to the blade, its point bursting through his unarmoured torso. Blood ran down the blade's fuller and the Viking coughed dark, oozing crimson into his beard. He crumpled to the sand and Beornoth stood and let the dying man's weight drag his body off the blade.

'I am Beornoth!' he roared, and charged at the mass of Vikings before him. They had dashed from their beds, and so were unarmoured. Some held weapons, and some were rubbing the sleep from their eyes, barely able to comprehend what unfolded within the safety of their beachside camp. Beornoth flicked the tip of his sword at a snarling face and that man yelped as the sword point sliced through the gristle of his nose. The surrounding warriors jerked away as blood sprayed from the

wound. That lunge turned into a two-handed cut down another
warrior's chest, and suddenly the Vikings leapt back from his
fury. They were shouting and cursing and made a baying half
circle around him, backing away from his vicious, blood-soaked
sword. Beornoth breathed deep, his chest heaving beneath his
byrnie. He held his sword two-handed and stood ready with bent
knees, standing on the balls of his feet. Beornoth was one man,
facing a horde of Viking warriors. He saw a large group peel off,
racing towards the ebbing tide. Those men were shouting and
waving frantically, urging others into the waves to rescue their
precious warships, which were slipping inexorably into the pull
of the sea. Beornoth knew he must die here, alone in the darkness. There were too many enemies for him to fight. Warriors
circled him now: big men, the lovers of battle. The grim-faced
warriors of the front rank come to kill the impudent Saxon who
had raided their camp. Beornoth smiled again. At the moment
when his death seemed so close; he hoped it would re-unite him
with Ashwig and Cwen. He longed to see their joyous, little,
round faces once more. In that fleeting moment the thought
occurred to him that if he did not believe in God, how would he
ever see them again?

   Two warriors came for him, both armed with spears. The leaf-
shaped blades thrust at him and Beornoth swayed away from
one, and batted the second aside with his sword. He brought his
blade down hard with the power of his two-handed grip, onto the
wrist of that spearman, and sawed the edge back to slice skin and
break bone. The spearman bent over and grunted with pain, and
Beornoth swung his sword overhand and brought it down hard
on to the top of that Viking's skull. He quickly brought the sword
up to parry a lunge from the second spearman's weapon and
danced away from an axe swing aimed at his chest. Beornoth was
panting. The brave men had come to the front to fight, and the

rest of the Viking warriors shrank back. In the darkness, all was chaos and shouting as the Norsemen tried to stop their ships from drifting out to sea, the weight of the warships' hulls too much for the warriors who hauled on the severed mooring ropes.

Beornoth beckoned them on, knowing that each moment bought Alfgar, Osmod and the prisoners more time to escape. The spearman came on again, and Beornoth blocked a lunge and changed his grip on the sword to bring the blade back with a deft turn of his wrist to slice open the throat of his attacker. The Viking dropped his spear and fell, clutching at his neck where his lifeblood pulsed out onto the sands. Two axemen came on, the first in a wild flurry of blows and a bold war cry, and Beornoth edged backwards as he parried the furious swings, barely able to fend off the strength and speed of the warrior's attacks. The second axeman came at Beornoth and grabbed for his arm, trying to hold him so the other warrior could strike, and Beornoth thought his time had come as he felt himself yanked off balance. Suddenly, a scream erupted from over Beornoth's shoulder, and the warrior who held his arm dropped as a spear point slammed into his eye, killing him instantly. A dark shape charged past Beornoth, cannoning into the first axeman, sending him crashing to the sand there as the roaring spearman stabbed him in the guts and retreated to stand with Beornoth.

'Couldn't leave you to die alone, Lord. Not when there're Vikings to kill.' It was Osmod, and Beornoth grinned at his oath-man, pride welling within him. It was a stupid thing to charge back across the beach to face certain death, but it was brave. Osmod had come far since the days when Beornoth had first met him, when the Branoc's Tree man had been afraid to strike and embrace the violence which must come with being part of the household of a Saxon Thegn. The mass of Vikings heaved and more men came forward. Beornoth and Osmod struck at them, slashing and cutting until Beornoth's muscles ached and his arms screamed at him to drop his sword. He ducked under a spear thrust, and danced away from the swing of an axe, darting forward, holding his sword firm in two hands and cutting left and right. Warriors fell away, and others came to take their place. Blood rushed to Beornoth's head and his ears rang with the thrill and ecstasy of battle.

Beornoth felt a blow between his shoulder blades and staggered forwards. Osmod sprang at the attacker behind and Beornoth hoped his byrnie had stopped the blow piercing his flesh.

'They are all around us,' said Osmod, backing into Beornoth. The two men fought as one, back to back and whirling in a circle, striking with sword and axe. Vikings fell back from them, a mass of bearded, growling warriors hungry for their blood but wary of the bite of their steel. The Viking throng parted, and their flaxen-haired leader, Skarde, marched into the space between his warriors and Beornoth. He was dripping wet and wiped water from his eyes. Seawater, Beornoth presumed. From where Skarde had joined the attempt to stop his precious ships from drifting into the waves. He barked an order and four men barged through the darkness and into the torchlight. These men brought shields and Dane axes, long-handled and vicious. Beornoth straightened and let his sword hang by his side. Skarde was as clever as he was savage. The Viking chief saw that the easiest way to stop Beornoth was to trap him between shields, and then it would be a simple matter to push cold steel into his body whilst he could not swing his sword. Beornoth grabbed for his locket, his hand shaking from the fight's exertion and slick with dead men's blood. He kissed the soft wood for what he thought would be last time and readied himself for death.

The shield men came on and Beornoth charged them. One

man raised his brightly painted shield and shoved Beornoth backwards, and another barged him from the side. He tried to cut at their legs, but the four men closed him in tight as though he were stuck in an ale barrel. He heard a cry, and he peered over his shoulder to see Osmod tumble to the sand with a spear in his guts and an axe in his back. Beornoth kicked, jerked and snapped his teeth at the enemy, but a dull thud exploded at the back of his skull and pain sent his vision flashing like lightning. Beornoth felt himself slipping, falling from consciousness, and his heart leapt, hoping he was on the way to see his children once more.

## 18

The pain in his head pulsed like a hammer beating on an anvil, and his body ached with burning fatigue. Beornoth groaned and raised a hand to hold his skull. It felt as though a horse had kicked him and he could feel dried blood matted into his hair. He spat sand from his mouth and licked a dry tongue over cracked lips. Beornoth's heart sank as the realisation and disappointment washed over him that he was alive. He was still within his body and had not ascended to the afterlife. He let his face rest on the damp sand, eyes shut tight, trying to cope with the brain-thudding headache. Beornoth heard coughing and spluttering next to him, and allowed one eye to open a slit to look around. Osmod was sitting there, leaning against a fence post. His face was as white as fresh milk, and blood spattered his beard.

Beornoth pushed himself up to sit next to his oathman. He felt a stabbing pain in his ribs and up across his shoulder. He remembered feeling a blade strike his byrnie at his back, but the mail had held, because the injury was bruising rather than a stab wound. Swelling on his face had reduced one of Beornoth's eyes to a slit, and daylight punched into his brain like a knife blade. He saw he was in the same fenced pen from which he had freed the slaves the night before, and only he and Osmod now occupied it, which he hoped meant that Alfgar had successfully led the prisoners to freedom. That at least gave Beornoth cause to smile a little. It meant the dead Thegn's children were free. They had avoided the fate of the Viking slave markets and Alfgar would be at River's Bend by now, or so Beornoth hoped.

Osmod's eyes flickered to Beornoth, and he nodded slightly to see his Lord awake and sitting next to him. Beornoth placed a hand on Osmod's arm.

'You fought like a champion yesterday,' Beornoth said. 'Bloody foolish to come charging back like that. But it was brave, and you honoured your oath.'

'I'm dying, Lord,' whispered Osmod. Beornoth had to lean close to hear his words. They were so faint that the morning sea breeze almost whipped them away. He looked at Osmod's stomach, but his folded arms covered the wound. Beornoth saw a dark pool of blood-soaked sand around Osmod's legs. Behind Osmod, blood stained the post he rested upon, leaking from the wound at his back. He was dying, and Beornoth could see it in the ashen greyness of his long face.

'Alfgar must have escaped with the prisoners. Your bravery saved the lives of those who needed your protection,' said Beornoth.

Osmod coughed again, and crimson bubbles appeared at his mouth. 'Promise me something, Lord,' he whispered. Beornoth drew closer to hear his words. 'Swear on my bones that you will kill this bastard Skarde, and throw his Viking wolves back into the sea.'

Beornoth reached over and grasped Osmod's hand, the skin cold and clammy. He looked his man in the eye, made sure Osmod saw the honest determination there.

'I swear it. If I get out of this mess, I will make sure that Skarde dies on my blade and that I will cast his men from these shores drenched in their own blood. I swear it, Osmod,' he said, and Osmod smiled for a moment, before his body shuddered and his head lolled onto his shoulder. A stream of thin blood trailed from his mouth to drip onto the sand. Beornoth ground his teeth, another good Saxon soul lost to Viking steel. He meant what he had said to Osmod. The East Saxon had showed bravery charging into the Viking camp, knowing he must surely die in the face of overwhelming numbers, and Osmod's actions had saved Beornoth's life, for without that charge he would surely have succumbed to the Vikings' blades. Beornoth cast his eyes up at the morning sky. It was grey and overcast and a gull circled above him, its broad white wings floating on the sea wind. He hoped that whatever God there was in Heaven would accept Osmod into his gates. His sacrifice had saved the lives of women and children, and that surely was worthy of a place in Heaven.

'Your friend is dead,' said a voice speaking in Norse. Beornoth turned and saw Skarde staring back at him. He had long golden hair, plaited on each side of a long, hard face. Skarde had piercing blue eyes, and a wide slash of a mouth, and his cheeks, jaw and nose were all angular and harsh like the rocky coast of his homeland. 'You can understand my words?' he asked.

'I can,' said Beornoth.

'Where did you learn to speak as we do?'

'I am from the north, close to the Kingdom of York. West Northumbria.'

'I had family in York, once,' said Skarde wistfully, looking out to the sea. 'We got our ships back. It took all night.'

Beornoth stood and brushed the sand from his hair and beard. He was still wearing his byrnie, and he thought it strange that they had not stripped him of so valuable a piece of war gear.

His knife and sword were gone, and he suddenly realised he had lost most of the Heriot granted to him by Byrhtnoth. He had left Ealdorbana tied in a field beyond the dunes, and his sword was now in the hands of the Vikings. All he had left of what the Ealdorman had granted to him was his byrnie. He didn't care that this bloodthirsty Norseman had once had family in York. Beornoth wanted to shout at him, tell him of his own loss at the hands of Viking warmongers. There was little point in that, he knew. If Skarde had once had family in York, then more than likely they had seen death or loss at the hands of Saxons. To talk of loss and family with a man who worshipped Odin and Thor, Gods who thirsted and rewarded warriors who sought war and battle, was futile.

'Where is my sword?' he said.

'We are looking after it for you, you killed or injured many of my men with that blade last night.'

'And you killed my man here, and countless others. You burn villages, kill innocent people who cannot defend themselves and take women and children as slaves.'

'I am Viking,' said Skarde, and shrugged. 'You must be hungry. Come and walk with me.'

Beornoth thought about telling Skarde to throw himself in the sea, but his stomach growled, and if he was alive, then he might as well eat again before they killed him. Beornoth was all too aware that his capture would likely end in torture, and he steeled himself to that thought, knowing that enduring the pain without screaming could well be his last battle against the Vikings. He walked to where Skarde stood. He put one hand on the low fence and vaulted over it, his headache pounding and his wounds stinging each time he moved. Two heavily armed warriors stood behind Skarde, and they bristled as Beornoth came to stand facing their leader. Beornoth just smirked at them.

Skarde bent and picked up a skin from the sand and handed it to Beornoth. He took the stopper out and drank deeply. It was cool, fresh water, and it felt like the finest of royal wines slipping down his throat to quench his thirst. The liquid dripped down into his beard, and Beornoth handed the skin back to Skarde.

'Fighting is thirsty work, no?' said Skarde, and laughed a deep belly laugh. Skarde set off at a brisk walk through the camp, and Beornoth followed him, weaving between the organised lines of sailcloth tents thrown up on the beach behind the safety of the ditch and palisade still under construction. Warriors sat beside small cook fires, eating their breakfast. As they passed, men rose and bowed their heads to Skarde. Some said 'Lord' and clapped their fists on their chests. Most scowled at Beornoth, some even spat in his direction. Beornoth could smell roasting fish and baking bread. His stomach turned over and growled at him. Bearded faces, some tattooed and scarred, stared up at him. Piles of spears, leaning upright together, stood neatly like bushels of wheat, and men combed their hair and beards with combs made of horn and bone. Beornoth could hear warriors working at the palisade, the chopping of wood and shouting of orders rippling across the beach above the caw of gulls, and gentle rumble of the sea. These were professional warriors, organised and serious. They were not pirates here in the land of the East Saxons for easy plunder and a spring jaunt along the Saxon coastline. They were soldiers, and a shiver went down Beornoth's spine as the realisation dawned on him that Skarde's crews were indeed part of a larger force. The Norse warlord, Olaf Tryggvason, was probing the south and east Saxon coastline, looking for weaknesses and assessing their fighting capacity. Which surely meant that either this summer, or next summer, Olaf would bring the full force of his Viking army down upon King Æthelred and the people of Saxon Britain. That would bring suffering and death on a scale not seen by the Saxons in a hundred years.

Skarde reached a fire close to the shoreline, at the centre of his line of ships, all safely moored and secure once more. The fire crackled and sparked, and Beornoth rubbed his hands and held them towards the warmth, his shoulders relaxing as the heat ran through his face and chest. Five men gathered around the fire, drinking ale from skins, and eating a meal of fish and bread. The rich smell of baking bread filled Beornoth's nostrils and, combined with the pungent fish, he thought he had never been so hungry. The five men turned to look at Skarde and rose to their feet. Four were men of an age with Beornoth, all having seen at least thirty-five summers, big-shouldered and grizzled. The fifth man was small and whip-thin, with dark eyes in a hollow face. He wore a cloak hung with feathers that jangled with small bones as he moved. He made a strange sign with his hand and covered one eye as he stared hard at Beornoth.

'Don't mind Rolfr. He is a holy man, as you Saxons would say. He does that to ward off your evil spirits,' said Skarde with a smile. Beornoth just stared at the little weasel of a man. Though small, he emanated a strange power. Beornoth shuffled his feet and scratched again at the sand in his beard. One of the big men handed Skarde a wooden plate of steaming fish alongside a hunk of fresh bread. Skarde handed it to Beornoth and bowed his head.

'You do me great honour, by serving me from your own hand,' said Beornoth. He had seen the respect with which the warriors in the camp had saluted and acknowledged Skarde, and clearly this group of men here by the fire were the leaders of his crews. It told Beornoth that Skarde was not only a fine warrior, which he knew from trading blows with the Viking himself at River's Bend, but also that he was a man of great importance.

'I honour you as a fighting man. I respect that, your courage.

You stood alone against many, so your man could run away with the slaves. I remember you, from the fight last year.' Skarde smiled and accepted another plate for himself and thanked his man.

Beornoth took a bite of fish, the white flakes soft and succulent in his mouth. His injured ribs ached as he swallowed, but the taste of the fish more than compensated for the pain.

'And I remember you. Did he get them away?' asked Beornoth, not looking up from his plate.

'We let him and the slaves go. You earned their lives.'

'Thank you for that,' said Beornoth. Skarde inclined his head.

'You are an Ealdorman?' said one of the big men, a black-haired warrior with a gruff, hoarse-sounding voice.

'A Thegn,' said Beornoth. 'You are a Jarl, Skarde?'

'I am a Jarl, yes. From the north. These are my men, Ulfketil, Brand, Einar Ravenhair, and Sigurd Bearskin.' Skarde pointed to each of his leaders as he said their names, and the men nodded to Beornoth.

'I am Beornoth,' he said, and bit off a chunk of bread, washing it down with a mouthful of watered ale. The ale tasted good, the old familiar liquid warm in his belly. He didn't want to drink it, having not taken a drop since leaving the north, but he didn't want to refuse the drink and insult his hosts either. 'You are treating me well. I expected to die last night.'

'We honour bravery, and daring,' said Einar Ravenhair.

'The Gods smiled upon you last night, but your people are doomed. Your God is weak and feeble, Odin will cast him asunder and use his skull as a drinking cup,' hissed the little man.

'Is that why you are here?' said Beornoth.

'We are here to avenge the death of Bloodaxe and our kin. My Lord Olaf will take these lands, and we will bring our people here to live on your fine soil and in your forests teeming with game.

Your King is a usurper, he killed his brother and stole the kingdom and is not loved by his people,' said the man introduced to Beornoth as Sigurd Bearskin. He was a hulking brute of a man, with white hair and eyebrows above bright blue eyes, his face covered in dark blue tattooed whorls and beasts.

Olaf Tryggvason was planning an invasion. That much was clear in the certainty of how Sigurd spoke of his master's intentions. Beornoth finished his food, feeling the eyes of the others on him, waiting for him to retort. He took his time using his bread to mop up the juices from the fish. Beornoth laid the plate on the sand and drained the skin of watered ale. He looked up at the sky, the early morning grey giving way to white clouds shot through with shafts of bright sunlight.

'Thank you for the food,' he said, bowing his head to the five men, before resting his eyes upon Skarde and his harshly angled face. 'I swore to my man Osmod, who lies dead in your slave pen. I swore I would kill you, Jarl Skarde, and that I would throw your murderous, raping, sons-of-whores, bloodthirsty warriors back into the sea to limp back to your stinking home of rocks and seal shit.'

The four warriors all stepped towards Beornoth, hands falling to their war axes hanging from loops at their belts. Skarde raised a hand to calm them.

'You had best kill me now, and should have let me die last night. I'll fight any of you dogs now, right here. Just give me a blade,' said Beornoth, and he grinned at them. A humourless, grim smile. He wanted them to know that he did not fear them. Beornoth hoped that if he challenged them to fight, he could avoid the fate of death by torture. He wanted them to see what a Saxon Thegn was made of, and to drive fear into their hearts with his belligerence and certainty in his own ability.

'A fine boast, friend Beornoth,' said Skarde, clapping

Beornoth on the shoulder. 'But you won't be fighting me, or any of these men, today. We have fought before, you and I. Last summer we fought, and I remember the clash as though it were yesterday. I hope Odin saw us fight that day, and I hope one day we will fight again. But today you will fight for your life. We have just the man for you to pit your strength against.'

The little Odin priest, Rolfr, cackled and hopped from one leg to another, his bones and trinkets jangling. The four Vikings smiled and nodded to each other, and Beornoth frowned. If he was going to fight for his life, he knew the man they put before him would be a warrior to fear.

## 19

The sea's relentless rhythmic power crept up the shale to envelop the moored warships which bobbed peacefully on the ebb and flow of the incoming tide. Beornoth felt a chill breeze from the sea blow across his face and tasted salt on his lips. He sat in the slave pen and rested his aching body. The morning passed, and Beornoth watched the Vikings busily completing the construction of their camp. A man brought him a plate of roasted pork when the sun reached its highest point in the sky.

He hoped the dead Thegn from the raided village was looking down from the afterlife, and that his soul could find peace now that his children were safe. Beornoth also found some comfort that the other children he had rescued would now be back with their bereft families. Beornoth supposed it didn't matter who those women and children were in the slave pen. What mattered was that the vulnerable, and those in need of his protection, were safe. He thought again of his own lost family, and of his wife living a lonely existence inside of her head, locked away for her own protection in the convent. Life was hard, and Beornoth would have been content to have died in the fight on the beach.

He was almost bereft that he had woken at all. At least, he supposed, he would get a chance to kill another Viking when he fought their champion. A fight to the death was a better way to die than the grim prospect of torture. Beornoth assumed he would fight once the Vikings had taken their evening meal, and that Skarde would put on a show for his men. He watched men come and go, wondering if any of them would be the man he would face. Vikings loved duels and fighting of any kind. Beornoth had seen it many times in the lands around York. They fought Holmgang duels to settle disputes or over points of honour. Such things were highly ritualised, with a square of a certain size laid out with hazel rods, seconds appointed and strict rules of how the duel was to be fought, and what would happen to the winner and loser, with compensation to be paid to families and such.

Beornoth hoped Byrhtnoth was marching his forces towards the beach, to fight Skarde before he could attack elsewhere and pour his spear-and-axe Vikings deep into the Saxon countryside, stabbing into Essex and Wessex like a knife into soft flesh. The Viking leader had treated Beornoth with respect. He was well fed and Skarde had sent a slave woman to wash and clean Beornoth's wounds, which was a strange kindness at odds with his viciously warlike nature. Skarde was a formidable man, to become Jarl and lead these ferocious worshippers of battle meant that he was more than the average warrior: he was clever, violent and skilled in the arts of war. The spectacle of Beornoth's fight to the death against their champion would be a welcome distraction for the Viking warriors in the camp, whilst they waited for the next stage in their campaign. These men had braved wild and dangerous seas to sail to Britain, and they came in search of wealth and reputation. They would be restless, wanting to fight and fill their purses with silver, and a fight to the death would occupy their minds for a few days, giving Skarde time to scout the land and make his plans.

It would be a great service to all Saxons and Christians when Beornoth fulfilled his oath and tore the life from the flaxen-haired Jarl. Beornoth had to admit, however, that he could not dislike Skarde. There was no arrogance in the man, and it was clear his men respected him. He was quick to smile, and Beornoth had seen at River's Bend that Skarde fought in the front lines, risking all alongside his men, not waiting behind the lines to issue orders and let his men put their lives on the line for his glory and reputation. He was, therefore, the exact opposite of Osric. That Osric was now an Ealdorman, Aethelhelm's heir, and that the apple had fallen so far from the tree, stuck in Beornoth's throat. There was little or nothing to be done about that, and the fact that Osric was undeserving of his lofty station was irrelevant. That was the right of noble birth, to succeed one's father. Beornoth thought that Alfgar would make a better Ealdorman than Osric. Alfgar had grown and changed over the last year at Branoc's Tree. He was no longer the callow youth, afraid to speak and raised in the ways of the Church. Alfgar was now a brave warrior, skilled with spear and axe, and he had what most did not; the ability to use his head. He was much more like his father than Osric would ever be.

Beornoth's thoughts slipped back to Skarde, and he had the strange idea that he and the Viking leader might have been friends in a different life, if they were not on opposing sides. He respected all that Skarde was as a warrior and leader, but Skarde was a Viking, a worshipper of Odin, and determined to take Essex for his Lord at all costs. So, they must be enemies. Beornoth smiled at the fates of men, and how God played with them. He had sworn to kill Skarde, so kill him he would, if he survived the fight to come. Beornoth had also sworn, years earlier, to kill as many Vikings as he could whilst his strength and life lasted, in vengeance for his dead girls. Beornoth watched the white tips of the waves out towards the horizon and wondered if he would not have made a better Viking than a Saxon. He was not a holy man, and God had never shown him any kindness, and Beornoth knew very well what he was, a brutal and ruthless killer. Those traits were better suited to the worshippers of Thor and Odin, where war fury and battle skill were beloved of the Gods and rewarded in the afterlife. But Beornoth also knew that his people needed men like him. There were too many sheep and lambs in the flock. God and Christ taught peace, and forgiveness, and Beornoth's life had shown him that the world snarled at peace, and stamped its foot on the throat of forgiveness. Beornoth knew his place and also knew that the people needed him now more than ever. The people of Branoc's Tree, and the people of Essex, needed his sword and his viciously brutal temperament to protect them from men just like himself, these wolves of the sea who came for blood. So he would protect them, he would bleed and take his sword to the invaders, he would kill and maim so that the good people, the families who tilled the earth and tended to sheep and cow, could live in peace. But first, he must fight Skarde's champion.

The sun grew low in the sky, visible only as a glowing red slit between a clutch of dense grey cloud. Its red hue cast an eerie glow across the beach and up on to the hill, which rose where the beach ended in an outcrop bending away to the south. The Vikings filtered back into the camp, their day's work labouring on fortifications, foraging or on patrol at an end, with the men on evening watch taking their places around the perimeter. The Vikings laughed, ate and drank together. Beornoth could detect no fear or apprehension amongst them. It was a stark reminder of how little they feared the Saxons. They were almost dismissive of the threat posed by a Saxon attack. The Vikings all walked straight-backed, took care of their hair and beards, and kept their armour and weapons clean and polished to a sheen. They cared about how they looked and their reputations. That monstrous pride, combined with their belief that death in battle was a glorious and noble thing, was what made them so successful in war. There is no fear in a man who believes death in battle is the pathway to Heaven. Those factors, and their sleek, shallow warships, had led the Vikings to riches and glory across Britain, Ireland, Frankia and the lands of the Scots for well over a hundred years. Beornoth watched them milling around him, casting amused glances in his direction. He worried for his people, for the men and women of the East Saxons, and for all Saxons. They would need strength, discipline and forceful leaders if Olaf Tryggvason managed to turn these raids into a large-scale invasion.

A shadow fell across Beornoth's face, and he looked up to see Skarde smiling down at him.

'It's time,' he said, and nodded his head to show that Beornoth should follow him.

'Time to dance, Saxon,' grinned Sigurd Bearskin, as Beornoth climbed over the pen's fencing and grunted at the pain in his ribs. Beornoth followed the men as they led him through the camp. Just as earlier in the day, the men of the Viking crews bowed their heads to Skarde as he passed. Beornoth felt their eyes upon him. He saw men nudge each other and point in his direction. More than once he saw hacksilver change hands, warriors no doubt betting on the outcome of the fight Skarde had planned. Beornoth did his best to stride with his shoulders back and his chin up. But he felt the fear in his belly. The coiling worm of battle fear turning and twisting inside him, spreading its poison to his mind, telling him to run or to beg for his life and avoid the

fight. He would not do that. He would turn that fear into anger
and fury and use it against the man he must face. What was
bravery but the overcoming of fear? He wondered who it was he
would face in this fight for his life. Beornoth was a big man, taller
than most and broad in the shoulder, so he did not fear facing a
man of equal size. He knew that often the size of a warrior was
not the most important thing in a fight, often it was the size of the
fight in the warrior rather than the size of the warrior himself.

They rounded a line of tents and all Beornoth could see
before him was a clamour of warriors. They faced away from him
and were standing on tiptoes to see over the heads and shoulders
of the men in front of them. It was a sea of warriors, moving and
swaying with a rumble of voices hovering above it like the mass of
men were a great ocean of mail, leather and anticipation.

'Out of the way, lads,' bellowed Sigurd Bearskin, and the men
before them turned to see Skarde, Beornoth and Sigurd
approaching. The men parted collectively, shuffling backwards to
make a pathway which cut straight through the throng, as though
a plough ran through them to make a furrow ready to seed. The
Vikings fell silent, and Beornoth saw hard faces staring at him.
Each man seemed to hold his breath in anticipation of the fight to
come. Beornoth clenched his jaw, fighting hard to keep the coils
of fear in his belly under control. Outwardly, he tried to look as
hard and cold as he could, meeting the eyes of the warriors as he
marched between them. Inside, he wanted to turn and run. He
clenched his teeth, the muscles in his cheeks working beneath his
beard, and took deep breaths.

At the end of the pathway, Beornoth could see a rope spanning a cleared square on the beach within the camp. Beyond that
rope, a figure came into view. It was a warrior stripped to the
waist, his torso muscled and dark with tattoos. The warrior had a
head shaved clean around the sides, and a long ponytail of

twisted blonde hair hanging from the top of his head. The warrior's arms were thick with the rings Vikings wore as a sign of their martial prowess, and the man prowled the beach like a starving bear waiting to be released from its cage.

The tattooed man caught sight of Beornoth through the crowd. He pointed at Beornoth and let out a roar so loud the fish in the sea must have heard him. He turned in a circle, waving his arms at the crowd around the fighting square. Suddenly, the eerie quiet erupted into an ear-splitting wall of shouting and roaring. The warriors raised their hands and pumped their fists towards the heavens, calm faces became twisted grimaces of anger and hate. Beornoth felt a hand on his shoulder.

'The men want to see you fight our champion. A great Saxon warrior against a great Viking warrior. They raise enough noise so that Odin will watch your fight today. He will see your bravery and one of you will die. This is the way of the warrior,' said Skarde.

'Then you and I should fight,' growled Beornoth, and he heard Skarde laugh. Beornoth was breathing heavily, his shoulders rising and falling, feeling the weight of his byrnie, and tensing his muscles. He realised his hands had clenched into tight fists, and his pace had quickened. The twisting in his belly was gone, the fear worm devoured by the twin monsters of anger and hate.

'We will fight again, my friend. I think the Norns have twisted the threads of our fates together. But today you fight Agnar. If you can kill him, then you will live. You will go back to your army and we will meet again, on the glorious field of battle.'

Beornoth turned to Skarde, and he saw the happiness on his face. He was grinning and raising his arm towards the sky with the rest of his warriors. Beornoth sighed, and he feared again for his people. These lovers of war and blades were here to kill and burn in honour of their Gods. They lived and breathed the clash of arms, and they had sailed their fast ships here to Essex to burnish their reputations with the blood of his people.

Beornoth reached the rope and stepped over it. He glared at Agnar and the Viking laughed and shouted a prayer at the clouds above.

'You must take off your mail,' said Skarde, shouting above the din, and the Jarl helped Beornoth pull the heavy byrnie over his head. Skarde handed it to Sigurd and marched to the centre of the fighting square and a hushed quiet fell over the crowd.

'Today, we will witness a contest between champions, a duel to the death worthy of Odin!' Skarde said, and the crowd roared their approval, faces red and arms reaching to the sky once more. 'Agnar, victor of countless Holmgangs, hero of the battle of Vallheim, will fight Beornoth, the Saxon warrior who attacked our camp single-handed last night, cutting loose our ships and killing our brothers. He is a Jarl of the Saxons, and his death is a great honour for us, to show Odin what we are achieving in his name. These champions will fight to the death!'

The Vikings cheered their approval, clapping one another on the back, and Beornoth saw skins of ale doing the rounds amongst the crowd. Agnar still paced the fighting square. Every so often, he would let out a bellow and raise his hands to the crowd, then his head would shake and his face twitch. Beornoth watched his opponent, allowing the anger to build within him, the fire spreading through his limbs and his muscles tensing and shoulders bunching. Agnar was broader in the chest and shoulder, and he looked to be ten years younger than Beornoth. But Beornoth had a lifetime of fighting, a lifetime of hefting weapons, wearing his heavy byrnie day in and day out, so he did not fear the Viking's strength. Beornoth had quashed his fear, and it had been what all men fear. The fear of death and pain. His wounds pulsed and ached, but he let that discomfort feed his anger, allowing it to grow and strengthen him.

Beornoth's locket lay on his chest, and he stroked the smooth timber casing. He told himself that Agnar had been there that day with the Danes, even though he could not have been given how young he looked, but that perhaps he had been the man who set the fire in his Hall that had burned his children and made their beautiful smiling faces into shrunken charred corpses. Beornoth realised that he too was prowling now, his breath coming deep and heavy. He was ready to fight.

Skarde took a length of rope from Sigurd and tied one end of it to Agnar's left wrist. He came across the square and tied the other end to Beornoth's left wrist.

'You will fight in the way we do it in the far north, Norse island fighting. Harder than a Holmgang, but more entertaining for the men,' Skarde said, and winked at Beornoth.

'Just get on with it,' hissed Beornoth, and his arm yanked forward as Agnar pulled on the rope. Beornoth pulled back to take the strain. The rope was as long as three men, and it drew the two warriors together. Agnar had rotten brown teeth beneath his beard and his eyes were wide and glaring. Skarde smiled at them both and strode to the edge of the square. He pulled a long knife from the back of his belt and held it up to show the crowd; they roared their approval again and he tossed the weapon up in the air where it twirled, catching the evening red of the setting sun. Beornoth watched it, horrified as he realised there would be only one weapon between them. They must fight for control of the blade, tied to each other in a fight to the death. In those few swift heartbeats, as the blade turned in the air, Beornoth allowed the beast of his anger and hate to take over him. He knew Agnar would wait for the blade, try to get to it first to cut and slash at Beornoth's face and torso. He also knew the Vikings lived by the warrior code of honour. 'Piss on your honour, you murderous bastards,' Beornoth said under his breath, and he was already charging towards Agnar. The flashing blade transfixed the tattooed Norseman, now on its downward arc, and he stepped forward to catch it in his meaty fist. But his throat met Beornoth's fist instead, which the Saxon had made into a spear shape, his middle finger knuckle protruding into a point. Beornoth drove his fist hard into Agnar's throat, and the Viking's tongue shot out, and his hands came up to grasp at his injured windpipe. Beornoth ignored the knife, hearing it crunch into the sand behind him, all sound of the baying crowd drowned out by his focus on killing Agnar, the embodiment of the Viking raiders who had burned his children long ago.

Beornoth crouched and thundered two punches into Agnar's stomach, and the warrior collapsed into the sand, rolling up into a protective ball. Beornoth tried to stamp on his throat, but the Viking's huge forearms took the blow, so he tried again, but this time tried to stamp on Agnar's skull. The Viking's leg shot out, however, and hooked beneath Beornoth's standing leg, and now it was his turn to tumble to the sand, where he landed heavily on his back and the wind rushed out of him, leaving him gasping for air. Beornoth felt a heavy blow on his chest. It felt like a war hammer pounding down upon him, but it was Agnar's elbow. The pain flashed across Beornoth's chest bones and he rolled away from the attack. Something dragged his arm savagely backwards, and he looked up to see Agnar had regained his feet and he had pulled the rope between them taut. Beornoth tried to suck in gulps of air to regain his wind, and his heart sank as Agnar held the knife before him, grinning and twirling the blade, then raising it to the crowd who roared their approval.

With his tied hand Agnar beckoned Beornoth to stand, and he pushed himself to his feet and shook the dizziness of the blow to his chest from his head. Agnar yanked the rope, and Beornoth pulled back to take the strain. He circled Agnar in a crouch, and the Viking did the same, still grinning and showing his rotten brown teeth and holding the knife before him, ready to strike. The Viking lunged twice, not fully committed attacks, mere feints to feel out Beornoth's agility. Beornoth sprang back from the blows. Agnar was fast. For a man his size, he moved well on the balls of his feet, and Beornoth knew he would need to get close to the man, if he was to survive. As if to confirm that thought, the blade lashed out faster than Beornoth would have thought possible and sliced across Beornoth's forearm. He grunted with the pain, but tried not to show the sting of it on his face. They circled again, and the blade flashed out like an arrow shot and it forced Beornoth to parry it with his open palm. Blood spurted from a cut across his hand. Twice more Agnar cut him, once across the chest, when he was too slow to leap away from a strike, and once across his arm again.

Beornoth swallowed hard. He felt strength leaving him with the blood seeping from his wounds onto the sand. He was out of breath and he knew he couldn't last much longer against the younger, faster warrior.

'You are slow, like an old woman,' growled Agnar, and he raised his blood-smeared knife to the crowd and basked in the glory of their cheers.

Beornoth gritted his teeth and darted in towards the Viking, and sure enough the knife shot out in a straight stab, but at the last moment Beornoth twisted away, feeling the searing pain of the blade slicing across his ribs. But he was inside Agnar's guard now, and he crashed his forehead into Agnar's nose and hooked his tied arm around Agnar's knife arm, locking it in as tight as he could, feeling the wet of his own blood on Agnar's flesh. The Viking tried to wheel away from the pain of the headbutt, but

Beornoth kept him close with his armlock. He punched Agnar twice in the ribs and hooked his free hand around Agnar's back to grab his ear. Beornoth tore at it, using all the strength built up across a lifetime of war, and Agnar yelped as his ear tore away from his skull in a sickening spray of dark blood. Agnar jerked violently, trying desperately to get away from Beornoth's savagery.

'You killed my children. Bastard!' Beornoth roared into his opponent's face, spittle flying into his beard. He knew, of course, that Agnar had not been there that day, but other Vikings had been, and Agnar would now face the wrath of Beornoth's anger at those men. He grabbed hold of Agnar's flailing rope of hair and yanked back on it, twisting his head savagely to one side. The Viking was off balance and Beornoth let go of his hair and grabbed his knife arm. He drove it down with as much force as he could muster and bent to one knee, bending Agnar's arm backwards at the elbow. The arm crunched, like the sound of biting into a crisp summer apple, and Agnar roared with pain and dropped the knife. Beornoth stood and yanked on the rope, which still tied them both together. Agnar cried out again as his broken arm flopped uselessly on the end of the tether.

Agnar lay in the sand, clutching one hand to the side of his head, where the wound of his torn-away ear pumped blood through his fingers into a dark pool on the sand. Beornoth picked up the knife and yanked on the rope again, and Agnar yelped from the pain in his broken arm. Beornoth looked at the crowd, and he smiled as he saw how their faces had changed from joyous cheers for their hero to masks of anger and hate as they saw their man laid low. He realised he was still holding Agnar's ear, and he tossed the grotesque flap of skin into the crowd and held up the knife to taunt them. He edged cautiously towards Agnar, wary that the warrior was still alive and snake-fast. Beornoth wanted to fall upon him and drive the knife into his heart, but Agnar's leg flashed out just as Beornoth suspected it might and he caught it in his tied hand and slashed the knife blade underneath Agnar's leg, hamstringing him. The Viking moaned, immobilised and grievously wounded. There was a groan from the crowd as they realised their champion was done.

Beornoth circled behind Agnar and yanked the rope to pull on the broken arm. As Agnar rolled towards the pain, Beornoth knelt and wrapped his free hand around Agnar's jaw and pulled his head back to expose his jugular. He was about to rip the blade across his throat when he heard the crowd chanting.

'Give him a blade,' they chanted in unison, over and again. Beornoth paused. He had beaten Skarde's man and won his own life, but it was a fine line between humiliating their champion and winning the fight. Beornoth knew that if he went too far in humiliating Agnar, then the crowd would turn and, for all his promises of life and freedom, there would be little Skarde could do if the throng fell upon Beornoth.

Beornoth reached down and pressed the knife into Agnar's hand. The warrior looked up at him and Beornoth saw relief on his blood-smeared face. Relief that he would die with a blade in his hand and in honourable combat, securing his place in Valhalla. Had Beornoth cut his throat, and the champion died without a blade, it would condemn him as a nithing, forced to wander the underworld until the end of days. Beornoth was not a heathen, but nor was he a lover of God, so he would allow Agnar to die with honour, which he hoped would placate the baying Viking warriors.

Agnar grasped the blade and closed his eyes tight. Beornoth, without hesitation, yanked hard with all his might on Agnar's head and broke his neck. Agnar went still, lifeless but on his way to Valhalla.

The crowd cheered again, and Beornoth rolled back on his

knees. Bleeding and exhausted, but alive. Skarde stepped into the fighting square with his hand on his axe, and for a moment Beornoth thought the Jarl would attack him, but he smiled and Beornoth took a breath of relief. He looked around at the fierce faces, and wondered if they really would let him out of their camp alive, or if there was some fresh ordeal he must suffer before Skarde would keep his word and allow him to leave.

# PART III

---

# PROTECTOR

.

## 20

'They just let you go?' said Alfgar, wiping his hand across his long face and shaking his head.

Beornoth winced, touching gingerly at the knife wound on his ribs. It was mid-morning. The Saxon forces at River's Bend had camped at the same location for days, and so the grass which had once been lush and green was now a brown, muddy, churned-up smear on the riverbank. The stink from the massed warriors and their filth overwhelmed any of the more pleasant smells of springtime. Beornoth had rode into the camp on a horse provided by Skarde, and found Alfgar and the rest of his men amongst a patch of cleared trees, where they had stretched cloth across nearby boughs to create makeshift tents to keep the rain off the men's heads. The men had also erected lean-to stacks of branches here and there for the same purpose. Fires, or the ash remnants of old fires, dotted the land between forest and river.

'They let me go,' confirmed Beornoth. 'They made me fight one of their warriors. Then fed me, tended to my wounds, gave me these arm rings, my weapons and mail, a fresh horse and sent me on my way.' Beornoth raised his arms, and the rings jangled against themselves. Alfgar's mouth fell open, and he stared at the craftmanship of the silver and gold rings about both of Beornoth's wrists. The rings had belonged to Agnar, and Skarde had said that, following his victory, anything that had belonged to Agnar now belonged to Beornoth by right of combat. They were beautiful things of silver and gold, twisted coils and writhing dragons and boars' heads carved intricately into the shining metal.

'I thought you were a dead man, you and Osmod. I prayed for your souls. You sacrificed yourselves so that we could get away,' said Alfgar.

'Osmod died.' Beornoth did not want to speak of the oath he had made to Osmod, of what he had promised to do as Osmod took his last breaths. To give voice to that promise now would turn it into a boast, and Osmod deserved more than that.

'God bless his soul, but he gave his life so the women and children could go free,' said Alfgar, and made the sign of the cross. He gestured over his shoulder at the women and children rescued from the Viking slave pen. One child caught Beornoth's eye and smiled at him. He was a young boy with a curly head of shaggy nut-brown hair, and he was playing with a small wooden horse, which he lifted to show to Beornoth. Beornoth noticed Wulfhere sat amongst them, whittling away at a chunk of wood with his small knife. The big warrior was crafting wooden toys, and he was laughing and talking to the children, both he and they enjoying the day as though nothing had happened.

'I am glad they are safe,' said Beornoth. His heart warmed to see it. The pain of his wounds was worthwhile to see the people who needed his protection safe.

'Wulfhere is good with the little ones, and we made it back to the horses. Ealdorbana is here, with the other mounts.

'Why hasn't the army marched? Is Byrhtnoth here?'

'He is. I was summoned by him not long after we got here. I

told him of the Viking camp and that you had given your life to save us. I told him you cut their ships loose, and how many men they had at the beach.'

Beornoth scratched at his beard, and slowly clenched his wounded hand open and closed, feeling the freshly forming scab stretching. 'Did you tell him their fortifications were not yet complete?'

'Yes, Lord.'

'What did he say?'

'Nothing. Not to me, anyway. Men go out on patrols and to search for food. But we have been here for days now, with no sign of any advance or that we will fight.'

'The army can't stay here for much longer. The fyrd will melt away little by little. Men will need to get back to their farms and their families. We must fight now if we are going to beat Skarde.'

'Will we fight, or go back to Branoc's Tree?' asked Alfgar.

'Where is Byrhtnoth?' said Beornoth, knowing that he must persuade the Ealdorman to move to action, or risk losing his army.

Beornoth found the Ealdorman at the western end of the Saxon camp. He stood watching a line of his warriors practising shield wall manoeuvres. They moved through the standard shield wall formation drill, shields overlapping and banging together, alongside a clipped shout from the men as they moved as one. The warriors then raised spears to rest overhand and upon the iron rims of their round, painted linden wood shields. They moved forward in unison, and as Byrhtnoth shouted his orders, the line wheeled away or charged as he commanded.

'Ah, Beornoth, back from the dead,' said Erkenwald, a crooked smile splitting his clean-shaven face.

'Beornoth?' said Byrhtnoth, turning around. 'They told me you were dead, that you charged alone into the Viking camp.'

'I survived, Lord.'

'I can see that. But how?'

'I fell, whilst we tried to rescue the prisoners. When I awoke, they forced me to fight their champion.'

'I hope you killed the heathen dog,' said Byrhtnoth. He turned to fully face Beornoth, and placed his hands on his hips, eager to hear the tale. Beornoth told Byrhtnoth and Erkenwald of the duel, and how Skarde had let him go.

'They might be pirates, murderers and thieves, but they have a sense of honour, these Vikings. I'll give them that,' said Byrhtnoth, and he looked to Erkenwald, who nodded in agreement.

'We could march today and be at their camp tomorrow, Lord,' said Beornoth. He took a step closer to the Ealdorman. 'Their fortifications are not complete. There will never be a better time to fight them.'

'We will fight them, Beo. Don't worry about that. Look at my warriors here. They are ready for the fray. Are they not well drilled?'

'We can launch a surprise attack, Lord. They do not expect it, they do not fear us. If we can attack them now, before they drive further inland, then we can kill them all.'

'Surprise attack?' said Byrhtnoth, and he looked at Erkenwald with raised eyebrows. 'We will meet them in the open. God will grant us strength and victory on the glorious field of battle. We shall meet them with honour, in battle lines, and show the heathens how God graces his followers with valour.'

Beornoth sighed. 'We cannot keep the men here much longer and King Æthelred has not summoned the northern Ealdormen and their Thegns. If the Vikings are reinforced they will outnumber us. Surely we must attack now?'

'I await their move. Once they strike out from their fortifica-tion, we will drive them to a field of our choosing and strike them down,' said Byrhtnoth. He puffed his chest out, and his cheeks reddened. Beornoth made to speak, but Byrhtnoth raised a hand to silence him. 'The King has summoned his Ealdormen from across Wessex and Mercia to help him protect the south coast, and there are other threats in the north. When I want your advice, Thegn, I will ask for it. A messenger came for you today, some sort of trouble on your lands.'

'Where is this man?'

'Leofstan!' Byrhtnoth shouted, and a boy came running. 'Show Beornoth where his messenger is.'

The boy nodded and bowed. He beckoned Beornoth on, and before Beornoth could bow his head, Byrhtnoth had turned back to watch his men at their practice. The Ealdorman seemed offended that Beornoth had tried to offer him advice, but Beornoth was astounded that Byrhtnoth could not see the merit in attacking the Vikings whilst their beach camp was not yet fully fortified. He followed the boy and looked at their own encampment as he walked. No ditch or palisade, only the river at their flank providing any sort of barrier for the Vikings to overcome should they attack. Beornoth shook his head. If an attack was to come from the invaders, it was as like to come from the river and their shallow-draughted dragon ships than from the land. The boy scurried along, his bare feet squelching and slipping in the slick mud. The lack of preparedness, the inability to strike at the right time, summed up the difference between the professional and disciplined Viking warriors, and the part-time landowners and farmers of Saxon Britain. In the northern shires, Beornoth's people were used to constant fighting, whether it be small-scale family disputes and feuds between Viking and Saxon landowners, or raids across the north-west coast from Irish Vikings, or Northmen howling down from Strath Clota or further north. The men of Wessex, Essex and Sussex had grown soft since the days of King Alfred and King Athelstan. Victory over the Danelaw had brought peace, and peace had slowly swept away the fear and harsh reality of war and Viking attacks. Beornoth worried for his people. How would they cope if this Olaf Trygvasson launched his invasion?

The boy pointed to a tall, thin man who worked briskly, brushing a dappled mare amid a line of horses. Boys hurried here and there, tending to the mounts. Some were mucking out, shovelling up the piles of shit to barrow them away from the precious horses who provided mobility for the army. Some boys were forking fresh hay and fodder for the horses to eat, and others were brushing and tending to the huge warhorses at the end of the line. Ealdorbana would be there somewhere, and Beornoth would pay him a visit once he had received this message from Branoc's Tree.

As Beornoth approached, he recognised the messenger as a tenant of Branoc's Tree. He was a lantern-jawed man with a bulbous nose. Beornoth could not remember his name, but recalled that he held a hide of land and had a family. The man heard the sounds of Beornoth's boots in the mud, and as he turned, his face turned pale. He swallowed, the ball in his throat visibly rising and falling. The man licked his lips, and Beornoth frowned.

'What news of Branoc's Tree?'

'A messenger came, Lord. From the north.'

'From the north?' Beornoth asked, and the man shuffled his feet.

'Yes, Lord. A man came, a warrior on a fine horse. He came two days ago. He said that a northern Ealdorman had sent him, and well, he said that, well...'

'Out with it,' growled Beornoth.

'He came from Ealdorman Osric, Lord. The messenger said

the Ealdorman wants his bastard brother returned. He said he
wants him returned, or your wife will pay the price.'

Beornoth felt his blood rushing in his ears, and a tightness
grew in his chest. 'This man came to Branoc's Tree,' he said
slowly. 'And said Ealdorman Osric wants his brother, Alfgar,
returned or my wife will pay the price? Those were his exact
words?'

'Well... not exactly, Lord.'

Beornoth stepped closer to the man. 'Tell me what he said,
exactly.'

The thin man wrung his hands and looked at the floor. 'He
said Ealdorman Osric wants his bastard brother returned to him
before the moon grows full, or your mad wife will pay the price.
He said the Ealdorman would give her to his men, whore her to
his warriors just as the Vikings had whored her.'

Beornoth closed his eyes. He wanted to snatch the messenger
and punch him, not because he blamed him for his words, but to
take his anger out on someone, anyone. He breathed slowly,
battling to control his fury. 'Did he say Osric has my wife now?'

'He didn't say, Lord, I have told you all the man said before he
rode away. The Lady Aethelberga sent me to find you straight
away.'

'Get Wulfhere, and Alfgar. Round up my men and bring them
here. We ride, now.'

The thin man bowed his head and ran to find Wulfhere and
the others, slipping in the mud as he went and barely keeping his
footing in his haste to get away from Beornoth's wrath.

Beornoth rested his hand on a tree trunk. His stomach heaved
and he thought he would vomit, but kept the contents of his guts
down. His head spun, breaths coming short and sharp. A
memory of Eawynn came to him when they were young together.
Her shining dark hair, and deep brown eyes, round and warm.

She had been the light of his life, so full of laughter and joy. That vision faded, and he closed his eyes, wiping a hand down his face. He opened his eyes and saw another memory of her. She was giggling, playing with their girls, tumbling and skipping on warm summer grass. She had been so happy then, and so had he. He should have brought her south with him, to the safety of Branoc's Tree, not left her in a convent to suffer alone. Beornoth had made many mistakes in his life. With matters of the sword, he was decisive and confident, but in other matters, he was weak, clumsy, and found wanting. Beornoth cursed himself. How could he have left her there when he had a new, safe home at Branoc's Tree? He needed a drink; he needed some ale.

Beornoth looked to the sky and rubbed at his eyes. An army of troubles pressed down upon him with the weight of a blacksmith's anvil. Vikings on the coast, prowling and poised to ravage the Saxon coast. His wife threatened, if not already taken by Osric. He had to leave the army; he had to leave his Lord Byrhtnoth and go to Eawynn. Heriot be damned. He had let her down once already when she needed him most, on the terrible day long ago, and now he had let her down again. He was supposed to be a protector, a sword to protect his people and loved ones. He couldn't even protect his own wife. The entire world was on fire, and Beornoth knew he had to charge into that flame, sword in hand, and make his enemies suffer.

## 21

'You have six days, Beornoth,' shouted Byrhtnoth, a deep frown furrowing his forehead. The Ealdorman wagged a ringed finger in Beornoth's direction. 'I could force you to stay, you are oath-bound to me, but I'll give you six days. If you aren't back by then, and we have to fight without you and your men, that which was given will be taken away.'

'If the heathens fall upon us, and a Thegn and his Heriot are not here to protect the people, then you and your men will be excommunicated,' came a shrill voice from behind Byrhtnoth. It was the Bishop of Essex, a small, wiry man with tightly curled grey hair sprouting from either side of his Bishop's mitre.

Beornoth nodded at the Ealdorman and his Bishop, and clicked his tongue to urge Ealdorbana forward. Behind him came the line of his household troops and the fyrd men of his tithings at Branoc's Tree.

'The Ealdorman believes you are deserting him,' said Wulfhere, riding alongside Beornoth.

'I don't care what he believes,' growled Beornoth. 'He knows I am no coward.' He picked up the pace and nudged Ealdorbana into a canter. They left the mud and stink of River's Bend and rode along the winding riverbank, past the reeds and drooping willow trees and across the bracken and heather of the East Saxon countryside.

'The men will fear for their souls, with that threat from the Bishop. I will fear for my own soul if we are to be excommunicated. We will all go to hell. It's a fate worse than death, Lord,' grumbled Wulfhere.

'They need not fear. We will be back before the six days are up. If Byrhtnoth hasn't attacked Skarde yet, whilst his defences are under construction, he won't do it now. He wants to fight a battle, he wants a shield-wall clash worthy of a poem to burnish his honour before the King and God.' Beornoth looked behind him and saw Alfgar clutching the cross around his neck and praying so hard his eyes might bleed. To a pious man such as Alfgar, excommunication was a truly terrible threat.

'What if the Vikings attack Byrhtnoth before we return?'

'Then we should be glad that none of our men will have lost their lives.'

'Why don't we just ride for your wife now? You and I can go, the others can ride to Branoc's Tree. We will be there and back in six days,' said Wulfhere.

'I have to make sure Branoc's Tree is secure. If Osric wants to attack me, then he could already be there, waiting. The messenger could easily be a trap to lure us all into that one place. To make it easier for him to kill Alfgar and me in one fell swoop. I doubt he has made the ride south, but we should be ready just in case. In war, I have learned to prepare for the worst.'

'But what if she is still there, in the convent? We could get her out before Osric takes her?'

'He wouldn't have made the threat if he didn't have her,' said Beornoth. He felt his locket banging against the skin of his chest as he rose and fell in time with the rhythm of his horse. It was as though it was tapping him, nudging him. As if the memories of his family urged him to action. Beornoth's belly soured as a cloak of shame descended upon him. What kind of man was he to leave his wife exposed to his enemies? He couldn't protect his family years earlier, and he still couldn't protect them now. He tried to shake it off. 'Besides, we have women and children with us to think of. We need them safe in Branoc's Tree, and preparations made to make the place secure before we ride north.'

'So we will ride north, then?'

'We will ride,' said Beornoth. He glanced over his shoulder where amongst the ranks behind him were the prisoners rescued from Skarde's camp. The women and children rode with the warriors, either perched in front of them, or clinging to the riders' backs.

'Will you bring Alfgar north?'

'I don't know yet.'

'But you wouldn't give him to his brother?'

Beornoth just frowned at Wulfhere, who raised his hand to apologise for asking the question. He hoped his men knew him better than that, especially Wulfhere, who had been his man for over a year. Beornoth knew he was not a kind or friendly man. He was surly, difficult and belligerent. But he hoped he was at least honest and tried to be an honest Lord to his men.

'He seems too close to that woman,' said Beornoth, looking over his shoulder at the red-haired woman who rode behind Alfgar, clinging tightly to his waist.

'Aye. They killed her husband and father in that village where the Vikings took her as a slave. He has barely left her side since he returned to River's Bend.'

'He's an Ealdorman's son, whether he likes it or not.'

'So?'

'So, it's all right for him to have a quick tumble with a maid at the summer fair, but he must use his head before he takes a wife. He has a chance, maybe, to be an Ealdorman one day.'

'Maybe he doesn't want to be an Ealdorman, or find a marriage for power. Maybe he wants to find a woman he loves?'

'Don't be a fool,' snarled Beornoth. 'Love doesn't come into it. If Osric dies without an heir, then Alfgar is the Ealdorman in Cheshire. He must marry accordingly.'

'Which is why Osric wants him dead.'

'Even though he's a bastard, he is still next in line to be Ealdorman. So, yes. His brother wants Alfgar dead.'

'He likes that redhead, though,' said Wulfhere, and laughed. 'We'll get your wife back, Lord.'

Beornoth felt his shoulders bunching with the tension. It ate at him like poison, that knowledge that he was riding away from Skarde, whom he had sworn to kill, and that he was riding to take care of his lands and Heriot rather than riding straight for Eawynn. Doubt gnawed at his mind. There was no straightforward decision, and Beornoth had to follow his gut feeling. If he stayed with Byrhtnoth, then Osric would hurt Eawynn, and he could attack Branoc's Tree. Osric had sent men to raid Branoc's Tree before. If Beornoth rode straight for Eawynn, then he could leave Branoc's Tree vulnerable. So, he must risk losing his Heriot and leave Byrhtnoth, secure Branoc's Tree in case of attack, and then ride hard to free Eawynn from Osric. He had only six days to do it, and get back to Byrhtnoth or he would lose his Heriot. Osric would try to kill him, of course, but men had tried before.

They arrived at Branoc's Tree as evening drew in. It was late Spring, turning to early summer and as the Sun made its descent, a chill wind blew across the fields, and Beornoth and his warriors wrapped themselves in cloaks and huddled over their horses as they reached the stout wooden walls. They dragged the gates open and Beornoth ducked as Ealdorbana rode underneath the gate lintel. A boy came racing over to take the bridle and walked alongside the horse until Beornoth came to a halt in the open square at the centre of Branoc's Tree. Wulfhere shouted orders at the people gathering in the square to greet the returning warriors. He bade them prepare food and ale for the warriors, and find lodgings for the rescued prisoners.

Beornoth left Wulfhere and Alfgar to make the arrangements for the men and stalked to his Hall. He pushed open the oak doors and closed his eyes as the welcome heat of the roaring fire at the Hall's centre hit his face like the breath of a dragon. He pushed his cloak back and rolled his shoulders to loosen the tightness in his neck. The people in the Hall scattered to the dark corners as they saw their Lord, sensing his malevolent presence. A grey-haired woman in a brown woollen dress brought him a mug of water, and he barked at her to bring him some ale. It had been so long since he had taken a proper drink, and he told himself he would only drink one. His eyes were stinging, and his throat dry. The weight of the decisions he must make lay heavy upon him, as did the risks he faced, and he thought for a heart-beat about asking the woman to bring back the water, but she returned having replaced the mug's contents with ale and he raised the mug and drained its contents in three gulps. Beads of the gloriously sweet and frothy drink dripped into his beard, and Beornoth wiped them free with the back of his injured hand.

'Bring me another,' he said, and the woman bowed and shuffled off to obey his command. Beornoth took off his helmet and touched gingerly at his wounded ribs. The ale had already spread its warmth through his chest and throat. He had not drunk for so long, and he needed some ale to help him think clearly. Beornoth told himself that he would not rest for long, he would have one more drink of ale at his fire, then he would make preparations for the defence of Branoc's Tree before nightfall, and then ride hard for Eawynn.

The woman returned and handed him the mug, and again Beornoth drank it down in swift gulps. He felt the tightness in his neck and shoulders relaxing, and he sighed. 'Another.' He sat on a high-backed bench by the fire and stretched out his legs, enjoying the warmth seeping through his boots and on to his feet. He would take one last drink, and then see to the defences. The woman returned, and Beornoth drained the cup. 'Another, and bring a jug this time, and some food.'

A door creaked open at the rear of the Hall as the woman laid down a jug of ale, and a plate with cold cuts of pork, some pungent-smelling cheese and a chunk of dark bread. He poured himself another cup and took a drink before taking a bite of his food. He was aware of someone approaching, but Beornoth did not raise himself from his ale.

'Welcome back, Lord Beornoth,' said Aethelberga, coming to stand next to him. 'You got the message, then?'

'I did,' he replied, and drained the cup before filling it again.

'Your enemies have your wife. They might attack us here at Branoc's Tree.'

'I said I got the message.'

'So, what will you do? What should we do?' She fussed at the wrists of her dress, and came to stand between Beornoth and the fire, frowning down at the jug of ale.

'I will get my wife from that bastard Osric, and we will prepare Branoc's Tree in case of attack.'

'Do you think this is the right time to be drinking by the fire, Lord?'

Beornoth drained his cup and stood, towering over Aethelberga, her head reaching only to his chest. 'Leave me, woman. Make sure the prisoners we rescued from the Vikings are cared for. There are children amongst them.' He leant forward and looked her in the eye. 'When I want your advice, I will ask you for it.'

Her face went crimson, and she bowed her head and strode towards the double doors and out into the courtyard. Beornoth sat again, and finished his jug of ale, calling for another. He regretted using his size to intimidate Aethelberga. She did not deserve that. She was right. Now was not the time to be drinking ale by the fire. But the ale was strong, and the fire was warm. Beornoth's mind became fogged, dark thoughts clouding his thinking. He stared at the dancing flames and he saw Byrhtnoth threatening to take away his Heriot and lands. He saw Skarde leading his Vikings into battle, cutting and slashing with a bloodied war axe, raiding and pillaging to soften up the lands of the Saxons for Olaf's invasion. Then he saw Eawynn amongst the flames, as she was when they were young together: beautiful, strong-willed, and full of fun. They would spend days together, riding in the valleys and forests around his father's lands, talking and laughing. They were the best times of Beornoth's life, and now he felt like a different person to the one he had been when he was young, and when he had been a father to his girls and a husband to his wife. A tear rolled down his cheek as he thought of the evenings spent bouncing them on his knee, playing with their dolls made from straw and tied with cloth, of watching them sleeping so peacefully. Then seeing their shrunken, twisted, blackened bodies in the ash remnants of his burned Hall.

So many people needed him and depended on him. Beornoth owed them all so much. When she needed him the most, he owed Eawynn for not being there. He owed Byrhtnoth for making him a Thegn again and appointing to him a Heriot, restoring his family's honour. He owed Osmod the oath he had sworn in his death throes, to kill Skarde and throw his horde back into the great grey sea. The burden was too heavy, and Beornoth doubted he was the man to see it all through. How could he fight Osric, now an Ealdorman, and win? How could he rescue Eawynn, and what if she was already dead, or suffering at the hands of Osric's warriors?

Beornoth drained the jug of ale and shouted for another. All those faces looked at him within the flames, disapproving and judging. More ale came, and he drank it, each cup banishing the faces further into the shadows and bringing him closer to the oblivion he craved, and that he had so often found at the bottom of his cups.

'Lord,' he heard Wulfhere say over his shoulder. Beornoth turned and slipped from his bench, chuckling to himself as he sat back up.

'What is it? Have a drink with me, Wulfhere.'

'I cannot, Lord. There is much to be done. We must decide who to leave here at Branoc's Tree and who will ride north with us. We must appoint guard shifts, arrange for patrols to watch out for attack, make sure there is enough food in case our enemies dig in outside the gates. The horses need preparing to ride out. Will you not come outside, Beornoth? The men look to you for command.'

Beornoth waved a hand. 'Have a drink, sit down.' He patted the place next to him on the bench and held up the jug to Wulfhere with a shaky hand.

'Forgive me, Lord. But your wife needs you. We must ride out with haste.'

Beornoth roared with fury and surged to his feet, dropping to one leg as his ale-fuddled mind went dizzy. He pushed himself to his feet, banging his injured ribs on the bench as he rose. Beornoth flung the jug at Wulfhere, but it flew well wide to crash on the floor beyond him. 'Everybody needs me. Have I not done enough? Have I not killed enough men? Did I not fight alone against the Vikings this very week with these very hands?' He held his hands out to Wulfhere, then tore at the bandage on his cut hand, fumbling and missing the cloth and belching loudly, the sound echoing around the rafters.

'Will you come out and command the men, Lord?'

'You command them, you order the defences. What use is it making you captain of the household troops if I have to do all of the bloody work myself? Earn your keep, you lazy bastard. Now piss off out of my sight.'

Wulfhere's mouth fell open, and he shook his head. He bowed to Beornoth and left the Hall without saying another word. Beornoth grumbled to himself and sagged down onto the bench, roaring for more ale and food. He drank and ate and stared into the fire, losing himself in the welcome hollowness of the pit of inebriation.

## 22

Beornoth gasped at the shock of the ice-cold water hitting his face. He pushed himself up on to his elbows and his breath came in quick gasps. The thumping pain in his head made him wince, and he retched at the foul sourness in his stomach. He opened one eye into a tiny slit, but stabs of lightning shot through his skull, caused by shafts of daylight streaming in from the firehole above him in the thatch. Aethelberga stood before him, an empty bucket in one hand and a scowl on her face. She dropped the bucket to the hard packed-earth floor, the corners of her mouth twitching slightly at the loud clang, which made Beornoth's head ring like a church bell.

He retched again and doubled over to vomit next to the dwindling embers of the Hall's fire.

'A fine Thegn and Lord you are to your people. Drunk and useless. Enemies on all sides, and your wife taken prisoner. Do you have no honour?' said Aethelberga.

Beornoth covered his face with his hands as a wave of guilt and shame washed over him. He thought about running, bolting out of the doors, finding the nearest horse and riding out of

Branoc's Tree and away from everything. He could go far away, where nobody could find him, he could hide from his unworthiness and the people who needed him, and whom he had let down. No more responsibility, no more blades and death, no one to depend on him.

'I can't do it,' he moaned, dropping to his knees and keeping his face from Aethelberga.

'Yes, you can. You should have thought of this plight before you downed your body weight in ale and self-pity.' She came towards him and placed her hands firmly on her wide hips. 'You have to do it. I know you have earned your reputation in battle, and so do all your people. You are Beornoth, scourge of the Vikings. Hero of River's Bend. The warrior who charged into an army of Vikings to rescue women and children. We need you now. Your wife needs you. Pull yourself together, strap on your sword, and do what you were born to do. Snap yourself out of this hole you have dug for yourself. It does not become a Thegn and a warrior. Do it now, or get out of this place and never return.'

He looked at her, and pulled himself to standing, squinting his throbbing eyes at the sunlight. 'It is morning now?' He shook his head and wiped vomit from his beard. 'It is already too late. I would need to reach the north by tomorrow, find Eawynn and get her away from Osric in less than a day, before riding back in less than two days. Or the six days will pass and Byrhtnoth will grant my Heriot to another. My family honour, so recently restored, is to be lost again. They will excommunicate my men and me. It can't be done.'

'It can be done. Take two horses for each man and ride hard. Do not stop, find your wife, don't get yourself killed, and get her back here. You can be back with Byrhtnoth and the army before the sixth day,' said Aethelberga. She picked her way around the debris of spilled food and empty ale jugs to collect Beornoth's sword and seax from where they lay in the floor rushes. She handed them to Beornoth, and he took them, shaking his head and stifling another bout of retching.

'I need another drink,' Beornoth groaned, and crouched to find a jug with some ale left within.

'One thing you most certainly do not need is another drink. Why is it a man so strong in war looks to hide at the bottom of an ale jug when things become difficult?'

Beornoth slumped down onto the bench and ran his hands through his hair. 'For the emptiness it brings. The dark dreamless sleep, without memories or thoughts.' He whispered those words to himself more than to Aethelberga.

'It was unspeakable, what happened to you and your family, Beornoth,' said Aethelberga. She sat next to him, talking softly. 'But we must face such things as an enemy. Drinking to escape the memory of terrible moments in our lives is not the answer.'

'What is the answer, then? How can I forget my children, dead at the hands of Viking raiders, or my wife, attacked and driven mad?'

'Do not forget them. Honour them. Fight for them. Remember them as they were, and live your life in their memory, not trying to escape them.'

'I wish I had died with them.'

'Well, you are not dead. You are alive, and our people need you. So put down the ale, and pick up your sword. Use the Heriot the Ealdorman has granted you, my late husband's Heriot, to vanquish our enemies. Or leave us. Run away and climb into a bottomless jug of ale and never come back.'

Beornoth stood, realising that she was right. He had spent so long wallowing in the pain of all he had lost, when he should live his life with their memories close to his heart. He had already wasted too much time wallowing in self-pity and he should already be on the road north if he was to get Eawynn away from Osric and to safety, in time to get back before Byrhtnoth took his lands away. 'Your words have struck me like a blow to the head,' he said. 'I will fight for the honour of my lost family.'

'Good. You are a good man, Beornoth. Use your strength to protect the people. Will your enemy, this northern Ealdorman, attack Branoc's Tree?'

'I don't think so. He's a young, arrogant fool. But I don't think he is foolish enough to bring his warriors on to Byrhtnoth's lands and strike at one of his Thegns, especially when Byrhtnoth is at war with the Vikings.'

'But he might attack?'

'He might,' Beornoth allowed. 'But I will leave the warriors here to protect Branoc's Tree. You will not be unprotected.'

'Do what must be done, then.'

Beornoth nodded his thanks to Aethelberga. Her words were harsh, but her meaning was kind. He wanted to tell her how strong she was, and that he knew how hard it must have been for her to adjust to a new Thegn coming into the home she and her husband had built together. Beornoth saw the deep sadness still there behind her fierce eyes, the loss of her husband still fresh and painful. He wished he had been more respectful to Aethelberga's husband and his deeds. The people of Branoc's Tree clearly respected him and missed him. Beornoth was a different man. He knew he was not a man of kindness or encouraging words. He was a man of war. Beornoth couldn't find the words to tell Aethelberga what he wanted to say. So he just looked into her eyes, and hoped she knew, at least a little, how much he respected her.

Beornoth set his jaw and consciously banished the feelings of shame swarming within his ale-skewed brain. He had done those things she spoke of, brave and noble deeds, and it made him proud to hear it come from the mouth of so strong a woman, a woman he respected. Beornoth strapped on his sword and hooked the seax scabbard to the back of his belt. He must be strong, and he must use his strength to get out of this impossible situation. He could fight and he could kill, and Beornoth hoped that would be enough. Eawynn was in danger and could already be Osric's prisoner. He had to go to her now, with all haste. Before Osric hurt her, Byrhtnoth took his lands away, and the Bishop excommunicated Beornoth and his men. The risk and danger in what faced Beornoth was overwhelming, but it must be done.

'I ride now,' he croaked, voice cracked and hoarse. 'I must be back here in five days' time.' He marched past her towards the door. Two days' ride north, and two days back. That left one day to check the convent, hoping Osric was bluffing and Eawynn was still there, or get inside Osric's fortress and get Eawynn out of his hands. It could be done. He would need to ride hard and he would ride into the jaws of his enemy and it was more likely that he would die than succeed, but it could be done.

'Beornoth,' Aethelberga called after him. He stopped and turned to her. 'Make them pay if they have hurt her. Then come back here and kill the Viking murderers who plague our lands. Protect your wife, and protect the people of Branoc's Tree and Essex.'

Beornoth strode out into the morning light, ignoring the sickness in his belly, the pounding in his head, and the ache of his wounds.

'Wulfhere, Alfgar,' he bellowed, so that all the folk within the walls would hear. 'Wulfhere and Imma will ride north with me. Alfgar will remain here to take command of Branoc's Tree.' The courtyard was already a busy hive at the morning's work, fetching water and firewood, grinding oats, and tending to animals. At Beornoth's orders, the place erupted, men dashing here and there, and then Wulfhere appeared, bleary-eyed and fresh from his bed.

'So, we ride?' Wulfhere said, smiling and scratching at his beard.

Beornoth walked over to him and placed a hand on his shoulder. 'We ride, you, Imma and I. Just three of us to take back my wife. Ready two mounts each because we must ride hard.'

'Three of us?' said Wulfhere, his head rocking back as though someone had slapped him.

'Three of us. The rest must stay here. Osric could have a force on the way to take Alfgar here, or Skarde could strike this far inland. The men will protect the people. And we will be back in five days. With one day to spare to rejoin Byrhtnoth.'

Wulfhere nodded and grinned. 'So we ride, and Alfgar stays?'

'He stays. We need a clever warrior here to defend Branoc's Tree in case Osric or the Vikings attack whilst we are away. We return in five days, then we join Ealdorman Byrhtnoth and kill the cursed Viking invaders!' Beornoth roared, and the men of Branoc's Tree shouted their approval. Beornoth felt the hairs stand up on his neck at their roar. A boy brought him a skin of water and he drank it down, slaking his ale-thirst. He strode to a water trough and stood upon it so all the people of Branoc's Tree could see him. 'I am your Thegn,' he said, and waited as heads snapped around to look at him and the people stopped at their tasks. 'I have not spoken to you together before because I am not a man of words. Ealdorman Byrhtnoth made me Thegn here for one reason, because I fight and kill Vikings. I might not show the kindness and warmth of your previous Thegn. But I have this.' He drew his sword, the blade rasping on the scabbard's throat, and held the shining steel up for all to see. 'This is what I bring to Branoc's Tree and the East Saxon people. I must go now, back to my home in the north. Men there have attacked my family and

made threats against one of my oathmen. I will punish those
men, and then I will return and bring this blade to strike at the
hearts of our Viking enemies before they make our people suffer
any further. You all knew Osmod, he died fighting next to me. He
was a fierce fighter and a brave warrior.' Beornoth saw the people
nodding and exchanging glances with each other. 'He died next
to me, having given his life to protect you, and to rescue our
people destined for a life of slavery. Before he died, I swore an
oath to him, and I will keep that oath. I swore I would scourge the
Vikings from our lands, and so I will. Prepare yourselves and man
the walls. Keep a keen eye out for any danger, and in five days, I
will return.' The people raised their fists and shouted their
support. Beornoth kept his sword raised and looked each person
in the face, so that they understood his determination and the
truth of his words.

Alfgar came dashing from his quarters, pulling on his clothes
and hair sticking up like an old brush. 'We are going north, Lord?'

'You will remain here. I ride with Wulfhere and Imma,' said
Beornoth. He handed the water skin back to the boy and took his
cloak from another. He clasped the heavy wool cloak at his
shoulder with a plain bronze pin.

'Why am I not going with you, Lord? Have I not proved myself
a warrior?'

'You have. More than proved yourself. Which is why I need
you here, to protect the people.'

'It is my brother who has taken your wife, and my life that is
threatened. Let me fight with you, Beornoth.'

'I need you here, because I trust you.' Beornoth put his arm
around Alfgar's slim shoulders and turned him around. He
pointed with his other hand at the people in the courtyard and
swept around to show him the children playing with wooden
toys, whittled and crafted for them by Wulfhere. The rescued

children were amongst them. Then Beornoth pointed to where Aethelberga, and the red-haired woman rescued from Skarde's camp, were setting up a weaving loom on the porch of the Hall. 'I will be back in five days' time, or I will be dead. Either way, your brother could attack here with his forces, or Skarde could strike deep inland and bring his savage warriors to the gates of Branoc's Tree. These people need you, Alfgar, they need your spear, your knife and your cleverness. Use all that you have learned to keep the people safe. If men come who want to burn, kill, rape and enslave them, you must protect them. I leave you in command.'

Alfgar rubbed his hand down his pale, long face. He looked at Beornoth with his dark, ringed eyes and nodded. 'I will protect the people, my Lord.'

**23**

Beornoth leant over the saddle and whispered his thanks in Ealdorbana's ear. He stroked and patted the warhorse's muscular neck as the beast bobbed his head. White lather flecked the horse's chest and flanks. Beornoth had ridden the animal harder than a warrior should ride a beast bred and raised purely for war. He groaned at the pain from the still fresh wound across his ribs and stretched his back and thighs, which burned and ached from the hard ride.

'Less than two days,' grinned Imma next to Beornoth. Imma rode a smaller chestnut mare, and behind him the spare mounts were roped to his saddle, already ridden to the point where they were almost blown.

'Let's see if the Lady is still in there, then,' said Wulfhere. He poured water from a skin on to his hands and washed it into his beard and over his bald head.

Beornoth clicked his tongue, and Ealdorbana lurched towards the convent. The building lay in a glade, high timber walls sat where a light forest of beech and elm gave way to a pasture filled with the bright yellow of dandelions and lush green grass. Bees buzzed around the hives dotted around the outside of the walls.

'It doesn't look like it's been attacked,' said Imma.

'Who would attack a convent?' asked Wulfhere, and both he and Imma made the sign of the cross.

'You wouldn't need to attack it. It's not defended,' said Beornoth. If he had come to this place to take a woman, he would simply knock on the door and if they refused entry, he would force his way in. No broken walls, no fires, no hurt or dead sisters, just a big man taking a little woman against her will. But Beornoth would never come to a place to take a woman, nor would any warrior with honour or reputation. He came to the gate, hope and fear competing for control of his emotions. Beornoth hoped the gate would open, and he would go inside and see Eawynn looking out of her wide window, at peace. He feared she was gone, taken, being mistreated somewhere by men who knew nothing of her delicate mind, and of the horrors which had broken it.

Beornoth slid from Ealdorbana's back and stretched his own back again. It had been a hard ride, pushing the horses to the point of exhaustion, only stopping to change mounts and when it grew too dark to ride safely. He knocked on the gate, and moments later heard voices and the shuffling of feet beyond. A small wooden window in the gate scraped open, and a wrinkled face peered out at him. Bright blue eyes sat within a brown face, as wrinkled and worn as an old leather boot.

'Lord Beornoth,' she said. Her voice cracked, and she bit her bottom lip. Beornoth's heart sank.

'Lady Eawynn?' he said, heart pounding in his chest.

'Gone, Lord. Men came for her. Forced their way into this very gate, into a house of God, holy and devoted to the Blessed Mother.'

'Can you describe these men, sister?'

'Big men, warriors. Northerners, like you, Lord.'

'Did they hurt you? Was Eawynn hurt?'

'They pushed us around. They slapped Sister Breda. Wait a moment,' she said and slid the window closed. The gate screeched on its hinges as the little sister pulled it open; she took a step out and put a small hand on Beornoth's thick forearm. She was a tiny woman, barely reaching Beornoth's chest. She looked up at him and gripped his arm tight.

'Eawynn was frightened and confused. They dragged her out. She was screaming and desperate. They were not gentle. They told us to tell you, if you came, to bring your man Alfgar to them in Mameceaster. I am sorry, Beornoth, that we could not keep her safe.'

'Thank you,' was all Beornoth could say. A tightness gripped his chest, and the gorge in his throat rose. He patted her little hand, and she pulled it away, shaking her head, and started to cry softly. Beornoth turned away and beneath his iron byrnie his muscles tensed and the flame of furious anger caught fire.

'What will you do?' she called after him.

Beornoth paused and turned back to her. 'Get Eawynn back and kill anyone who gets in my way.'

They left the convent and rode hard towards Osric's lands. They had barely slept and Beornoth's muscles ached and his eyes looked like piss-holes in snow.

'So we're not in Mercia, then?' said Imma, the young warrior pulling the hood of his cloak around his face and frowning up at a malevolent sky of shadows and swirling cloud. A bitter rain spat above their heads as Beornoth, Wulfhere and Imma rode carefully along a steep-sided gorge covered by an ancient, dark forest. They were travel-stained and weary; their horses moved laboriously, exhausted from the hard ride north.

'It's hard to explain,' said Wulfhere, tipping his head back to catch the cool raindrops on his tongue. 'This land used to be part of Northumbria in the old times. Then it was the Kingdom of York when the Danes ruled here. Then Mercia, when Eric Bloodaxe was killed, and now Cheshire since the Lady Æthelflæd made it so.'

'So Osric is Ealdorman of Cheshire?' asked Imma.

'He is. The Lady Æthelflæd created Cheshire to sit between her precious Mercia and the lands of the Danes, who stayed on in the Kingdom of York after Bloodaxe's death. Cheshire is the borderlands, the Badlands. Always war, constant raids. Vikings coming across from Ireland, or howling down from the north.'

'Did the Danes not leave when Bloodaxe was killed?'

'No, more's the pity. Most stayed. Many of them have been here that long that they are men of God, like you and me. Third generation here, their grandfathers and great-grandfathers were Viking raiders and invaders.'

'So why not just drive the Danes out?' said Imma.

'Easier said than done. They are wealthy landowners, and often married into the great Saxon families. They are part of the place now. And they fight like hell,' said Wulfhere.

'I think I understand now. So, the Lady Æthelflæd created Cheshire as a strip of Badlands between the Danes of York and the Saxons of Mercia, to allow Mercians to live in peace and without fear.'

'You're not as daft as you look, lad,' said Wulfhere with a grin. 'She made Osric's father Ealdorman to fight, and keep the borders of Mercia safe.'

'And Lord Beornoth, you were a Thegn here?'

Beornoth leant forward as his horse kicked her way up a slope and onto a piece of rocky headland. Below him, the forest sloped down towards the River Medlock, and to the west, in a great sweeping hook of that river, perched Mameceaster. Her walls were red and bright in the rain-soaked gloom.

'I was,' said Beornoth. 'South of here. My forebears lived through all those years of war. Northumbria, Danelaw, Kingdom of York, Mercia and now Cheshire.'

'So that's Mameceaster,' said Imma, bringing his horse alongside Beornoth's. 'It's a stone-built town. How in all bloody hell are we going to get in there?'

'The Rome folk built it. Great men who built like Gods. Not the rotting timber buildings we build now. That's cut stone and brick down there. Old and hard,' said Beornoth wistfully. He remembered walking the walls with his father when he was a boy, the great bear of a man holding his small hand in his huge, calloused paw. His father had told him of the Romans, how Mameceaster had been a great fortress to defend against the savage Britons who ruled these lands before Beornoth's ancestors came across the sea to take this land for themselves. They had restored the fortress in Beornoth's father's time, patched here and there with stone pillaged from other Roman buildings nearby and made strong again.

Mameceaster was a square of high brick walls, with four gates on each side, perched on a broad hill and protected on three sides by the river's meander. The main gate faced to the south, where a cobble path led into a high turreted barbican with two arched gateways below it. From each gate, straight pathways cut the fortress into four sections, with timber-built turrets dotted around the walls to give archers the high ground, and a grand Hall at the centre where the pathways crossed. It was a town and a fortress, and Beornoth saw smoke rising in twisting wisps from dozens of hearth fires within the walls.

'How the bloody hell are we going to get in there?' asked

Wulfhere, echoing Imma's question, and made the sign of the cross against his own blasphemy.

Beornoth shifted his weight in the saddle and shivered as rain dripped underneath his byrnie to trickle beneath his padded leather jerkin and roll down his back. 'Be thankful that we are not here with an army. To attack that place would be a murderous task. We are just three men. We can just ride in, like any other merchant or traveller.'

'Just ride in?' said Wulfhere, his eyebrows raising so high they almost jumped off his face. 'Surely someone will recognise you, and they will capture us? Should we at least wait for dark and climb the walls or something, stay hidden?'

'We don't have time,' said Beornoth. 'Not if you don't want to be excommunicated. We have to get Eawynn out today. So, we go in now. They won't be expecting a few men alone. Osric knows I am a Thegn again, and so I have men. He will expect me to approach with a war-band and seek to talk with him, to barter and beg for Eawynn's life. He hopes I will hand his bastard brother over to him in exchange for her life.' Beornoth did not mention his fear that Eawynn would react as she often did whenever he visited her. He could fight his way in to free her, and she might not want to come with him, she might attack him and they would all be killed. Knowing that fear would not grant Wulfhere or Imma the courage they would need to get out of Mameceaster alive, Beornoth allowed it to eat away at him silently.

'But we will not talk, or barter,' said Wulfhere.

'No. We won't,' said Beornoth, and he nudged his horse with his heels and made his way down the hillside.

Before Beornoth, the walls of Mameceaster reared up, with the turreted gateway as high as four men. The Rome folk knew their business. Mameceaster's high gate would allow the defenders to pepper an attacking force approaching the town with arrows and other missiles from atop the walls, and the crenulations in the tower's top would provide perfect cover for bowmen. They rode slowly towards the town, rain lashing them as it fell mercilessly, pounding into the surrounding earth. It was mid-morning, and the entrance road to Mameceaster was busy with everyday people at their work. Beornoth reined his horse in, and watched as a merchant's cart, heavy with clanking earthenware pots, ambled through one of the two arched gateways, followed by a trio of riders all armed with spears and wearing green wool cloaks. From the right-hand archway people emerged from the town, a shepherd leading out a flock of goats, a woman walking with a yolk across her shoulders with two empty buckets on either side.

'Those riders could be Osric's men,' said Wulfhere. He leaned forward in the saddle with his arms crossed, peering through the sheeting rain at the town.

'A patrol maybe. There are guards at the gate there, look,' said Imma, pointing at two men armed with spears and wearing wide-brimmed straw hats to keep the rain off their faces. The gates were not barred, and the guards did not check the merchant's cart, nor question any of the people entering or leaving the gateways.

'They aren't guards, they are just making sure people only use one gate for entry and one for leaving. They aren't expecting trouble. Wulfhere, you and I will ride in. Imma, you wait here with the spare horses.'

'But Lord, I...' said Imma, throwing his hands into the air.

'You stay here,' growled Beornoth. 'When we come out, if we come out, we will come howling like the wind. We will need those spare horses if we are going to make it back to Branoc's Tree before Byrhtnoth punishes me, and his Bishop excommunicates you.'

Imma sighed and nodded, wiping a hand across his brow to flick away the rainwater. 'Very well. So you are just going to ride in?'

'We are,' said Beornoth. He slid from the back of his mare and climbed up on Ealdorbana. Beornoth loosened his sword in its scabbard at his waist and made sure his seax was secure at his back. Wulfhere was already atop his spare, larger horse. They had not trained her for war like Ealdorbana, but she was still big enough to put the fear of God into any man who faced her broad chest and muscled flanks.

'Leave that,' Beornoth said. Wulfhere had untied his helmet from his saddle. It was a simple bowl helmet, riveted around the rim and with a nasal protector attached to the front.

'I don't fancy dying in this place with a split skull,' said Wulfhere.

'What man of peace rides across country to visit a town wearing a helmet?' asked Beornoth.

'A man expecting a fight,' chuckled Wulfhere, and tied the helmet to his saddle again. 'You know this place, Beo. Where will they keep Eawynn?'

'I knew it well, once. I spent a lot of my childhood here. When I first took up the spear, I learned my trade in Osric's father's warband.' For a moment, listening to the raindrops slapping into the cobbles below, Beornoth remembered himself as a boy, brought here by his father whenever Ealdorman Aethelhelm called for his Thegns. He would run through the streets with the other boys, barefoot and filthy and in search of excitement. He had fought with the local boys. Sometimes he would get a thrashing by bigger, older boys, but more often than not, it was he doling out the beatings. Beornoth and the sons of other Thegns would try to steal an egg, an apple or a loaf of bread from the merchants, which often led to a wild chase through the busy streets. Then,

when he had passed his sixteenth summer, Beornoth's father had
sent him to join Aethelhelm's war-band. Beornoth had served
with the warriors of Cheshire for three years, and they were years
filled with fighting and war. There was always trouble, with the
Danes on the northern borders, landowners in the Kingdom of
York and constant stealers of Saxon cattle. The Vikings from
Ireland and the north raided intermittently, and then on the
Chester side of the shire, the Welsh were always spoiling for a
fight, stealing livestock or brooding over land disputes. Those
were the days when Beornoth learned how to fight. His father's
retainers had taught Beornoth weapon skill since the time he
could stand, but in those years in the war-band, he had learned
how to kill.

'Osric will have Eawynn in his Hall,' said Beornoth, snapping
out of his daze. 'He will want other men to see that he has my
wife. He is an arrogant man, and will think to burnish his reputation by daring me to come to him, but that I do not.'

'Does he not know of the Viking attacks in the south? Should
he not lend us aid?' asked Imma.

'He knows. The King's Ealdormen all send one another
messages, written words with the goings on around Britain. He
won't care, though, he will only bring his men south if the King
orders it,' said Beornoth.

'The King should order it, then. We need warriors,' said
Imma, his rain-soaked face bright with indignation. He saw
Beornoth's scowl and lowered his eyes.

'The King does as he sees fit. He's the King. You are a lowly
spearman. So stay here with the horses, and be ready when we
come hurtling from that gateway,' said Beornoth, and he nudged
Ealdorbana forwards.

He and Wulfhere rode slowly towards the gates, the horses'
hooves clip-clopping loudly on the stones, and the rain beating

down around them. Beornoth leant over and stroked Ealdor-bana's nose and scratched his ears. 'I need you to fight with me today, boy. I need all your strength and bravery,' he whispered into the horse's ear. Ealdorbana snorted and shook his mane, and Beornoth smiled. He knew he could trust the beast to snap his teeth and use his powerful legs to help him in what he must do. Beornoth pulled his cloak around him to cover his mail and weapons, and he kept the smile on his face as he rode past the spearman at the gate.

'Good morning,' said Beornoth, grinning at the guard closest to him. He was a young man, round-faced and glum, his jerkin sopping wet beneath an old leather breastplate. The guard took a step back, surprised at Ealdorbana's size, but he nodded at Beornoth.

'Bloody rain never stops,' the guard grumbled. Beornoth laughed and ducked his head as he rode underneath the ancient Roman archway. Inside the town, the streets were quiet, the rain forcing most people to find shelter. Beornoth let his cloak fall to his back and sat tall in the saddle. The pathway turned from cobble to mud, and rivulets of rainwater ran down either side to merge into a fast-flowing deluge. Ahead, Beornoth saw the great Hall, with a long plume of smoke rising from its smoke hole, its thatch dark and soaked through.

Beornoth drew his sword and let the blade rest at his side, enjoying the weight of it in his hand. People in the road moved out of his way, and he urged Ealdorbana to quicken his pace a little. Beornoth felt his own heart quicken, his breathing becoming deeper. Eawynn was close. Osric was close.. Beornoth blinked at the tiredness in his eyes and rolled his neck to loosen the tight muscles there. Wulfhere caught up and rode beside him.

'When I go into the Hall, you wait outside. Get your axe ready and don't let anyone enter. I won't be in there long,' said

Beornoth. He didn't give Wulfhere time to reply, and rode around
the street and into the square which lay at the intersection of the
four main roadways. Across the square, there was a low span of
timber fencing, with a gap at its centre which led up to the great
Hall. At that gap, four warriors lolled, leaning against their
spears, and holding their shields above their heads, keeping the
rain off. Beornoth was not a good man. He had allowed his grief
and loss to overwhelm him into a pit of drunken self-pity. He
knew that the spiral of ale and despair had laid him low. He also
knew that he was a cruel and brutal man. He had abandoned his
wife to the convent when she needed him. He had let her down
twice, once at the mercy of Viking raiders, and now to the power
of his enemy. Beornoth might not be good, but he knew what he
was. Mounted and armed on Ealdorbana, he was a Lord of War, a
savage killer with skill and experience. Osric's warriors were not
ready for him. They would not expect a lone horseman to attack
them in their own stronghold. Yet here he was, thirsty for
vengeance and to spill the blood of his enemies.

Beornoth grunted and urged Ealdorbana into a canter. The
four men heard his approach and peered out from underneath
their shields. Each of their jaws dropped open, and they were
about to lower their shields when Ealdorbana crashed into them,
sending each man spinning into the rain-soaked, muddy pathway. Beornoth swung his sword backhand, and the blade
slammed into a recovering warrior's neck at the point where it
met his shoulder, and Beornoth sawed the blade to spray blood
bright in the grey morning. Beornoth wrenched on the reins to
bring Ealdorbana around, and the stallion snapped his
monstrous teeth at a warrior who leaned away, only to be stabbed
in the throat as Beornoth lunged across the saddle. The warrior
clutched at the blade and fell away, gurgling as Beornoth ripped it
free.

Beornoth heard himself shouting amidst the chaos. All around him was panic, and the cries of injured and dying men filled the air. A third warrior was scrambling in the mud, dashing towards the Hall, and Beornoth rode after him, leaving the fourth warrior to Wulfhere. The running warrior turned to look desperately over his shoulder and screamed just as Ealdorbana rode him down, the man's bones crunching beneath the power and weight of the war stallion's hooves. The great timber doors of the Hall stood before Beornoth, they were closed with huge black painted hinges, and Beornoth pushed Ealdorbana towards them. The horse reared and kicked his forelegs, beating against the doors, and Beornoth leant forward to cling on to his horse's back. Beornoth felt a blast of hot air wash over him as the doors flung open. He ducked to ride beneath the door frame, and the inside of the Hall erupted in screaming and shouting. Beornoth had come for his wife, and he had come for vengeance.

**24**

Beornoth wheeled Ealdorbana around, and the horse's thunderous steps echoed about the Hall, rising above the screams of the people who ran before him. Merchants, warriors and women scrambled, faces drawn, shocked and terrified of the monstrous black stallion amid their feasting Hall, and the baleful warlord sat atop him, sword dripping blood into the floor rushes. Rainwater steamed from Ealdorbana's flanks and he snorted a spray of mist into the Hall. Beornoth saw a roaring fire at the centre of the long room. They had cleared benches to the sides of the Hall so people could gather around the fire to eat breakfasts of porridge and ale. He saw the raised platform across from the fire, and there he stood, pointing right at Beornoth. Osric. His golden hair and long nose were unmistakable even in the Hall's smoky darkness.

A brave warrior charged at Beornoth, sword drawn and a snarl on his face. Beornoth recognised Egbert, Osric's man, who had ridden south with him a year earlier. He brought Ealdorbana around, and the beast's chest barged Egbert aside, sending him stumbling. Beornoth brought his sword down two-handed, letting go of his reins to add force to the blow. Egbert raised his own blade to parry, but Beornoth was striking from above, and he put all his hate and strength into it. His sword crashed through the parry, and smashed into Egbert's skull with a loud crack, splitting his head open in a spray of gore and dark blood. It was a terrible wound, and Egbert fell away to spill the contents of his head onto the hard packed-earth floor. Women screamed, and men groaned in terror. That blow was enough to send any other attacker fleeing for their lives, and Beornoth rode Ealdorbana across the Hall towards Osric. He snarled at the folk who fell away from him, enjoying the looks of terror and fear on their faces. These were the people who had taken his wife from the safety of her convent. One of these men had struck her and one of the sisters. Beornoth let the hate and anger flow through him. His wrath consumed him. He was here for Eawynn, and for vengeance.

Ealdorbana snorted and stamped his forelegs. Eager for battle, Beornoth dug his heels in and the warhorse charged forwards, his size heightened by the smoke-filled rafters and enclosed space. He was like a monster from legend, a beast from the depths of the earth come to Osric's Hall. The young Ealdorman was shouting at his household warriors to attack and kill Beornoth. But they were not in their byrnies and most were unarmed. Some tried to form a line, brandishing knives. Beornoth let his anger burst forth into a roaring war cry, and charged at them. The line scattered, and one man leapt to the side and tried to slash at Beornoth's leg with his knife, but met the tip of Beornoth's sword with his gullet. That man made a low mewing sound as Beornoth drove the blade down his throat and on into his chest, ripping the sword free in a gout of blood. The women huddled in the dark corners of the room shrieked with horror at the horrific injury.

Beornoth saw Osric's face pale and staring, his eyes wide and hands wringing. He clicked his tongue and the warhorse slammed his forelegs onto the raised platform, the thump of his weight as loud as lightning in a winter storm. Osric tumbled, and all the men on the platform fell back. Beornoth rode Ealdorbana around to the rear and leant down to rest the point of his gore-spattered sword on Osric's chest. The Ealdorman lay in the rushes, and closed his eyes tight, holding up an arm to cover his face.

'Where is she?' Beornoth roared, holding Ealdorbana steady as his legs pounded the earth around Osric. The Ealdorman quivered and shrieked as a great hoof landed a hand's breadth from his head. 'Where is she?' Beornoth repeated, and flicked the sword so its tip made a shallow cut on the cleft of Osric's chin.

'She is in a room at the back of the Hall. She has been treated well,' Osric said, so quiet that his voice was almost a whisper, a shaking arm pointing behind him.

'Fetch Eawynn here, now. Or I'll cut him open like a pig at Yule and dance in his guts,' Beornoth shouted, and he saw two men run into the darkness of an open door in the rear wall. He glanced down at Osric. The young, arrogant Ealdorman was lying prone beneath his blade. A simple flick of his wrist would lay open Osric's throat, and it tempted Beornoth. Osric had taken away the promise of a Heriot and dreamed of laying Beornoth low, he had tried to kill Alfgar, and taken Eawynn prisoner. But to kill an Ealdorman would surely make him an outlaw, ordered to be hunted and killed by the King. For now, he thought, his actions were defensible. Osric, though an Ealdorman and above any law save the word of the King, had kidnapped his wife. Beornoth was taking her back. No man in the land could dispute his right to do that. So he stayed his hand, but let the wide blade hover above

Osric's chest, so close to his face that Osric would smell the iron tang of his own men's blood upon it.

'I would have exchanged her, for Alfgar,' said Osric, his wide eyes darting from the sword, to Ealdorbana's forelegs, and to Beornoth. 'I didn't hurt her.'

'You took her. One of your men struck her and manhandled the good sisters.'

'That was regrettable, I...'

'I want that man. The one who hit her.'

'Alfgar, is he here?'

'Your brother is not here. I am here, and you will give me Lady Eawynn and the man who struck her.'

'I am an Ealdorman,' spat Osric, finding his courage and rearing up on his elbows. 'How dare you enter my Hall like this? I'll have you...' He swallowed his own words as Beornoth allowed Ealdorbana to stomp closer to Osric's head, making him freeze and cover his face again with his hands.

The two men emerged from the rear doorway, between them walked Eawynn. They held her at her elbows and Beornoth's heart sank to see the look of fear stretched across her face as she looked around the Hall, plainly not knowing where she was or what was happening to her.

'Bring her to me,' Beornoth roared. Movement caught the corner of his eye. The warriors in Osric's Hall were banding together, a group of four or five men edged towards him. Beornoth recognised Streonwold as the warrior who led them, the captain of Osric's father's troops.

'Come any closer and I'll gut your Lord where he lies,' Beornoth said, and the men stopped in their tracks.

'You can't just charge in here like this, you will pay for it, Beornoth,' shouted Streonwold.

'Drunken bastard probably doesn't know where he is,' said another.

Beornoth ignored them, but he knew that if they charged him in numbers, they would overwhelm him. The key to getting out of Mameceaster alive was surprise and speed. Beornoth knew Osric would hate him even more now that he had assaulted and shamed him in his own Hall. If he fell into Osric's hands, he would die badly, most likely by long and painful torture, and capture would also surely mean the end for Eawynn.

'Bring her to me,' he said to the two men. They brought Eawynn towards him, and Beornoth saw her eyelids fluttering, and her eyes darting from side to side. She looked up at him, and her lip quivered. He held out his left hand and hauled her up behind him. She cried out as he pulled her, and for a moment Beornoth panicked, worried that she wouldn't willingly climb onto Ealdorbana. If she pulled away, Beornoth would be off balance and it would be easy for Osric's warriors to attack and overwhelm him. He thought she might attack him, clawing and scratching at his face, but he sighed with relief as she grabbed his wrist and hauled herself up, kicking her leg over the saddle behind Beornoth and wrapping her arms tight around him. Beornoth felt her warmth through his byrnie, an old familiar warmth. He must get her to safety. He owed her that.

Beornoth pulled on the reins, and Ealdorbana turned. The sound of his hooves striking the floor and the noise of his snorting filled the Hall and echoed around the smoke-stained rafters. Beornoth dug his heels in and the warhorse sprang forward towards the entrance door. Eawynn gripped him tighter around the waist. The Hall's doors were still open and daylight shone there like an ethereal doorway to another world, ready for him to ride out into the open. But Beornoth snarled, and he turned the horse around again in the centre of the Hall, next to the crackling fire, its glow passing over Beornoth and Ealdorbana to cast monstrous shadows on to the walls.

'I am Beornoth, Thegn. You took my wife, so I came for vengeance.' Ealdorbana stomped and turned in a circle, and Beornoth held his blade aloft. He saw Osric get to his feet and his warriors dashed to support him, helping him stand and brushing the floor rushes from his clothes and hair. He pushed them away petulantly and wiped at the blood on his chin. 'Who is the man who struck my wife?' demanded Beornoth.

'Seize him, call out the warriors. I want his blood and I want his head. Take him!' shrieked Osric, finding his courage now that Beornoth and especially Ealdorbana were out of striking distance, his face twisted into a rictus of hate. Beornoth wanted the man who had struck Eawynn, but he also wanted to live. So, he nudged Ealdorbana forwards and the warhorse rode for the doorway.

Beornoth emerged into the glare of daylight, closing his eyes tight as it stung his vision in sharp contrast to the smoky gloom of Osric's Hall. He forced them open, and saw that the rain had stopped, but ahead, a band of spearmen had Wulfhere surrounded. Osric's men had rallied towards the shouts and screams of the townspeople. Beornoth killing the warriors outside the Hall had roused them, and Beornoth saw more warriors running along the muddy pathways which led to the crossroads at the centre of Mameceaster. Six men jabbed at Wulfhere with spears. He had blocked the fenced entrance to the Hall with the bulk of his horse and was batting away spear blades with his axe. Beornoth could see stripes of blood on Wulfhere's arms and legs where those spears had torn at his flesh.

'Hold tight, and close your eyes,' Beornoth said over his shoulder. He felt Eawynn tighten her hands on his waist, and her faced pressed into his back. He dug his heels into Ealdorbana's

flanks and the warhorse leapt forward. Beornoth gave the horse
his head, and he charged towards the gateway in long, powerful
leaps. Ealdorbana leapt over the fence to land in the mud-slick
path and Beornoth felt the thump of the landing, and Eawynn let
out a small yelp at his back. The horse clawed its hooves in the
mud and came around to face the enemy warriors. They turned
to Beornoth, and Wulfhere shouted a war cry as he buried his axe
blade in the chest of one of his attackers.

Before the warriors could react, Beornoth was amongst them.
Ealdorbana charged two men out of the way, and Beornoth cut at
one man's shoulder with his sword, then swung the blade over his
horse's neck to smash the point into an attacker's face. The tip of
the sword punched through the man's nose and into his skull,
spraying Ealdorbana's flanks with blood. Beornoth ripped the
blade free, and gore spattered the surrounding warriors who
leapt away from Beornoth and Ealdorbana's savagery.

'We have to keep moving, ride for the west gate,' Beornoth
called to Wulfhere.

'I thought you would never come,' said Wulfhere. 'Did you
kill him?'

'The bastard is still alive, and we have Eawynn, so ride!'
Beornoth leant into Ealdorbana's neck and the warhorse
pounded forwards along the pathway. He guided him in a turn to
the west, nudging the horse's flanks with his heels and calling
words of encouragement into his ears. Beornoth knew that the
huge double gateway would likely be closed now that the town's
warriors knew the Ealdorman was under attack, and he also
knew, and hoped, that the smaller gate on the western side of the
fortress would be left unguarded and unlocked. It faced on to the
river and so was rarely closed, to allow the townspeople access to
come and go to the river. Townspeople and warriors alike fled the
pathway before Ealdorbana's unstoppable charge, the warhorse

churning up clods of mud as he thundered through the town. The howls and shouts of Osric and warriors rang in Beornoth's ears as they tried to organise themselves to pursue him.

The small gate came into view, and Beornoth breathed a sigh of relief to see green grass beyond its square opening. He charged through it and out into the grass beyond. A thin verge of turf ran around the hillside on which Mameceaster perched, just wide enough for one rider, and so Beornoth allowed Ealdorbana to reach his full speed as he raced alongside the deep red bricks of the ancient Roman walls. He could hear the pounding of Wulfhere's horse behind him, and he raced out into the open space beyond Mameceaster's main gate. He glanced at the town and saw the gates were still closed. It would take some time for Osric to saddle and mount his men and set off in pursuit. Imma was where Beornoth had left him, and Beornoth nodded as his oathman leapt up onto a horse's back, and set off at a gallop, leading the three spare mounts in a line behind him.

Eawynn was free, and Beornoth and Wulfhere had made it out of Mameceaster alive. Beornoth rode hard, Osric would chase him like a maddened boar, and he had two days to get back to Byrhtnoth or lose his Heriot. He sheathed his blood-smeared sword, and held one hand on the reins and one over Eawynn's warm hand, where they clasped together tightly at his waist.

## 25

Imma wrung water from the cloth and dabbed at the wounds across Wulfhere's arms and torso. The young warrior had collected a helmet full of water from a brook, which babbled noisily as it ran through the forest, and the water in the helmet was now stained pink with blood as he washed Wulfhere's wounds clean.

'Easy, lad, that one's deep,' hissed Wulfhere, sucking in air through the gap in his teeth. He sat stripped to the waist, chewing on a piece of hard baked bread they had brought from Branoc's Tree. Beornoth watched Imma tend to his oathman. Wulfhere had taken some spear cuts in the fight at Mameceaster, but his injuries were not serious. Beornoth looked to the small fire they had allowed themselves to kindle within the deep bowl of an upturned tree, where winter winds had ripped the ancient oak from the earth, leaving a cave of exposed roots and rich, dark soil. The fire crackled, and smoke trailed up into the leafy canopy above them. They had found no dry branches or timber for the fire, so it was green and damp wood which burned in the tree's cavernous bowl, which gave off more smoke than Beornoth would have liked. Had he been alone, he would not have risked the fire, but Eawynn, Imma and Wulfhere needed the warmth and comfort after the risk they had taken that day. There was a danger that Osric's men would see the smoke, but Beornoth thought they had put enough distance between them and their pursuers in an afternoon of hard riding to risk the fire and its restoring warmth. Imma and Wulfhere had ridden hard for two days, changing horses to keep them fresh and allow them to maintain a hard pace, and they had stood with Beornoth whilst he attacked Mameceaster, which was at best a risky plan. They were good men, brave and determined, who had stuck hard to their oaths and done what most men would not believe possible. They had risked death, and pushed hard to make the long journey north in two days. So, they had earned a fire and some warmth before the journey continued at first light.

'Your wounds are all clean. You can put your jerkin back on now,' said Imma. 'You are lucky one of those spears didn't kill you.'

'For a moment back there, I thought I must die. That they would overwhelm me. All I could do was try to keep the spear points at bay with my axe,' said Wulfhere, and he pulled on his jerkin slowly, careful not to let the padded leather rub too hard against his wounds. He grinned over at Beornoth. 'I said a last prayer to God, and then you burst through the doors, Beo, and I knew we would live.'

'It wasn't God kept us alive. It was iron. My sword and your axe.' Beornoth laid his hand on the hilt of his sword where it lay next to him, unbuckled from his belt and resting on the leaf mulch of the forest floor. 'Now, we have two days to get back to Branoc's Tree and then to Byrhtnoth, or he will take everything from us. My Heriot, my ancestral honour, and your God. We have cheated death, and Eawynn is safe. We must push hard and get to

Essex before the week is up. When I can, I will reward you both with silver and gold. Men will talk of the deeds you accomplished this day. They will tell their children at firesides of brave Wulfhere and Imma, the warriors who rode to the north, faster than a man can travel, to storm a Roman fortress.' Beornoth struggled with the words. Kindness and praise did not come easy to him, but the words were true and the men needed to hear them. Beornoth would not forget what they had risked for him.

Eawynn sat to Beornoth's left. She had her knees pulled tight up to her chest, and her arms folded tightly around them. Eawynn rocked gently and stared wide-eyed into the dancing flickers of red and orange as the fire crackled and spat, the glow casting strange shadows on the planes of her face and neck. She looked thin and pale.. The terrible scar across her throat seemed darker in the firelight, and her dark eyes were deep black pools.

'Eawynn, I am so sorry. My love,' he whispered. He had longed to say those words for so long. In the depths of drunken despair, at his lowest moments, those were the words that echoed around in his mind, torturing him. Beornoth's past haunted him. That he was not there when the Vikings came to their home. He had been away fighting for his Ealdorman, following orders. But his first duty should have been to protect his family. He was sorry. Guilt and sadness had ripped him apart for years, tearing at his mind like the talons of a devil. He should have been there when the Vikings came, and he would never forgive himself. She didn't take her eyes from the fire, and he didn't think his words had penetrated the darkness in her head. At least she was safe now. Beornoth would get her back to Branoc's Tree, and Aethelberga would look after her, and he would be close to her. She would never be in danger again. He would make sure of that.

Imma cut a chunk of cheese in two with his knife and threw it across the fire. Beornoth caught it and ripped a chunk from it. He held it out to Eawynn, but she did not acknowledge him.

'You must eat. The ride will be hard. You will need strength,' he said, but she just maintained her fixed stare on the flickering flames. He withdrew his hand and took a bite himself.

'Osric will hate you even more now, Lord,' said Imma.

'An Ealdorman for an enemy is a dangerous thing. He can do as he pleases. He could strike you down without fear of retribution from any Lord,' agreed Wulfhere.

'He was my enemy, anyway. I insulted him. He didn't like it. I took his half-brother in, trained him to be a warrior. Osric didn't like that either. He wants me dead, and he wants Alfgar dead,' said Beornoth. 'I have killed his men and struck at his home. He can come for me if he chooses, but I dare say I am not an easy man to kill.'

Imma and Wulfhere laughed at that, and they tucked into the food. Imma and Wulfhere talked together, reliving the events of the day, talking of the fear in their hearts as they raced away from Mameceaster knowing the enemy would be on their heels. Beornoth left them to their talk, and ate his food quietly, the warmth of the fire welcome on his face.

'You came for me.' It was only a murmur, a whisper of a voice almost buried beneath the sounds of the forest and the fire. It was Eawynn. Beornoth's breath caught in his chest and he turned to look at her. She still stared into the fire. 'You came for me, Beo,' she said again.

'A messenger came to me. Told me they had taken you. I went to the sisters, and they told me Osric had taken you, and his men had hurt you. Eawynn...' Beornoth wanted to say more, but the words died in his throat. He was afraid of her. He had been afraid of her since the Vikings came to their home on that fateful day. Afraid of what she thought of him, of what she might say to him, afraid because she was the only woman he had ever loved, and he had failed her.

'They couldn't hurt me, I am beyond that,' she turned to look at him. 'But you came for me.'

'I did. But I should have come for you sooner. I am a Thegn again now, with a Heriot and lands. I will take you there. You will be safe.'

'You were a Thegn before, and we were not safe.'

'No, we were not.'

'Nowhere is safe, not in this world. Our girls, Beo. So small. They wait for me in Heaven.' A tear rolled down her cheek, a solitary bead of water running down the curves of her face and around her chin, where it ran down across her scar. The jagged line of raised white flesh the Vikings had left as their mark on her forever. They had cut her throat, but not deep enough to sever the windpipe. She had survived, to become trapped in a living hell inside her own head ever since.

'They were the lights of my life, and I miss them every hour of every day,' said Beornoth. He handed Eawynn a piece of bread, and she took it. She said no more, but she ate and drank, which encouraged Beornoth. He wanted to go to her, hold her in his arms and watch her fall asleep. But he just watched her, and remembered when they had been happy and in love, so long ago. Before the cruelty of the world had torn their lives apart.

## 26

The army of the East Saxons had broken camp by the time Beornoth and his men returned to River's Bend. What had once been a green, lush field beside a fast-flowing river was now a brown, filthy scar on the landscape. Like some great dragon from the stories of old had nested there and left it torn and riven with his fire and claws. Beornoth sat astride Ealdorbana at the top of a ridge, looking down upon the valley, and he saw Byrhtnoth and his warriors mounted and at the head of a long line of warriors marching upstream, away from the coast.

'They are marching away from the enemy,' said Alfgar, shaking his head. Beornoth had reached Branoc's Tree the previous day, and was now ready to rejoin the army within the deadline imposed on him by Byrhtnoth. Aethelberga had welcomed Eawynn into the Hall, and Beornoth's wife seemed content to be somewhere where she was welcome, and could roam the grounds as she wished. She had not spoken to Beornoth again on the hard ride south, but she had also shown no signs of her old madness and fury. He had said goodbye to her before he left, and she had just stared at him. She did not seem afraid, or angry, so he had left her there in Aethelberga's care.

'Byrhtnoth must have news,' said Beornoth. 'Skarde must be on the march, or the Vikings have struck elsewhere. I'll find out what's occurred when I let the Ealdorman know that we have returned.'

'There might have been a battle already, Lord,' said Wulfhere.

'No,' replied Beornoth. 'We would have run into the survivors by now, fleeing across the countryside. There has been no battle yet.'

'Do you think he will attack?' said Alfgar.

'Who, Skarde?' said Wulfhere.

'My brother. Do you think he will attack Branoc's Tree? Looking for me, and for retribution on you, Lord.'

'There will be a reckoning, sooner or later, with Osric,' said Beornoth. 'He won't come now. If he brings a force of men here to Essex, and attacks Byrhtnoth's lands, it would be bad enough, but to do it whilst the Vikings are here and not to join his men to Byrhtnoth's would be a serious matter. A matter for the King. So, Osric will wait until this war with the Vikings is over, then he will come.' He had thought of little else since leaving the north. Beornoth too had been concerned that Osric would attack his lands in Essex in a furious rage at the insult Beornoth had committed in his Hall. But he was sure the young Ealdorman would wait until the timing was better. Nevertheless, he would come. Such a display of violence and insolence against an Ealdorman in his own Hall could not go unpunished.

They rode down the hillside and alongside the marching column until Beornoth reached the riders at its head. Byrhtnoth rode there on his fine warhorse, flanked by his Bishop and by Erkenwald. The Ealdorman turned in the saddle, alerted to Beornoth's approach by one of his captains.

'Ah, Beornoth. So good of you to come back to join us,' said Byrhtnoth with exaggerated fondness. 'We go to press the heathen, to fight them on open ground.'

'I am back, Lord. Just as you requested,' said Beornoth.

'You have resolved your family problems?'

'I have, my Lord. I am here now to fulfil my oath and my Heriot's obligation.'

'You are here to kill Vikings, Beo. We will need your sword. There will be a glorious battle, reputations to be made, and the poets will sing of our deeds,' said Byrhtnoth. Erkenwald caught Beornoth's eye, and the warrior raised his eyes to the heavens.

'Have the Vikings left their beach camp, Lord?' asked Beornoth.

'They have struck inland, north of here. We go to meet them.'

'Have they taken their ships?' asked Beornoth. If the warships remained moored in the bay, then it was only a raid up the coast, but if the ships had gone, then the Viking army was on the move, looking for another place to strike and punish the Saxons for the missed opportunity of attacking them when their camp was under construction.

'They have sailed away, abandoned their camp. We will seek them out,' said the Ealdorman.

Beornoth and his men fell back to find the fyrd men from his lands and ride alongside them in the marching line.

'Do you think there will be a battle, Lord?' asked Alfgar.

'There must be. Byrhtnoth wants it. He doesn't want to strike at them like they strike at us. He craves the glory of a pitched battle,' said Beornoth.

'Won't the Vikings just keep avoiding us, raiding and getting rich off our lands?'

'I would, were I Skarde. But his task here is to feel out the land for a full-scale assault by his leader, this Olaf Tryggvason. So, maybe we can lure Skarde into a fight. If he weakens us now, it makes it easier for Olaf should he wish to land the rest of his army on the shores of Essex.'

'Let's hope the bastards just sail away,' said Alfgar.

They rode in silence for a time, marching across the river at a shallow ford where the waters babbled across shining stones before striking north. Beornoth listened as the men of Branoc's Tree chatted to his household troops. News of the families at Branoc's Tree were exchanged, and he heard more than one tale told of the attack of Mameceaster.

'Out with it, lad,' Beornoth said, after the feeling of Alfgar's eyes on him became annoying.

'Osric, Lord,' he said, mumbling and stuttering the words.

'Your brother, the Ealdorman. Yes?'

'Does he really want me dead?'

'He does, you alive is a threat to him. He will come for you again.'

'Did you really ride into his Hall and kill his men?'

'I did.'

'Could you have killed him?'

'I could.'

'Surely he will complain to our Ealdorman, to Byrhtnoth, of your actions, and seek justice?'

'He might,' allowed Beornoth. 'But first he would need to explain why he took my wife from a house of God and assaulted the sisters there. He won't want to do that. The King might hear of it, and the King is a pious and godly man.'

Alfgar pressed him no more on the matter, and Beornoth hoped that what he said was true. Osric could approach Byrhtnoth for justice, and Beornoth could see how appalling it would sound, the tale of him riding into Osric's Hall, killing his warriors and humiliating the Ealdorman. The only way in Beornoth's power to protect himself from that possibility, and the retribution it would bring, was to raise his favour in Byrhtnoth's eyes. To make himself too important to give up to Osric. The only way Beornoth could see to make that possible was to come up with a way to lure Skarde out to fight. To give Byrhtnoth what he wanted, and bring Skarde to fight a battle. Then, Beornoth would make sure he fought in the front rank, as he always did, but where Byrhtnoth could see him. He must burnish his worth into Byrhtnoth's mind like a cattle brand. Beornoth could fulfil his oath to Osmod, and make himself indispensable to Byrhtnoth. He must kill Skarde where the Ealdorman could see him, and throw the Viking invaders back into the steel-grey sea.

## 27

Beornoth stood on a patch of sodden earth, looking out across a gaping coastal estuary. He had come through a sprawling maze of rivulets and canals carved into the land by the relentless rise and fall of the tide down the ages, to look across the bay at the most eastern point in Saxon Britain. The sky rang with the calls of cormorants and gulls rising above the wind's bluster and the crashing of the sea. The birds glided on the breeze, suspended in the sky as though daubed on a war banner. In every direction, all Beornoth could see were mudflats and salt marshes, no hills or valleys anywhere on the horizon. It was a wide, flat land, treacherous and pitted with secret paths and waterways. Beornoth stared at an island across the estuary. The island lay at the mouth of the River Blackwater and was low and broad; a golden beach faced south towards Beornoth, topped by dark heather. A clutch of Viking drakkar warships sat on the sea-facing end of the beach, drawn up so their beast heads snarled landwards, like great sea beasts crawling from the deep in search of prey. Skarde had abandoned his beach camp and sailed his warships north to occupy the island, known as Mersea Island. The Saxons had missed a chance to attack the Norsemen whilst they secured their raiding position on the beach, and now Skarde had moved his force to Mersea Island, protected from a landward attack by the sea on all sides, and in a perfect location from which to pour his savage warriors upriver and into the heart of Essex.

'There's a church on the island,' grumbled the fisherman. He was a bent-backed, leather-faced man with wisps of white hair blowing from his balding head. He had poled Beornoth, Wulfhere and Imma through the mudflat channels aboard a narrow canoe to give them a good view of the island from the south.

'Well, I hold little hope for the poor holy men,' said Wulfhere, making the sign of the cross.

The island had a fishing village on its western side, and during the journey around the complex system of channels and river around the flats, the fisherman had explained that there was once a salt farm on the island, and it was now rich in oysters and other shellfish prized by the wealthy people of Essex. The fisherman himself made his living by setting withies around the channels, and using his canoe to retrieve his catch to feed his family.

'They look safe on the island, not much chance of a battle with no ships of our own,' grumbled Imma.

'Why is Byrhtnoth so hungry for a bloody battle? We had one already, last year. It was terrible,' said Wulfhere.

'He wants to fight the Vikings in a pitched battle. The Ealdorman wants to prove himself as a war leader and kill the Vikings,' said Beornoth. He understood the Ealdorman's reasons. War was all about reputation and ambition. That was what drove Skarde and his men to attack the Saxon coast, and it was what drove Byrhtnoth to seek his battle. Reputation would increase his standing with the King, giving him more influence and power.

'He is already well known as a great war leader,' said Wulfhere.

'How else should we fight the Vikings?' said Beornoth, pointing across the estuary at the three warships moored on the east side of the island. 'They are too fast. They can sail and strike anywhere. Without the King's fleet, we can only try to keep up with them, riding along the coastline. But they would outrun us and be free to raid wherever they please. The best hope Byrhtnoth has is to coax Skarde to fight, and kill enough of them to send the bastards back to their homelands. With too few men, they can't continue their raids and will be gone. For this summer, at least.'

'Let's hope we can get them to fight, then,' said Imma, and he threw a stone into the murky waters. 'I still don't see how we can attack that island, though.'

The fisherman coughed and wheezed. Beornoth stared at him and was about to aid the man as he seemed like he was choking, before he realised the old man was actually laughing. The fisherman pointed a gnarled finger towards the western side of the island, and then up at the sky.

'What's so funny?' asked Wulfhere.

'The strood,' said the man, and he bent over to rest his hands on his knees because he was laughing so hard.

'What is he talking about?' Wulfhere said to Imma. Beornoth and Wulfhere were from the north, and Imma was a man of the East Saxons. The shires and tithings of the Saxon kingdoms were a patchwork of dialects and accents, but Imma and the fisherman were both men of Essex.

'I don't know.' Imma shrugged.

'The strood,' repeated the fisherman. His laugh had turned into a wracking cough, and he hauled up a mouthful of phlegm, which he spat into the water. Imma grimaced, and Beornoth shook his head. 'It's the full moon. When the moon is full there is an island, but as the moon wanes, it's not an island any more. Do you follow?' The little fisherman hopped from scrawny leg to the other and rubbed his hands together.

'You mean when the tide goes out?' asked Beornoth.

The fisherman nodded and grinned to reveal two browned teeth jutting from his gums at odd angles. 'Yes, the tide. When the moon wanes, you can walk there. It's only underwater now because the tide's in.'

'So, when the tide goes out, we could walk on to the island?' said Beornoth.

'Yes,' said the fisherman, and he broke out into another fit of laughter.

## 28

'Are you sure about this?' said Byrhtnoth later that night. He grimaced and sighed, his breath steaming out of his mouth in the frosty night air. Beornoth rode beside the Ealdorman at the head of a long column as they marched their way across the flat marshlands on Essex's east coast.

'I'm sure,' replied Beornoth.

'God will guide us,' piped up the Bishop over Beornoth's shoulder.

'We can march over to the island?' asked Byrhtnoth, which Beornoth was sure was the fifth time the Ealdorman had asked him.

'As the sun comes up, Lord, the tide will go out. When it does, we can march to the island and form our shield wall on the beach. We will march as close to where they have moored their ships as possible. They will have no choice but to face us.'

Byrhtnoth nodded and pursed his lips. Beornoth knew he wasn't on the Ealdorman's good side since he had left the army to make the journey north. But he was sure now that he had found a way to get himself back in his Lord's good graces. The fisherman had told Beornoth the pattern of the tide's rise and fall over the next day as the full moon waned. So Beornoth knew that during the night was high tide, and then after morning prayers the waters would be low enough for the army to cross. The Vikings would wake to find a Saxon force on the island, lined up and ready to fight, and they could not escape to their ships and avoid that confrontation. Also, Beornoth knew Skarde from his time in the Viking camp and, being a man of honour, Beornoth doubted the Viking leader would refuse battle if they laid it out before him. They were not so different, Byrhtnoth and Skarde. Both outstanding leaders, warriors and men of monstrous pride.

To ride and march at night was a dangerous undertaking, and no commander would choose to do so unless there was no other choice. Horses could lose their footing and become lame. Stragglers or units carrying heavy baggage could become lost and detached from the main force. Tonight, however, the shining moon provided enough light for the warriors and fyrd men of Essex to march under its eerie half-light, across the salt flats and marshland, and approach Mersea Island in the deepest of night. Some men grumbled the spirits would come for them during the full moon, that the shadow walkers or night goblins would emerge from the mudflats and drag them down into the deep. These were old stories, tales told by the people of Britain since the time before the Romans came. Beornoth didn't pay heed to such tales, just as he didn't trust in God any more. But he did not deny the men their grumbling, better to worry about monsters and ghouls, than worry about the ferocious Vikings they would face in the morning, in that terrible shield wall clash where men die, and the man opposite you will do all he can to push his axe or spear blade into your face, neck, belly or groin. Many of the men around Beornoth would die tomorrow, or suffer the crippling wound, that awful wound that would reduce any man instantly to a life of beggary and dependence. A lost leg or arm renders a warrior useless, and with no other skills to offer, he becomes reliant on his Lord for food and shelter for the rest of his days. Such thoughts were enough to make a man fearful, to make him panic at the thought of the fearsome shield wall. So, let them have their shadow walkers, better that than to face the reality of the horror of what awaited them at sun up.

Erkenwald called a halt to the march within sight of the sea, and across the estuary the island loomed like a dark silhouette against the horizon, like the curved back of a magnificent beast sleeping in the deep. Beornoth could feel the sour mood growing across the army. Their grumbling and chatter was understandable. They were tired from the night march and their feet were cold and wet from tramping through the bog, and they were anxious about the fight to come.

'The men should try to sleep for a few hours, so should you. No fires, though,' Beornoth said to Alfgar and Wulfhere. Wulfhere nodded and rode back down the column to where the men of Branoc's Tree marched. Alfgar stayed with Beornoth, staring out across the bay.

'Do you think they will fight, Lord?' asked Alfgar.

'They will have no choice,' replied Beornoth.

'Do we have more men?' said Byrhtnoth's Bishop. Beornoth turned to see that he and the Ealdorman were close.

'We have more men, but they have more warriors. Every man aboard those dragon ships is a warrior. That's his life, his profession and how he feeds his family and people. Like you and I, like Byrhtnoth and his warriors, and the other Thegns and their household troops. When I was in Skarde's camp, I thought they had somewhere between one hundred and fifty and two hundred men. Most of our men are from the fyrd, farmers, potters, millers and the like. We are the warriors: Alfgar, my men, Erkenwald's men, Byrhtnoth's men. We are the ones who must fight at the front. We are the ones who must break the Viking line.'

'What if they break our line?' asked Alfgar.

'If they get amongst the fyrd?' said Beornoth. 'Then there will be a great slaughter, and the Vikings will be free to sail up the river to raid as they please. If they break us tomorrow, many of our people, our women and children, will die or become sold into slavery. That is what we fight for, to protect the people, to use our blades and our skill to fight for those who cannot fight for themselves.'

'Do we have to kill them all?'

'No. I have never fought a battle where all the losing side were killed.' Beornoth saw Alfgar blow out a sigh of relief, his question as relevant for a Saxon defeat as it was for the Vikings. 'We will need to kill enough for them to break, to run. When that happens, they will make for their ships, if they can. Their ships are their lifeblood, and they will fear that we will capture their drakkars and we will strand them here to die.'

'You have fought many battles, Lord?'

'Many,' Beornoth replied. 'Too many.' Visions of past slaughters flashed through his head, making his stomach twist at the memories of bloody wounds and screaming warriors.

'What is it like?'

'You have fought in the shield wall before at River's Bend. Keep your shield up, protect the man to your left. Strike with your spear when you can, but your principal task is to keep your shield up.' Beornoth didn't tell Alfgar the rest. The blood, the screams, the pain and the horror. He would discover that for himself, for at daybreak tomorrow there would be a battle, and many men would die.

'Will they not have sentries on the other side, watching the beaches and such?' said the Bishop, wringing his hands and licking at his thin lips. The leaders of the Saxon force stood on an outcrop of marshland, topped by weeds and grass. They waited at the point where the causeway would appear from beneath the water, and allow them passage on to Mersea Island. The sun was not yet up, but a sickly yellow glow across the sea promised its coming, pushing back the night's darkness.

'Maybe we should send swimmers across, to kill the sentries before they shout a warning and rouse the Vikings?' said a broad-shouldered Thegn.

'It doesn't matter if their sentries see us, I want them to come out and fight,' said Byrhtnoth. The Ealdorman was grim-faced and looked huge in his byrnie and war helm. It was a fine helmet burnished to a shine, with cheek pieces, a carved horse's head nasal protector, and at its crest was a wrought-iron boar. The Vikings would know him for a wealthy man, a Lord of War. Their champions, and ambitious men who hungered for reputation and glory, would be drawn to him on the field. To kill such a man and take his armour and weapons would make a warrior rich and famous for life. Byrhtnoth welcomed that. He was a great lover of battle himself, and Beornoth saw no fear on the Ealdorman's face or in his hard eyes. 'If Beornoth is right, and we can get across, then it will be too late for them. There will be a fight whether or not their sentries see us.'

'Look,' said Erkenwald, and he pointed down at the rippling water. A rock had appeared beneath the brown, lapping water, and another further ahead. 'The road appears.'

There was a murmur across the gathered leaders. Beornoth ground his teeth. The fisherman had been right. Soon they could make the crossing, and soon he could kill. Beornoth touched his smooth locket underneath his byrnie. He thought of his dead daughters, and Beornoth wanted to kill Vikings. His hate and fury against the northern raiders would never be sated. He wanted to cut them, stab them and hurt them, to punch them and kill them for what they had taken from him. Beornoth drew his sword and took a step forward. He leaned out and plunged the tip of his blade into the water, and sure enough, he hit a hard surface. He turned and nodded to Byrhtnoth. The huddled warriors peered down at the water, faces long and mouths open, as though it was magic or wizardry Beornoth conjured with his sword.

Byrhtnoth stared at him, his powerful jaw fixed and expectant, and Beornoth knew he had to restore the Ealdorman's faith in him. He must remind the Ealdorman why he had granted him the Heriot, and why he had made Beornoth a Thegn of the East Saxons. He stepped forward, and his boot plunged into the icy seawater, the cold of it making his toes curl and his shoulders shiver. The water only came up to his ankle. He held his breath and took another step. Again, his boot sank into the water but found hard stone at ankle depth. He realised he had been holding his breath, so Beornoth breathed out slowly. He took another step. If he fell into the water, or if the fisherman was wrong and there was no causeway ready to appear with the ebbing tide, then Beornoth would be dragged to the bottom of the estuary. His heavy mail byrnie, his helmet and weapons would drag him down like a stone to the bottom of the sea where his lungs would fill with cold, salty seawater and he would drown. Beornoth flexed his hand on the leather-twisted sword hilt in his hand and held the blade aloft. He pointed it towards Mersea Island and strode forwards, watching the sea in front of him, trying to make out where rocks were poking through the surface of the lapping tide. He marched for sixty paces, and his boot crunched on the tiny shale pebbles of the island's beach. Beornoth looked behind him, and Byrhtnoth led the rest of the army across the Strood causeway – the name given to this strip of land which appeared at low tide. The Ealdorman came to stand with Beornoth and clapped him on the back.

'By God's grace, you were right, Beo. Now, let's see if we can't get these cursed heathen Vikings to fight,' growled Byrhtnoth.

## 29

Beornoth watched as four Viking sentries ran frantically up the beach, their shapes dark silhouettes, and their arms waving above their heads. They shouted and whistled, trying desperately to wake their shipmates, who slept peacefully, believing themselves safe from attack on an island, safe from the Saxons whose fleet was with their King, far away. Beornoth marched up the beach with Byrhtnoth, towards where the Viking warships were moored, black and grey shadows against the wan morning light.

Soon the Vikings would come pouring over the beach, armed and ready to kill. But they would be groggy from sleep, surprised by the Saxons on Mersea Island's beach. Beornoth allowed himself a smile. War was not just a weapon of skill and strength; it was also cunning and trickery. He smiled because there cannot be any better feeling than surprising an enemy who wants to kill you, who uses his own cunning to strike where you are weakest, but then is outfoxed himself in return. The Vikings thought they could strike inland, without opposition, deep along the wide River Blackwater and raid Saxon towns and villages, but now they had woken to find a broiling force of Saxon killers on their island haven, here to kill them. Beornoth was ready. He held the hilt of his sword where it rested in his scabbard, the grip strong and comforting. He was ready to kill and fulfil his oath to Osmod, and to remind Ealdorman Byrhtnoth of his value as a Thegn.

'There is as good a place as any,' said Byrhtnoth, pointing with his spear to a long spot on the beach where shale gave way to dark sand. 'Better footing. They will have the hill, such as it is, but we have our families and our people at our backs.'

Sunlight crept through the strange other-worldly gloom of the full moon's darkness, and now Beornoth could make out the Viking's drakkar ships clearly where they bobbed on the tide. He also saw that the beach gave way to long spiky grass along a shallow hill, which then led on to the island's interior. On the crest of that hill, which was no taller than a man, as the Vikings mustered he could see heads bobbing and spear points wavering, like a hedgehog waking from its slumber. The Saxons were between the Viking force and their precious ships, and there was no way out for the Norsemen other than to fight. He marched with Byrhtnoth to the wide strip of clear beach between long pockets of shale. Beornoth twisted his feet in the sand and the grip was good. It was a fine place to stand, they would make this the front rank, and he would fight at the front, where the dangerous men, the lovers of battle in the Viking ranks, would come to kill him. Soon, they would bring their fearsome axes, bright spears and sharp swords to cut and slash at him, to cut his throat, or open his guts and put him into the ground forever. They must be stopped, this heathen horde of violent Norsemen. If the Vikings won this battle, then the East Saxon people would suffer the horrors of war. The Vikings would raid and burn, kill and enslave the people without opposition.

The Saxon warriors formed ranks, with Byrhtnoth and Beornoth standing at the centre of the front line. The men were quiet, Beornoth could hear their feet crunching in the shale, and their clank of shields and spears as they crossed to the sand and made ready, lining up and finding their place to stand. They would stand with friends, men from neighbouring farms, or warriors from the same hearth-troop, and they would bleed and die to protect their families from the Viking invaders.

'We will fight together today, Beo,' said Byrhtnoth. He stuck his spear into the sand before him and took his shield from a man behind him. 'If you fight like you did at River's Bend, then we can't lose.'

'I seem to remember you fought hard yourself that day, Lord,' said Beornoth, recalling how Byrhtnoth had fought in single combat, and spurred his men on to greater feats of bravery.

Imma handed Beornoth his shield, and he passed his hand through the leather loop and gripped the wooden handle which spanned the bowl behind the shield's boss. Beornoth sheathed his sword and took a spear from Imma. It was the long-hafted æsc spear of the front rankers, its shaft was of smooth ash wood, and its blade was wide, forged into the shape of a leaf. The first two ranks of Byrhtnoth's shield wall held with the long spears. Imma carried the shorter, thinner atgir spear of the rear rankers: throwing spears which they would launch over the heads of the warriors who toiled in the front lines.

'Here they come,' growled Byrhtnoth, pointing to the beach-head with the blade of his spear. 'Form ranks,' he shouted, and they echoed the order up and down the Saxon lines. Warriors shuffled into position, shields banging on iron weapons, and a hum of anticipation drowned out the sounds of the gulls and the waves lapping gently behind them. The men of Byrhtnoth's household warriors tried to barge into the line between Beornoth and Byrhtnoth, but Beornoth held his place. He must fight well in full sight of the Ealdorman to ensure his Lord saw he was worthy of his Heriot. Beornoth's plan had worked so far. The Saxon army had marched across the strood and now the Vikings poured over the low sand dunes, and their fate would be determined by the battle Byrhtnoth craved.

'Looks like numbers are even,' said Wulfhere, pushing himself into place on Beornoth's right. Wulfhere too held the long æsc spear, and the front line now spanned twenty warriors wide.

'We'll have to break them. Sea behind us, and no room to fall back. If we break, we must run for the strood, which won't be pretty,' said Beornoth.

'So, we won't break, then,' grinned Wulfhere. 'Alfgar is two ranks behind us, with Imma and the others.'

The Vikings were now thick on the dune's grassy top, and they streamed on to the sand ahead of the Saxon army. A clutch of warriors forced their way through the centre and marched across the sands to stand across from Beornoth and Byrhtnoth.

'Skarde,' said Beornoth. The flaxen-haired Viking leader stood at the centre of his men, armed with spear and shield.

'I remember him, from River's Bend,' said Byrhtnoth. 'Looks like he wants to talk.'

'Those men are his captains. I met them when I was a captive in their camp. Einar Ravenhair, Sigurd Bearskin, Ulfketil, and the little one is a holy man named Rolfr.'

'Holy man? Pagan scum, more like,' Byrhtnoth spat into the sand. 'What names they give themselves, these Northmen. I come to fight, not to talk. Tell them as such, Beo, you speak their language.'

'I see you have brought some friends to visit us,' shouted Skarde in Norse, his strong voice travelling across the sands. Both Saxon and Viking hordes went silent at his words, the quiet sweeping across both forces as though a great hand had passed over the island to hush them. 'Beornoth, you look well. We don't need to fight today. Many good men will die. Just pay us silver and gold, and we will sail away.' The Viking Jarl's hatchet face creased into a smile; his wide slash of a mouth filled with white teeth in his golden beard.

'My Lord Byrhtnoth has not come here to talk or barter. He comes to kill you, Skarde,' Beornoth replied.

'Brave words,' said Skarde. 'Your men look weak. Most are not warriors, I think. If we fight, you will all die today.'

'So we die. But I will seek you on the field, Skarde,' said Beornoth. Skarde laughed and raised his spear to salute Beornoth. The Viking leaders turned and marched to their men, and organised their shield wall.

'What did the bastard say?' said Byrhtnoth.

'He asked us to pay him off, and that if he did, he would sail away.'

'I don't pay thieves and murderers. We fight.'

'Which is what I told him, Lord. I told him we have come to kill, and that I will look for him on the field.'

Byrhtnoth chuckled. 'Then God help him. Bishop, say your blessing, and then get yourself to safety. Death is coming to this beach.'

The Bishop shouldered his way through the warriors and came to stand before Byrhtnoth. He made the sign of the cross and Byrhtnoth kneeled. The whole Saxon army followed his example and knelt on the damp sand. Beornoth sighed and also dropped to one knee. The Bishop placed a hand on Byrhtnoth's helmet and said a prayer. Then he raised his crosier and shouted the word of God, so that all the Saxons could hear.

'To kill a heathen is not a sin! It is the pathway to Heaven. God wills it, he wills you to bring vengeance and justice to the heathen defilers!' the Bishop shouted, spittle flying from his mouth and his face as red as a robin's breast.

'Praise be to God!' the Saxons said as one, and they rose as one. The Bishop scuttled away, likely to hide at the rear, as far away from the heathens as possible. Beornoth had knelt with the other men, but he did not seek the protection of God, nor did he pray to him for victory. He trusted in his spear and his sword, and his hate. Beornoth rested his shield against his shoulder and reached behind his byrnie to touch his smooth timber locket. He closed his eyes and conjured the image of his daughters running and laughing in the sun. Then he allowed himself to remember their little burned bodies, twisted and shrunken in the ashen remnants of his Hall. He remembered Eawynn, throat cut and raped in the ashes. Beornoth tucked the locket back safely behind his mail and his padded leather jerkin. He took deep breaths, the fire of vengeance and fury kindling in the pit of his stomach like a blacksmith's forge starting up for the day. His chest heaved and his muscles tensed.

Beornoth raised his spear to the sky. 'Death to the heathens, death to the Vikings, kill them all!' he shouted, and the warriors behind him let out a roar, a hate-filled murderous sound which made Beornoth's heart stir. Byrhtnoth strode out before the army and turned to face his men. A hush swept over the lines again.

'Men. We are here to fight our enemy, to fulfil our duty as warriors and men of the fyrd. But more than that, we are here to protect our people. Our children and our wives, the ones who cannot defend themselves. Those men across the sands want to take everything from you. On this beach, they want to rip your life from your chest. They have sailed from their cold homes in the north to come here, to our home. They want to kill you, burn your home, take your wife and enslave your children. Then, they want to bring their own people here to live on your land. So fight hard today, kill your enemy. There will never be a more important fight, men. Are you ready to fight for your homes?' Byrhtnoth spoke to the entire army, striding up and down the line. At his last question, the men exploded, red-faced and roaring. They banged their spears on their shields in unison, and so the war music had begun. Beornoth felt it, he felt the rage of the warriors around him coursing through his veins, and the battle-drum sound of weapon on shield stirred them all to the fight.

'Shield wall!' Byrhtnoth roared, and he fell in beside Beornoth. They overlapped their shields, as did Wulfhere on his right. The Saxon army raised their shields to present one long, solid wall of wood and iron to the enemy. 'Spears!' shouted Byrhtnoth. Beornoth and the rest of the front two ranks slid their long spears across the top of their shields to make a line of shining spear points, sharp and glinting in the morning sun.

Across from the Saxons, the Viking lines parted. Rolfr ran through their centre and capered in front of the enemy line, dancing and thrusting his hands towards the Saxons. Sigurd Bearskin followed him, dragging a flailing figure behind him. The Saxon battle cries dimmed to a sigh of despair, as they realised that the man Sigurd dragged along by the hair around his tonsure was a Saxon priest. The Viking hauled the priest to his feet and turned him to face the Saxons. Rolfr continued his hopping dance and approached the shaking priest. The holy man whipped a dagger from his sleeve and sliced open the priest's throat, sending a spurt of bright blood to splash on the brown-yellow sand. The Saxon lines went quiet. Sigurd held the priest upright as Rolfr brought forth a bowl and used it to collect the lifeblood pumping from the priest's cut throat. Sigurd then let the priest fall, and Rolfr daubed the fresh blood across Sigurd's bare chest, and now it was the Vikings' turn to bellow their war cry and rattle their arms. More bare-chested warriors came forth from the Viking line to have themselves daubed with blood.

'May God strike them down, but they are evil. That must be a priest from the island's church,' said Byrhtnoth, making the sign of the cross.

'They are a brutal people. Those bare-chested bastards look like madmen. Those must be the wicked men, the dangerous ones,' said Wulfhere.

'They are the ones we must kill,' said Beornoth. He raised his voice. 'And they have no armour. So they will die easy, despite their madness.' The men around him beat their war music again.

'Attack,' came the order from Byrhtnoth. He had seen enough, and the lines moved forward. Beornoth marched in time with the Ealdorman, left foot and right foot, keeping pace and keeping shields locked together. Wulfhere did the same on his opposite side. The sun was up now, and despite the chill morning breeze cutting in from the bleak grey sea, Beornoth was sweating beneath his helmet. The leather liner beneath the iron helmet was already wet and clammy in his hair. Rage burned inside him, hot and vicious, and he puffed out his cheeks and clenched his teeth. There is a fine line between battle fury and fear, and Beornoth had seen many a fine warrior succumb to that fear in the horror of the shield wall. He knew, however, that the fury came from the fear, so he let himself fear the bare-chested, war-mad Vikings and the axes of their Norse crews. He feared them and he hated them, and now he would have vengeance for his murdered family, and the chance to fulfil his oath to Osmod.

The enemy lurched forward, Skarde knowing that to stand still in the face of an attacking shield wall would push his men back, bowing their line and spoiling spear thrusts, so they came on to meet the steady Saxon charge. Beornoth could see their eyes peering over their shields, white and wide. Their spears were sharp and coming for his throat, and behind that front line he could see the bare-chested warriors, Sigurd Bearskin amongst them. Those men looked feral, they chomped their teeth on the edges of their shields and their beards were flecked with the spittle of madmen as they whipped each other into a crazed war-frenzy.

'Throwing spears, loose,' Byrhtnoth shouted. The clipped roar of approval came from the rear, then the collective grunt of twenty men. The short throwing spears whistled over Beornoth's head and flew across the sand in an arc, there was a heartbeat of silence, and then a thud and crack as the throwing spears struck the Viking lines. Cries of pain rang out, and the Viking march stuttered.

'Archers, to the flanks,' Byrhtnoth called. Ten bowmen dashed from each side of the Saxon lines, and began to pour arrows into the flanks of the enemy, forcing their men into the centre, making space there tight and hard for the front rankers to keep their spears straight.

'Charge,' roared Byrhtnoth. There were only ten paces between the lines now, and the Saxons surged forward. Beornoth gripped his spear, knuckles white, and put his shoulder into his shield, for the battle had begun.

## 30

Beornoth wanted to close his eyes and crouch behind his shield before the snarling wall of Viking iron and their murderous, bearded faces. But he kept his eyes fixed on the man opposite and snarled himself. He waited until he could smell their leather and the acrid stench of their sweat, until he could feel the oppressive weight of the battle line almost upon him. Then Beornoth lunged with his spear, veering it right at the last moment so that the man opposite him raised his shield, but the spear tip plunged into the bright blue eye of the warrior opposite Wulfhere. That Viking screamed, and Beornoth yanked his weapon back to leave a ruined face, running with dark, thick blood and the jelly of a ripped-out eye dripping down the Viking's cheek. Beornoth pushed his shoulder into his shield and took the impact of the Viking line. It was a shocking force, jarring his whole body as though he was holding back a mountain. He shoved back, as did Wulfhere and Byrhtnoth on either side of him, in a furious test of Saxon and Viking strength and will.

A Viking spear thumped into Beornoth's helmet, the blow blackening his vision for a moment, then the spear came again, this time slicing just wide of his cheek. Beornoth glanced over his shield, where a greasy-bearded Viking with a scarred face brought his spear back for another thrust. Beornoth lifted his left boot and raked it down the Viking's instep, causing the enemy to howl and pause his strike. That pause cost him his life, as Beornoth drove his own spear into the greasy-bearded man's throat, above the line of his byrnie. The Viking gaped and dropped his weapon, and Beornoth twisted his spear savagely, tearing flesh to spill a gout of blood washing down the Viking's chest. An axe came from behind the dying man to chop down on Beornoth's spear, severing the spearhead, and a bare-chested warrior, face and chest daubed with the dried blood of the sacrificed Saxon priest, replaced the dying Viking in the line. That wild-eyed warrior thundered his war axe onto Beornoth's shield, the boards held, but Beornoth had to brace it with both his hands. All was chaos, and Beornoth felt his senses heighten, the noise and panic of battle, the shoving, stabbing, screaming hell of the shield wall.

Wulfhere was shouting incoherently as he shoved against the Viking opposite him, their shields locked in a life-threatening match of power and will. Beornoth looked to his left and saw Byrhtnoth striking overhand with his spear, but two Viking spear blades jabbed at Beornoth, one slipped over the rim of his shield to strike his byrnie mail at the shoulder, and another cut across his cheek. Beornoth yanked back the broken shaft of his æsc spear and pulled his arm back to give himself room. He reversed his grip and looked beneath his shield to see where his enemy's foot was. A leather boot peeked underneath the bottom rim, twisting in the sand for grip as the enemy beat again upon Beornoth's shield with his axe. Beornoth stabbed down with the shivered timber end of his spear, and it connected with the axeman's boot. He shrieked and jerked away from the blow, so

Beornoth brought the rim of his shield up to smash the iron strip into the Viking's face, bursting his nose like a ripe tomato. The Viking howled in pain, and Beornoth reached to his back and whipped his Seax free. He pushed forwards and stabbed upwards with the wicked broken-backed blade to pierce beneath the Viking's jaw, and the Seax passed through the soft flesh and up, punching through his mouth and up into the skull beyond. A huge wash of blood poured from the man's head and down Beornoth's arm, and the axeman fell away, dead.

Before Beornoth could reset his stance behind his shield, Byrhtnoth leapt into the gap the axeman had left, and launched his spear into a Viking's chest, then he pulled his sword free and bellowed his war cry, using the space to lay about him with his blade. The Vikings shrank back from the Ealdorman, and for a moment Beornoth thought there might have been enough space for him and Wulfhere to drive into them behind Byrhtnoth and split their line. But an animal howl filled the air, rising even above the din of battle, of dying and injured warriors falling to the sands. The Vikings had not fallen away. They were simply making space for one of their champions to fight. The pressure on the shield wall broke off, and a line appeared between the Saxons and Vikings, and opposite Byrhtnoth, Sigurd Bearskin faced the Ealdorman. The Viking was still daubed in the priest's blood, and his axe dripped blood from the men he had already struck in the shield-wall fight. Erkenwald stepped forward to take Byrhtnoth's place, but the Ealdorman waved him back. Beornoth was breathing hard, and his muscles ached from the exertion of the shield wall. He saw the lines had swung, that the sea was no longer at the Saxon's back. Skarde had been clever. He had put his biggest and heaviest warriors on his left flank, and the strength and weight of those men heaving at the Saxon flank had turned the lines so that the Vikings now had their warships at their back. Skarde had learned his lesson, and there could be no attempt to cut his ships lines this time.

Beornoth saw Byrhtnoth roll his shoulders, and he flicked up his sword to beckon Sigurd on to fight. It was a brave thing for the Ealdorman to fight again in single combat; he was a wealthy and powerful man and could have sent any of his champions out to fight Sigurd, but he did it himself, risking his life in front of his warriors. He was a Saxon warlord and a leader of men, but he risked not only his own life by fighting Sigurd; if he won, then the Saxons would glory in their leader's victory and it would spur them on to fight with full hearts, but should he fall to Sigurd's axe, then the Saxon warriors would despair, and without their leader would likely collapse and succumb to the professional Viking force. Byrhtnoth had fought and won in single combat at River's Bend, but Beornoth saw Sigurd was a warrior to fear. A bare-chested madman come to slay the prideful Ealdorman.

Sigurd Bearskin came on. His blue eyes were absurdly wide and his face drawn taut, muscles standing out on his bare torso. He quivered as he approached Byrhtnoth, and the Vikings behind him roared and clashed their weapons for their champion. Beornoth shivered to see the strange look on Sigurd's face. It was as though a demon possessed him, as though his spirit were no longer of this world and his mind was in thrall to some war demon from the Vikings' god-world. Byrhtnoth did not hesitate, nor did he seem perturbed by the strangeness of Sigurd's appearance. The Ealdorman clashed his sword on the boss of his shield and went to meet his adversary. Sigurd screamed, a blood-curdling, high-pitched keening, and launched his attack. He came on, swinging his axe in a huge overhand arc, and Byrhtnoth took the blow on his shield. Sigurd swung his axe around again, but Byrhtnoth barged him with his shield, pushing Sigurd off balance, and cut the edge of his sword across Sigurd's exposed chest. Sigurd looked down at the red line carved into his flesh, and he grinned at Byrhtnoth. He came on again with wild swings, and Beornoth was surprised because they were the blows an inexperienced warrior or a fyrd-man might make. Whatever madness had taken hold of Sigurd had plainly made him forget the cuts of the axe he must have learned when he was a boy.

Byrhtnoth raised his shield and charged Sigurd. The Viking beat his axe, kicked and clawed at the Ealdorman's shield, shouting with spittle showing at his mouth and in his beard. Byrhtnoth took the blows, and Sigurd's chest heaved, and his breath came quick and shallow, wasted in his misplaced fury. The Ealdorman broke away, as though to take a step back to catch his own breath, but it was a feint and the Ealdorman came at Sigurd with his shield high and bullying Sigurd's face. Byrhtnoth's sword snaked out beneath his shield and pierced Sigurd's bare stomach. The Ealdorman roared as he drove the blade deep, and his great strength lifted the Viking from the ground when the sword tip burst from his back to spray blood at the Viking lines. Sigurd cried out with shock and pain, and he brought his axe around in his death throes to strike at Byrhtnoth, but the blow was spoiled on the shield, the blade cut a shallow slice across Byrhtnoth's face, a line of blood stretching from forehead to chin, but the cut missed the Ealdorman's eye. Byrhtnoth let Sigurd drop to the sand, put his boot on the Viking's chest, and ripped his sword free. He flicked the gore from its tip at the Vikings, spat on Sigurd's twitching body, and brought his shield up again, ready to fight.

The two enemy lines were quiet: Vikings shocked at the defeat of their war-crazed champion; and the Saxons in awe of their leader's brutal victory.

'Shield wall!' shouted Byrhtnoth, and the Saxons burst into a raucous cheer for the Ealdorman. The lines went forward, and

Beornoth brought his shield up to overlap with Byrhtnoth's and Wulfhere banged his shield on to Beornoth's and so they made the wall anew across the Saxon lines. The Vikings too formed their line, and the two armies came at each other again to begin the clash once more.

'Axes, Lord. Watch the axes,' shouted Wulfhere from behind his shield. The spears had disappeared from the Viking front rank, and Wulfhere was right. No sooner had the words left his lips than a Viking beard axe hooked over the edge of Beornoth's shield.

'Axes,' Beornoth roared, and he hoped the front line heard the warning, for this was the Vikings' greatest battle trick. A second ranker would use the hook of his axe blade to pull down the shields of the Saxon lines, leaving the Viking front rankers to strike at the unprotected faces and necks of the Saxon front line. Beornoth heard shouts and screams up and down the line and knew that it had worked, that Saxons were dying. He held on tight to his shield, and felt the force of another axe blade thundering upon it, the force of the blow shuddering his arm and shoulder. He felt a stinging hot prick on his calf, and Beornoth looked down to see a long knife point snaking beneath his shield, looking to slice at his legs and groin. One warrior attacked him from above, another tried to rip his shield away, and yet another tried to kill him from below. Beornoth's heart was racing, and the burn of fear grew tight in his chest. The clamour of the shield wall was overwhelming, bodies tight against others, sweating and grunting with the effort of pushing back against the enemy and trying to stay alive. Beornoth could not see beyond Byrhtnoth to his left, or Wulfhere to his right, only the two warriors like him, stuck in the press and trying to fend off killing blows from the enemy.

'We have to break the line,' Beornoth shouted at Byrhtnoth,

and the Ealdorman nodded at him, a grimace twisting his blood-washed face. 'We can't hold on much longer. Our line has already been turned. If they break though, we are finished.'

'Essex!' bellowed Byrhtnoth, and heaved with his shield, throwing the Vikings back and creating space for him to strike with his sword. Beornoth stamped down with his foot to pin the hand that struck at him from below and he shouted with rage, gathering all his strength to heave his shield upwards against the axe which tried to drag it down. As the axe raised, he crouched and lunged his seax underneath it at the belly of the Viking opposite him. He pushed hard, but the Viking's mail held. He aimed lower, and felt the soft give of flesh as the seax found its way into the enemy's body, warmth as blood spilled from the wound, and elation as the pressure on his shield fell away.

That space would be short-lived, the Viking ranks would fill it in a heartbeat. Beornoth had a moment to strike forward, to risk everything and make a wedge into the Viking line. He knew that Byrhtnoth and Wulfhere would follow him, Erkenwald too. Beornoth slammed his shield down onto the head of the warrior, whose arm remained trapped under his boot. He brought his shield down again and heard a sickening crunch. He let the shield go. Beornoth held his breath, passed his seax to his left hand and ripped his sword free. To let the shield go was foolish. If one of his household warriors did such a thing in shield-wall practice, he would scold them and urge them never to do that in battle. Battles are won by organisation and discipline, but lines are broken by wild ferocity and courage. So Beornoth let his shield go and gave himself over to the war fury and battle luck. He charged forward, stepping on the shield and crushing the Viking beneath him to leap at the Viking line. As he sprang forward, he slashed with his two blades, landed and slashed again. He felt the sword and seax strike, but didn't wait to see what damage he had done. The Vikings were tight around him now, foul ale breath and stinking leather, and long, plaited beards. They cut at him. He felt blows on his byrnie, on his arms and head, but he cut back. He headbutted, elbowed, bit and stabbed at them. Pressure came at his back. Byrhtnoth and Wulfhere were forcing him forward with their shields and he kept moving, killing and injuring and fighting for his life.

The cloying horror of that charge pressed on Beornoth. He became like an animal, all violence and fury, surging through the Viking lines like a wolf through a flock of sheep, propelled forward by Wulfhere and Byrhtnoth.

'Beornoth, we are through,' he heard a voice shout desperately, the sound muffled and hollow in the depths of his mind. A hand shook his shoulder, and he turned into it, raising his blood-soaked seax with a snarl. 'It's me, Beo, we've done it,' said the voice. The war-haze cleared and Beornoth's eyes came back into focus. Byrhtnoth stood before him grinning, his face a grizzly mask of torn flesh and dried blood from his fight with Sigurd. Beornoth looked around and saw they had broken through the Viking lines, and had torn their force in two. He saw Wulfhere, huge and baleful, hacking at Vikings who were stunned to see their famous bare-chested warriors thrust aside by the Saxons. Erkenwald was with him, and the Vikings fell back before their blades.

Beornoth's shoulders sagged, and his weapons felt heavy in his hands. Cuts and bruises stung and ached all over his torso and arms, and his head throbbed where the enemy had struck at his helmet. His breathing was ragged and laboured. But he was still alive. The beach was a maelstrom of individual fighting, the organised lines of battle were gone, and the Vikings and Saxons fought each other in rolling pockets of death and savagery. The sands churned and were stained dark with the blood of the fallen.

'We need to get warriors to the fyrd. The Vikings are amongst them,' said Beornoth. A clutch of Viking axemen were hacking into the men of the Essex fyrd, the farmers and millers armed only with spears and billhooks. Byrhtnoth nodded and marched in the direction, calling Erkenwald, Alfgar and Wulfhere to march with him. Alfgar's face was ghostly pale, and his weapons bloody. He had fought in the rear lines, but had made his way to the front. Beornoth knew Alfgar had become what he needed to. He had become a killer. Beornoth gritted his teeth and swallowed the pains of his body. He steeled himself to do that which must be done. This was his place as a Thegn, as a landholder of the Saxon kingdom. He held that land and his Heriot to fight and kill to protect the people and the lands of his King and Ealdorman. He lurched forward, flexing the tight muscles in his hands and gripping his weapons.

A Viking screamed his war cry and lunged at Beornoth with a spear. He deflected the blow with his sword and ducked inside the spear's reach. He banged his shoulder into his attacker's chest and rammed the wicked point of his seax into the Viking's groin, twisting and ripping at the man's insides. That enemy fell away, and Beornoth turned to follow Byrhtnoth towards the fyrd, when from the corner of his eye he saw a familiar flaxen-haired face. A hard, clever face. There, through a press of fighting men, was Skarde. He was flanked by Einar Ravenhair and three bare-chested warriors with the same crazed look on their faces as Sigurd Bearskin. Beornoth knew he should follow and protect Byrhtnoth, and get between the Vikings and the men of the fyrd, but he had also sworn an oath to Osmod in his death throes. That oath was to kill Skarde and to cast the Vikings back into the sea. So, he turned away from Byrhtnoth, and strode towards Skarde, to fulfil his oath.

## 31

They had broken the Viking battle line, and Beornoth knew from experience that once that breakthrough was made, the warriors of the army whose front lines had collapsed would panic. The men at the back, the warriors who stood in line but did not crave war, who did not live for the clash of weapons and the chance to burnish one's reputation with the blood of his enemies, those men would flee for their lives. Then running would become as contagious as a plague, and the army would break. But not today. Skarde's men had rallied after the Saxons had ripped their lines open. They had realised that though the numbers of Saxon and Norsemen were equal, the Vikings had more warriors. Fighting in the chaos of the broken lines suited them. Beornoth saw that they were overwhelming the Saxons, hunting in packs to attack and kill Saxon warriors, and butchering the men of the fyrd.

Beornoth saw all of this and made his way towards Skarde. The Viking leader fought with an axe in his right hand and a long knife in his left. Even in his byrnie, he moved fast, like a sea serpent slithering and striking at his prey. A Saxon warrior met Skarde, and there was a flurry of blades, of sword and axe. Skarde bobbed and weaved around sword strikes and took his opportunity to strike, disembowelling the Saxon with a sweep of his knife.

'Skarde,' Beornoth called, his voice rising over the thunder of battle. Skarde's head snapped around, and a grin flashed across his angular face. He charged at Beornoth, and Beornoth met him with a feint of his sword and a lunge with his seax. Skarde flowed around the blow and Beornoth grunted as he felt Skarde's knife scrape across the back of his byrnie. In the maelstrom of battle, he could not tell if the blow had broken through the links of his mail, and there was no time to worry about wounds or pain. Beornoth followed Skarde's movement and struck with his sword, forcing Skarde to parry the blow with his axe. The Viking knelt under the weight of the attack, and Beornoth kicked him full in the chest, sending Skarde sprawling in the sand. Beornoth leapt forward, poised to plunge his sword into Skarde's throat, and he felt the elation of victory rising within him, but a warrior barged him out of the way. A bare-chested Viking faced Beornoth as he regained his balance. He was a short, lithe man, corded with muscle and with the same frenzied look in his eyes as Sigurd Bearskin. He stood between Beornoth and Skarde, and even though Skarde roared at the warrior to leave Beornoth to him, he came on swinging his axe in elaborate circles, laughing with battle-madness.

Beornoth met the twirling axe with his sword, but a deft kick from his attacker swept away his leg, and Beornoth found himself off balance and falling over the Viking's outstretched knee. The mad face appeared above him, howling his victory, and raised his axe to strike, when his chest burst open with a spurt of blood and torn flesh as a spear point punched through his body, killing him instantly. The warrior fell, and Imma held a hand out to help Beornoth to his feet.

'You saved me, lad,' said Beornoth, clapping his oathman on

the shoulder and turning to face Skarde once more. As he caught sight of the Viking, a blow struck Beornoth in the face as he turned. The haft of Skarde's axe cracked him across the nose and cheekbone, sending his vision black. Beornoth swung blindly about him with his weapons, trying desperately to clear his vision, but Skarde was not there. Pain enveloped his face, and he could taste the iron tang of blood in his mouth. The blackness faded, and Beornoth snapped his sword into a defensive position. Skarde was five paces away, the battle raging around him, and with Imma kneeling at his feet. Young Imma, brave and light humoured, a good man with his life in front of him. Skarde's knife was in his belly, and the Viking sliced the blade of his axe across Imma's throat and pushed the young warrior to the sand with his knee. Beornoth roared with anguish and hate. He dropped his seax and gripped his sword in two hands, and threw himself at the Viking leader. Skarde met him, and they exchanged blows, each thrust, parry and block executed with bone-numbing power and speed. Beornoth felt power and strength flowing through him, the heightened sense of battle, the war-lust overtook him, and Beornoth welcomed it. He drove Skarde back, wielding his blade with both hands, made each blow stronger and he shouted and roared his defiance in Skarde's face.

Skarde's face became taut, stretched with exertion and fear, fighting for his life against Beornoth's savage onslaught. Beornoth kept moving, his attack relentless. Skarde's axe came up to meet an overhand strike, and Beornoth leaned into it, pushing the axe down and drawing close to Skarde. Beornoth grabbed the Viking Jarl by the throat, his huge paw of a right hand snapping around Skarde's neck like a shipbuilder's vice. Beornoth let his sword fall and used his left hand to grip Skarde's axe, forcing it out wide. Skarde thrashed in his grip, kicking and bucking, but Beornoth squeezed his hand tight. A lifetime of weapons practice, battle, hate and murderous fury pulsed into the muscles in Beornoth's right arm. He roared and lifted Skarde from the ground and drew him into a vicious headbutt, smashing the gristle of Skarde's nose to pulp. Skarde's eyes bulged and his face turned purple, and Beornoth clenched his hand tighter, throttling and strangling his enemy to death. Skarde kept hold of his axe. Like all Vikings, he feared dying without a blade in his hand more than he feared dying itself, and Beornoth watched as the light slipped from Skarde's eyes and felt his body go limp.

Beornoth let Skarde's body fall to the sand. He picked up his sword and held it aloft, shouting his triumph to the heavens, to whatever God deigned to watch that grim struggle of life and death on Mersea Island. The Vikings saw their leader dead, and they saw the baleful blood-soaked figure of Beornoth standing above him. Beornoth was wounded, cut, slashed, stabbed and bruised. But he was alive and had fulfilled his oath to Osmod. The surrounding Saxons erupted into a cheer of victory, and the Vikings fell back, running to their ships and away from the victorious Saxons.

'We've done it, we've beaten the bastards,' said Wulfhere, standing next to Beornoth and wrapping a heavy arm around his shoulder. Beornoth nodded and leant on his sword, thrusting its point into the sand.

'Imma is dead,' said Beornoth. The boy's body was only a spear's length away. His eyes were open and staring out to sea. Erkenwald lay nearby, an axe buried in his chest, and his byrnie ripped open by the blow to reveal the red-purple of his insides. The feeling of elation and victory was fleeting. Now that the fighting was over, Beornoth felt bone weary. He closed his eyes. The smell of blood was overpowering, tinged with the stench of the voided bowels of the dead, and Beornoth wanted to be away from it. His face throbbed, and his body ached. 'He was brave.'

'He is in God's hands now,' said Wulfhere, and made the sign of the cross above Imma's body.

'What God?' said Beornoth, and he spat the dryness out of his mouth. He could not understand how Jesus, Mary or God himself could witness the carnage he saw on the beach before him and allow so many souls to be killed in so wretched a way. He looked out at the white-tipped grey sea: the Viking warships were under oars, thrashing against the tide to beat their way to safety and away from the Essex coast. Not all the Vikings had made it safely aboard their dragon ships. A dozen of them wallowed and screamed in the shallows, where Byrhtnoth and his household warriors hacked at them, their thirst for death unquenched and the sea turned to red by their butchery. Beornoth reached with a shaking hand to grab the locket at his chest. He brought it to his lips and kissed the warm wood. It came away smeared with his blood. 'Ashwig, Cwen,' he whispered. He had killed and maimed on Mersea Island's beach. He had done his job. He allowed himself the naïve hope that at least some men who fell to his sword had been there that day, long ago, when happiness and hope were ripped from his world. Beornoth had done his duty, he was a Thegn and a warrior and his people were protected.

## 32

Ealdorbana crunched the carrot, and his mouth tickled Beornoth's hand where the horse bit as much of the vegetable as he could without munching on Beornoth's hand. He stroked the warhorse's nose and brought his head to rest on Ealdorbana's forehead. He patted his flank, and Ealdorbana whinnied, his nose soft and his jaw slack.

'Good boy, rest now. You've earned it,' said Beornoth. He left the stable's shade and walked out into an early summer's day, the sun warm on his face and neck. He watched as a gaggle of children danced across the courtyard, playing with wooden flutes Wulfhere had crafted for them with his whittling knife. Beornoth yawned and grimaced where his face still ached from the blow Skarde had struck him.

Against the Hall front, they had brought a large loom outside to rest against the timber planking of the Hall's gable. The threads were brightly coloured, and three women worked at it, using a thread picker to push the strands together into tightly woven material. The woman at the centre of the three was short, with dark nut-brown hair gathered in plaits at the top of her head. To see her there, busy and talking quietly with the women of Branoc's Tree, made Beornoth's heart swell. It was Eawynn, and she seemed to have found peace, in her own way. She was not the woman she had been, years ago, but nor was she the woman Beornoth had placed into the care of the Church for her own safety. She turned to watch the children play, shielding her eyes from the sun with her hand. A hint of a smile played on her mouth. She saw Beornoth, and her gaze lingered on him for a moment, and then she turned back to her work. Since he had returned from the battle with Skarde, they had shared a few words, polite exchanges of good morning, or good evening. It was enough. Beornoth could see her every day. She had accepted the families of Branoc's Tree and they had accepted her.

A voice carried on the dry breeze, and Beornoth saw Aethelberga giving a group of young women a stern talking-to. They were grinding oats and wheat, a relentless task which was to be done every day. She scolded them because she had found tiny stones in the porridge and flour.

'She's a fiery woman, that one,' said Wulfhere. He was in his jerkin, sleeves rolled up and a smile cracking his wide, brutal face.

'She is as fierce as any warrior,' agreed Beornoth, and Wulfhere laughed. She was strong and proud, and had shown kindness to Eawynn, and Beornoth would never forget that.

'She is happy that you let her remain as the Lady of the house.'

'She is the Lady of the house.' Beornoth saw Wulfhere look over to where Eawynn worked. His wife could never run Branoc's Tree. The Eawynn of old would do it standing on her head, but now she had too many demons to fight, too much hurt to live with.

'I think Alfgar wants to marry his woman,' said Wulfhere.

'Bloody fool. Where is he?'

'Off in the fields somewhere. He's a good lad.'

'He is, but he's still a bloody fool.'

'There's worse things a man can do, Lord, than find a woman he loves. Noble or not,' said Wulfhere. Which Beornoth thought was true. 'His brother will not forget what we did to him.'

'No, he won't. Nor will he forget that he has a brother to kill.' Osric would come for them, Beornoth knew. Sooner or later, the Ealdorman would send men, or find some way of attacking Beornoth and Alfgar. They were enemies, and Osric was a proud and arrogant man. Beornoth had ridden into his Hall, killed some of his men, and embarrassed him in front of his warriors. That hate would run deep, and there could be no forgiveness on either side for what had happened. 'Your leg looks better,' said Beornoth.

'It feels good. The limp has gone.' Wulfhere had taken a spear thrust to his thigh at the battle on the beach, and for a while he had limped and moaned about his injury.

'You are a fine warrior, and a good captain,' Beornoth said, looking his oathman in the eye. 'I am lucky to have your axe at my side.'

'Thank you, Lord. We have come a long way since you dragged me naked across Offa's Crag,' he said, grinning. Wulfhere ran his hands through his hair and his arms clinked, where his warrior rings clashed against each other. Beornoth had rewarded Wulfhere with four silver rings, beautifully crafted arm rings taken from the Viking dead. Wulfhere was as rich now as any warrior in Essex below the rank of Thegn, and he had earned it. 'So, now we get to rest for a while,' said Wulfhere.

Beornoth grunted at that. Osric loomed in the north, and Olaf Trygvasson held ambitions of taking Saxon Wessex and Essex for his own, the Viking dream of conquering Saxon lands would never die. There could be no rest, no peace.

'Lord, Lord,' came a shout from across the courtyard. A boy was scrambling through a gaggle of hens running towards Beornoth.

'Calm, lad. What is it?' asked Wulfhere.

'Someone has stolen cows, Lord. From old Wicca's place at Pear Tree Wood. Five of them I heard, armed and dangerous men, Lord,' said the boy, his face red under a shock of curls.

'Get my sword, and saddle up Ealdorbana,' shouted Beornoth. There were always more men to fight, men who wanted to bring violence and pain to places where there was peace and harmony. Beornoth was a Thegn, just like his father, and his father before him, and he would use all his skill and ferocity to protect his people from those that would do them harm.

# HISTORICAL NOTE

The period in which this story takes place is a point in the history of England where one of its most well-known Kings, Æthelred the Unready, came to power after an unusual period of peace and prosperity in the Viking Age. The history of the years leading up to Beornoth's time is essentially the building and unification of what we now know as England. That process began under the rule of Alfred the Great, who ruled from 871AD until 899AD, and was completed by King Edgar, who ruled from 959AD to 975AD, which is very close to the time of this story, set in 989AD.

History has given Æthelred a bit of a rough ride. His epithet 'the Unready' implies a weakness in his character, when it is actually an Anglo-Saxon pun. The name Æthelred means 'well advised', and *unræd* in Anglo-Saxon means 'poorly advised.' When Æthelred eventually succeeded his father, King Edgar, in 978, he was only a child. The timing of his succession was unlucky for Æthelred, because it saw the return of Viking raiders, who seemed to have left England unscathed during the reign of his father, King Edgar.

The Vikings of Denmark and Norway found an England

weakened by its years of peace, and struck in increasing numbers throughout Æthelred's reign, coming to a head in the 990s. I set this story in the years leading up to that larger attack, and specifically two years before the Battle of Maldon in 991. That battle shocked the English court and led to new policies which would halt the Viking conquest, at least for a time.

Byrhtnoth and Olaf Tryggvason are historical characters, but Beornoth is fictional. He is a man of his time, a brutal warrior whose existence revolves around his skill at arms. His role as Thegn is to serve his Ealdorman, and the King, as a warrior and to fight for them when required and to protect the laypeople of his shire. In return for that service, his Lord granted the Thegn land from which he earned his living. The major difference between a Thegn and a Ceorl, or freeman, was that a Thegn owned at least five hides of land, a church and kitchen, a bell house and a castle gate. These requirements, and how society was structured in the tenth century, are recorded in the contemporary 'Promotion Law', or 'Concerning Wergilds and Dignities'.

The Heriot which Beornoth loses and fights to restore was a sort of death-duty, or will, by which a Thegn or other member of the nobility in the tenth century paid back to his Lord the gift of sword, spear, horses and horse trappings he was held to have received when he took up or inherited his position. Evidence for this practice comes down to us in the will of a man called Ketel in the eleventh century. In it, he bequeaths his Heriot to his Lord: 'I grant him my Heriot, a helmet, and a coat of mail, and a horse with a harness and a sword and spear...'

The north-west of England was a place of border skirmishes and constant small-scale fighting in the time following the killing of Erik Bloodaxe in 954. The Kingdom of York became absorbed by England, and Viking rule in the Danelaw effectively ended. There were, however, undoubtedly many Viking families and landowners spread across northern England who did not leave the country following Erik's death. They had been living in the north since the Great Heathen Army arrived in 865, and many had been there for generations. We can see it in place names across Yorkshire and Lancashire to this day, York is the most well known, but Wetherby and Scunthorpe are also good examples. So, it is into this maelstrom that Beornoth is born and raised to a life of sword and shield.

The story of England in the late tenth century is one of Viking invasion and warfare, leading up to the St Brice's Day massacre, and eventually to the attacks of Sweyn Forkbeard and his son King Cnut in the early eleventh century. Beornoth's fate is to be at the heart of that conflict, so his battles are far from over.

# ACKNOWLEDGMENTS

Thanks to Caroline, and all the team at Boldwood Books for their belief in the story, and in me as an author, with special thanks to Ross and Sue for all their effort and undoubted skill.

# MORE FROM PETER GIBBONS

We hope you enjoyed reading *Warrior and Protector*. If you did, please leave a review.

If you'd like to gift a copy, this book is also available as an ebook, digital audio download and audiobook CD.

Sign up to Peter Gibbons' mailing list for news, competitions and updates on future books.

https://bit.ly/PeterGibbonsNews

# ABOUT THE AUTHOR

**Peter Gibbons** is a financial advisor and author of the highly acclaimed Viking Blood and Blade trilogy. He comes to Boldwood with a new series Warrior and Protector, set around the 900 AD Viking invasion during the reign of King Athelred the Unready. He lives with his family in County Kildare.

Visit Peter's website: https://petermgibbons.com/

Follow Peter on social media:

twitter.com/AuthorGibbons

facebook.com/petergibbonsauthor

instagram.com/petermgibbons

bookbub.com/authors/peter-gibbons

# Boldw**oo**d

Boldwood Books is an award-winning fiction publishing company seeking out the best stories from around the world.

Find out more at www.boldwoodbooks.com

Join our reader community for brilliant books, competitions and offers!

Follow us
@BoldwoodBooks
@BookandTonic

Sign up to our weekly deals newsletter

https://bit.ly/BoldwoodBNewsletter

Printed in Great Britain
by Amazon

20122905R00188